CHURCH

A DARK ASYLUM ROMANCE

THE BOYS OF CHAPEL CREST

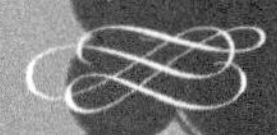

K.G. REUSS

BOOKS FROM BEYOND

Church: The Boys of Chapel Crest 2022

Published by Books from Beyond

Cover Design: Moonstruck Cover Design & Photography, moonstruckcoverdesign.com

Cover Photography: CJC Photography

Cover Model: Jordon Deno

Second Edition Printing 2023

For those wandering through the darkness.
There will be light.
I promise.

FOREWORD

Dear Reader

If you are reading this book anywhere but from Kindle or have downloaded it from anywhere but Amazon, you are reading a stolen copy and need to stop what you're doing and get the book legitimately. Stealing isn't right, and it hurts authors and could end in them being banned and unable to finish your favorite books. Do the right thing. The world has enough liars and cheaters in it. Don't add to the heap.

This is a work of fiction. If you aren't able to separate from reality for this wild ride, this book isn't for you.

Suspend disbelief when reading this.

This story is twisted. If you're curious about how twisted, please check my website https://www.kgreuss.com Every deed for the series is listed there. If you find any of them bothersome, navigate away.

This is a dark bully asylum academy reverse harem. These aren't nice, sweet boys. These boys are fucked up and ready to eat you whole. No one is a hero at Chapel Crest. Everyone is out to get you. Never trust anyone. Never turn your back. And above all else, know your limits.

Are you sure you're ready?
Like, really sure?
If so. . .
Let's go to Church ;)
-K

PROLOGUE

SIRENA

Eight Years Ago …

"Wanna know a secret?" Seth's blue eyes raked over me.

"I don't know. Do I?" I looked from the small, white mouse in his hands to his face, shivers rushing through my body.

Seth Cain was my neighbor and best friend. We played together every day after school and often spent the nights together on the weekends, underneath our blanket fort, giggling over ghost stories and talking about the latest video games.

I loved to sing and dance, and he'd even made up a song to hum for me that I added words to. He hummed it all the time, even when I wasn't singing. We called the song "Roses and Whiskers". Or actually, I did. He rolled his eyes at the name I picked out, but it fit the words I saw in my head for his tune. A curious kitten nosing through the roses and getting scared when a thorn caught her paw.

He'd gotten in trouble at school a few days ago for humming the song during a test and had been sent to the principal. It had made him angry. So angry that he'd thrown his book at Mrs. Baker. He'd been getting weird since his dad moved out a year ago.

Hateful. Cruel. Terrifying. Sometimes he talked to people who weren't even there. It scared me.

But he'd been my best friend since we were in diapers. If anyone could help him, it was me. Whenever Seth got into a fight at school or got mean, I was there for him. I swore to him I always would be. I always tried to draw his attention away from the invisible people he spoke to. I didn't want anyone to think he was strange because he was perfect to me.

I let out a shaky breath.

"C-can I hold Oscar?" I asked, cupping my hands to accept the mouse his mother had purchased for him for fifty cents down at the pet shop.

Seth said it was her way of keeping his mind occupied and teaching him responsibility. Plus, it gave him someone real to talk to when he was alone. Seth was already responsible as far as I was concerned. He practically raised himself since his parents were always working. And now with his dad gone, his mom worked two jobs.

Seth cocked his head and narrowed his blue eyes at me, his dark hair falling across his forehead before handing me the tiny creature.

He glanced to his right and frowned, talking to someone who wasn't there just like he'd done at lunch today. "She won't hurt him. She loves him."

I took the mouse, breathing a sigh of relief and ignoring his words.

"Hey, little fella," I cooed into my cupped hand, hoping whatever gloomy thoughts going through Seth's head would go away.

Seth turned his attention back to me and watched wordlessly. I could see the wheels spinning in his ten-year-old mind.

"We're moving," he said after a beat. "That's my secret. Mom doesn't want me to tell anyone. *No one does.* She met someone new. His name is Philip. *I hate Philip*. We're leaving in the morning."

I looked up at him in surprise. "Where are you going?"

Seth hadn't mentioned a Philip before. But I had noticed a strange man coming into their home over the last few months though. Seth also hadn't let me inside his house for the past two weeks either, claiming his mom was busy cleaning. I guessed that meant packing. It was unlike Seth to keep secrets, especially big ones like this, from me. My tummy ached when I realized I might be losing my best friend.

He shrugged. "I don't know. Somewhere. It won't be anywhere good. Philip is a bad man. *We all know it.*" His expression darkened with his words. "I don't think I'll be able to see you anymore."

"Maybe you'll go with your dad?" I asked hopefully, ignoring how he said *we,* like it was more than just him.

He frowned and shook his head as he addressed someone who wasn't there. My heart raced as I thought about what him leaving meant. His dad still lived on the other side of town. If Seth stayed with him, we'd still be able to see one another.

Seth scowled and focused on me again. "No. Screw him. Mom said he left us for someone half her age. I guess I'm getting a brother or sister and a new mom and dad because of the people they left each other for. It's messed up."

I winced. My dad had left my mom when I was seven. I remembered wondering where he went and why he never came back. Mom told me he was dead to us and to never think of him again.

As if reading my mind, Seth spoke, "It's different for me, Rinny. Your dad just disappeared. Mine found someone better and decided I wasn't good enough, so he's having a whole new baby. Then my mom started seeing Philip. He touches. . ." his voice trailed off as he schooled the pain from his face. "I'm going to get revenge. *We are.*"

A storm cloud passed over his face as he gestured to whatever invisible things he saw.

"Revenge? How?" I frowned, wondering what Seth was cooking up in what had become a gloomy mind. All I knew was if someone was hurting my friend, I needed to get him help.

"I'll kill the baby." He shrugged like it was nothing. "Then they'll take me away, and I won't have to see Philip. Killing someone is a good plan. *They* said so. It's not like anyone cares about me anyway."

I wet my lips, worry creeping through me. This wasn't my best friend.

"*I* care about you. You can't kill a baby, Seth. It'll be your new baby sister or brother. You're supposed to love it and teach it things. Like with me and Cady. I taught her how to braid her hair yesterday."

He was quiet as his breathing rate increased, his serious gaze fixed on me. He jerked and glanced to his right, a frown marring his lips again. His hands shook as he swallowed. He stood silently for a moment before he spoke, "A-are you sure?" he asked in a soft, worried voice. He seemed to be listening for a moment before he said, "O-ok."

I took a tentative step back as his focus snapped back on me. Seth had never turned his violence on me. He'd always been kind and sweet, taking care of me as much as I took care of him.

Something seemed to break within him in that moment. It was like a lightbulb had gone off over his head.

"I don't want to love the baby." He glared at me before closing the distance between us and shoving me.

I cried out as I tumbled to my backside. I hit my head on the concrete floor, making my vision swim and my tummy churn. Oscar fell out of my hands and scurried off, squeaking as I struggled to sit up.

"Don't you get it, Sirena? I hate it. *I hate everything.*" He kneeled beside me for a moment.

I reached out to him, thinking he was going to apologize and help me up, but he surprised me again and fisted my hair. I let a wail out as he tugged so hard, I thought he'd pull all the dark strands from my head.

I fought back, slapping at him. He drew back and punched me in the face, dazing me. Seth was stronger by a lot and twice my size. Even at ten, he looked a few years older than other kids our age.

If the hair pulling wasn't enough, the hot trickle of blood flowing from my nose let me know this wasn't one of Seth's wrestling games. He'd never been mean or cruel to me before.

"Stop. Stop!" I cried out, struggling beneath him as he shifted to straddle me.

He released my hair, but his fists kept flying at my face.

"Seth! Seth!" I tried to cover my head as my best friend in the whole world went crazy and beat me on the dirty, cracked cement of the old shed on the back of his parents' property.

I was no match for Seth Cain though. Black spots dotted my vision as my arms fell limply to my side.

Seth's sobs and his soft words tickled my ears as I lay beneath him, my body hurting. "You'd be better off dead, Rinny, than to spend another moment in this stupid world. *They told me that. They said I'm saving you.* It's what friends do, right? Sirena?" He stopped hitting me. His warm breath washed over my face as I stared up at him through bleary eyes. "I love you, Rinny. You're my best friend in the whole world. *I'm saving you.* I promise I am. Wait for me to get there, OK? In heaven? Things will be better then. We'll be best friends always. I swear it. No more hurting here. I don't want anyone to ever hurt you. I'm so sorry. You'll be safe forever. Mom says angels always go to heaven. I promise I'll find you."

Relief flooded my body as he moved off me. The sounds of shuffling and scraping made me wince before I managed to crack my eyelids open to find Seth looming over me with a shovel.

"Roses and whiskers
Don't stop the purrs, mister.
This world is too big
To go it alone
So follow me through the thicket
And just try to fit through the thorns.
I'll be right behind you.
No need to be alarmed."

He sang the song in a shaky voice before the words faded away and became a hum. A soft song I used to adore so much.

As much as I wanted to stop what I knew was coming, my body felt like lead. I had to make the effort though. I rolled onto my stomach and made a feeble attempt to crawl away. It was useless. The shovel swished through the air, the humming louder. With a crack the shovel came down on the back of the head, sending me to my tummy hard.

The last thing I saw before the darkness claimed me was Seth's white shoes, my blood splattered on them.

As my vision faded, so did his words.

I'll be right behind you

No need to be alarmed.

SIRENA

PRESENT DAY

I stared out my bedroom window into the shadow-filled woods in the distance, my heart in my throat as I listened to my mother talk with my sister as they packed my bags.

"Do you really think she'll be OK? I mean, you know. . ." Cadence's voice trailed off.

I could feel my younger sister's blue eyes on the back of my head as I continued to peer out the window without moving. I loved my little sister. Even though she was almost two years younger than me, we were close. She took care of me when I couldn't find the effort to do it myself.

"Jerry thinks it's for the best. Nothing else has helped her. Jerry thinks the Lord can save her. That maybe the therapy they offer there can help. It might make her normal again."

"She *is* normal," Cadence said with a sigh. "I wish you'd stop saying she isn't. I don't think sending her away because of that holy roller is the best idea. She needs *us*, not some asylum moonlighting as a damn religious school."

"What she needs is God." Jerry's heavy footsteps thumped into my bedroom.

I didn't bother to look at him, opting to continue staring at the forest beyond my window.

"The devil has his demons nestled deep in her soul. God and his angels will work them out of her at Chapel Crest. If the therapy doesn't work, then the word of God will. It's that simple."

I could feel his smirk. I ground my teeth. I hated the smug bastard. My mom decided church was the way to go after my miraculous rescue that she owed to the power of prayer. That was where she met Jerry, a diehard religious nut job—a prayer circle for me before I was found. Praise Jesus and all the angels. Or whatever. She'd married Jerry a year later, and we'd been forced to move into his home across town. Not that I minded the move. Not having to look out my window to see the shed my barely alive body had been stored in for nearly a week was a relief. Being stuck in a locked, metal toolbox there for days hadn't done me much good except screwed my head up.

I hadn't spoken since the day Sheriff Joe pulled me out of my metal prison. But hell, I wasn't even conscious but for a minute to see his face. I never told them who'd done it. There'd been sightings of a strange man in town, a wanderer. People thought it was him. Poor bastard had a reputation he didn't even deserve.

Maybe I didn't tell because I wanted Seth to think I really was dead so he wouldn't come back to finish me off. From the stories I'd heard, Seth's mom, Carrie, had been questioned since I was found on their property. When nothing concrete came back—and why would it, nobody suspected a ten-year-old and Carrie had an alibi—she was cleared and never heard from again.

I had no idea if Seth knew I was alive. Fear and trauma were excellent motivators to keep my lips sealed. But now, I was being forced out of the safe cocoon I shared the past seven years with my sister and being taken to Chapel Crest, a place Jerry swore would exorcise the demons out of me and give me my voice back. Since I was almost an adult, he was getting worried I might never be able to live independently.

To my mom's credit, at least she'd convinced him to let me try intensive therapy for three more months before giving up and signing the papers when I still wasn't able to communicate.

Truth be told, I thought Jerry just hated the stigma of being the mute girl's stepdad. He was a prominent figure in town. He didn't like having me underfoot. I saw his forced smiles and endured the ugly words he spouted whenever Mom and Cadence weren't around to save me.

Little bitch. Mute whore. Worthless cunt. Waste of life. You need to atone for your sins against our Lord. He doesn't punish the innocent! He did not send ME to punish the innocent.

Jerry also liked to hit me when Mom and Cadence weren't around to try to beat the demons out of me. I took it soundlessly, crying myself to sleep afterward. And I never told.

I was silent. It was safer that way.

If I shared with everyone all the nasty things people said and did to me, Cadence would end up in more trouble than she was already in. She'd gotten into a lot of fights on my behalf since my near-death experience. She'd take on anyone. She'd been suspended twice last year for defending me.

"Well, everything's packed." Mom blew out a breath and walked around my bed to kneel beside my chair. "We're going out for dinner as a last family meal. Cadence thinks Italian would be best since you love the bread so much. Does Gino's sound good?"

I stayed silent. I never answered her, never even looked at her. It was just the way my head was now.

I continued to peer out the window.

She licked her lips and reached for me, taking my face in her hands and turning me to look at her. "I miss you, Sirena. I hope Chapel Crest brings you back to me."

A tear slid down her cheek. I wanted to wipe it away so it wouldn't ruin her makeup. Instead, I just stared back at her, wordless.

"I guess that's it." Mom cleared her throat and rose to her feet. "Cady, help Sirena get dressed for dinner. Meet us downstairs in thirty."

I was grateful when Jerry didn't put in his two cents. Instead, I listened as he stomped out of the room, my mom on his heels.

"I hate that douche," Cady muttered, going to my closet. She grabbed an outfit Mom had left out for me and came around to stand in front of me. "You're lucky, Sirena. You get to escape. I'm stuck here listening to Reverend Fuck Stick quote Bible verses at me while I think of twenty ways to screw up his day."

She reached for me, and I took her hand, allowing her to help me to my feet.

"This dress is hideous." She stared down at the mint-colored, ankle-length dress she held before a smirk tipped her plump lips up. She pushed her dark hair away from her face. "Want to have fun?"

I gazed at her curiously, and her grin widened.

"That's a hell yes, huh, Sis? I'll be right back."

Cady left my room quickly and returned within moments with another dress in her hands. It was much shorter, hitting just above the knees, with a wide neck. Tiny pink rosebuds snaked along the dark material.

"I've always thought this dress would look super cute on you, Rina. I'm giving it to you to wear tonight and to take with you to Chapel Crest. God knows you're going to need something cute to wear that isn't one of those ugly nun outfits Jerry made Mom buy for you. You can also take my boots. They look killer with the dress."

I took the items she handed me and proceeded to dress as she left the room. She came back a few moments later as I sat at my vanity staring at myself. My long, black hair hung in soft waves to my waist. I was born with partial heterochromia, meaning my eyes were blue with a ring of green and starbursts of gold in the centers. They were startling because the colors were so rich. It was always the first thing anyone noticed about me. Mom liked to tell me I was extra special, and God put a little more magic into me when he created me. Cady and her friends gushed over my eyes and lashes whenever they were around me. My frame was small, but I guessed I looked OK because Cady always talked about how boys stared at me in school, even though Jerry made me dress like a sixteenth-century maiden with skirts to my ankles. Cady didn't dress like that. She fought too hard for Jerry to deal with. He used me instead.

But it was OK. I liked seeing my sister happy. She was far too pretty to be stuck dressing like a house elf, so I took the burden of Jerry's clothes wraths myself.

It didn't matter anyway. I didn't want the boys to look at me. Boys scared me. Men scared me. Dad left me. Seth tried to kill me. Jerry hurt me. Yeah, I was good on the male front.

"You look great. I got you something," Cady said as she placed a package in my lap.

I examined the pretty, pink package before I lifted my head.

Her smile was so bright, it sparked excitement within me. "Go on. Open it. You're going to need it. You need to raise some hell for me in other parts of the state that way we can both drive Jerry nuts."

I opened the package and stared down at the pink, pleather bag.

"It's makeup. A whole bag of it. I used all my birthday money to get it for you. It's the good stuff too."

I ran my fingers over the zipper. I didn't wear makeup. I didn't even bother learning how to put it on.

Cady snagged the pouch from me and opened it, displaying all the pretty colors and containers inside.

"I'm going to show you how to put it on, OK? I don't want my sister to run off and not know these things. You're going to see cute boys at Chapel Crest, and you're going to want to have some fun. At least, I would. You know, let them put the devil inside me." She giggled as she pulled out the bottles and containers.

I watched and listened as she explained the purpose of each one and how to use them. It seemed fun, and I really liked it. It reminded me of painting. I loved painting. I'd sit for hours, creating art with all the colors. It was my only outlet it seemed. That and reading. The doctors explained to my mom both activities were escapes from reality, but I shouldn't be allowed to do it too much. That was why I had a certain amount of time each week I could paint and read. The rest of the time I sat staring at walls in silence or being beaten by Jerry.

Once we were done with my makeup, Cady beamed at me.

"Of course, you have to text me if you have any issues. I know you don't communicate at all, Rina, but it would be so cool if you would. Or could." Her bottom lip quivered as she stared at me. "Just a text. A letter. Something so I know my big sister is still in there somewhere. I miss you." She sniffled and wrapped her arms around me in a gentle embrace. "Do you remember when we used to do karaoke nights with Dad? You sang the loudest. You were so good. I remember Dad wanting to get you lessons. Mom said we couldn't afford them, but Dad got that part-time job just to send you. I was so proud of you whenever you went on stage and sang. I wish you'd sing again, Rina."

My bottom lip trembled, but I held back my tears as I sat staring at my reflection, Cady's arms around me. I wasn't that girl anymore. That little girl screamed for help in a metal box for days until she could scream no more.

Cady pulled away from me and wiped her eyes. "OK. Enough of that or I'll have to redo my makeup." She gave me a smile and held her hand out. "Come on. Let's go before Reverend Shit Lips has a meltdown."

I took her hand and followed her slowly out of my room. I'd had a lot of physical therapy, but there were still moments where it hurt to walk. Or maybe it was the memories that hurt me, the steps reminding me of how I'd become a seventeen-year-old, mute invalid without a soul, heading for a religious asylum prep school to get the demons out of me so I could be normal again.

They say to be grateful for what you have. The only thing I was grateful for was that Seth Cain was gone.

I silently prayed every night he'd stay that way.

SIRENA

At Gino's, I happily munched on bread and stared at my plate. To everyone on the outside, I was lost in my own head. But I wasn't. I heard everything from the whispered concerns between Mom and Cady to the server asking if I wanted a refill to Jerry disregarding me completely when some of his friends stopped by our table. I even heard one woman telling Jerry about how the Lord worked in mysterious ways.

Things in my life certainly were a mystery. One I didn't know how to solve.

Later that night, I lay in bed, staring up at the ceiling, thinking about everything. Absentmindedly, I rubbed the sore spot on my arm where Jerry had pinched me hard when he saw my outfit earlier. The pain was worth pissing him off. I let out a soft sigh and rolled over, making sure my covers were pulled up tight around me. The thought of leaving home, even if I'd be leaving Jerry the douche behind, made me nervous. I didn't have any friends. Cady was as close as I got to having one. I was a good student, but I struggled because it seemed every year, I wound up with a teacher who thought they could fix me and so focused on tormenting me during class with questions and projects which required me to speak in front of everyone.

But as much as I wanted to whisper, to talk, to sing, to scream, it just wasn't in me anymore. I hadn't even tried after everything happened. It was like my voice had died the day Seth had hurt me.

Closing my eyes, I focused on the breathing exercises my therapist taught me to do whenever I felt stressed.

Deep breaths. In through your nose, out through your mouth. With intention. Again. Focus. Everything is OK. In through your nose, out through your mouth. Count. One. Two. Three.

Eventually, I drifted off to sleep, only to be woken right before daybreak by Jerry snarling my name. I sat up quickly as he tugged my long braid so hard, I winced.

"Get up, you little devil slut," he commanded, his muddy brown eyes dull. "It's bad enough we've been stuck with you and your sins, but now I have to take time out of my day to drive your ass across the state to get rid of you."

I flinched again as he released me. I hated getting my hair pulled. My chest heaved as I tried to calm myself.

One. Two. Three. Four. Breathe...

"Do you know how happy I'll be to be rid of you?" He was in my face, his breath hot on my cheeks as I trembled. "No more of your sins contaminating my house. I know what you are, girl. You lured a man to your unholy *cave*, and God made you pay the ultimate price. Life will be better for all of us once you're gone." He reached out and clamped his hand painfully around my face and squeezed, his eyes flashing.

"You've got a pretty mouth. Too bad it's good for nothing." He shoved me back, releasing me.

I fell onto my back as he moved away, my heart pounding hard.

"Get dressed. I want you out of my house within the hour."

He marched out, leaving me quivering on the bed. At least he hadn't tried to beat the devil out of me this time. That was usually how our little visits went. I'd spent a lot of time nursing the wounds he gave me over the years. Bruises never got the chance to heal in my world. They were simply replaced with new ones. But never anywhere that could be seen. Apparently, God also commanded for me to have my beatings in inconspicuous places, like my back and thighs.

Hefting myself out of bed, I quickly showered and put on the pretty dress Cady had given me the night before. I knew it pissed Jerry off to see me in it because he said I was *trying to tempt men to my woman cave.* What a load of crap. He never gave Cady a hard time for dressing pretty or accused her of trying to tempt men. Probably because he knew she'd raise hell. My little sister would sing like a canary the instant Jerry looked at her wrong. That was why the focus was on me. I was an easy target. A silent one he could use to beat and control because all I wanted *was* the silence. I'd take those punishments without so much as a tiny whimper. I didn't want the drama. I didn't want to be the center of attention.

But it hurt so much. It broke me. It made me more fearful and withdrawn. Therapy never went well. I listened while my latest therapist talked about tackling the things I was scared of. She diagnosed me with selective mutism brought on by trauma, plus PTSD, depression, and generalized anxiety disorder. She recommended I be placed in a state hospital so I could get more hands-on help. That was when Jerry stepped in with Chapel Crest as the best option for me, citing how it was both an asylum and a school. They took care of kids with mental illnesses and troubled youth. They offered onsite medical care. I'd never be alone. And Bible studies were the center of all their curriculum because if medicine couldn't fix it, God would. So that was how I found myself about to leave my home and my family.

Methodically, I put my hair in a long braid down my back and stared at myself one final time before going downstairs. Cady had already put my suitcases down there. I had a long year ahead of me. I'd be eighteen soon, and after graduation, I planned to go to college. Maybe I'd get a business degree and open my own art gallery. Wherever I ended up, I knew it would be far from Jerry and his whips and heavy fists.

"Good morning," Mom called out, strolling into the living room to find me staring down at my things. "I was just getting ready to make an early breakfast."

Jerry stood behind her and gave a silent shake of his head.

Right. One hour.

I opened the front door and grabbed one of my bags, hauling it down the front steps. My mom's sighs followed after me, but it was whatever. The sooner I was away from the bullshit of Jerry the Bible Thumper, the better.

I loaded my suitcase into the back of the new, silver Volvo Jerry had bought my mom and started to go back inside, but Cady came down the front steps with two more suitcases—one mine and one I didn't recognize.

She loaded both into the back as Mom brought out a duffel bag and placed it atop the suitcases.

"It has bedding in it for you," she explained with a smile. "I thought you'd like something nice and new. I also have some art supplies in it for you. It's a limited amount since you need to stay in reality like your therapist says. The supplies are separated, so it should be fine."

"And the extra suitcase is something I packed for you," Cady said with a wink. "It's so you actually have decent things to wear. I made sure your makeup bag was packed too."

"Cady," Mom admonished. "Sirena *has* nice things to wear."

"She wears what Jerry says she can wear. He treats her like crap, Mom. I wish you could see it." Cady glared back at the house before giving it the finger.

"Cadence Renee," Mom hissed, slapping her hand down. "Jerry has given us so much more than anything I could give you girls on my own. He's just... set in his ways."

"Yeah, his ways of being a douche canoe," Cady grumbled, the sour look still on her face.

Mom closed her eyes and breathed out before plastering a smile on her face. "We'll stop and get breakfast on the way since Sirena is so excited to get to her new school. I'll grab my purse." She strode back to the house, leaving me with Cady.

"Listen, I also packed some snacks for you in there in case everything sucks at this holy roller school Jerry is sending you off to. There are a few cute outfits, some shoes, and heels. I also put your bank card in there. Dad deposits money in the account for us every month even if he doesn't bother to visit or call. May as well use the money. I mean, break yourself in, Sis. Have fun. Please. For me." She stared back at me with luminous eyes.

I swallowed, knowing damn well I wouldn't.

She sighed. "You'll do great. Text me. You never use your damn phone. I packed it in your bag. Charger and laptop too. Oh, and your Kindle. Don't tell Mom though. I was supposed to leave it on the counter, but I think it's just stupid. You should be able to read for fun if you want. And I know I've said it before, but I just. . . I just want you to talk to me, Rina. I wish you would. *Could*." She hugged me. "You'll be OK. I know you will."

"Enough of that," Jerry called out with sneer as he sauntered out of the house with Mom. "She's going to school, Cadence, not to the gallows. Please keep public displays minimal. We don't need the neighbors talking."

"You don't think they're going to talk once they notice Rina is gone?" Cadence taunted.

"Get in the car before I change my mind about letting you come with us," Jerry snapped. "You're behind on your Bible studies. You didn't attend on Wednesday. . ."

He was off and running. I tuned him out as I got into the backseat, snapped my seatbelt into place, and stared out the window. It was still warm out, despite it being Michigan and near fall. The leaves hadn't started changing yet, but I figured it had more to do with the strangely warm weather we were having.

Chapel Crest started a week earlier than my public high school and was located in the Upper Peninsula on Lake Superior. I knew how cold it got up there and wished I'd thought of packing a jacket and boots. Not like it mattered though. I didn't typically spend a lot of time outside. I assumed that aspect wouldn't change.

The drive from Detroit to the northern part of the state was a long one. I didn't even bother staring out the window since I-75 was a boring drive. When we reached the Mackinac Bridge, the suspension bridge separating the upper and lower peninsulas of Michigan, I perked up and gazed out over the Great Lakes. The view was truly stunning. The water seemed so blue and calm. I imagined running along the beach and laughing. Happy.

I slumped back in my seat and closed my eyes as we neared the end of the bridge. Cady had fallen asleep somewhere around West Branch while I'd listened to Jerry talk with Mom about some church gathering they were going to over the weekend.

Eventually, the droning of Jerry's incessant chatter put me to sleep. I didn't wake until Cady shook me gently. Prying my eyes open, I glanced out the window to see a massive, stone building that resembled a castle. Hastily, I got out of the car and gawked up at it, feeling lightheaded due to its sheer size.

"Damn. This place is huge," Cady said as she stood beside me, staring up at it.

Old ivy hung off it in some places. Some of the stones were darker than others, making it look like a place where horrible things happened. Like vampire attacks. I shivered at the thought of Dracula living in the basement. *Was it living? Being dead in the basement?* Didn't matter. I didn't like the idea at all, considering this would be my home for the next year.

After a moment, I glanced around and noticed there were other similar buildings on the property.

"I bet they're dorms," Cady said, following my gaze. "That's cool. You'll get to sleep in a small castle. Hope they aren't haunted. They look haunted."

I had the same thought.

"Come get your bags. I'm not carrying them," Jerry called out.

Cady rolled her eyes. "Of course, you're not, Saint Dinkus," she muttered under her breath as I followed her to rear of the car.

We tugged out my bags, me taking one suitcase and the duffel bag and her taking the other two suitcases. Then we followed Mom and Jerry up the stairs and into the building.

A burly security guard directed us to the main office, his dark eyes drifting over me. Probably wondering what I was being brought in for. I paused and placed my luggage down as we entered the main hall so I could stare in amazement. Marble floors, dark tapestries, pillars, a sweeping staircase leading to higher levels.

"Welcome to Chapel Crest. Can I help you?" a guy about my age dressed in a navy blue school uniform asked, smiling at us.

"Yes, my stepdaughter is enrolling here. We need to get her settled in."

Jerry was stiff and formal as always. He was a judge in our city. He had zero tolerance for anything and felt that weakness never got people anywhere. Jerry was a grade-A jerk in all situations. Except church. That was where everyone kissed his ass.

Cady said she thought I was being sent off for his political gain because he was considering a run for mayor, so he didn't need me underfoot. She was probably right. Cady usually was.

"Ah, new student." The guy turned to me and perked up. He was handsome with copper-colored hair, hazel eyes, and a bright smile. "I'm Bryce Andrews. I'm on the student council, so I do a lot of tours for new and prospective students. What's your name?"

I stared back at him, wordless. He seemed absolutely normal. Too normal to be in a place like Chapel Crest. He lifted his brows.

"Her name is Sirena Lawrence. She doesn't talk." Cady shifted to stand beside me.

"Oh!" Bryce's eyes widened, and his cheeks flushed. "My apologies. Uh, well, we don't have any students here who sign—"

"She doesn't sign. She doesn't do anything," Jerry said with a disgusted grunt. "I've already discussed her issues with Headmaster Sully. He's aware of them and informed me that her teachers and the medical staff know. He says he has a place for her here." The way he said it made my skin crawl.

"Right. Excellent. I'll just grab her information and show you all where she'll be staying." Bryce turned on his heel and gestured toward the leather chairs outside an office.

Before I could take a seat, he motioned for me to follow him. He looked uncomfortable, and I couldn't blame him. He didn't know how to communicate with me. I was used to it. It happened a lot.

I followed him into an office.

"This is Mrs. Douglas. She's our secretary," Bryce said, indicating the elderly woman in pearls and a Chapel Crest sweater behind the desk.

She glanced up at me disinterestedly.

"Mrs. Douglas, this is Sirena Lawrence. She's new here. I'm just going to get her schedule and room assignment and then give her a tour."

Mrs. Douglas grunted and went back to her Bible reading. It was just as well. It wasn't like I had anything to say to her.

Bryce tipped his head for me to follow him again.

"This is Headmaster Sully's office. He's not in right now. He'll be back on Sunday for mass. If you ever need to talk to him, don't. He's not the friendliest of people. What you'll want to do is go to Vice Headmaster Atkins. He's far easier to deal with and just down that hall when he's actually here." He pointed in the opposite direction before opening a drawer and thumbing through it quickly. He grabbed a file with my name on it.

"I need to get a photo for your school records and your badge, so you'll be able to get into the library and anywhere else on campus you need to go. It also serves as your identification for med passes," he said, snagging a camera off the top of the filing cabinet and turning to me. "Um, stand against the wall for me."

I did as instructed and faced him.

"Smile," he said.

I didn't bother as he snapped the photo. He moved over to a computer, quickly uploaded my photo, and hit print. A moment later, a school badge popped out with my photo and name on it beneath the Chapel Crest logo of a cross and roses.

He handed it over and slid a copy of the image into my school file before grabbing a handful of papers and nodding for me to follow him.

"Do you want your parents to come with us to your dorm?" he asked, peeking over his shoulder at me as we strolled to the door.

When I didn't answer, he stopped and studied me.

"I-I'm sorry, Sirena, but it's hard to figure things out. I know you can hear me, but I'm at a loss as to what to do. Should I just have them come with us? It's a bit of a walk, and, really, parents don't typically visit the dorms. Students meet up with family in the great hall or monastery for events. I can have someone help with your bags. What do you think? Parents or no parents?"

I gaped back at him, my anxiety kicking in.

Count, Rina. One. Two. Three. Breathe. In through your nose, out through your mouth. Four. Five. Six. . .

Bryce scratched his head. "I'll just tell them to go. If it's not OK, you can stop me. I just don't want to step on any toes. I know leaving your family is hard and all."

I stared down at my feet as I tried to keep my breathing even.

"OK. Yeah," he mumbled, turning and pushing through the door. "Sorry it took so long. I wanted to show Sirena around the office and let her know how to reach out to our headmaster."

Jerry got to his feet and glared at me like I'd done something wrong. I averted my eyes back to the floor as Bryce continued to speak.

"Normally, parents don't accompany students to the dorms. You're more than welcome to come along, but I'll also be showing her around. It's a lot of walking and talking, so I won't be offended if you guys wanted to take off." Bryce gave my family a mega-watt smile.

"That sounds like a good idea. I have a lot to get done tomorrow, and it's a long drive back," Jerry said. "She has everything she needs at the door."

He didn't elaborate. He simply turned and marched back to the entrance.

"I love you, Sirena." Mom wrapped her arms around me tightly. "Cady said she put your bank card and all you'll need in your suitcase. If you need anything, *please* text me. I'm so nervous leaving you." She held me for a moment longer before pulling away and beaming down at me, tears in her eyes. "Get better, baby." She drew in a quick breath and looked to Bryce, giving him a nod before squeezing my hand and going to the front doors without a glance back at me.

Cady rolled her eyes.

"Sorry about him. Jerry. He's a dick," she said to Bryce.

He dropped his proper attitude and snorted as she grinned at him.

"Listen, I want you to know my sister isn't an idiot, OK? She went through some nasty stuff as a kid, and she doesn't talk because of it. She can understand you just fine. She's normal. Make sure she's treated that way. I'll come back here and kick your ass if she gets hurt. Got it, pal?" She poked his chest for emphasis.

Bryce blinked several times before stammering, "Of course. No worries. I mean." He glanced at me then back at Cady whose arms were folded over her chest. "We do have a few students who might make life hard here. And the nuns aren't the friendliest, but I'll do what I can. It says she's a senior, so it's just a year. She'll be OK for a year."

The way he spoke made me think I definitely might not be OK for a year.

"Better hope so," Cady grumbled. "I'll seriously burn this place down if anything happens to my sister." And with those sweet words, she grabbed my hand, turned, her dark hair whipping behind her, and pulled me to the front door.

I looked behind me to find Bryce gawking with his mouth open.

Yeah, Cady had that effect on people.

CHURCH

"What the fuck?" I snarled, shoving the bitch sucking my cock away from me.

She landed on her ass with a loud thud, spit dribbling down her chin.

"S-sorry—"

"You scraped my shit, you dumb fucking whore."

When I glared down at my softening cock, an ugly, red streak showed where her teeth had marked me. I hadn't even bothered to remember her name. I beckoned, and the girls came. I didn't need to know their names.

"I told you she sucked," Stitches said with a grin from his spot on the couch where another girl was blowing him. "But not in the good way. Ask Sin. He would've told you."

Shaking my head, I let go of my dick and stared down at the whimpering girl on the floor. Stitches let out a soft groan. *Lucky fucker.*

"Come here," I demanded, getting to my feet.

The girl crawled back to me, her mascara smeared on her cheeks.

"Kneel and open your mouth."

She did as commanded.

I took my dick in hand and began pumping it. "Show me your tits."

Her eyes widened as I jerked myself off in front of her. Quickly, she removed her shirt and slipped her tits out of her bra.

Small. Barely a handful. I sighed. *What a fucking waste.* Maybe the bitch would be good in bed. But at this rate, I doubted I'd bother trying her out.

I stroked my cock faster, eager for a smoke. With a groan, I blasted her face with my release, soaking her.

She raised her hand to wipe her face, but I smacked it away.

"Leave it. Let it dry." I grabbed her shirt off my floor and pitched it into the lit fireplace. "Now get the fuck out, and I suggest learning how to properly suck cock."

She rushed out, sobbing, as Stitches buttoned his pants and grinned at me.

"Why are you such a dick?" he asked, slapping the girl on the ass who'd been on his dick as she got dressed.

She giggled as she bent down to kiss him.

He quickly jerked away and tutted at her. "You know the rules. You suck my cock, and then you leave."

"Stitches," she whined, pushing her chest out.

He chuckled and tugged her onto his lap. His lips closed around one of her hardened nipples. She moaned like a whore.

I didn't have time for this. Reaching out, I grabbed her by the hair and dragged her off his lap. She let out a startled cry and stared up at me with a sheen of tears in her eyes.

"You suck cock, and then you leave," I repeated dangerously. "Now get the fuck out."

She quickly gathered her clothes and left us alone in our private dorm that wasn't really a dorm. It was actually private housing that my great-grandfather a shit ton of times removed had built when this hellhole started. I was a legend at Chapel Crest. A fucking god. My family had attended the school since its beginning nearly a hundred years ago, back when it was an actual school. Now it was a fucking asylum under the guise of a school.

But it was my home. I did whatever I wanted here. I owned the place. If anyone dared say otherwise, they knew the wrath I'd bring down on them. My crew and I were the boys of Chapel Crest. The gods of its hallways. The crazy lurking in the shadows.

I shared my small paradise with my best friends Malachi "Stitches" Wolfe, Sinclair "Sin" Priest, and Asher "Ashes" Valentine. We each had our own bedrooms, plus a kitchen and living room. The only downside was we only had three bathrooms. A pity, but I figured since it was only four years of our lives, we'd survive. I'd made sure the house was updated before I started here freshman year. It was our fucking palace. I came from money. Nothing was out of reach for me. Except my sanity. I was working on that though. *Mostly*.

"Man, come on," Stitches groaned.

"Let's smoke." I tossed him his shirt and moved past him to our back patio, which overlooked Lake Superior. It was a bit of a secluded place, nestled at the back of campus along the lake. We had insane parties out there, which no one said shit about because they were *our* parties. Not security, not the nuns or cunt of a priest, not the therapists or medical staff. *No-fucking-body*. If someone wanted to survive here, they got in my good graces and did what they were told. It was that simple.

Stitches joined me a moment later, and I handed him the lit joint after taking a deep drag. He hit it before blowing it out a moment later.

"Ashes said he and Sin would be here soon. They stopped in St. Ignace for something."

I nodded, looking out at the lake. "What the hell could they need in St. Ignace?"

"Probably hitting up a smoke shop or something. You know how Ashes likes those fruity vapes, man. One of his cousins works at the one in town and hooks him up."

I rolled my eyes. Ashes preferred vaping over hitting a joint. It wasn't like he didn't smoke; he just didn't do it as often as we did. It probably had something to do with being too close to a potential fire. He had some impulse control issues and OCD. While weed tended to chill him out, his vape hit his sweet spot. I figured it was because he could count the fucking rings he blew out. Ashes liked to count. Or rather his disorder made him count. Fives were his thing. Drove me nuts to watch him tie and untie his shoes five fucking times every morning. Or puff out five rings of cherry-scented bullshit before every meal. At least the rings didn't stink though, which was one of the reasons why we didn't give him too much shit about it.

"We having a party on Monday?" Stitches handed the joint back to me and leaned against the railing, studying me with his dark eyes. Stitches and I had been friends for a long time. He didn't come from money. He came from violence, neglect, and trauma. My old man adopted him when we were kids. We were brothers now. But hell, all the watchers were my brothers. Best friends until the end and all that shit.

I took a hit and held it, enjoying the burn and rush. I blew out the smoke and coughed. "Fuck yeah. When do we not? It's tradition to meet the fresh meat. Need to let them know early on they have no say here."

Stitches nodded. "Hope we get some new pussy. I'm getting bored with the same ol' shit we have now. You know, I fucked Daria in the ass last night. Swear she's a nympho, and cock is her medicine, but fucking these bitches is really getting old."

I let out a snort. "Weird you say that. I did too, but it was yesterday afternoon."

"I guess that explains why her shit was worn out. It was like throwing a hot dog down a fucking hallway," he muttered, running his fingers through his shaggy, black hair. The tattoos on his arm peeked out from beneath his long-sleeved, dark shirt.

"Why the fuck are you wearing long sleeves?"

He shrugged. "It's cold, man. The breeze off the lake makes me shiver."

"Christ. Don't say *shiver,* you pansy ass." I handed him back the joint.

Stitches was a different breed of crazy. While I was simply off my rocker, he was bipolar, his moods shifting like a current. He'd been good lately, though. Thankfully. I hated it when he went manic. One episode at the end of last year, he'd spent three days not sleeping and digging a fucking hole in the backyard. I ended up having a small pool installed since it seemed a shame to let it go to waste. Of course, the flipside was the depression. I hated it more. Luckily, that didn't come along often.

He took another hit and laughed. "Fuck you, Church. If you wouldn't have kicked what's her name out, I'd be nice and warm and balls deep in some pussy right now."

"Whatever. She's trash like the rest of them." I propped my arms on the rail and stared out at the water again. I'd never cared enough about any girl to keep her around. They were for fucking and blowing my load on. None had ever captivated me enough to *feel* anything. I never empathized with their tears. In fact, the more they cried for me, the harder my dick got.

"Let's go get some food. I'll Door Dash some shit here. I feel like pizza. We'll have to meet them at the gates," I muttered, shoving off the railing.

"Sure. Order enough for Ashes and Sin too. Oh, and breadsticks. That shit slaps from Carmine's."

I nodded and pulled my phone out. Carmine's did have good food. I placed the order and stuffed my phone back into my pocket.

"Let's go. By the time we get to the gates, they should be there." I turned and went back into the house.

Stitches followed, and we left, going out the front door and making our way down the cobblestone path.

Chapel Crest was hell, mostly because my crew and I made it that way, but I was certain we made it more tolerable than any of the fuckers running the place would have. The nuns were cunts, and I had a sneaking suspicion that Headmaster Sully was involved in some shady shit with Father Emerson, the asshole who ran our masses.

Yes, my crew ran an *initiation* of sorts for new students, but I felt like the men in charge might run their own form of initiation behind closed doors. No one ever spoke of it. Maybe I was simply paranoid. Wouldn't be the first time I'd been accused of it.

Chapel Crest was a place for tears and secrets. It started with everyone's personal issues and then had some fucked-up, trickle-down effect. It gave the fuckers who ran this place hard-ons as they tried to treat us and make us better with sing-alongs and therapy sessions. It was all bullshit.

We strolled down the path, wearing our street clothes. Classes hadn't started yet, and it wasn't like we were sticklers for the bullshit uniform. I typically didn't even bother to tie the shitty ties or button the white dress shirts all the way. I let my tattoos peek out without a care in the world.

"Looks like Bryce has some fresh meat," Stitches said with a low whistle.

I followed his gaze to where Bryce was walking with a girl who had a rocking body. Her black hair was in a thick braid over her shoulder. As we got closer, my mouth practically salivated to taste her. We didn't have girls who looked like her here. Her short sundress put her long, lean legs on display for us, and her creamy shoulders made me want to take a bite of her flesh and swallow her down while she screamed for me to stop.

"Fucking dibs," I growled, knowing Stitches was about to call it.

"Dick," he muttered as they approached.

"Who's this?" I asked in a stone-cold voice as Bryce stopped chattering about the architecture of our buildings to her.

His eyes widened in surprise when he saw us.

"Oh. H-hey, Church," he said, clearing his throat. "I didn't realize you were back already."

The little bitch looked like he was going to piss his pants as he gazed up at our towering forms. Everyone in my crew was over six feet tall and made of muscle. If our behaviors and fucked up psyches didn't intimidate people, our sizes would.

"I asked you a question," I snapped at him, settling my gaze on the beautiful creature at his side.

My pulse thundered in my ears as her oddly-colored eyes widened at me before she quickly looked to her feet. I'd never seen eyes like hers before. So. . . colorful. Vivid blue. Moss green. Gold starbursts.

Fuck, that's nice.

"What's your name?" Stitches asked her.

She didn't answer, opting to continue examining the ground.

"H-her name is Sirena Lawrence. She doesn't talk," Bryce said, clearing his throat again.

"Why not?" Stitches asked, circling her.

I smirked as she visibly flinched

"Cat got your tongue, angel?" Stitches stopped in front of her and waited for her to speak because maybe Bryce was pulling our dicks—not that he'd be brave enough to, but hey, stranger things had happened.

Stitches stepped back and glanced at me with a lifted brow. I surveyed her for a moment before taking his spot. Reaching out, I tilted her chin up and cocked my head at her.

Fuck, she was beautiful. Thick, long, dark lashes framed her unique eyes. Skin that looked like porcelain. The faintest of crimson on her cheeks. And those plump, pink lips. My dick twitched in my pants as I thought about how fucking gorgeous she'd look with those lips wrapped around my throbbing cock. *Breathtaking.* Just like my own little Snow White. She was a perfect doll. *A perfect princess for my kingdom in hell. Or a queen.* I shook the thought off.

"Speak," I commanded softly. Dangerously.

"Church, she can't. Her family left her like twenty minutes ago. She went through some traumatic shit and doesn't talk now. I haven't seen her medical records because they're sealed like everyone else's, but I talked to her sister. I saw her academic file though—"

"She can hear?" I looked to Bryce.

He nodded stiffly. I smiled and focused back on her. Softly, I ran my knuckles along her jaw. She quivered beneath my touch.

Who would dare harm such a stunning creature to make her this way? She was my kind of crazy. I was intrigued. It amped up my desire. If there was one thing I loved, it was pretty, broken things. Things I could play with. Things I could finish off. Things I could smash to bits.

"Sirena," I murmured, watching as her lips parted slightly, her bottom lip trembling. I leaned in, and she stiffened as I spoke into her ear, my lips brushing against her skin, "We're going to have lots of fun together."

I stepped back and lifted her long, thick braid off her shoulder. "Hmm. Pretty."

I laid it gently back on her shoulder and eased back further.

Run. I love the fucking chase. The hunt. The screams. Please. Fucking run from me.

Bryce gaped at me like a startled deer caught in the headlights of a semi-truck.

"Why are you still standing there?" I snapped at him, finally pulling my attention from the girl in front of me.

"S-sorry. Sirena," he said, nodding for her to follow him.

She stepped around us. Stitches and I spun to watch her go. She cast a quick peek at us from over her shoulder, her brows crinkled before looking ahead.

"Fuck, man. I want that," Stitches said with a groan, letting his head fall back. "She's gorgeous. Did you see her eyes?"

"Yeah." I chuckled softly and clapped him on the shoulder. "Let's introduce her to Sin and Ashes tomorrow. Maybe they'll be interested too."

"Going back on dibs now and remembering our arrangement?" Stitches asked.

I snorted. "I'm just playing nice." I ground my teeth. "For now."

He grinned. "Are you thinking what I'm thinking?"

"Claim," I said, my heart hammering hard in my chest.

We hadn't ever officially claimed anyone before because we hadn't found someone the four of us were interested in enough to commit that way to. The perfect addition to our little band of crazy. Someone we could share and care for and fucking own. Someone who would complete us instead of trying to come between us. We'd talked about the possibility after everything went down with Isabella a few years ago. It looked like we might have finally found our unicorn. I rubbed my hands together in anticipation. If she was the one, we'd make it official. Throw a fucking party and present her like a queen, letting everybody know that if they messed with her, they'd invite our wrath. And then we'd make her ours. Together.

"Fuck yes. I'm in."

"Then let's tell our boys, shall we?" I said with a wicked smile, turning to go to the gate.

You weren't truly broken until we broke you. Those were the rules.

Lucky Sirena Lawrence, the girl with no voice.

SIRENA

"Sorry about them," Bryce said as we continued along. "They're a big deal here—Church and his crew." He glanced over at me. "Stay away from them if you can, Sirena. I was hoping you'd stay off their radar because they can really mess with you. That guy back there—the blond one with the nose piercing, earrings, and tattoos—he's Dante Church. He's their leader."

Bryce leaned his head closer to mine and lowered his voice, "He's ruthless. Totally insane. I heard he was actually diagnosed as like, a sociopath or something. We just say he's a psychopath though. He's nuts. There are rumors he hunts animals in the woods with his bare hands and then eats them raw. And that he keeps a jar with their eyeballs in his bedroom. *No one* crosses him or his crew."

He blew out a breath before continuing, "Then there's Malachi Wolfe, the guy who was with him. They call him Stitches. I don't know why other than he sometimes gets in fights and people end up with stitches from his fists when he loses control. Old money like Church in a way. He's Church's adopted brother. Stitches is definitely bipolar. Last year, he dug halfway to China in their backyard during one of his manic episodes. He's all over the place. You never know what mood he'll be in, making him volatile and dangerous since I'm pretty sure violence is his favorite drug. Asher Valentine and Sinclair Priest are the other two members."

I grimaced at the information, worry creeping through me. I had every hope in the world I'd be overlooked by them, but there was something else niggling at me. Something I didn't quite understand.

We turned to the right, walking between two buildings.

"Seeing one or two at a time is bad, but getting the entire crew is a death sentence." He paused for a moment, peering around cautiously.

"They call Asher *Ashes* because he's a pyro. Last year, he set off like six trash cans and then the library. Sinclair they just call Sin because he's seriously just screwed in the head like Church. I swear the devil sent Church here to give us a taste of hell. The four of them refer to themselves as the name the watchers. They have spies all over the damn place here, doing their bidding." He sighed and shook his head.

That must be why Bryce kept swiveling his head to make sure no one was nearby to hear what he said. I swallowed hard, fear making my heart pound.

Both guys were breathtaking and frightening. Dante with his piercings and tattooed arms plus the hint of ink on his chest where he'd failed to button his shirt. He screamed bad boy in neon letters. And Malachi Wolfe. Looked just as sinful with his messy, black hair and piercing dark eyes. He had tattoos and earrings too. Jerry would have a heart attack if I brought either of them home.

My lips tipped up at the image of Jerry losing his shit. The idea became more appealing.

We reached a stone building similar to others we'd passed.

"Just try to watch yourself, OK? I hope Church doesn't decide to play. He was looking at you like you were his favorite meal. Not a good thing." Bryce pushed the door open and stepped inside. "I'm pretty sure he has the makings of a serial killer. Same with Sin, but you haven't met him yet. Hopefully, you don't have to."

I followed him, my anxiety creeping up. It hadn't slipped past me how Church and Stitches had looked at me. It had frightened me, making me feel like that scared ten-year-old girl again.

Crazy or not, I had to admit, they were two of the hottest guys I'd ever seen. Church had a dimple in his cheek when he smirked. It looked unnatural once he actually spoke. Both guys were built like walls. There must be a gym on campus because there was no way they got that ripped from hanging out in their rooms reading scripture. If Cady had been there, she would've gushed over their looks.

But me? I was terrified about whatever they were planning.

We're going to have lots of fun together.

I hoped their idea of fun meant leaving me alone and never speaking to me again. Something told me that wouldn't be the case though.

"So, you're on the top floor," Bryce said, drawing my attention back to him. "There are tons of stairs if you want to take them, but there's also an elevator, which I recommend unless you're trying to kill time. Jack's probably already put your things in your room." Bryce had called a guy named Jack earlier to take my luggage to my room.

The place was basic. Dark walls, portraits of saints, maroon carpet that might benefit from being replaced. The space didn't invite light into it. In fact, it made me feel tired.

"Med pass is at seven in the morning and seven in the evening if you take meds, so make sure you're in your room at those times. The last thing you want is to be taken to Headmaster Sully. The staff also does bed checks around eleven and then periodically throughout the night. The doors auto-lock. The security staff have master keys if they need to get in. Your student ID badge is also your key. No one can get into your room without the universal key from security or your student badge. You're safe here. Mostly."

We rode the elevator in silence. I logged Bryce's information away, grateful I at least had a lock on my door. I sent a silent prayer that I wouldn't have someone out in left field for a roommate.

When the elevator stopped on the fifth floor, I followed him out and to a room at the end of the hall. My shoes sank into the thick, plush carpet lining the hallway. I bet it made it easier for students to sneak out since no one would hear them creeping around. Paintings of biblical scenes graced the dark walls. Light flooded in through the stained-glass windows on either end of the long hall. Overall, the place was dreary with all the dark flooring and decor.

"Room 555." Bryce smiled at me. "That's an angel number if you're into that sort of thing. Might be a good omen for you, Sirena."

I stared ahead, waiting for him to just open the damn door so I could go inside and set my room up. I wanted to relax.

He must have sensed my impatience because he finally opened the door and stepped aside to let me enter. I moved forward, and he followed.

It was a good space. I'd assumed I'd have a roommate, but there was only a single bed in the room.

"This floor has private rooms. Your stepdad paid extra so you could room alone. You even have a private bathroom. Most of the rooms here are regular dorm rooms, and everyone shares a large community bathroom on each floor. These rooms are reserved for people who can, uh, afford them."

So Jerry actually shelled out money for me. It was probably just his way of keeping me as far from other people as possible. At least in this instance, I needed to thank him. Or maybe my mom had something to do with it.

"As you can see, you have a queen-sized bed and a sitting area." He gestured to a circular tower part of the room where there was a window seat and a leather chair facing the lake. "Your own bathroom is right through there." He pointed at a closed door. "There's a bit of a kitchenette for you. Counter and sink. Storage drawers. Oh, and a mini fridge too." He nodded to the black appliance on the countertop before he strode over to a wardrobe and tugged the doors open. Inside was a small flatscreen TV.

"You get cable in these rooms, which is cool because the regular dorm rooms don't have TVs unless students bring them from home. And since there's no way for those with regular admission to get cable without it being part of their tuition, it's pointless. Each common room in the dorm buildings does have a big screen and furniture. The only thing they play though is some twenty-four-hour church services and the old *Ten Commandments* movie."

He grew quiet as we stood there, likely having run out of steam needing to carry on a whole conversation on his own. My suitcases were lined up against the wall by the door. I was eager to start unpacking so I could be alone.

"So, uh... what I was saying about Church and his crew... They really are dangerous. It would be smart of you to try to lay low if they're looking for you. You don't want to be caught up in anything concerning them. *They* run this place, not the teachers, medical staff, security, or headmaster. *It's them.* Every year they host a party at their private house just a bit up the trail from here to celebrate the start of a new year. Everyone important or trying to be important goes. They initiate the new students. It's seriously messed up." He shuddered as he considered it. "Just stay away from them if you can. I can't stress it enough."

I stared at the wall, and he sighed.

What could have possibly brought Bryce to Chapel Crest? He seemed completely normal to me.

"Well, I think I covered everything important." He placed the folder he'd been carrying down on my bed, his voice dragging me from my thoughts. "That's your welcome packet. A campus map, your schedule and a few other important things you should take a look at are inside. There's a media center in the main hall that I didn't get to show you, but you can't miss it if you're on the second floor. It's the first door on your left. If you need to print anything or use a computer, you'll find everything in there. Other than that, welcome to Chapel Crest." He shuffled over to the door and gave me a quick smile. "I wrote my number on the front of the folder in case you need anything. I'm always available."

He hesitated for a moment, probably waiting to see if I'd say anything. When I didn't, he blew out a breath, gave me another half-smile, and left my room.

The moment the door clicked shut, I let out a heavy sigh of relief. I set to work unpacking everything. I wanted to start with my bed, so I unzipped the massive duffel bag and pulled out the new bedding

Mom had gotten me. It was cream and lavender with tiny flowers on it.

After my bed was made up, I moved on to dealing with everything else, noticing my mom and Cady had also sent silverware, plates, bowls, cups, bottled water, tiny boxes of cereal, and snacks. I dug out the sugary treats Cady had stashed in my bag and placed them on my counter. With the food stored away, I started hanging my clothes. I didn't have a ton. Most of my things were ugly because of Jerry. But the suitcase Cady had sent me with was loaded with all sorts of cute tops, shoes, skirts, jeans, and dresses. She'd even thrown in a curling iron, a blow dryer, and some styling tool I'd seen her straighten her hair with.

I set my makeup and hair items on the counter in the small bathroom, grateful I had my own private place. The tub was deep, which was fantastic because I loved taking bubble baths while reading. And Cady had even sent my favorite bubble bath and soaps along. I hung my two towels and washrags on the rack.

This wasn't so bad.

After I left the bathroom, I noted the time on my alarm clock and realized I'd been working for over two hours. I set my laptop on the bedside dresser then flopped down on the mattress and pulled out my cell phone. When I turned it on, there were two messages—one from Mom and one from Cady.

I opened Mom's first.

Mom: Hey, hon! I hope you check this. We made it to the hotel safely. Jerry was tired, so we're staying in Gaylord for the night. I'm so proud of you and how brave you are with going to a new school so far from home. I really think it'll help you come out of your shell. You know we're only a phone call or text away. I love you, Sirena. I already miss you.

I loved my mom. I didn't necessarily like her choice in men, but what did I know? I knew Jerry gave her a better life. I still hated him though.

I opened Cady's message.

Cady: Text me! Call me! Even if it's just so I can hear you breathe. I'm worried about you and no one being there to stick up for you. Find the biggest bad asses on campus and befriend them. Seriously. They'll protect you. And if they don't, let me know. I don't care if I have to run up Jerry's credit card Ubering my ass up there, I'll come and take down any bastards who hurt you. I love you, Sis. Be safe, OK? XO- C

I shook my head as I read Cady's message before darkening the screen. I grabbed the remote and channel surfed before settling on a rerun of *Friends*.

The sky was starting to get dark beyond my window, which was just as well. I dressed in my new tank top and short pajamas Mom had gotten me and settled back in bed, hugging Mr. Fuzz—my old teddy bear from when I was a kid—to my chest. I loved that old bear. It had been a Christmas gift from my parents the year before Dad left. I guessed I probably kept it around because it reminded me of better times. Happier times.

With those happy memories in my head, I closed my eyes, telling myself I needed all the sleep I could get.

†

THE CLANG of church bells roused me from a deep sleep right at daybreak. I punched my pillow and tugged the covers over my head in an attempt to drown out the noise. Classes didn't start until Monday, so I didn't have crap to do all day.

If I were a more enthusiastic person, I'd go exploring, but I figured I'd leave that for later. Bryce said a majority of the students would be arriving today and tomorrow and that I'd need to be at morning mass on Sunday.

I figured I'd paint a little today. I'd already set my easel and paints up by the tower window and was excited about painting the sunrise on the water. Since the damn bells woke me up, it seemed like now was a good time to get started, so I got out of bed and did my bathroom routine before yawning and settling in front of my easel, my paintbrush at the ready.

And then I let my hands and soul do the work of speaking for me.

STITCHES

"She wasn't on campus all day. I looked." Church paced the living room, his blond hair a mess from dragging his fingers through it.

"Why are you so obsessed?" Sin grunted, settling back on the couch and watching Church with his narrowed, gray eyes. Today he'd decided to pull his hair back in a long ponytail, letting his shaved sides be seen. The black snake tattoo slithering up the side of his neck, the gauges in his ears, and piercings in his lip made him look like a son of Satan, instead of the good boy his mama hoped he'd be.

"I'm not obsessed," Church snapped, shooting a glare at Sin who took it in stride, a dark brow quirked. "She's. . . different. I like that."

"Everyone at this hellhole is different. Ain't none of us normal, that's for damn sure. Plus, she's a fucking mute, dude. It's no fun if they can't scream." Sin offered a dark smirk as I laughed. He had a point.

Ashes shook his head and flopped down at the other end of the leather sectional, his black shirt partially unbuttoned.

"It's not polite to refer to people that way," Ashes said, cracking open his bottled water and taking a sip before recapping it.

"Shut the fuck up, Ashes. Wasn't it you who called Jasmine

Reynolds a come-guzzling, gutter slut this morning?" I asked from my spot on the leather ottoman. I shifted in my seat, already uncomfortable from sitting too long.

Trying to be still made me ache inside. My brain always wanted to go, go, go, but whatever the fuck part of it that housed my logic told me I needed to chill. The constant war in my head exhausted me. Eventually, one of the moods, or whatever they were, would win, and I'd spiral before it all happened again. I'd already taken my lithium for the day. Hell hath no fury like a bipolar who forgot his meds.

"Might have been. But, in my defense, she really is. She's swallowed so much come I'm surprised she doesn't sweat it," Ashes said.

"Nasty. Can you imagine a bitch sweating come?" I looked to Church who'd gone back to pacing.

Church had gone off his meds a long time ago. Hell, I didn't even know if he bothered to ever take them in the first place. His form of medicine was running through the cemetery and woods in the middle of the night, hunting small animals like a lunatic. To be fair, he *was* a fucking lunatic. We all were in some way. Our crazy brought us closer together though. We were nothing without each other.

"No." Church grunted before stopping. "Did Andrews say which dorm she was going to be in?"

"No, that fucker was barely keeping the piss in his dick," I said with a snort. "Besides, I don't know what you're freaking out about. A girl who looks like her probably already has a boyfriend."

"Well, *now* I'm interested." Sin sat forward, letting his borderline personality disorder and psycho shine through. "I like it when I can get a girl to cheat."

"Your name's not Sin for nothing," Ashes muttered, finishing his water and hauling out his vape.

"Damn right." Sin nodded solemnly.

"*I* want her," Church said. "I think we'd have fun with her. Or at least I would."

"Right. A chick who can't talk." Sin rolled his eyes and sank back again, his interest gone. "Sounds fun. I'm not interested in a bitch who can't scream when I fuck her. Boyfriend or not."

"If she can't talk, then she can't bitch," I pointed out.

Sin nodded thoughtfully.

"Listen, she'll have to be at mass tomorrow. Why not just see her then?" Ashes glanced between all of us. "Sin and I don't even know if she's worth the trouble. I mean, I'm sure she's worth something, but for us? We're not easy to get along with. Girls don't last long with us. Our crazy tends to scare them off. We'll see her tomorrow and get a look at her. Who knows? We may not want shit to do with her."

"Ashes has a point. Besides, I'm tired of bitches lately," Sin said. "Another year of the same pussy is getting old. Melanie. *A-fucking-gain*? I think we've torn that pussy up enough. It's like trying to fuck open air, so loose nothing grips my dick. We could use a new toy. Plus, I heard she went on an eating binge this summer and gained fifteen. So much for her body dysmorphia and anorexia. Guess the fucking gods at this place helped heal her."

"Tired of bitches? So you're interested in cock now? You can suck mine, Sinclair." I grabbed my junk for him through my jeans.

"Pfft, you'd suck mine, *Malachi*."

I rolled my eyes at him. "Whatever. Maybe she gained the pounds in her tits and ass. *That* would still keep me interested, open air or not. Can still fuck her ass and mouth." I looked over to Church as Sin snorted. "Church, I'm with Ashes. Let's just chill until mass. We can see her then. *Talk* to her. See if she'd be a good candidate for us to claim. She might just be a good one-and-done fuck, you know? For now, I want to play some Madden and eat some leftover pizza or something. So fucking chill."

Church was always worked up over something. Everything pissed the psycho off or set him off. He had a way of flying off the deep end about most things in life. We'd all been best friends since we were young. And Church had always been fucking nuts. Even when we were toddling around, barely able to talk, he was crushing bugs and laughing gleefully as their guts exploded out their asses.

Of course, Sin was a close second to Church. He liked to do dark shit. Pain and torment seemed to motivate him as much as they did Church. Of course, where Church was just nuts, Sin was a logical type of crazy, always weighing the outcomes of his actions. I was surprised the two of them didn't get together and start a cult just so they could watch members drink the Kool-Aid and laugh about it.

And Valentine. Mr. Candy Hearts himself. Ashes was probably the nicest out of all of us, if one could call any of us *nice*. If you were in the mood to beg with positive results, Ashes would be the one you called out for. He tended to give a shit more than the rest of us. He was the All-American poster boy with his dark crew cut and blue eyes. Add his mega-watt smile, and most girls creamed themselves just looking at him.

"I'm going to play Xbox. You pricks in?" I peered around at my friends.

"Sure. Loser sucks my dick," Sin said.

Church grunted and slumped down in his chair. "Any of us probably suck cock better than that fucking bitch who was here yesterday."

"Cami? Scrape your dick?" Sin nodded knowingly. "I fucked her mouth before the end of last year. She has a bad gag reflex too. Puked all over the place when I blew my load down her throat."

"Gross," Ashes muttered, grabbing a controller.

I grinned. "Sounds like Sin was into it."

He shrugged. "Just exorcising her demons, boys."

†

"Fuck." I squinted my eyes as sunlight streamed into my room.

We'd stayed up way too late playing video games and planning our welcome back party. I hauled my sorry ass out of bed and grabbed a quick shower before slipping on my navy blue and white uniform. I downed my meds for the day. Being the watchers, we didn't need med passes. We did our own shit. I doubted there was anyone with big enough balls on campus to try to force meds on us if we decided to stop taking them completely. With money and power came a heaping shit load of doing whatever the fuck we wanted. I didn't bother with my tie, knowing Headmaster Sully would glower at me the entire time. It was the little things that made me smile.

I sauntered out to the living room to find the guys already suited up and lounging around.

“Almost late. Trying to get that vein in Sully’s forehead to burst?” Ashes asked.

“You know it,” I said, snagging the waffle off his plate and stuffing it into my mouth. "I mean look at the rest of you, in uniform for the most part, ready to make an appearance like good, little boys."

I winked at him. Ashes looked the most put together out of all of us. His tie was at least half-assed knotted, while his white shirt was tucked in, and his blue blazer was in place. Hell, even his pants were pressed. Church’s tie hung limply around his neck, and his shirt was untucked. Sin had only fastened half his buttons and left his tie dangling from his back pocket, his long hair pulled up into a bitch biscuit atop his head.

Sin chuckled at me as Ashes scowled and flicked the empty zippo he carried around five times.

“Let’s go,” Church called out, shoving his phone into his pocket.

We followed him out and down the trail, watching all the students trudge along at the ungodly hour.

“Hey, Munson, you still owe me fifty bucks,” Sin called out to a skinny mother fucker wallowing along with dark, greasy hair. “I want it by end of the day, or I’ll take my payment out of your baby sister. She's starting this year, isn't she? Heard she’s a cutter. She might enjoy my brand of punishment.”

Munson paled and picked up his pace.

“His sister looks like him. May as well just fuck him.” Church narrowed his green eyes at Munson’s back. “No tits. Built like a fucking stick.”

I let out a soft laugh while Ashes just shook his head.

When we reached the cathedral, students stepped aside for us so we could go in. We took our seats in the back like we always did, foregoing all the bullshit holy water and forehead dabbing.

"Place is a fucking prison." Sin sighed, peering around. "Check them all out."

"Melanie is looking good. That fifteen did go to her tits and ass," I said, eyeing the blonde in her short navy blue, plaid skirt.

We'd all fucked her. Separately, of course. She considered herself our number one. Our claimed, even though we hadn't said she was. At least, she knew how to suck cock. Supreme bitch though. Decent rack that was better now with the added weight. She was a narcissist with image issues, which made her hard to fuck. She liked to twist shit on us. Fucking her was like fucking a skeleton from the cemetery. Next to us, she was probably second most important and popular person on campus if we considered the four of us one entity.

"Boring," Church said, his green eyes keen as he examined everyone who passed by.

"Looking for someone?" a deep voice called out.

I let out a snort and glared over at Seth Cain, the asshole we all loved to hate. If we were being honest, Seth was probably the third most important person on campus. But what a fucking douche. The guy was an enigma. He was fairly quiet, but for some reason, chicks flocked to him. He did give off a bit of a bad boy persona, but we just did it better. Maybe it was because there were more of us and only one of him. Word in the halls was he suffered from some of the same shit we did but with a fun twist—Seth heard voices. He saw things no one saw. Total schizo who tried to kill his stepfather with a fork when Seth was thirteen. Heard the dude lost an eye in the attack, and Seth stomped on it while his neighbors phoned 9-1-1. He spent some time in a state hospital before they sent him here a few years ago, deeming him well enough to rejoin the ranks of the mildly insane.

"Looking to put you in the ground," Sin said easily, trailing his gaze over him. "Figured someone would've done me the favor by now."

"Come on, Sinclair, you know I'm not easy to kill," Seth muttered.

Girls giggled as they passed by him. But they snapped their mouths closed when they caught our glares.

"Why are you here?" Ashes demanded from the far end of the pew as he flipped open his Bible five times before snapping it shut.

"It's been a long summer. That's all. Figured you assholes may have missed me."

"Hardly," Church grumbled. "Now get fucking lost before I kick your dick in, Cain."

"We've missed you too," he said, backing away with a dark laugh.

I watched as he sauntered down the aisle, his dark hair brushing against his shoulders. In a perfect world, Cain would've been one of us, but the guy was an unpredictable prick. Church was already our unpredictable prick. We didn't need two. And we especially didn't need someone capable of carving our eyes out with a fork at dinner.

"Where the fuck is she?" Church growled as the last few students trickled in.

"Maybe she really can't hear." I laughed softly. "She didn't know she had to be here."

Father Emerson started with his droning, silencing the room. The security guards clad in their all-white lurked in the dark corners of the church. *Armed to the tits with tranquilizers in case someone gets out of hand.*

My head fell back, and I stared up at the cathedral ceiling probably thirty feet above me, images of some biblical bullshit painted on it. The stained-glass windows lining both walls sent shards of colors scattering across the students and pews.

Emerson was halfway through the morning prayer when the doors behind us slammed shut. Heads swiveled to gawk at the fool who dared enter mass late, disregarding the prayer Emerson led in his droning, monotone voice.

The beauty Church was obsessed with darted into the packed cathedral. All the seats were pretty much taken, so she'd be hard pressed to find a place to sit without causing more of a disruption.

The only empty spot was in our row where only our crew sat.

I grinned, knowing how this was going to turn out.

Finally. Some excitement.

SIRENA

I'd gotten caught up painting and lost track of time.

I rushed as fast as I could to the cathedral, but the doors were closed. It took me a moment to get inside, and then, of course, those damn heavy doors had to slam closed, making nearly everyone turn and stare at me. There had to be a few hundred people there, gawking at me.

And there wasn't a damn place to sit.

I peered around, catching the angry glare of Father Emerson, a few faculty members, and security off to the side who I recognized from the staff directory in my folder.

Damn it!

A quick scan of the place for Bryce made me realize there was no way I'd find him in the sea of students. The only place to sit was next to the guys he'd warned me to stay away from. It was either sit or run, and I was too scared to run, so I quickly moved closer to the guys and begged with my eyes for them to let me sit beside them. Fear coursed through me as the blond one, Church, gazed up at me with a raised eyebrow. A low murmuring rippled around the room.

"It'll cost you," he said softly.

I said nothing, staring down at him desperately. Everything in my body screamed for me to run. I even shuffled back as panic began to creep its way up my throat.

What if I ran? Everyone would know. But if I stayed, I'd have to sit with them. . .God, they terrified me. One. Two. Three. Breathe. Breathe. BREATHE!

The one who'd been with him yesterday—Stitches—let out a soft laugh. "It's your funeral, angel."

I quickly peered past him to see two other guys. One had a man bun. His uniform strained against his muscles, and his shirt was partially undone, showcasing his tattoos. He stared back at me, his gray eyes dark and narrowed with a look of pure disgust on his face. The other one—dark crew cut—seemed to be put together and far nicer than the other three. His blue eyes darted between Church and me before he scooted down. The guys followed, except Church.

Instead, he gestured to the space between him and Stitches.

"Welcome to hell," he murmured.

I swallowed and took the spot quickly, forcing my fears down because my therapist told me I needed to learn to face things head-on.

Don't run from your problems, Sirena. That's not how we heal.

It only took a moment for me to realize I'd made a very bad choice. Students whispered, casting looks back at me. I stared down at my hands, realizing I'd forgotten to grab my Bible on the way out.

The priest began talking again, calling order back to the room. "Please turn in your Bibles to John 20:22."

A Bible was slid onto my lap, and I peeked over to find Stitches with a tiny smirk on his lips.

"That's two," the guy with the bun muttered softly.

Church let out a quiet chuckle, confusing me. I didn't know what was so funny. But everyone here had a mental illness or behavioral issues of some sort, so maybe blurting random things was that guy's deal.

With shaking hands, I opened the Bible and followed along, rising to my feet and standing silently while students sang when prompted—everyone but the guys in the pew with me. They didn't sing. They stood stone still, their overwhelming presence sending chills rushing through my body. They dwarfed me in size. I felt like a child standing amongst them. They were easily over six feet tall and would tower over Jerry.

I felt suffocated by their intensity. Breathing was a struggle because each inhale filled my nostrils with their intoxicating scents. Crisp. Clean, but smoky.

My leg bounced as I tried to keep my anxiety down.

Stupid. So dumb. Damn it, Sirena! Control your breathing. There are tons of people around. You won't be hurt. Breathe. Breathe. BREATHE.

Everyone here is crazy though! What am I doing? You gotta go. You need to run. Run, Sirena! Damnit! RUN!

I blew out a shaky breath as I tried to take up as little space as possible.

I flinched when Church's warm palm moved to rest on my jittering leg, pushing it down so I'd be still. He didn't look at me, and he didn't remove his hand from my knee. I stared down at it like it was a hot iron on my skin.

I wanted to scream. I should've ran.

Please don't touch me. Please. Please.

I dragged in a few strangled breaths, recognizing I was about to completely lose it. I was about to have a full-blown panic attack right in the middle of the damn sermon. A meltdown like last year's when Garrett McGregor got too close to me in the hallway and pushed me against my locker as he grabbed my breast. I'd crumpled to the floor and curled into the fetal position, silent tears pouring from my eyes as I'd hyperventilated. Of course, no one knew what had happened since I didn't talk. And Garrett McGregor hadn't said shit. I'd been taken away in an ambulance, and Mom had met me at the hospital. I'd spent two weeks in a psych ward for that episode.

The congregation stood again to sing. I could barely get up. My legs trembled beneath me as I clutched the back of the pew in front of me, my head dizzy.

I didn't pay attention to the rustling coming from my right, but I jumped when a warm hand was pressed to my back and the dark-haired guy at the end was where Stitches had been. He nodded to the aisle.

"Go," he urged softly as everyone sang without paying attention to us.

I stepped around Church who peered at me impassively.

"That's three," the guy with the bun called out loudly enough for me to hear.

Stitches snickered as the dark-haired guy escorted me into the aisle and out of the building. The moment I was outside, I hauled in a deep breath and sank to my butt on the top step, my arms wrapped around myself as I rocked.

"Are you OK?"

I continued to sway. The guy cleared his throat and sat down on the top step a foot away from me.

"My name is Asher Valentine. Everyone calls me Ashes," he said in a deep voice. "What's your name?"

I didn't answer. I concentrated on getting myself under control.

"Right," he muttered. "You don't talk. Stitches and Church said that. I know you probably want to get the hell out of here right now, but I'd advise against it. If you aren't present for mass, they'll ding you. It's a bitch to deal with. I'll spot you this once. But don't make a habit of it, OK? Just stay until everyone leaves. I'll make sure it counts as being here for you."

My body stopped moving, and I let out a shaky breath.

"We'll stay out here until the service is over, but you need to be at the next one. All the way through. Sin has started taking a tally."

It took me a moment to realize he was talking about the man bun guy. He'd been counting. He said I was at three. I had no idea what that meant, and I didn't find myself caring at the moment.

"This is weird," Ashes muttered. "Do you shake your head or nod or anything?

I swallowed and hugged myself tighter.

"Am I bothering you? Do you want me to go?"

A tear slid down my cheek. I hated feeling this way. My therapist said I needed to learn not every male was out to get me. That some really were kind.

Maybe Ashes was one of the nice ones.

"OK. . . well, I don't know how much you know about Chapel Crest, but this place can be brutal. Watch yourself. Not many here are cut out to be your friend. It's probably a good thing you don't talk. No one can accuse you of running your mouth. That sort of thing can get you into a lot of trouble." He glanced up at the clear sky for a moment. "You're a secret keeper."

Ashes grew quiet, and I chanced a peek at him. He was beautiful, just like the other three guys he'd been sitting with. It didn't take a genius to figure out that he must have worked out like the others. I averted my gaze before he caught me staring. Bryce said Ashes was a pyromaniac. The idea intrigued me.

"I'm glad you've relaxed." He looked behind him and sighed. His phone buzzed in his pocket. He pulled it out and read his text message. Quickly, he thumbed out a message and then seemed to be going through his social media. It was just as well. It was awkward just sitting there with nothing to do.

I got up and brushed off my bottom. With my eyes trained on the ground, I moved down the stairs and over to the edge of the cathedral. A cemetery was just beyond it. A shiver raced through me when I surveyed all the old, cracked headstones. A crow cawed in the distance as I rubbed my arms despite the warmth of the morning.

"The cemetery extends all the way to the woods," Ashes said from behind me, making me jolt. His warm hand rested on my back for a moment to steady me before he stepped beside me to peer through the wrought iron fence. His fingers held a silver Zippo, which he flicked five times in succession.

"The place can be pretty creepy. They say it's haunted. The campus was built about fifty years after the cathedral and cemetery. The place started out as a religious school and somehow morphed into what it is today. A place to hide away the crazies in the world."

He paused for a moment before continuing, "It was once a small logging town. People moved on though. Sicknesses took over." He pointed to some of the stone buildings in the distance. "Those are mausoleums. Houses for the dead in case you didn't know."

I swallowed and gaped up at him.

He stared down at me, his brows crinkled. "You have beautiful eyes. I've never seen eyes like it before. They're. . . mesmerizing. I wonder what you've seen, what you've been through."

Cady's advice about finding the scariest guy on campus to befriend shot through my head. Maybe Ashes could be my friend.

I'd have to get used to him though. Guys scared the shit out of me now. Surprisingly, Bryce hadn't frightened me. He was almost comforting, but I knew his reach wasn't far at all. I wasn't sure how much protection he could offer me aside from his presence.

The doors to the cathedral banged open as we stood staring at one another. Students poured down the steps, laughing and talking. A few screamed and several of the white-clad security guards surged forward and took hold of them to lead them away.

Ashes glanced over my shoulder and nodded his head.

"Figured you'd be out here," Church's deep voice rang out. He stepped beside Ashes and swept his gaze over me.

Stitches and the guy I guessed was Sin joined him, creating a semi-circle around me. A few passing students shot me quick looks and whispered behind their hands.

"What do you think?" Stitches asked, folding his arms over his chest as he shot me a smirk. With high cheekbones and shaggy jet-black hair, he was quite beautiful to look at. He looked like an angel, albeit a fallen one.

I focused on my feet, wondering if I could just walk away without any consequence. The panic grew again, tightening my chest and narrowing my throat. It wouldn't be long before it won, and I was on the ground in the fetal position, frozen by fear.

"I'm with Church," Ashes murmured.

"Are you fucking kidding me?" Sin snorted. "Not happening."

"Why not?" Church asked as I glanced up at him.

"She's a secret keeper," Ashes said. "Tell her your secrets, and she can't tell anyone else. She's pretty perfect actually."

"Plenty of people keep their mouths shut if you cut out their tongues," Sin said darkly, his gray eyes sweeping over me. "Right, new girl?"

"Party tonight?" a deep voice rumbled, cutting off whatever Sin planned on saying next as I shook, gripping the wrought iron fence behind me.

My breath caught in my chest as I glimpsed Seth Cain. His blue eyes swept over me for a moment until that light bulb look that haunted my nightmares washed over his face.

I stumbled back into the fence, my chest heaving as I struggled to suck in air.

"Sirena?" Seth's shocked voice met my ears.

The other guys glanced between us as I breathed hard. Seth was beautiful. Hair black as pitch. Blue eyes. As big as the guys surrounding me.

And here. So very much here.

He took a step toward me, and I squeezed my eyelids closed for a moment before pulling myself together and darting away. I staggered as I tried to get away, my chest heaving as I tried to breathe.

No. No. No. No. NO. Not here. Please, not here.

I broke past Sin, my elbow knocking into him as he grunted his discontent. Or surprise. I wasn't sure which, and I sure as hell didn't care.

Seth Cain was here which meant I needed to not be.

ASHES

I wanted to reach for her as pure terror swept over her pretty face. Instead, I watched as she struggled to inhale before she ran from us, nearly falling onto the cobblestones, but not bothering to look back or slow down.

"What the fuck?" Sin frowned. "She should join the track team."

"Do you know her?" Church focused on Seth who stared after her with his mouth gaping open. He cleared his throat and shook his head.

"Uh, yeah. I mean, I used to. We went to school together when we were kids," he mumbled.

All the swagger he usually had was gone and replaced by what seemed to be discomfort. It was difficult to tell on him since he kept his shit together most of the time.

"Yeah? What the fuck is wrong with her? She's hot as hell but doesn't talk. Apparently, some bad shit happened to her and now she doesn't speak," Stitches said.

"I don't know." Seth cleared his throat. "So…party?"

"You know we are. Now, what's the deal with that crazy bitch?" Sin pressed, jerking his head in the direction Sirena had fled in.

"Man, I don't know. I heard she died." He swallowed, his Adam's apple bobbing.

That explained why it looked like he'd seen a ghost. What the hell had happened to her?

"Andrews!" Church shouted.

Bryce Andrews flinched at the sound of his name but came over to us.

"What dorm is specter in?" Church demanded.

"Specter?" Bryce crinkled his brows.

"The mute chick," Sin snapped, making Bryce wince again.

"Oh. Um, Sirena Lawrence. Right. She's in Esther Hall. Room 555."

"Nice. Private room." Stitches nodded. "Perfect."

"Why do you want to know?" Seth pulled himself together again and glared, a muscle thrumming along his jaw.

"Why do you think?" Stitches popped a brow at him.

"Harder to hear them scream when they don't have a voice," Sin added.

"I've gotta go." Seth grunted, backing away. "Stay away from her." He still had that deer in the headlights look about him.

"Whatever," Stitches said, waving him off. "*We* run this place. Not you. We'll do whatever the fuck we want. Go take your psych meds and fuck off."

Seth clenched his jaw as his gaze darted among us. He said nothing before he backed away and loped off in the direction Sirena had gone.

"Andrews, would you be so kind as to inform the new girl that her presence is requested tonight at the gathering I'm having? I'd hate to not welcome her properly." Church gave Bryce a Cheshire smile.

Bryce looked sick but nodded before scurrying away.

"Did you get her to talk?" Stitches asked.

I shook my head, wanting to get to the bottom of whatever Seth had going on with her. Guy was completely weird as shit.

"No. She had a panic attack and rocked herself until it passed, then we stared at the cemetery."

"Best fucking date you've ever been on, eh, Ashes?" Stitches joked.

"Might be. You jealous?"

"Nah. I'll tap that pussy soon enough. Church called dibs though. He's first in line for that train ride." Stitches rolled his eyes.

"I'm not interested. She's all yours," Sin said. "Bitch seems crazy, and I'm the only one allowed to hold that title."

"Church is crazy," I pointed out.

"I prefer insane." Church's green eyes glinted with his ill intentions.

I wasn't much for prayer, but in this instance, I knew Sirena Lawrence was going to need one.

†

"WHAT'S THE PLAN?" I asked as I flopped down into my usual spot on the leather sofa in our living room and flicked my Zippo five times. "Same shit we do every year?" I sucked deeply on my vape and puffed out five perfect, cherry-scented rings into the air.

"Yes. I think the initiates for Chapel Crest will just go through the standard procedure," Church said as he typed away on his laptop.

"What the hell are you doing?" Stitches peered over Church's shoulder.

"Research," he muttered, tapping and scrolling some more. His gaze skittered across the screen, and his fingers slowed to a stop. "Well, well, well."

"What is it?" I got up, my curiosity getting the best of me.

Church was always up to something.

"I found out what's wrong with specter." He pointed to the screen and gazed up at us.

Ten-Year-Old Detroit Girl Found Alive but in Critical Condition

I quickly read the article about Sirena Lawrence.

"Fuck," I muttered, running my fingers through my hair and reading the screen again.

Locked in a metal toolbox for nearly a week... Beaten by a weapon that was never found... Critical condition... Life flighted to a children's hospital...

"Damn. That's some fucked up shit." Stitches stepped away as Sin entered.

"What are you cunts up to?" He cast a cursory glance in our direction.

"Finding out why Sirena Lawrence doesn't talk," I said.

"Why's that? Cat got her tongue?" He snickered at his own joke.

"Someone tried to kill her." Church swiveled the computer around so Sin could see.

He skimmed the information, shaking his head. "Well, she needs to get over that shit."

"She was stuffed in a dark fucking box," I snapped at him.

"So? I was shot in the chest and choked nearly to death on my own blood. You don't see me crying about it." Sin stomped over to the chair and sat down.

"No, instead you've got some buried PTSD and loads of issues with your personality disorder," I fired back.

Sin's jaw went slack before he spoke again, "Either we bring her out of her shell, or we move the fuck on. While I enjoy having play-things, I can't see where I'd get any joy out of this."

Sin had major issues forming relationships with women. He tended to lose control if he got attached, as we'd seen with the last girl who was dumb enough to fall for him. His fear of abandonment—something he had issues admitting—made him difficult to love. Instead, he simply fucked girls and without forming connections. We knew him well enough to know he'd find joy in this if he'd let go a little bit.

"Oh, I can think of a few ways." The way Church's eyes glinted with darkness and the curling of his lip made me sigh.

"Initiation," Stitches said knowingly.

"Cemetery," Church added.

Sin leaned forward, smiling sinisterly, his interest piqued.

"Mausoleum," he growled.

"The perfect spot for little, dead girls." Church grinned.

I should've said no, but I wasn't part of the gang for nothing. I also liked pretty, broken things. Maybe it was their suffering that reminded me I was human. I needed the screaming. The begging. The crying.

It made me feel.

Just *what* I felt was sometimes the problem.

And that led me to believe I had a bit more issues than my diagnosis suggested.

SIRENA

I stared down at the cell phone in my hand, knowing I couldn't call anyone. No one knew what Seth had done to me. No one would save me.

A knock at my door had me dropping my phone and backing away, fear rushing through me as I envisioned Seth with a shovel behind the heavy, wooden door.

Go away. Go away. Go away. Breathe, Sirena. One. Two. Three. Four. . .

"Sirena? It's Bryce."

I blew out a breath and swallowed hard before taking a shaky step forward.

Could Bryce help me?

"Hey, uh, I need to talk to you. Can you open the door? Please?"

I shuffled slowly toward the door and peeked through the peephole to make sure he was alone. When I saw he was, I pulled the door open.

"Hey." He smiled widely at me. "May I come in?"

I stepped aside for him and quickly closed the door as soon as he crossed the threshold. He moved to the center of my room and glanced around.

"It looks really nice in here."

I walked to my bed and smoothed my skirt down as I sat, trying desperately to remain calm and not appear as if I were in the middle of a major meltdown. *Who knew what would happen?* I was sure security and the medical staff would rush in to give me a shot that would make me itch and feel numb inside.

God, I didn't want that fucking shot. I hated that shot.

"Yeah. So..." He offered me a quick smile. "I'm supposed to let you know the watchers are demanding your presence at their party tomorrow night."

I stared at him, confused. *Who were the watchers?*

"Right, you don't really know who they are. I told you about them. Church, Stitches, Sin, and Ashes." Bryce came over and eased down beside me on the mattress.

I drew in closer to myself at his nearness.

He didn't seem to notice. "You see, every year they throw a party to welcome students back, but it's more than that. They initiate the newbies. Some of them make it through the ordeal. Others are deemed unworthy and become slaves of sort. And then some are ignored because they lose interest. Obviously, you want them to lose interest in you. Anyway, Church sent me to make sure you show up tomorrow night."

This couldn't be approved by the staff here at Chapel Crest. It sounded like some form of torture.

I stared at my hands in my lap. There was no way in hell I was going to any parties. I had every intention of not leaving my room except for classes, and I'd be making damn sure my door was properly shut so the lock engaged every night. The last thing I needed was for Seth to get near me.

"This is a big deal, Sirena. If the watchers want you, they'll take you. They'll select a few to torment. You don't want it to be you. Do whatever you have to do to keep yourself away from them. But you'll need to show up. Shit will be bad if you don't. They prey on the weak."

Bryce sat for a moment longer before getting to his feet.

"I know you're afraid, but I'm not the one you need to fear. You have my number. Text me, and I'll try to help you. I-I read your file. I know I wasn't supposed to, but I couldn't help it. I know how you were hurt. I know guys frighten you." He licked his lips and swallowed hard. "Just. . . stay safe, OK? I don't have much pull here, but I can keep you company." He moved to the door. "You can't stay silent forever. The watchers have a way of making people scream. If you're in their sights, eventually, you'll scream too. Everyone at Chapel Crest screams."

He twisted the knob and walked out. The moment he was gone, I shot up and checked the door, my chest heaving with the new information.

I fucking hated it here.

†

I DIDN'T SLEEP. I lay in bed and stared up at my ceiling. When the sun rose, I got to my feet like a zombie and got ready for the day. With my uniform on, I slung my backpack over my shoulder and trudged to the main building on campus. I left thirty minutes early, hoping no one else would be out. The last thing I wanted to do was run into Seth. Or those watcher guys.

When I got to the building, I went upstairs to my first class of the day, opting to skip going to my locker. I figured extra stops would increase the odds of running into Seth.

My first class centered around scripture. I groaned inwardly. *What a way to begin the day*. I knew I'd be struggling to stay awake within ten minutes of it starting.

I let out a breath and strolled to one of the windows overlooking the courtyard. Students were starting to gather down there. Some of them laughed and chatted, while others moved toward the doors to enter the building. Security milled about, watching students. Leaning against the wall, I slipped my phone out of my bag when it buzzed and found a message from Cady. She was grinning in the picture with a message attached.

Have a great day, Rina!

"Make sure your phone is on silent," Bryce called out as he approached.

Startled, I looked up at him and quickly turned my phone off and stuffed it back into my bag.

"Do you text?" he asked, his gaze sweeping over me quickly. He paused before speaking again, "Sorry. I forget you don't talk at all. Or give any sign that you even hear me." He let out a sigh. "I'm in Sister Claire's class this morning with you. In fact, I shuffled all my classes around to be in as many of your classes as I could. We won't have calculus or group therapy together. Hope that doesn't sound creepy or stalker-ish. I figured strength in numbers and all that. Swear I'm not crazy." He offered me a bashful smile.

While it did strike me as weird, it also gave me some relief. Bryce seemed OK. I didn't get super nervous around him, so it had to mean something.

"Sister Claire is strict. All the nuns and teachers here are, but she's one of the rougher ones. The Brothers and Sisters and some of the other teachers live here on campus. They're housed a bit far off the main path, so once classes are out, we don't tend to see them. Not that it matters. The watchers run this place mostly anyway. There's security, but I'm pretty sure they're afraid of the watchers. The medical staff come and go in shifts. Past that, we're on our own."

A shiver ran through me at his words. Typically, I'd view being on my own as good, but not with someone capable of murder running loose on campus. I was pushed into Bryce as some tall blonde strutted past me, her high heels clicking. His arm immediately snaked around my waist to keep me from tumbling over as my hands landed on his chest.

"Well, if it isn't Andrews and the angel. Why am I not surprised to see you two clinging to one another?" Stitches smirked at us as he came to a stop and leaned against the wall near us. His dark eyes took in Bryce's arm still around my waist, and a muscle feathered along his jaw.

I pushed away from Bryce, heat filling my cheeks.

"Did Andrews tell you about the party tonight? You're going to be our guest of honor," Stitches continued, his dark gaze sliding over my body. "I've been meaning to ask you, angel. What's the deal with you and Cain? You both looked like you'd seen a ghost yesterday."

He stared me down, waiting for an answer. When I didn't give him one, he continued, "I asked him. He said he knew you from when you were kids. To me, it seems strange that you'd be so nervous around someone you already knew. If anything, I'd think it would bring a sense of comfort." He pushed off the wall and stood directly in front of me.

I inched closer to Bryce on instinct, my pulse thundering in my ears.

"Then we looked you up. Or rather, Church did. He can *obsess* sometimes." He smiled and reached out to lift my braid off my shoulder.

Bryce's arm snaked around my waist again as I drew in tighter to him.

"Someone tried to kill you. That's. . . insane." His smirk widened as I moved so close to Bryce that I was tucked neatly beneath his arm, clinging to him. Stitches leaned in as both Bryce and I stiffened, his mouth near my ear. "I bet you're afraid of the dark now, aren't you?"

He let out a soft chuckle, his warm breath blowing over my skin. Goosebumps popped up along my flesh as he moved back.

"This is cute," he said, gesturing between Bryce and me. "I mean, it's not going to happen, but it's cute. Don't forget, angel. Party tonight at the Sanctuary. Skipping it isn't an option."

He finally backed away as Sister Claire opened the classroom door and disappeared inside.

"It'll be OK," Bryce mumbled. "I hope."

So did I, but things weren't looking good. At all.

SIN

I blew out the smoke from the joint I was toking and watched as she floated across the courtyard with Andrews by her side, her head down as he chattered away.

Sirena Lawrence.

I hated the girl, and I didn't know why. To be fair, I hated pretty much everyone, but something about her just twisted my normal hatred into a knot of something dangerous. Something lethal.

Whores were a dime a dozen here at Chapel Crest. She'd end up being another one if any of the bastards slinking down these halls got to her.

My attention was drawn to the guys on campus as they watched her walk past in her tiny, plaid skirt, her ass swaying. Either the girl didn't know her own beauty or she did and knew how to play it up with the mute, innocent act. Either way, I'd enjoy watching her be broken down. If there was anything in this world I loved, it was creating blood and tears. And screams. God, I loved fucking screams.

I hoped when she finally cracked, she'd scream until her lungs turned black.

I was fucked up. I didn't try to hide it. Docs said I had a borderline personality disorder as a result of my environment as a kid. That I had some PTSD from shit.

I knew it was just the tip of the iceberg though. I had a lot of issues the docs at these places couldn't even fucking touch. My real dad was insane. I assume he was the devil himself. He'd knocked up my ma. When she'd asked for a divorce from his abusive ass, he'd taken me and held me captive. He'd phoned her to let her know we weren't coming back. He'd kept her on the phone as he'd beaten me to a bloody pulp while I'd screamed for mercy. I could still hear her crying my name in my head sometimes at night when I closed my eyes.

"Tell her goodbye, Sinclair. Tell her we're going on a trip to hell. Tell her how much it hurts and how scared you are. Give her the best goodbye memory a boy can give his ma."

He'd ended up shooting me in the chest as she'd begged for him to stop before turning the gun on himself and blowing his brains out just before midnight on my eleventh birthday. I'd watched as his brains splattered against the wall of a dirty hotel room before my eyes closed. He'd died, and I'd lived.

It was as fucked up as it came, but that was my story. After they pulled my ass off life support as a means of letting me go, I started breathing on my own and opened my eyes. A miracle created from sin. Ma said it was the power of prayer.

A year later, she'd married a banker by the name of Rudy Duncan. *What a fucking laughable name.* She'd met him when she went out on one of the cruises she took every year with my aunt. I'd scared Rudy so much he'd convinced Ma to send me to Chapel Crest so I could get the help I apparently needed. He thought I was like my father, the devil. He'd never said it, but it was in the way he'd cowered around me, how he'd watched me with fearful eyes, the way he'd never let Ma be alone with me. He thought I needed God because of all the shit I'd gotten into.

He was going to be real fucking surprised when he realized I was a fucking god.

I finished what was left of my joint, my body buzzing from the high, and pushed off the table I was sitting at. I didn't know where I was going, but my feet seemed to. So did my fist. My right hook came out and cracked Devin Morris in the jaw, making him stumble back.

I fisted my hands around his lapels and glared down at him. "Don't fucking look at her. Don't think about her. Don't even fucking learn her name," I snarled down at him. "I'll fucking kill you. Got it?"

"S-sorry," he stammered. "I-I- won't, Sin. I didn't know she was claimed by the watchers."

I grunted and released him. He stumbled back into his two friends, the three of them booking it out of the courtyard without a backward glance.

She hadn't been claimed. *Yet.* I knew Church wanted her. Hell, so did Stitches. Ashes was harder to read, but if I knew him like I thought I did, he wouldn't say no once Church got her on her knees. He'd said he was in. That didn't necessarily translate into how *in* he was.

And me? Everything told me no. My past experience with women screamed for me to run the opposite direction. I didn't want to be caught in that storm again. I refused, but if we were just going to fuck her while we were at Chapel Crest....

"Hey," Seth called out as he approached me.

Silently, I watched him approach, his hands in his pockets. Seth Cain was nearly as fucked up as I was. He may have played Prince-fucking-Charming, but I recognized my own kind when I saw them. He battled his own invisible demons.

I said nothing, waiting for him to continue.

"Are you guys claiming Sirena Lawrence?" He stopped and surveyed me.

"I don't fucking want her," I said with a grunt, some weird feeling taking hold of my heart. I brushed it off. "But Church and Stitches do. Probably Ashes too. Why?"

Seth swallowed. "I'm interested in her."

I raised my brows at him. "Nostalgia?"

"You could say that."

"She have a tight pussy?" I asked, curious about his reaction.

His eyes darkened, and his mouth morphed into a deep frown. "I wouldn't know. We were ten the last time I saw her."

I nodded. "Well, I bet she does have a tight pussy. I'll let Church know you're wondering. If you have enough cash or secrets, he might even let you watch him fuck her bloody once he claims her. He won't let you play though."

"Sirena isn't that kind of girl. She won't fuck him just because he tells her to."

"No?" I raised my brows. "She won't get much of a choice in the matter. When Church wants something, he takes it. You know that. Besides, who said anything about her having a choice in it?"

"That's why I'm coming to you to ask for a favor."

"What's that?" He had my curiosity piqued. "You know, secrets and favors can be the cost of a soul."

Seth scoffed. "I have no fucking soul." He swallowed before continuing, "I really do want her. I want claims. I knew her first. She was my best friend when we were kids."

His Adam's apple bobbed. I'd never seen the pretty boy look so . . . vulnerable.

"Really?" I murmured, narrowing my eyes at him.

He nodded. "I'll pay for her."

"The only payment you could possibly give me that would interest me is making her scream. Can you do that? Make her scream?"

"Yes," he answered softly, licking his lips as a dark expression crossed over his face.

I surveyed him quietly, taking in the darkness of his eyes before I spoke. "You know, I find it strange. You can have pretty much any pussy on this campus, but you want the mute."

"I told you. I've known her for a long time," he said. He swallowed and turned away from me.

"Yeah? Seems suspicious if you ask me. Ten, you say?" I nodded, rolling the details around in my head. "She was hurt when she was ten. Almost killed. She hasn't spoken since. Never outed her attempted murderer."

He licked his lips, his gaze darting around.

"I'm no detective, but I bet you know something about that, don't you?" I circled him and stopped in front of his face. "Maybe someone let their crazy out."

"I want claims first," he repeated softly. "I don't know shit other than that."

"Maybe. I'll run it by Church. But I doubt he'll say yes. Her tight little ass and big tits have him a little crazy right now. Come to the party tonight. We'll see what happens. Sound good?"

"I'll pay, Sin."

"Sure, you will." I patted his cheek. "But we don't auction off girls here. We play with them. Maybe Church will let you have her once he and Stitches have had their fills."

"You know Sully will probably call her into his office," he called out as I turned.

I froze for a moment before I stalked back to him.

"You know the rumors. Let me have her before he gets her. He won't touch her if she's claimed."

"If she's *claimed* by a Watcher. Not a second-rate pretty boy," I snarled at him. "Don't come at me with bullshit. Rumors. That's all that shit is anyway. Shit created by angry, crazy people. You don't want to make our fucking list, Cain. I suggest you back the fuck off and wait to see what we decide. Got it?"

He nodded, his glare hard. "Yeah. I got it."

"Good. Now get the fuck out of my face. Oh, and stay away from her until we say otherwise. Understand?"

"Yes," he grumbled, backing away from me.

Something told me he didn't have it, and I'd probably have to beat it into him.

And I would because that was the sort of shit that got my dick hard.

MUSIC BLARED out of the sound system. Church had taken the measures to have our sanctuary soundproofed when we started here. A godsend really with all the fucked-up shit which took place within its walls.

"Gather 'round, you fucking ingrate pussies," Church bellowed as he strode down the staircase, a drink in his hand and Melanie tucked beneath his arm.

She sent out a beauty pageant smile to all the students gathered. I scoffed. The bitch thought she was our claimed for good. Like there was no competition. And to be fair, there hadn't been until Church saw Sirena. All we'd done was pass Melanie around and fuck her. It stroked her narcissistic ego.

We didn't even need to ask for what we needed. She just got on her knees and sucked cock like she was some come-starved whore who'd die without her next meal. She liked to get us off. It made her feel special, but it was dull. Fucking her never got me excited. It was simply a means of passing time in this hellhole.

"Tonight, we initiate you new pricks. If you're new around here and got our memo, line up on the back patio. Everyone else, get on the lawn. You know how this works." Church moved away from Melanie as he reached the bottom step and high-fived Stitches.

I glanced around the crowded place and didn't spot a sign of Sirena Lawrence. I caught Asher's eye across the room. He lifted his brows in a *well, she's fucked* sort of way.

She sure was. I grinned, excited at the prospect.

CHURCH

I glared at the handful of students before me. When we initiated new students, we picked the ones we thought might offer the most fun or who'd step out of line the easiest. It was the punishment that got my dick hard. It was a part of my brain I couldn't manage to turn off. I loved the hunt. The conquest. The fucking blood and tears. I'd bathe in that shit if I could.

If we missed one or two arrivals because they arrived late, it was easy enough to remedy. We also liked to initiate the students who might be useful to us later on. Fifteen of the newbies fidgeted as they stared nervously at me, my watchers at my side. I knew every new enrollee's record. We had a kleptomaniac, a handful of depression zombies, a couple of borderline personalities, some with eating disorders, a schizophrenic, some with impulse control disorders, a sex obsessed kid, and one with an intense fear of heights that turned into terrible anxiety. I hoped to add fear of the watchers to their list of ailments.

My heart thudded hard when I reached the end of the line of students and saw no Sirena Lawrence.

I curled my hands into fists and tried to breathe easy.

Where the fuck was my specter?

"Don't worry. It'll be more fun this way," Sin said softly from beside me. He'd made it very clear he wasn't interested in her, but I knew Sin. If nothing else, he was in it for the potential stress relief. So long as it didn't lead to him attaching and obsessing over someone because that always ended badly with him. His fear of abandonment had heightened in the last few months. He denied having abandonment issues, but we, watchers, knew better. We'd known him long enough to know all his quirks. The things that made him tick. Those that made him explode.

They were all fucking glorious.

"Clothes off, heads up," Stitches shouted, grinning at the students like a maniac.

They exchanged looks with one another.

"Now," I bellowed, grabbing my yardstick and smacking it against the railing of the patio.

The students quickly stripped down to their undergarments. We surveyed them for a few moments as the crowd behind us laughed and snickered.

"This won't do," I called out, shaking my head. "Ashes."

Ashes marched forward and began doling out packages to each of the newbies.

"Inside those bags are what we want you to go put on. Go inside and change. Then get your asses back out here. Don't touch anything but your clothes and packages once you're inside. I'll beat the shit out of you if you mess with anything else. Even you girls." I gave them a wicked grin before they scurried off.

"Angel bailed," Stitches commented, lifting his dark brows at me.

I nodded, my jaw clenched. No one defied me. Ever.

"Plan?" Sin asked, lighting a joint and taking a hit before handing it over to me.

"She doesn't like being locked in dark places," I growled. I'd already seen her file. I couldn't handle not knowing what made my little ghost tick. "*Nyctophobia.* Maybe she should find herself in one again."

Sin let out a soft, dangerous laugh.

Ashes shook his head. "That might be too far. She's traumatized—"

"My cousin hit his head when he was a kid. He had seizures for years after. Then one day, he fell off a ladder." I gazed out at everyone having a good time in the yard and took another hit of the joint I held before passing it off to Stitches.

Every one of these fuckers was medicated to hell. And if they weren't on pharmaceuticals, they were self-medicating with the alcohol and weed. Chapel Crest was a place meant to break you, not save you. It was hell on Earth. The world of medicine didn't make money on the healthy. Riches were in the sickness. Chapel Crest spread its disease deeper into the students. To be fair, so did I. A psycho needed something to pass the time with though.

I blew out a ring of smoke and continued, "After he fell and smacked his head again, the seizures stopped. Maybe the hair of the dog that bit her would be her saving grace."

"Or maybe it'll fuck her up more." Ashes locked eyes with me. "We could pick anyone else—"

"Do you not want to make her squeal and beg?" I cocked my head at him.

He snorted and hit his vape, puffing out a cherry-scented ring. His fingers tugged his hair five times before hitting his vape again as he fidgeted with his lighter. "I didn't say that, but if you're going to fuck with her like that, then don't be mad when I do my own thing."

"And what thing would that be?" Sin took the joint from Stitches and popped an eyebrow at Ashes.

Ashes shrugged. "Pick up the pieces."

"You fucking dog." Stitches chortled. "Prince fucking charming, eh?"

"Probably get me further than Church's plan. He can lock her up anywhere he wants to. I'll just make sure I'm the one to offer her a helping hand."

"And a helping of cock." Sin let out a belly laugh and inhaled before blowing out the smoke.

"If that's what she needs." Ashes grinned. "But I think we should go easy on her. Everyone needs saving sometimes."

"I don't think we should go easy on her," I said, shaking my head. "She disobeyed. Not only did we tell her, but so did Andrews."

"Andrews had his hands on her this morning," Stitches broke in. "Before Claire's class. She curled into him like a sweet, little kitten. He ate that shit up too."

"What?" Sin straightened, his gray eyes glinting. Sin may have said he didn't want shit to do with Sirena, but the way he'd been acting suggested otherwise.

I heard about him threatening people for just looking at her. He was bending whether he realized it or not. It was just part of his sickness. He craved her. Before long, he'd be the one in the hole, the place where they put those who'd snapped went. He'd be tightened into his straitjacket just like Stitches had been a few months ago when he broke during his mania.

Stitches nodded as Ashes swore.

"Cain came up to me today too and asked if he could have her," Sin continued.

I did a doubletake. The threads which barely kept my anger in check threatened to snap. "Why the fuck does he want her so much?"

"He said she was his best friend growing up. Gave me some bullshit talk about how she's some sweetheart or something. He wants her. He said he'd pay."

"Not happening." I clenched my hands into fists. "We break her. We own her. When she finally screams, it'll be our names, not Seth fucking Cain's name. Tell him to fuck off."

"Tell him yourself." Stitches nodded to Cain as he strode toward us, hands in his jean pockets.

I bit back my snarl as the initiates came back onto the patio. The partygoers took notice and quieted down as I turned my back on Cain, who paused to watch what was about to go down.

I wanted to get this shit over with fast. The only thing I could think about was finding Sirena and putting the fear of God in her sweet, tight, little ass. Maybe quite literally.

"The outfit you're wearing right now is to be worn all week. In classes. On campus. Even when you go to fucking bed. You will *not* change out of them. If you do, you'll pay dearly. Nobody wants to be on our shit list. Believe that." I raked my gaze over the trembling lot clad in their ridiculous outfits. "If you think you're fucked up now, wait until you piss one of us off."

"W-we have to wear our uniforms in classes," a skinny guy called out, shaking in his boxers that said *Eat Me* on the back.

Stitches had picked those out. He'd thought it was hilarious.

"So?" I stared evenly at him. "Only the strong survive here. If you get beaten and punished for it, then *get fucking stronger.* If the faculty here doesn't fuck your day up, then I will if you take off what you've been assigned to wear. May God have mercy on your souls."

I waved them off, and they scattered like cockroaches when the light shone on them. Some of the girls had tails on their tiny shorts and t-shirts that labeled them with clever sayings.

I suck devil cock was one of my favorites. Although, *crazy cunt* was a second. I was sure the faculty would love it too. They tried to parade behind their god and Bible, but I knew they were just as crazy as the people they ruled over. They got off on the torture just as much as I did.

"Personally, I like the one that says *I went to Chapel Crest, and all I got was anal,*" Cain said, approaching us.

Stitches nodded thoughtfully. "I like that one too. Sin picked it out."

Sin smirked before sneering at Cain.

"What the fuck do you want?" I turned to him.

"I saw Sirena wasn't here. I came to offer myself in place of her punishment."

Ashes snorted and turned away as I stared Cain down.

"Now why would you do that?"

"She's been through a lot of shit. I don't think she deserves more of it."

"Maybe that was just a warm-up. Maybe what she needs is to be broken so she can be repaired, don't you think?"

"What I think is you're making a big fucking mistake targeting her." Cain lost his cool calmness and glared at me.

I relished in his anger. "Good thing what you think doesn't fucking matter. We want her, and we'll take her. Nothing you can say or do will change that."

"Not if I get her first," he snarled.

"Are you challenging us?" Stitches stepped forward and glowered at him.

"I don't want to have to, but if you fuck with her, you're fucking with me."

"There is one of you and four of us. I think you know your odds," I said softly. "It doesn't seem like a bet I'd want to wager."

Cain let out a soft laugh. "Then you don't know me, Church, because I'm a little bit crazier than what you're used to."

I surveyed him. His nostrils flared as he eyed me back, his black hair windswept and blue eyes flashing.

I gave him a slow, calculating smile at the prospect of fucking his year up. "Then, by all means, make your move. We were itching for some excitement this year. We'll play for keeps. Winner gets the girl."

"The fuck?" Stitches snarled, stepping forward.

I held my arm up to stop him.

"Rules?" Cain demanded.

"Whoever gets her to scream, wins. It is, after all, the style in which you kill that matters most. Right, Cain?" I grinned at him as a muscle popped along his jaw.

"Trust me. I have style." He scowled at us for a moment before turning and sweeping away.

We watched him go before I turned back to my guys. This was going to be fun.

"We start tonight. Get ready."

SIRENA

"I think you'll like this," Bryce said, offering me a cupcake. "It's chocolate, but it has cherry flavored icing."

When I didn't reach for it, he placed it on the TV tray in front of me and grabbed his own out of the container he'd brought with him. He'd knocked on my door around eight that night and hadn't left. Instead, he'd told me about his day and what he wanted to do after college—own his own business—and then he'd proceeded to share sweets with me.

"I'm worried the watchers are going to come for you. They tend to get really pissed off when people don't do what they want. They were expecting you tonight."

I swallowed and looked down at the pink cupcake balanced in my palm that I'd picked up.

"Make sure you're watching your back as much as possible."

Our eyes locked when I peeked at him.

"I'll help watch it too," he said. "Strength in numbers and all that."

I wanted to thank him, but the words weren't there. Instead, I stared back down at my cupcake.

"My older brother is the golden boy," he said after taking a bite of his cupcake.

I lifted mine gingerly to my lips and took a tentative taste. The cherry and chocolate flavor exploded in my mouth, making me widen my eyes.

He offered me a knowing smile before he continued, "He was the quarterback of the football team. Got a full ride to state. Dates beautiful women. My parents were always satisfied with his mediocre grades because he has a bright future ahead of him. My father thinks my brother will end up drafted into the NFL." He placed his half-eaten cupcake back on the tray. His voice grew soft, "I got sent here because my parents think I'm gay."

He peered at me with wide eyes. So much sadness rolled beneath his gaze it made my heart hurt.

"I'm not gay." He fidgeted with his fingers. "My best friend back home is. He was spending the night at my place and kissed me. I didn't kiss him back. I didn't even know what the hell to do. My dad walked in and saw. I tried to explain, but he wouldn't listen. So here I am, a *disgusting sinner*. Someone he claims has mental issues that need to be taken care of." He blew out a breath before plowing on, "He told me no son of his would be a fucking queer. Like, what the fuck? Even if I were gay, I'm still the same person, you know? So that's why I'm here. I was labeled a mental case by my father. I'm here to be cleansed and reborn into someone he can be proud of."

I didn't move. I simply sat and listened while he talked.

"Truth of the matter is, I wish I had kissed Kevin back. At least then my old man would've been right. Instead, he hates me and refuses to even let me come home during breaks. I haven't seen my house since I got sent here freshman year. They visit me here, but my dad doesn't talk to me. He just glares at me. The last time he was here, he called me a faggot and told me to cut my hair."

My heart went out to Bryce. He was a beautiful guy, and I could tell his heart was filled with goodness. It pissed me off that his own father treated him that way. Not even thinking it through, I reached for his hand. His eyes widened when I held it.

"You-you're communicating." He breathed out.

I immediately withdrew my hand from his, but he reached for me again and twined his fingers through mine.

"Don't be afraid. I'm not like those other assholes. My end game isn't to hurt you. I want to help you. Your sister, well, I'm pretty sure she meant business when she threatened me. You'll be safe with me, Sirena. As much as you can be. I'm just a nobody here, so I don't have much leverage, but I'll do what I can, OK?"

I stared down at his hand in mine and let the tension fall away from my body.

"Want to watch a movie?"

He got to his feet and grabbed the remote, leaving my hand empty.

"Do you like comedies?"

My silence hung in the air, and he tilted his head at me, his gaze studying me. "I bet you like fantasy. *Lord of the Rings* it is."

He thumbed through some streaming apps until he found what he was looking for and hit play before taking up his spot beside me. He grabbed a bag of chips and set it between us on the bed. I settled back against my pillows with him next to me, feeling at ease around him. It was a feeling I hadn't felt in so long. It made me wonder what made Bryce Andrews so different.

"I'm breaking about a hundred rules being in your dorm with you," he said, glancing over at me. "My friend Jake lives on this floor around the corner in the guys' section. He's going to cover for me if I get stopped. It's a co-ed building, but co-ed rooms are off limits. Sully will skin me alive if I get caught." He grinned and shook his head. "I bet my dad would love that phone call. The headmaster calling my house to let them know I was found in a girl's room."

While I knew he was trying to make light of it, it still saddened me. I watched him while his gaze flitted over the TV. He really was nice to look at. I focused on the movie, feeling comfortable and maybe like I'd finally made a friend, even if he was a boy.

I WOKE up in the night because I thought I'd heard creaking outside my door. Bryce left after the first *Lord of the Rings* movie ended, and I'd fallen asleep while it was on. He'd crept out of my room, trying to be quiet, but I'd seen him close the door softly behind him. I'd rolled over and gone to sleep.

Knowing the watchers had their party going, I assumed it was just a late-night partygoer coming back, so I tugged my covers up and settled back against my pillows before closing my eyes. I drifted back to sleep almost immediately.

"You little devil slut," Jerry growled at me as I struggled to get away from him. His belt connected with the tender flesh of my back as he hit me over and over. "The devil has your tongue! You need to be cleansed!"

I thrashed wildly beneath him as he hit me repeatedly before his hand found my hair. With a tug, he hefted me off my bed and dragged me to the small toolbox in the center of the room.

I struggled in his hold and managed to twist and look at him. Instead of Jerry, it was older Seth's face which greeted me.

"It's what friends do," he choked out, shoving me into the toolbox. "Wait for me."

He closed me in as I desperately tried to free myself.

I can't breathe. I can't breathe. I can't breathe!

My eyes snapped open as I bucked against the four men shrouded in black inside my room. The scream on my lips rang silent as one of them tied a gag around my mouth.

"Just in case," he chuckled softly.

Stitches.

I scratched at them as they tried to contain me, my pulse thundering in my ears. My breath halted in my chest as one of the guys crawled on top of me and wrapped warm fingers around my neck.

"Don't fucking fight it," he snarled softly.

Church.

"It'll hurt a lot more if you do."

I stilled beneath him, and he loosened his grip on my throat and smiled at me through the dim light.

"Good girl," he murmured, letting his thumb drift along my trembling bottom lip.

"Let's go," Sin grunted, moving forward to the edge of my bed.

Church licked his lips as he gazed down at me. My chest heaved when he trailed his fingers down my chin and neck before he lifted the tiny, silver cross at my throat.

"Such a good girl," he mused softly. "But even good girls fuck up."

He shifted off me. Sin grabbed my wrists and hauled me out of bed. My tiny tank top and shorts left little to the imagination. I stared straight ahead as Stitches and Church drank me in, their glittering gazes traveling up my body.

"At least cover her," Ashes called out with disdain as warm hands brushed along my bare abdomen.

I shrank into myself, terrified of what was to come. I opened my eyes to see Ashes in front of me, his mouth twisted into a deep frown as he righted my top so I wasn't nearly hanging out.

If I were going to scream for help, Ashes would be the one I'd scream for.

His gaze locked on mine, and he smiled as Sin's hold tightened around me.

He leaned in, his muscular torso brushing against my body. "I'm sorry. Only God can help you now."

The silent scream clawed at my throat as a black bag was put over my head.

Ashes was a liar. God couldn't help me. He'd forgotten me long ago.

STITCHES

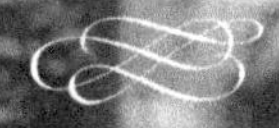

We waited around a corner as Bryce crept out of her bedroom.

"Looks like Andrews might have some game after all," Sin said with a soft snort as Bryce padded to the elevators at the opposite end of the hall, his head down.

Rage battled wild curiosity. Neither dominant. *Which did I feel more? Fuck it. Not worth figuring out.*

I want what's behind the door. For myself. Even for a moment.

"He's the least of my worries," Church muttered.

"We going in or what?" Ashes peeked around the corner again, clearly a little antsy.

"No, let's wait a bit longer. Make sure she's asleep so we can get inside." Church's mouth pinched in irritation.

Seeing Andrews coming out of Sirena's room had really pissed him off.

"I can't believe you let Melanie suck your dick again," Ashes said a few minutes later to Sin. "I thought we were moving away from her and working on Sirena."

Sin shrugged. "She offered, and I wanted to come. Seemed like a fair deal to me."

I chuckled. "I'd have done it too."

"We *are* trying to work away from her. She's getting clingy. She thinks she's our fucking queen. She's just a warm hole to fuck." Church grunted, peering around the corner again.

"You took her upstairs earlier," Ashes pointed out as he gave Church an eye roll and flicked his lighter open and closed five times.

"Yeah, to tell the bitch to chill on her shit. Then I brought her back downstairs with me because the last thing I wanted to do was leave her alone in my room. She actually had the nerve to ask me if we would make it official and declare her as ours." He snorted and shook his head. "She's got a decent enough pussy and is always up for fucking, but she's nothing to write home about."

"Well, if you guys would stop giving her the time of day, we wouldn't be having this conversation," Ashes said. "I haven't touched her since the end of last year."

"Which isn't saying much considering you were home all summer," I teased him. "Trust me, if you get hard-up here, you'll be balls deep in her snatch in the coming weeks too."

"Doubtful," he mumbled, letting the back of his head rest against the wall as he continued to flip his lighter open and closed.

"Let's go," Church said, stepping out from where we hid.

The hall was dimly lit, so we moved down it quickly to her door.

"You think she's one of those bitches who puts a chair under the handle or some shit in addition to keep the monsters out?" Sin asked, reaching for the doorknob.

"Maybe," Ashes answered.

I nodded. It made sense considering what we knew of her past.

"Open the mother fucker," Church hissed through the darkness.

Sin pulled a pin from his jacket and fiddled with the lock a moment before the click sounded and the door cracked open. He shot us a cocky grin and stepped into the room with us following. We gathered around her bed as she slept. A small lamp cast a pale yellow glow in the space.

"She's afraid of the dark according to her records," Church reminded us as he nodded to the light.

I didn't care about violence. Trauma. Sadness. Tears. Smiles. Someone's fucked up life. But knowing her story for some reason tugged at my heart. I hated that, but I also loved it. It was an exciting feeling I didn't think I'd get enough of. It created a high like a drug only better.

"Doesn't smell like sex in here," Sin whispered. "Guess Andrews didn't close the deal."

Church threw him a withering glance before looking back at her sleeping form. She seemed peaceful. Her lips were parted, and her sooty lashes lay gently on her porcelain cheeks. The blankets were twisted around her body, and fuck, what a glorious body it was. Those legs. . . I imagined them wrapped around my waist as I hammered away at her molten center. Her plump, pink lips kissing mine. Her unique eyes staring into mine. My name falling out of her mouth. Her face contorted with the pleasure I delivered. The flush I'd create along her breasts as I made her tighten around my cock while I thrust into her.

I swallowed and quickly pushed the lewd image from my mind and cast a glance at my boys. All of them wore varying looks of longing, even Sin who continued to vehemently deny any sort of interest in her.

She shifted in bed, drawing my attention back to her. Her head lolled on her pillow, dark silky waves tangling around her neck as she moved, thrashing violently as she fought some invisible threat.

We stood watching her silently as her face scrunched up and her chest heaved, her fingers twisted in her bedsheets.

"She's having a nightmare," Ashes murmured, transfixed on her as her back arched slightly.

"Wake her," he demanded in a tight whisper. Church stared down at her, a muscle feathering along his jaw and worry creasing his forehead.

I stepped forward and touched her arm. She flinched away from me, soundless even in her night terror. I peered up at the guys for direction, and Sin grinned at me. *Prick.*

With steady hands, I reached for her again and stuffed the gag into her mouth. Her eyes snapped open, wide with terror.

"Just in case." I couldn't stop the soft chuckle that fell off my lips. Not that I would have if I could.

†

IT WASN'T AS difficult as we'd thought it'd be to get her out of the dorms. She submitted pretty fast, a look of resignation in her eyes as we'd covered her head. A pity. I was hoping for some claws.

Once we were away from the dorms, Church removed the bag. It was only when she realized where we were taking her that she attempted to turn and run.

Sin caught her wrist before she'd even taken a step back.

"It's just a haunted cemetery," I teased, pushing the gate open with a screech and leading the way through the dark garden of tombstones.

Her gorgeous eyes darted around, the scream we all craved clinging to the tip of her tongue. All we needed to do was get her to scream. Call for help. Call us cocksuckers. *Anything*. Once she did, we'd show Seth Cain where to stick it and then own her right in front of him.

We trudged through the darkness, half pulling, half carrying our sweet, little captive through the night.

We finally stopped outside an old mausoleum nestled in the back of the graveyard.

"Sirena Lawrence." Church turned to her and smiled. "You were invited to our party tonight. You didn't show up. Very rude. You disobeyed my order. That's grounds for punishment."

She visibly swallowed and stared at all of us.

"Now would be a good time to beg," Sin offered sinisterly.

"You can use your words or just your mouth," I added, grabbing my cock through my pants to emphasize what I meant.

Anticipation had my heart in my throat as I watched her tremble. Something unfurled deep inside of me. Something dark and dangerous that made me want to shout into the night.

"Or both." Church brushed a strand of her dark hair away from her face. "Your choice."

She quivered where she stood, her bottom lip wobbling.

"Don't cry, pretty girl," Church murmured, circling her. He removed her gag and stopped behind her, pushing her hair over her shoulders.

She squeezed her eyes closed as she shook. Church leaned in and brushed his lips against the delicate flesh of her neck.

"Tell us to stop," Church continued softly. "*Beg us* to stop. If you don't, I'm afraid something bad might happen to our good girl."

We watched as she stood before us, wordless. She quaked so badly I was surprised she could even stand.

"She's not going to speak," Ashes said, his eyes raking over her. "Let's just get this over with. She looks like she's going to be sick."

"Last chance," Church said, moving back in front of her.

A tear squeezed out of her eye. Church leaned in and licked it away. He trailed his lips across her cheek before he rested his forehead against hers and exhaled. It took every ounce of self-control to not launch myself forward and devour her the way I wanted to.

"One," he said softly, his fingers pushing through her dark locks.

Sin had counted three occurrences she needed to pay us for before she'd missed the party. This would be the first one of four we'd check off our list.

Sin eased forward and opened the door to the mausoleum. Fear registered in her eyes. Church started to back away from her, but she reached for him, tangling her fingers in his t-shirt. Sin tried to tug her from behind, but she held onto Church, her eyes filled with panic, tears cascading down her cheeks.

"Fuck," Ashes muttered thickly at the sight of her silently pleading with Church.

I nodded. *Fuck* was right. She was gorgeous as she struggled, even though the fight normally wasn't my kryptonite. My cock thickened in my pants as I watched her cling to Church, her face wet with tears. Maybe crying girls didn't always make my dick hard, but this one sure did. I supposed there was a diagnosis there the quacks had missed over the years, but it wasn't something I wanted to be medicated for. It was something I wanted to fully embrace.

Church tilted his chin quickly at Sin who released her. She tumbled into Church's arms, her body shaking with silent sobs.

"Oh, pretty girl, what's wrong?" Church cooed softly at her as she pressed her body against his.

I swallowed down a growl of jealousy, eager to have her in my arms. Ashes shifted beside me, clearly having the same thought. I caught Sin adjusting himself from the corner of my eye. *You can run but you can't hide from the truth, and the truth was rock hard in my friend's pants.* He couldn't bullshit me. He wanted to sink deep inside her tight cunt and claim her just as much as the rest of us did.

"Talk to me," Church continued, raking his fingers through her hair. "It's all you have to do. That or get on your knees and show me how much you don't want to be locked in that dark room." He reached out and cradled her face.

She jerked away as her gaze darted around the darkened graveyard.

"There's nowhere to go," I murmured, stepping closer.

Fuck. Run. Please.

She glared defiantly at me for a moment before she shoved hard against Church. It caught him off guard, and he stumbled back. She took the opportunity to flee into the night, her black hair whipping wildly behind.

Yes!

I let out a whoop and raced after her, the guys falling in, full tilt into the night.

I leaped over tombstones, howling like a damn wild animal as the guys jeered. She had to be terrified out of her mind. The thought only drove me forward faster, eager to catch our weeping angel.

She was fast though and disappeared. After a few moments of us running our separate ways, we met back near a broken headstone with an angel guiding small children.

"Fuck. Where is she?" Sin snarled, squinting his eyes as he tried to search the shadows.

"Probably back to her dorm by now." Ashes grinned at Church.

"I thought she was afraid of the dark," I said, peering into the blackness of the night.

"I think she's probably more afraid of what's in it than the dark itself," Ashes muttered. "She may give us a run for our money, though."

"I'm counting on it," Church growled, pushing past me and creeping forward.

I spotted what he saw immediately. Movement behind a large, cracked gravestone.

Church lunged forward and disappeared behind the granite for a moment before he popped back in the glow of moonlight, a struggling Sirena in tow.

I had to hand it to her. She kicked and bucked like her life depended on it. And maybe it did. We were in the land of the dead, and none of us were as compassionate or as sane as we needed to be… as we wanted to be.

"Well, well, well. Look what I found," Church teased as he led her by her elbow back to the mausoleum.

When we reached it again, he released her roughly. She fell back against Sin and glared up at Church, her hands balled into tiny fists as Sin wrapped his hands around her biceps.

"This is going to end one of two ways. Get on your knees or get put there. Either way, I'm going to enjoy it." Church took a menacing step toward her.

Sin pushed her toward Church, who caught her easily.

With a look of defeat, she peered up at him, clinging to him for a minute before she resigned her fight and sank to her knees, her tangled waves falling forward around her as she hung her head.

Defeat had never looked so beautiful before.

Church unbuttoned his pants and pulled his cock out.

"You ever suck cock before?" he asked softly as he tilted her chin up.

She gazed up at him with those mesmerizing fucking eyes, her plump bottom lip wobbling.

"I'll take that as a no," he said breathlessly. "Come here. I'll show you."

She didn't move for a beat.

"You don't have to," Church said gently as he stroked himself. "But those who pass tests, don't need to retake them."

Her eyelids shuttered for a moment before they fluttered open, and she shifted forward on her knees. A triumphant smile spread over Church's face as he ran his cock along her lips.

"Open," he commanded softly, a tremor coursing through his body.

I'd have given anything to be him in that moment as she stared up at him with parted lips. If I had my way, it'd be sooner rather than later.

CHURCH

The moment I tried to push into her mouth, her hand shot out and hit me in the nuts, sending me to my knees, groaning. It wasn't a full on hit because I saw it coming, but it was enough.

Stitches and Sin cackled loudly as Ashes sniggered at me. If she had intentions on running again, she had about fifteen seconds before I got my shit together and showed her what happened when people didn't listen.

Sin grabbed her again and hauled her to her feet. She glared at me as Ashes and Stitches helped me up. I sucked in a few fortifying breaths and tucked my dick away before I stalked forward and took her delicate face in my hand, squeezing her cheeks. All that radiated from her was pure fury.

It was more fuel for my fire.

"You fucked up," I snarled at her.

If she cared, she sure didn't make a show of it like others would have. Anyone else would've been on their knees, begging for forgiveness, but not her. Not the silent, trembling girl before me. Instead, she stared me down, daring me to fuck with her.

"You know, I would've been merciful if you'd obeyed, but now?" I clicked my tongue at her. "I hope you enjoy your night. Welcome to Chapel Crest," I murmured, releasing her. I eased back and nodded at Sin, who wasted no time in hauling her away from me.

With wild eyes, she reached out. All her defiance was gone, only fear left in its wake.

And for a moment, a pang shot through my heart when understanding washed over her face that she wasn't going to be forgiven. But we both knew she would've been paid either way. A night in the crypt was a good welcome gift for anyone who failed to listen. It was the feeling in my chest though that made me hesitate. I'd never felt anything like it before. But I shoved whatever the fuck it was away.

"Bad boys lie, specter. Remember that." I gave her an even look.

"Fuck," Sin snarled as she clawed at him. He caught her hands in his, finally getting a firm hold on her and dragging her through the murky doorway. With a grunt, he tossed her onto the cold, stone floor and slammed the door behind her, locking it with a turn of the key.

He backed away, his chest moving rapidly as he wiped at his face. Her nails had caught him over his eyebrow, and he had a slight trickle of blood drizzling over his eyelid.

"She's strong," he muttered, wiping at the cut again.

I stepped around him and pressed my ear to the door. Silence reigned inside the windowless tomb. I expected she'd scream or cry, even bang on the door, but there was nothing.

"Tough chick," Stitches commented, coming over to lean against the brick wall. "She's got a dead ass body in there with her in the pitch black." He pulled out a flask and tipped it against his lips, taking a long drink before handing it off to Sin who wasted no time in taking his share.

Ashes slipped in the space next to me and rested his ear against the door. He pulled back a moment later. "This might make her worse."

I shrugged. "Or it might make her better."

"Play dangerous games, win dangerous prizes," he muttered, moving to take the flask from Sin.

"We aren't going to stay out here all night, are we?" Stitches shoved off the wall and raised his brows at me. "You almost got a blow job. Maybe the rest of us would like to get off before we crash tonight. Fucking around in a cemetery isn't going to make that happen. Unless Ashes wants to get on his knees." He shot a smirk at Ashes who gave him the finger and drank deeply.

"Cemetery worked for me." I smiled and shrugged. "Almost."

It was Stitches's turn to flip the bird. This time it was directed at me. I rolled my eyes and let out a soft huff.

"How was it? Getting that close with her?" Ashes asked the question I knew they all wanted the answer to.

"If heaven had a perfect set of tits and a hot mouth, then I'd just say I've almost been to heaven," I said.

"Really?" Sin looked interested as he surveyed me.

I nodded. "The anticipation alone was worth it. And the look on her face..." I rubbed my chest as that strange feeling I'd had moments ago resurfaced. Again, I pushed it away and gave my friends my trademark sinister grin.

Sin peeked back at the mausoleum before shaking his head and stepping away. "Then she nut checked your ass."

"Minor inconvenience." I waved him off, still a little pissed about her ruining the moment.

"How long are we leaving her in there?" Ashes asked.

"Overnight. Give her something to think about." I marched up to the door and called out to her. "Hear that, sweetheart? You're in there until the morning. Let it be a fucking lesson for you to do what you're told from now on. Fuck up and disobey, and it'll be worse. Sleep tight. Don't let the demons bite." I pounded my hand on the door before backing away.

"Let's go get some sleep. I'm fucking drained," I said, turning and going back the way we'd come.

The guys joined me. Ashes cast one final glance over his shoulder.

By the time we'd made it back to our place, I was running on fumes. I collapsed onto my bed, the memory of her parted lips against my dick on replay. I may not have gotten far, but it was a test.

Was it a dick move? Absolutely.

Would I do it again? Without a doubt.

I'd never claimed to be a saint. There wasn't a chance in hell I'd start now. I owned my fucking insanity.

ASHES

The next morning, I showered quickly and made my way to the cemetery. We'd done a lot of heartless shit in the past to other students, but this one probably took the cake. Recalling her on her knees with Church's cock pressed against her lips, with her hoping it would earn her freedom, made me feel like a shit human. I shouldn't have enjoyed seeing her like that, but I'd be lying if I said I wasn't sporting a hard-on that could rival steel as I watched Church try to fuck her mouth. Of course, he'd failed, which only increased my desire for her. Any girl who'd stand up to us was something to behold.

I picked up my pace, my fingers tight around my lighter, as I cut through the overgrown foliage in the forest on my way to the cemetery.

By the time I reached the mausoleum, my cock was as thick as a lead pipe in my pants. I had to take a moment before I unlocked the door and shoved it open.

I didn't know what I'd expected to find, but my heart flipped in my chest at the sight of her small body crumpled on the ground, her knees drawn up to her chest as she slept with her arms covering her head.

I crept up to her and kneeled.

"Sirena," I murmured, resting my hand on her shoulder.

Her body was like ice. She shivered beneath my warm touch.

"Sirena? Wake up. Come on."

She cracked her eyelids open, a sliver of blue, green, and gold peering up at me before she slid on her ass across the floor in an effort to get away from me.

"Don't be that way. I'm sorry about last night," I said, easing closer to her.

She flinched away when I reached out.

"Let's get you back to your room. I swear it's just me here. I'm not going to hurt you. I promise."

It was like trying to coax an injured kitten out of a corner.

She curled into a tight, trembling ball, flinching away from me again.

"Come on, love. I'm here to help you. I don't want you in here anymore than you want to be in here." I slowly extended my hand again.

She jerked away, but I persevered and finally snagged her hand in mine and hauled her to her feet. She shivered against me. Without contemplating the action, I shrugged my navy blazer off and draped it over her slender shoulders. Within the span of a heartbeat, she pressed against my chest, crying soundlessly again.

"I'm sorry. It was a bad idea." I'd never had a sobbing girl clinging to me like this.

Usually, if they were crying, it was because they were begging to stay, wanting to be picked by us. Sirena's tears were relief at being away from us. Of the knowledge that freedom, even for a moment, was near. Or maybe they were joyful because I'd rescued her. My heart stuttered at the possibility.

"Let me help you back to your dorm. You're a beautiful mess," I said softly, tilting her chin up so I could take in her face.

Dirt marred her perfect skin, and her hair was a tangled disaster. Tenderly, I guided her out of the mausoleum and into the cemetery, my arm around her waist as I led her barefoot through the maze of tombstones. She winced when she stepped on a twig. It snapped with a crack beneath her weight.

Knowing we'd already put her through hell, I tugged her to a stop and scooped her into my arms. She struggled at first, but I ended it fast.

"I'm sorry. I didn't realize we didn't give you shoes last night. The stones and twigs hurt to step on. Let me do this, OK?" I began walking with her in my arms.

She was light as a feather, her body tense in my hold.

I could probably carry her tiny ass all the way back to Detroit without breaking a sweat. Luckily, it was still far too early for anyone else to be roaming the campus.

Of course, it was a different story once I brought her inside her building. Two girls were outside their rooms—Hannah and April. I recognized them because I'd walked in on them sucking off Sin and Stitches last year in the library. Both were hot messes mentally. I never gave a shit to know their stories, but I was pretty sure one of them was a cutter. Their eyes widened as they took in the sight of Sirena in my arms, her face now buried in my neck. She had to be sleeping. Her breathing was deep and even.

When I got to her room, I gently deposited her in bed and plucked a dead leaf out of her hair.

"You should shower," I whispered when she cracked her eyelids open and took in her whereabouts. "Classes start in two hours."

I backed away, her eyes locked on me. The moment I was out of her room and the door closed, I let out a whoosh of air and flipped my Zippo open and closed five times. Nausea rolled through me. We were on the highway to hell, and poor Sirena was along for the ride.

I SAT AROUND, waiting for the guys to get up and moving. When they finally came into the living room, I stood.

"I took Sirena back to her room," I said. I flipped the top of my lighter lazily and surveyed the guys.

Church nodded as he snagged a cold waffle. "Figured you would. It's a good way for you to play the knight in shining armor."

"She blow you?" Stitches asked, grabbing a bagel from the fridge and taking a bite out of it.

I shook my head and snorted. "No. I found her curled in a ball in a corner. She was ice cold. I felt. . .bad."

I frowned at the feeling. It wasn't often that emotions of any sort rolled through my body. I hadn't let them in a long time. The therapists liked to tell me I compartmentalized things which hurt me, so I didn't feel as much. They said it was a trauma response after everything that had happened in my life. *Whatever.* Ignoring my feelings had always worked, but now? Now the feeling was nearly crushing me. I wasn't a fan.

Sin scoffed. "With the way she almost sucked Church's cock last night, you shouldn't feel bad. Since it was so easy to get her on her knees, it only proves my assumptions about her were right."

"And what were those?" I asked, folding my arms over my chest.

It was no secret among us that Sin harbored bitterness with females. He'd had a relationship once that went sour in a nasty way. Ever since, he'd been a pain in the ass about girls. He didn't trust them. It was why we'd come up with the far-fetched idea of finding a girl we could all claim together.

He shrugged and snatched Stitches's bagel from him. "That she's weak and a whore like the rest of the chicks here. She just doesn't realize it yet."

"She's not a whore. She was scared. Stop calling chicks whores. Last night, we saw a scared girl do what she thought she had to do in order to stay safe. What we did was pure torture." I sighed.

"Don't act all high and mighty, *Asher*." Sin shook his head at me. "She's clearly not all that smart if she thought for one second sucking cock would offer her immunity to punishment. Of course, she had to refuse. Another fuck-up on her behalf. She paid the price. It's that simple. Right, Church?"

Church nodded. "Yeah. Now she knows. That does remind me though. She paid one punishment. She owes us three more. So far."

Sin waved a butter knife at Church and swallowed a bite of his bagel. "He's right. Three *wishes* to go for us. Sucks to suck."

"I *hope* she sucks." Stitches laughed, his legs bouncing. That fucker always had a hard time sitting or standing still. Being excited only made him worse.

"She's going to be amazing," Church confirmed. "Seriously. We could train her just how we want it. It's perfect. Just looking at her last night on her knees. . ."

"Probably because she was in tears doing it." Sin snickered.

Church shook his head, which surprised me. "No, it was the feeling. The submission on her knees before her refusal. It was hot. I don't think I'll be able to stop once I get her. She should be very afraid."

I knew Church well enough to know he wasn't bullshitting. He probably would struggle with this bear of wanting her. I'd never seen his eyes glint the way they had last night. He wasn't fucking around. He meant business with Sirena. His obsession with her was a little concerning. It may even drive him more insane, if that were possible.

But I wanted her too. I was just a bit gentler in my approach. If one could call any of the shit I did or agreed to gentle. Part of me longed for her to want me back and not simply be afraid. Sirena intrigued me.

"Whatever. I just think we should give her time to recover mentally before we hit her with the next punishment." I grabbed my bag off the floor, feelings of worry for her rolling through me.

"I'm agreeable with that," Church said easily, scooping up his stuff. "She knows now not to screw up. She'll listen to us. We have all year to dole out the other three. I'll have a chat with her today. Make sure she plays by the rules. We still have Cain to deal with."

"That fucker isn't going to win and get her. We've scared the shit out of her. Plus, you saw the way she looked at him. She's more scared of him than she is of us." Stitches sighed. His eyes darkened, and his lips pooched out as a faraway look came over his face.

We didn't need him slipping again. Last year had been hell when he'd spiraled. It wasn't often students found themselves in the hole, but Malachi certainly made up for it during his severe bout of mania.

"And maybe *that's* something we should be worried about," I said, pushing the front door open as Sin and Stitches gathered their things to follow us. "Fear is an excellent motivator. We learned that last night when she got on her knees for Church. She might scream for Cain before she does for us because she's terrified of him."

The thought did nothing to calm me. In fact, my heart raced at the prospect of losing her to him.

"She won't." Church frowned.

But I knew he was thinking about what I'd just said. I had a strange feeling the next few months were about to get crazy.

Crazier. Shit at Chapel Crest was already *crazy.*

SIRENA

Loud pounding on my door snapped me out of the trance I'd been in for who knew how long.

"Wellness check," an authoritative voice shouted through the heavy wood.

I'd been zoned out long enough to have missed classes and cause a stir then. *Great*. I'd probably be in trouble now.

I shuffled over and unlocked the door, tucking my damp hair behind my ear and wrapping my arms tightly around my middle. The burly guy must have been aware of my file because his gaze swept over me without demanding a response. When he realized I hadn't physically harmed myself, he spun on his heel and left.

Last night kept replaying in my mind. I couldn't shut it off. Once I was sure the security guard wasn't coming back, I stripped down and got back in the shower, hoping to wash the memory away. I sat on the tile, folded in on myself as the water rained over me.

My adrenaline spiked as I recalled the helpless feeling that overwhelmed me when the bag had been put over my head. And then I thought about what had almost happened with Church. I hated to admit I may have liked it had it been under other circumstances. He was hot, and when he spoke tenderly to me and ran his fingers through my hair, it made butterflies come to life in my stomach. But he'd played me. They all had. I wasn't an idiot. I wouldn't have been free even if I'd opened my mouth and accepted him.

I ran the memory over in my head for what felt like the hundredth time.

The way my heart thundered. How some strange zing of electricity rushed through my guts. The heat between my legs as he ran his thick, velvety length along my lips. The fear. The excitement. The. . . want.

My head fell back against the wall as I squeezed my eyelids closed.

I was sick. So fucking sick. I needed to be here. If there ever was a doubt, it left my mind as those thoughts ran through my head.

It could've been worse. It could always be worse. I *could be worse.*

I've lived by that mantra since the day Sheriff Joe pulled me out of that God forsaken toolbox.

I turned the water off, stood up, and slowly dried myself with a fluffy towel. When I was in my robe, I wiped off the steam from the mirror and stared at myself. My eyes were dull. They hadn't sparkled since I was a kid. Dark circles rimmed them. My lips were turned down into a deep frown.

When was the last time I smiled?

Easy. Eight years ago.

I ground my teeth, anxiety welling in my chest as I thought about Seth lurking somewhere on campus. Truth be told, him killing me might not be a bad thing. After all, he'd pretty much killed me eight years ago. He just hadn't buried me deep enough. I hadn't lived since then. My life was a joke.

Why do I bother? Cady. Mom. Maybe. They'd be better off without me though. Cady endured a lot of shit at school because of me. I knew deep in my heart Mom blamed me for it. And Jerry.

The only thing I'd learned over the years was how to silently take up space. *What good was I beyond that?* I had a couple warm holes that might make me useful to a cruel boy as I'd come to realize after last night.

I shook my head. I needed a distraction. When my mind got into these funks, shit could get bad. I'd never acted on my dark thoughts, but if there ever was a time, I knew it was coming.

Would it hurt? Would I die slowly? Would anyone even miss me? Maybe Cady, but she'd learn she's better off. And Mom, but maybe she'd feel genuine relief.

Damnit.

They probably wouldn't find my body for days, considering Bryce was really my only friend here, if I could call a guy I'd just met a friend. Of course, maybe security would do a wellness check and find me. Maybe I'd be still clinging to this damn miserable life. I'd be saved and worse off.

Deciding it was best to occupy my mind with other thoughts before I got carried away, I sat at my easel. I dabbed my paint brush into the fresh paint I poured, and then I worked my way through my feelings, slashing colors onto the canvas.

I swallowed hard and blew out a breath as I stared at my work in progress a few hours later.

The mausoleum from last night. I'd painted the night sky behind it in swirls of colors, four dark figures holding a girl captive on her knees.

I was right back there again, my chest heaving from my sharp breaths. With a stroke of my brush, the girl reached for the boy she kneeled in front of. I painted him holding her hand.

Fantasy. Dreams. Art. *Not real.* Just what I wished because life would be easier if I were accepted as I was.

I felt dead inside. *How do you breathe life into the dead? Would I always feel this way? Would anything ever revive me?*

My phone buzzed with a call from Cady, completely tearing me away from my morose thoughts. I swiped it open and was greeted by her smiling face.

"Happy birthday, big sister!" she called out, a goofy party hat on her head.

She blew into a noisemaker and laughed. My mom leaned over Cady's shoulder and grinned at me, a party hat on her head too.

"Hey, honey! Happy eighteenth! I hope you're having fun today," she said. Her gaze seemed to rake over me through the screen, her smile not all that stable. "Make any new friends?"

I licked my lips. I'd been diligently ignoring the fact it was my birthday.

"Rina, we hid a gift in the side pocket of your suitcase. Open it," Cady said, bouncing in her seat.

I hesitated for a moment before I went to my closet to grab out the suitcase. I hadn't gone through the side pockets. I rooted around in it for a moment before I found a small, wrapped box. With the small package in my hand, I brought it back to my desk and sat in front of my phone again, which I'd propped up so they could see me.

"I hope you like it," Mom said as I tore the paper to get to the velvet jewelry box inside.

"We saw it in the mall and knew it was perfect for you," Cady added.

I opened the small box and stared down at a delicate, silver charm bracelet.

"What do you think?" Mom asked.

I removed the bracelet from the box and examined the charms—a microphone, a book, a ballet slipper, and a kitten. My heart swelled as I stared down at it. A tear trickled down my cheek.

"I knew you'd love it," Cady said, grinning. "Remember when we took that ballet class and I kicked Alan Weston in the face when he said I was too short? Then you kicked him in the shin when he laughed while I was getting yelled at?"

The memory surfaced, and I smiled inwardly. I did remember. It had been so long ago. Before Seth hurt me.

I closed my eyes and held the bracelet to my chest.

"I'm glad you like it, honey," Mom said gently.

Jerry shouted for Mom then, so she bid me goodbye, leaving me with just Cady.

"You cried today," she said softly. "What happened? You know I'll come kick someone's ass, Rina. Text me their name."

I swallowed. If I told her all the shit I was going through, I knew she'd end up being arrested. Cady was secretly my hero.

"It's OK. I'll find out when we come visit later this year," she continued.

We were both silent for a few moments before she sighed. Shortly after, she began telling me about all the juicy gossip from school and how Ryan Gates had asked her out. Football captain. Completely gorgeous. Everyone loved Ryan. He'd never bothered me, so I figured he was an OK human.

She spoke for quite a long time as I listened until she finally stopped and gave me a grin.

"I miss you. I can't wait to give you a hug. Be good, OK? I love you, Sis." She kissed her fingertips and pressed it to the camera lens before offering me a final smile. "Hope your birthday is awesome. Bye, Rina."

And with that, the screen blacked out asking me to rate my video call quality. I sighed and tucked the bracelet back into its box, not ready to wear such special memories on my wrist just yet.

I turned back to my easel and picked up my paintbrush. I stared for so long at the image of Church reaching for me with the watchers, that my eyes began to burn.

A sharp rap on my door startled me, making me drop my paintbrush. I quickly turned the easel around so the canvas faced the wall where no one could see what I'd painted.

Pulling myself together, I traipsed to the door and squinted out the peephole, hoping I wasn't going to be forced to the medical wing for an examination. I blew out a breath of relief when I saw Bryce standing on the other side staring at the floor. He lifted his head so I could see the concerned expression on his face as he knocked again, this time leaning against the doorjamb and shaking his head.

"Sirena? Hey, open up. You weren't in classes today."

I chewed my bottom lip for a moment before deciding I liked Bryce enough and didn't want him to worry.

I tugged the door open and stared at him.

"Are you OK?" His brows crinkled as his gaze swept over me. When I didn't answer, he spoke again, "May I come in? I-I heard Ashes brought you back to your room this morning. What happened? Everyone is talking, Sirena. Most people haven't even seen you yet on campus, but everyone knows about you now and that the watchers got to you. Please, talk to me. Write it down if you have to."

I backed away and let him step inside. The door clicked behind him, and he followed me to my bed where he sat beside me.

"What happened?"

I stared straight ahead until he reached out and gently turned my face to his.

"I'm not the enemy here, Sirena. Did they hurt you?"

My bottom lip wobbled as last night with the watchers came rushing at me again in full force. It was the fear that got me. Always the damn fear.

"Damn it." His Adam's apple bobbed as he swept his worried gaze over me. "What can I do? What will make it better?"

Nothing. The damage has been done.

We were both silent as we stared one another down.

"I-I know it's your birthday today, so happy birthday. I brought you a cupcake." He held out a pink cupcake for me.

I took it from him, earning a small smile from him.

"How about we watch the next *Lord of the Rings*? I-I can even stay with you tonight if it'll make you feel better. I'll sleep on the floor."

He got up when I didn't answer and grabbed my remote to turn on my streaming service. In seconds, the second *Lord of the Rings* movie loaded.

I rose, set my cupcake on the counter, and went to the small cupboards, removing two packages of microwave popcorn. Methodically, I put them in the tiny microwave. I didn't look at Bryce, but I felt his eyes on me when I dumped the popcorn into a large bowl and brought it back to my bed along with my cupcake. I set everything on my bedside table. He grabbed two cans of soda from my mini fridge and settled in next to me.

Silently, I handed him one of my two pillows and then pulled my blankets back, hoping he caught my meaning.

He seemed to because he slid beneath the covers with me and hit play on the movie.

"Let's go on an adventure to Middle Earth and forget about everything else, OK?"

And it was OK because really, what other option was there?

†

I AWOKE and blinked my eyelids several times as sunlight filtered into the room. I was warm and safe in my bed, Bryce beside me. I allowed myself a moment to take in his features.

He was handsome in a preppy, wholesome sort of way. Flawless skin peppered with day-old scruff. His hair was a mess. His lips parted slightly as he lay facing me on his side.

He must have sensed me watching him because his eyelids fluttered open, and he stared at me through narrowed slits.

"Hey," he greeted me with a soft, tired mumble. "You fell asleep early."

I had. I'd been exhausted. Trusting Bryce came easily, so I figured I'd better make use of my safety net while I could because he wouldn't be able to stay with me every night. I knew the rules. If one of those angry nuns, security guards, or even the medical personnel I'd seen on campus were to come barging in, we'd be metaphorically screwed.

"I need to get back to my room," he continued. "I can meet you out front and walk with you to class if you want. Sound good?"

I bit my lip and studied him. *Would saying yes be so hard?*

He was my friend. But I remembered what happened with my last best friend. Then again, he'd slept beside me and hadn't killed me.

"I'll take your lack of words as a yes," he said, chuckling as he climbed out of bed in his rumpled uniform, his hair a wild mess. He winced as he tried to flatten it before tossing me a smile and shrugging.

"See you in thirty?" He backed away to my door. "We're really going to have to work out a way to communicate. I'm going to assume everything is yes unless you tell me otherwise, OK?"

He opened the door and stepped across the threshold before calling out, "Thirty!"

The door clicked closed behind him, and I stared at where he'd been. Bryce Andrews was a godsend in this hell.

SIN

I stood beside Stitches in the commons area outside the main building. It was the area students congregated. Tables, vending machines, trash cans, bullshit flowers, and crosses—that was the commons area. My hair was tied back because the fucking bitches who ran this place griped more than I cared to hear. Even if we were the watchers, there were brave souls from time to time.

"We're only a few days into this shit hole year, and I'm already bored," Stitches grumbled, his gaze trailing over the mass of students as they walked through the commons or engaged with their friends.

Sirena hadn't been in classes yesterday. It had driven Church nuts, and if I weren't mistaken, even Stitches had been on edge. He was usually in a fairly decent mood when shit was going good in his head, but yesterday was a bitch having to listen to him and Church snarl at one another like rabid dogs. As often as I told them to fucking let the mute go, they refused. It only worked me up, causing me to bitch back. Ashes seemed to be the only one who had his shit together. Of course, Ashes had impulse control issues, so he could snap at any moment and burn this fucking place to the ground if the mood struck him just right.

"It's like this every year," I muttered, noticing Seth striding toward us. "Great."

Stitches followed my gaze and sighed, as he clicked his tongue ring against his teeth.

"Hey," Seth said, stopping beside us.

"What the fuck do you want?" I glanced at him.

The put-together prick had his pretty, bad boy look in order, complete with the earrings in his ears and strategically messed up hair.

To be fair, we really weren't supposed to have body jewelry here, but some of us ranked a little higher on the *don't fucking tell us what to do* totem pole. The hierarchy of insanity. It was way too hard for these lazy pricks to get our crazy back in check if we cracked. Best to lose an earring than an eye. Or a life.

"Wouldn't be fair if you guys were fucking around and cheating on our deal," Seth said, glancing between us.

Stitches snorted at him. "We don't need to cheat, Cain. We're already winning."

"Yeah?" His gaze raked over us, a muscle popping along his jaw. "Are the rumors true? Did she spend the night with Valentine?"

"Wouldn't you like to know?" I shook my head at him, enjoying watching his anger cruise just below the surface.

"Actually, I fucking would like to know," he fired back. "One against four is hardly fair."

"You already knew that. We pointed it out. You didn't seem to care if I remember correctly. So you mean you don't think you can get the girl with all your swagger?" Stitches let out a laugh, bouncing on the balls of his feet. "Thought you were a winner, Cain."

"Eat shit, Stitches. You know what I mean."

"It's not four against one." I said, spotting Bryce wading through the crowd of students with our favorite little, mute princess at his side. I bristled inside at the sight of them together. "It's more like four versus one versus one. Looks like Andrews wants to play."

"Fuck. Seems like Andrews is winning," Stitches grumbled.

We watched as Bryce said something to Sirena that made her look at him with what resembled humor on her face. He went along with it and continued talking, gesturing around him with a wide grin. I'd never seen the douche with a girl. I'd assumed he was into sucking cock, but fuck, what did I know?

Seth's eyes narrowed as he glared at Bryce.

"Easy, Mr. Asylum. Don't want to get knocked out of the game before you've started playing." Stitches stepped forward and turned to smirk at us. "I'll show you how to play. Take notes, Cain. You look like you're struggling. Maybe you should bring up your inability to close a deal in your group therapy session later."

Interestedly, my gaze tracked Stitches strutting his way over to the pair. He stopped them in the middle of whatever Bryce was saying. Seth cursed Stitches under his breath, his hands balled into tight fists.

Smoothly, Stitches reached out and lifted Sirena's dark braid off her shoulder and smiled down at her. She glared at him just like she'd done to Church. But at least she wasn't clawing his face off like she'd done to me.

"She won't fuck him," Cain snarled, stepping forward. "Or any of you."

"Well, I'd say she just might considering Church had his dick against her lips not long ago. Maybe you don't know her like you used to."

I was being a prick and exaggerating but fuck Cain. The guy's existence pissed me off.

"Besides, it's not about fucking her. It's about getting her to scream. I suppose they could be one and the same though, right?"

His fists shook by his sides as he glared at Sirena, Bryce, and Stitches, ignoring my words.

"Easy, champ. Even if she picks us, there's enough pussy around this place to keep you knee deep in it all year."

"I don't want anyone else," he snapped at me, shooting me a look of disdain, his chest heaving.

In all the years I'd known the guy, I'd never seen him react the way he was in that moment. I'd heard some stories though. The one about the fork in his stepdad's eye had even made me grin and have a bit of respect for him. I'd thought about stabbing Rudy at least a dozen times a day since my ma married him. The fact Seth actually did stab his stepdad made him tolerable in my book. Maybe not all the time, but enough that I didn't flat out punch him in the face.

"What's she got that you want so bad? A cherry-flavored pussy that showers you in gold flakes and a one-way ticket to heaven?"

"I could ask you and your assholes the same thing."

His gaze was still locked on Stitches as he draped his arm over Sirena's shoulder, blathering a mile a minute about whatever bullshit he was able to pull out of his ass. I imagined he was telling her how big his cock was and how he'd let her see for herself later. Judging by the looks Bryce was giving him, I'd say I probably wasn't far off my mark. Sirena appeared tense and panicked, which seemed to be her go-to.

"We just like a challenging pussy. A girl we can fuck and mess with who doesn't tell secrets? That's quite a treasure. We could fuck her raw, and she wouldn't tell a soul. She'd like it so much she just might shout it to the heavens. So we'd get that scream."

"She's not like that. I told you guys that."

"And I told you Church's cock traced her lips already. The way she and Bryce are going, I'd say he's got as good chance as you do of impressing her."

"Fuck off, Sinclair. You guys think because you can scare her, you'll win. I actually know her, so I'm steps ahead of you." He tore his gaze from Stitches, Sirena, and Bryce who were now walking into the school together.

I nodded and pushed off the table I was sitting on. "Yeah, well, I also noticed the fear in her eyes when she saw you. Pretty sure you have your work cut out for you, Cain. Good luck with that and whatever dirty little secret she's keeping for you."

"You don't know shit—"

I shoved him hard in the chest, tiring of his presence. I'd run out of tolerance. "I know a liar when I fucking see one. You probably keep secrets just as well as she does, huh? *Mr. Asylum.* The guy who's spent more time in state hospitals than he has a bathroom."

He glared back at me as I chuckled.

"Like I said, *good luck, you crazy schizo fuck.*"

I shoulder checked him hard when I marched past him and followed behind Stitches, Sirena, and Andrews into the building, keeping them in my sights. I didn't give a shit what had happened to her to make her clam up. All I really cared about was getting the guys to shut the hell up. The girl was beautiful, sure, but I didn't have the time or patience to deal with some bitch's crazy shit. The other guys liked to play with their food before they ate it, each of them with varying degrees of torment. But me? I liked to dive right in and get mine. Fuck playing around. I was ready for them to tire of her because I hated that she piqued my interest even a little.

If I had my way, this game would've been over before it started.

But even I had to admit there was an allure about her that I couldn't quite stay away from. It was gnawing at me, demanding me to take control of her. *To own her.* To fuck her with her own tears and make her choke out my name like a fucking prayer to the devil.

And that was really fucking dangerous. For everyone, myself included.

STITCHES

Making people uncomfortable. I loved it more than pretty much anything in the world. I didn't often filter what came out of my mouth, and I sure as hell wasn't going to start anytime soon. People's reactions did it for me, feeding the voracious monster that operated my brain. Crazy. Volatile. Unhinged. I enjoyed the silence that fell between the moments. The quiet where they tried to react. It made me all warm and fuzzy inside.

"You trying to get your dick wet with my girl?" I asked Bryce as we stopped outside our class.

It came off sounding teasing, but what I really meant was *don't fucking touch this perfect being*. She belonged to the watchers. The idea of some piss weasel sticking his dick in her made me vibrate with rage. Never a good thing. The last fucking thing I needed was to slide down that slope again. I couldn't deal. I *wouldn't* deal. I'd tumble and crash. Burn. Fuck. No one should touch her but the watchers.

Sirena flinched at my crude words, shooting me a look of annoyance as Bryce's cheeks reddened.

"Seriously. What's the deal? I saw him coming out of your room the other night. You fucking the Chapel Crest's math geek and not me, angel? That doesn't seem very nice of you."

She visibly swallowed as she stared straight ahead, the tendons in her neck tight from her teeth clenching. Unable to resist, I reached out and brushed my knuckles against her jaw. Ecstasy rolled through me. *Fuck yes. Her skin was soft.* She stiffened at my touch, but much to her credit, she didn't move away from me.

"Leave her alone. Why are you guys always trying to mess with people?" Bryce growled at me.

I looked over at him in surprise. A sliver of anger rumbled beneath my composure. Vibrating me. Like one of those little Easter chicks that wind up. I'd fucking clobber him. "*Are* you fucking her?"

"No," he snapped, glancing at Sirena. "But even if I were, it wouldn't be any of your damn business. She's only been here a few days, and you guys are already targeting her. She doesn't need this. I'm asking you to please leave her alone. She's done nothing wrong."

I stepped up to him and cocked my head. The anger cracked the surface. Fuck if I'd stop it. Moods were like the wind with me. Coming. Going. Fuck all. "*We* decide if she's done something wrong. And guess what. *She has.* She owes us for three more occurrences. She was sweet enough to pay one off in the cemetery with Church, weren't you?" I dragged my gaze away from Bryce to Sirena, my heart flopping as her big, colorful eyes focused on me. "I bet you can still taste his cock on your lips, huh, baby?"

Her bottom lip wobbled. Then my ears rang from the sucker punch Bryce landed on my jaw, sending me reeling back from the impact. Students gasped and screamed as Bryce faced me down, his body quaking. I had to hand it to him, the guy could hit.

I wiped at the blood on my lip and smirked at him. *Fuck yes. A fight.* "Nice. But you did it wrong. Try this next time." My fist collided with his gut, bending him forward as he gasped. Then I brought my knee up to meet his face but was shoved hard before I connected. I stumbled sideways, ready to kick ass. My vision swam in red.

Sirena stood in front of Bryce, her hands balled into tight fists as she glared me down.

A reaction.

My fury receded—something that had never happened to me

before. Usually, I'd snap, and it'd be game over. Not that I snapped often. I was probably the most lighthearted one of our ragtag group of basket cases.

I straightened up and studied her for a moment. Then she did something I didn't expect. She gave a slight shake of her head, letting me know she'd go to war for the dickhead behind her, and the only way to him was through her.

Communication. A silent scream for me to stop. God, baby, I'd never stop with you.

"So you want to fight?" I erased the space between us and leaned in so only she could hear me. "I'm going to hold you down and fuck you so hard you're going to scream my name for me. In ecstasy. You're going to fight me. And *beg* me for more. I'll show you heaven and hell, angel. Keep fucking tempting me. You're only making it *harder* on yourself." I grabbed her fist and forced her to flatten her hand as I pressed it against the hard length in my trousers. "Feel that? *That's* what your struggle does to me. I'm going to own you, Sirena. When this is over, I'll have my name tattooed across your skin just so everyone knows who you belong to. Stop. Fucking. *Tempting. Me.*" I released her, and she stumbled back to where Bryce was still bent over trying to catch his breath.

OK. So maybe I snapped a little. Normally, I wasn't the sort of guy who forced a girl to touch me. But fucking hell, she was doing something to my already fucked up head. In the infinitesimal amount of time I had to mull over my reaction, I realized I didn't regret it. I relished in it. I wasn't like Church or Sin who never felt remorse. I was still human in that way. But this? Not this. I wanted to fuck with her. She was a challenge, a puzzle, and a prize. I wanted to fucking win her. I wanted to make her tremble for me. I wanted her to understand how I felt about her right out of the gate. *Yeah, my dick is hard for you, baby.* No games. She needed to know she already had a place by my side.

"Mr. Wolfe, Miss Lawrence, Mr. Andrews. The headmaster's office. Now," Sister Elizabeth snapped at us as she came bustling down the hall with two of Chapel Crest's finest security guards.

They peered wearily at me. We all knew the command at me was for show, so I grinned at them and pushed past Bryce and Sirena, making my way to the headmaster's office, feeling really fucking awesome about how my day was going.

†

SIRENA AND BRYCE carried on a silent conversation with just their eyes while I watched. *What the fuck?* They simply stared at one another before he finally offered her a small smile that faltered before it could do much good.

Whatever they had going on, I wanted it. *I needed it.* My heart clenched in my chest as I stared. I wanted her to look at me the way she looked at him. Like he was her goddamn savior. I could save her, be her hero. *Give me a damn chance.*

A pang of sadness slithered through my chest at the thought. I shifted in my seat in an effort to detangle myself from the emotion. Feelings of sadness and hopelessness weren't good for me. I tended to plummet into their depths and struggled to break free. The last few months had been good after my severe bout of mania.

I was a type one bipolar case, which meant my highs were higher than fuck and my lows were lower than hell. I teetered a thin line between sanity and insanity because when I fell, I fell fucking hard and had a complete disregard for my safety or others. It was dangerous for anyone around me. The docs kept saying I was the most complex and worst case they'd ever seen. They'd even wanted to use me for a research study. Fuck that. I wasn't a damn lab rat. I had to get my shit together.

Do not go there, Malachi. Chill the fuck out. Get a grip. NOW.

"It's OK," Bryce murmured, giving her a slight nod of his head before squeezing her hand.

I snorted, pushing aside the emotions threatening to choke me. *And here comes the self-sabotage of any potential relationship in three. . .two. . .one. . .* "It's really not. She's in trouble, and you know it, and not just with the headmaster. I'm sure the watchers already know you decided to declare war. She's going to be punished."

"I was trying to protect her from you, you psycho. I'm not declaring war on shit," Bryce seethed back at me, his voice so low I had to lean in to hear him.

He glanced around to make sure the old bitch behind the desk wasn't listening. Sitting in the waiting room to see the headmaster wasn't unheard of for me, but Sully and the watchers had an understanding. Don't fuck with us, and we wouldn't fuck with him. So far, it had been going well.

"You should learn to control your temper, Andrews. Violence is never the answer. Don't they teach you that in group therapy?" *Practice what you preach, Malachi.*

He shook his head at me as he glared. I wanted him to speak again. He was digging a hole I couldn't wait to bury him in. The irrational side of my personality was trying to rear its head.

"What's going on?" Church's voice yanked me from my dark thoughts as he strode into the room like he owned the place. His gaze cut from me to Andrews before coming to rest on the angel between us, who was staring down at her hands, her small body rigid as she breathed in short, soft gasps.

I restrained myself from touching her. Shit, it was hard. I twisted my hands in my lap and bounced my leg.

"Well, if it isn't my silent, little cemetery specter." Church stepped forward and kneeled in front of her.

Andrews stiffened. I had to admire his dedication to keeping her safe. No one else would be fucking stupid enough to step up to us, but he was going all in. Guessed he was crazier than I'd thought.

Church reached forward and lifted her chin, so they were eye to eye.

"If you're in trouble, specter, all you need to do is ask for help."

Her fingers twisted in the hem of her skirt as she stared back at him. The serene look on his face even had me guessing his next move. Church was good at planning. I knew he had an answer to everything, which only made him more intimidating to everyone around him.

"Are you going to ask me?" he asked softly as he ran his thumb along her trembling bottom lip.

I ground my teeth at the motion, wanting to be the one to touch her while she quaked. Fuck, this girl was fire, and she was going to burn us all if we weren't careful. Even Sin who pretended he didn't want her would be ash if we ever got her to break. *Smoke in the wind. Dust. She'd obliterate us. I knew it.*

"Say it. Say, *Church, help me.* I can make it all go away. That's it. Three little words can change your life. If you don't ask me for help, the headmaster is going to punish you. Detention. Doing lines of scripture. The staff will get you. You'll end up with a new diagnosis and a whole lot of meds. You really won't enjoy what they have planned for you if you piss them off." His thumb froze on her lip, and he leaned forward to rest his forehead against hers.

She stiffened more, her breathing heavier.

"I'll even save your friend this one time."

I watched, mesmerized as she continued to tremble, knowing Church wasn't about to continue being nice for too long. He was too pent up like I was over her. He was going to lose his shit in three. . . two. . . one. . .

"Fucking say it!" he snarled. His hands shifted to grip her hair tightly as he pressed his forehead harder into hers. "Fucking *say it,* or I'll make you wish you were never born."

She remained silent. Andrews looked like he was going to shit his pants as he glanced from the old bitch behind the desk, who conveniently decided it was time for a coffee break and left the room, to me. I winked at him.

"Say it." Church breathed out again, releasing her hair.

Loose strands now hung around her face where he'd pulled some out of her braid. She looked like she'd been in a windstorm. He settled back and stared at her, clearly growing more pissed off that she wouldn't just break and say something.

Slowly, she lifted her gaze from her lap and peered back at him, her jaw flexed in determination before her middle finger worked its way up in front of his face.

I stared at her, shocked she'd made such a bold move. Clearly, Andrews felt the same because his mouth dropped open, gaping like a fish out of water.

And Church? He rose and stood stock still for a moment, and then he let out a snarl and grabbed her by her lapels, hauling her to feet. With ease, he lifted her off the ground and whirled around, holding her against the wall so she was eye level with him.

I got up because I knew him well enough to know he was close to tearing something apart, and I didn't want it to be her. Even Andrews stood.

Church released her gently, and she slid down the wall. He pinned her in place with his body as he gazed down at her. Just as defiant as before, she held his stare.

"Wrong answer, specter," he said softly, caging her between his arms. "Not for me though because you just made me want to up my game. Wrong answer *for you* because you could've ended this now. When you reach your breaking point, you'll come *to* me and *come for me*. I'll wait. Good things *come* for those who wait, right?" He gave her a wicked smile. "In the meantime, watch yourself. This place isn't the gateway to heaven. It's the road to hell. And we're just the demons along the way."

He pushed away from her and nodded at me as he stalked from the room without a backward glance.

"You should listen to what he says, angel. Some of us are in a better position to protect you." I winked at Andrews and tossed Sirena a smile before backing away and turning to follow Church out.

After all, I wasn't the one who was going to get punished.

SIRENA

Headmaster Sully took Bryce into his office first. I sat waiting for him, my leg bouncing and my mind running through my encounter with Church and Stitches. I had no idea why I wasn't falling in line for them. It was out of character for me. It probably had something to do with not wanting to be pushed around here. Cady wasn't here to fight my battles, and Bryce shouldn't have to. If he got kicked out because of me, I'd never forgive myself. That was why I'd stepped in front of him in the hallway. I'd wanted to stop everything before it happened. Of course, I was a little late on that considering the first punch had already been thrown.

And then Stitches had made me touch his dick through his pants. I swallowed at the memory. He was definitely hard. Butterflies had sprung to life in my guts, and they flapped now at the memory. Then Church had been forceful with me. He terrified me, but he also excited me. I hated I felt that way. There had to be more wrong with me than the therapists had suggested.

I jerked in my seat when the headmaster's door opened and Bryce came out, my thoughts of Stitches and Church scattering like roaches in sunlight.

"You can go in," he mumbled, stopping in front of me.

I got to my feet and gave the opening to the office an apprehensive glance.

"I told him it was my fault, but Sister Elizabeth already spoke to him. She said she saw you and Stitches, not me, so I can't be sure what's going to happen. The headmaster seemed adamant on talking with you, so just be careful. He's not a nice guy." He swept his gaze over me. "I have to go to class, OK? We'll catch up at lunch. You can sit with me. I'll find you." He turned to go and stopped before peering over his shoulder at me. "By the way, it was really fucking cool how you stood up to Church. It was dangerous, though. Watch yourself, OK?"

He left me, his words sending a shiver through my body. I knew I was in trouble with the watchers. I wasn't looking forward to whatever that meant, but there had to be some middle ground somewhere with them. I just had to find it. Out of the corner of my eye, I caught sight of a student without his shirt on wearing a rabbit mask over his face and chains draped around him as he skittered down the hallway.

What the hell?

"Miss Lawrence?" Headmaster Sully's deep voice yanked my attention from the shirtless, masked kid in the corridor who was now being pushed by someone screaming in a nonsense language while two security guards wrestled him away. Turning, I came face to face with a tall, middle-aged, handsome man with dark hair and a goatee standing in the doorway. He didn't seem concerned about the tussle outside the office. I guessed he was used to the weirdness.

I quickly shuffled into the room. The click of the door behind me made my heart jump.

"Please. Have a seat." He gestured to the leather chair in front of his large desk before he moved to his seat on the other side.

I sat, trying to take in the office. Dark wood. Fireplace. Degrees on the walls. Bookcases. No windows.

"Sirena Lawrence. Jerry is your stepfather, right?"

I snapped my attention back to him and remained silent.

"Right. He told me about your. . . issues." He clasped his hands together on his desk and studied me for a moment. "I went to college with Jerry. We were good friends. Still are one might say. We spoke in-depth about you."

I really didn't care and said a silent prayer he'd just give me my detention so I could go.

"So. . .not a word, Sirena? Not a text? A note? Nothing."

Nothing. Especially not for you.

I stared at a point over his shoulder, wondering where he could possibly be going with this. Of course, he knew I didn't talk. I was positive Jerry wouldn't have left that part out with their reunion chat. Jerry probably had a good laugh while he made fun of me for it too. Plus, it was in my records.

"That's really too bad." His chair creaked as he got to his feet and strode over to where I sat. He reached out for me. Confused, I peered up at him as his fingers smoothed down my messy hair from what Church had done to it earlier. My muscles tightened as I tried to keep my breathing under control. His fingertips skimmed along the bottom of my jaw, sending an electric current of warning through me. Moments before, I'd been locked in terror over how to deal with Church and the watchers, but now I could see they wouldn't be my only problem.

"Such a pity for such a beautiful girl to have been marked by the demons of her past," he murmured. "But God never puts anything in our paths that we can't handle, and I think I can handle this."

What?

"We heal people here. Through medicine and therapy. We do experiments and research in the hopes of finding a cure for the madness that cripples our students. No one is a patient here. They're all just students. Sent to learn how to be better. After all, it's in your mind." He tapped his head with a finger and offered me a smile, which did nothing to soothe my fear.

"Bad girls and boys get punished here, though, Sirena. Noncompliance isn't rewarded. It's punished, squashed out of the soul. God doesn't like the belligerent. It's harder to save a soul who wishes to side with the devil, you see."

He paused for a moment before continuing, "I heard you were a bad girl today." He stepped away from me, and I gulped in a mouthful of air, grateful for the distance.

He propped himself on the edge of his desk and studied me again. I felt like a bug beneath a microscope being dissected.

"We do things differently here, Sirena. Special students get special treatment. Our therapy tends to be a bit. . . old school. Our ultimate goal is to rid you of your demons through God, and of course, save your soul and sanity."

I swallowed, wondering where this could possibly be going. I had my doubts anyone would come to my rescue even if I did manage to scream.

"*And we never tell*. Naturally, you can't, which makes you perfect for what I have planned. Only the most special students get this sort of treatment." He licked his lips, making my stomach churn. "I looked at your schedule. You have group therapy at two, three times a week. I think you're also in need of additional one-on-one therapy. I'm known for my *cutting-edge* treatments. I combine the word of God with my lessons. And sometimes His rod." He smiled again. "Like I said, it's old school. Since Jerry and I go way back, and he asked me so nicely, I've agreed to give you my very special treatment."

I need to get out of here. How? What do I do? I wish Cady were here.

"When I was younger, they used to slap our hands with rulers when we needed to be punished." He moved back to his leather chair, picked up a ruler from his desk, and ran his fingers along the surface. "Punishment is therapy, you see? Negative reinforcement. Positive reinforcement. Operant conditioning. We do all that and then some here. We'll teach you to be normal again. You'll crave your sanity, and in turn, fall in line."

My heart thudded hard as I gulped down my anxiety.

"If God can't cure you, and medicine can't cure you—both I've heard you've tried—then my brand of therapy will. Jerry thinks you have demons nesting in your head. I don't disagree with him. All the students here do in one way or another."

What the hell. . . just do whatever he wants so you can leave. It's not like it's the worst thing you've ever been through.

He's crazy! Run, Sirena. Just leave!

You can't leave. Where would you go? You have to take the treatment. The punishment. Whatever fucked up therapy he has planned.

I held out my shaking hands, thinking maybe he'd get back up and smack them with his ruler.

A smile crossed his face as he chuckled. "Ah, no. I prefer to improvise. Come here."

I shuffled to my feet and went to him, wondering what the hell was happening and if Bryce had to go through it too.

He patted his thighs and stared up at me, a darkness glinting in his eyes. I started to back away, quickly realizing where this was going. He snagged my hand and hauled me back to him.

He was strong and had me bent over his lap within seconds, my skirt hiked up and my panties on display for him. I squirmed beneath him. He pressed his elbow into the middle of my back hard, making my eyes burn at the pain.

"This is what's going to happen. You're going to take your therapy. It'll be a two birds with one stone deal. We'll punish you for being a bad girl today, and we'll start exorcising those demons embedded in your soul. Of course, you won't say a word to anyone about this because if you do, you'll get sent home to Jerry, and he'll know. I think we both know that punishment will be worse if you upset him. Right?"

I squeezed my eyelids closed as Sully stilled for a moment. Finally, he let out a soft laugh as he stroked my backside with his large hand. I bit the inside of my cheek so hard I could taste blood as he brought the ruler down on my ass with a loud *THWAK.*

The sting raced along my skin as he struck me again and again over my panties. I wanted to tell him to stop, but I couldn't. There were no words in me, so I ground my teeth together hard enough I thought they'd break off. His thick erection pressed against my ribs as he continued his onslaught, each hit becoming harder and harder, his breathing heavy and ragged.

I balled my hands into such tight fists that my nails dug into my palms, making them bleed. The pain from those little cuts almost took me away from the pain in my ass. *Almost.*

"There," he said breathlessly as he stopped the beating.

I stayed on his lap, humiliation coursing through me while he rubbed my backside as a means to soothe it, but all I wanted to do was run from the room and never look back.

He pulled my skirt down to cover me and pushed me to my feet. I winced at the white-hot pain, wanting to die as a means to escape.

"It hurts, doesn't it?" he asked, rising to tower over me.

I didn't move, didn't acknowledge him. I simply gazed straight ahead, fighting the tears with everything I had. He had to have struck me twenty times before relenting.

"You're strong. I like that." He beamed down at me like he hadn't just nearly flayed me alive moments before or touched me inappropriately. "I expect you in my office every Friday after classes end for your *special therapy*. I swore to your stepfather I'd fix you. You'll be a new girl by the time I'm done with you."

He gripped my chin painfully and tilted my head up, so I was looking at him. "I don't need you to answer me right now. I only need your compliance. I'll see you Friday." He released me, sank back in his chair, and started shuffling through papers.

"You're dismissed. Go straight to class," he said, not bothering to look at me.

I didn't wait. I booked it out of there, wincing with every painful step I took. I didn't stop until I made it to my second hour class.

By the time lunch rolled around, I was even more sore and miserable. Bryce met me outside my history class.

"How was it? Did you get detention?"

I fell in step beside him, silently wishing I could just go back to my room and sleep the pain away.

"I hope you didn't," he continued as we walked. "Detentions here suck. It's always writing scripture or listening to it. Can't escape it no matter what. Sometimes, they throw you in the hole which is this dark room where no one can hear you scream."

Dark hole? No thanks. That was the last place I wanted to end up. Locked in the dark would kill me for good.

I'd closed myself off in my mind while I'd been in the mausoleum, rocking myself in the fetal position and singing in my head as I envisioned a bright playground. I wouldn't be able to do that again. I'd kept Cady and Mom in my mind. Cady rode the swings beside me. She laughed, and I grinned. Mom snapped photos. It wasn't a dark room. It was a paradise of light and laughter.

Bryce and I stopped at my locker, and I stuffed my bag inside before we went to the cafeteria. Food was the last thing on my mind as I waited in line with him. I tuned out most of what he was saying, not bothering to get anything to eat.

"You should eat," he said, glancing at my empty hands. "I can get you some food for your dorm if you want later this week so you don't run out. I have a few connections."

Had I been a different girl and this a different place, I would've laughed and teased him about his lunchroom connections. Instead, I ignored it and followed him to an empty table at the edge of the busy cafeteria.

I noticed the watchers had their own table in the front of the room, and they sat at it like they owned the place. From what I'd seen so far, they did.

I locked gazes with Ashes for a moment as he stared in my direction. He was definitely the nicest of the watchers, but still scary as hell. He cocked his head at me, his eyes narrowed. Sin caught him looking at me and tapped Church on the arm.

I immediately tore my stare away and focused on my hands again. Our table filled with other students. It didn't take long to figure out the cafeteria was set up like any other high school hierarchy. Geeks, nerds, weirdos at one end, and the closer you got to the front table, the cooler you were. Or maybe it was the more insane, since the watchers seemed to hold that title. No one here seemed terribly off their rockers. Or maybe they were just better at hiding it. I supposed the threat of Headmaster Sully beating their asses kept them in line.

"Sirena, this is Devon, Vic, and Lucy. Guys, this is Sirena." Bryce offered me a reassuring smile as his friends greeted me. "And you already know Jack from when he took your stuff to your room." He jerked his head toward the guy with the glasses and dark hair.

"Where are you from?" the one named Devon asked.

"Screw that. I want to know if the rumors about you hooking up with a watcher are true. Asher Valentine is hot." Lucy fanned herself, her dark curls bouncing with the motion. "They don't pick just anyone, you know. Everyone knows they practically claimed Melanie last year. She's a bitch, but she's a lucky bitch. Unofficially, of course."

"You'd be better off if you didn't get picked." Vic gave me a quick smile as he leaned in. "They're assholes."

I peered back at these people, surprised at how decent they seemed. Granted, we'd only just met, but at least they were talking to me and not teasing me.

"So... Where are you from?" Devon asked again. "What's your diagnosis? Let me guess. Depression? Everyone here is depressed. I mean, I'm depressed. Tried to bleed it out of me. Didn't work." He showed me his arms where ugly scars snaked along his wrists. "Kinda glad I didn't die. Today anyway. I also have ADHD. So I'm lying there in my own blood, and my brain is bouncing around, my focus on death but not really on death, you know? I was planning on tacos for dinner—"

"She doesn't talk," Bryce broke in, silencing him.

"Like she's shy?" Lucy appeared confused by the answer.

Bryce shot me a quick look before clearing his throat. "No, like she doesn't talk. Ever. At all. She's. . . mute. Is that an acceptable word for it?" He winced as he mulled it over.

"Do you use sign language?" Jack asked. He'd said hi to me when we met on my first day but had scurried off pretty fast and hadn't waited for my answer.

"She doesn't communicate. *At all.* She can hear you. She just doesn't speak or anything."

Lucy wrinkled her nose. "Dang. That sucks, girly."

"That's an interesting illness." Devon shoved a handful of fries into his mouth and chewed thoughtfully as he studied me.

I ducked my head again.

"You're really pretty," Vic said, his voice extra loud. He pointed to his eyes. "Your eyes. They're really cool."

"Idiot. I said she can hear," Bryce muttered.

"Sorry."

"Hey, losers," a girl said, stopping at our table with another girl in tow.

They were both the sort of girls I easily recognized. Cruel. Popular. Unrelenting. I guessed even in a place like this there were still mean girls.

Bryce scowled up at her in annoyance. "Melanie. Tasha. I think you're lost."

Melanie let out a fake laugh and flipped her blonde hair over her shoulder, Tasha giggling with her.

Definitely mean girls. Great. Just what Chapel Crest needed, more bitches.

"I just wanted to welcome the new girl to our little slice of heaven. I heard you spent the night with Ashes."

Her tone wasn't friendly. I knew girls like her well enough to know she was coming here to make a statement. And that statement wasn't a show of friendship.

If I'd been able to talk, I would've told her she was wrong. That I'd spent the night with all four of the watchers just to piss her off. But that was another girl from another time. Instead, I sat quietly, my leg bouncing, trying to keep myself from a total panic attack.

"I also heard you're like deaf or something," she continued.

"If she were deaf, that would make you an idiot," Lucy piped up. "I mean, who tries talking to someone like they can hear if they're deaf?"

Vic snorted and grinned at Melanie, who narrowed her eyes at Lucy.

"Her name is Sirena. She can hear you. She just doesn't speak," Bryce explained.

"Whatever." Melanie rolled her eyes and focused on me again. "I'm only here to say the watchers, *all* of them, are mine. I'm their girl. We're making it official soon. The next time I hear you're messing with my guys, I'll bury you. Got it?" All the sugary sweetness she'd spoken with before was gone, replaced by the pomp and circumstance of a raging, crazy bitch.

I didn't acknowledge her, opting to stare at a spot over Devon's head as I counted in my mind.

"Bryce, make sure you remind her. I think the little, weird-eyed bitch is having a seizure or something." And with that, she left, taking her sniveling dog with her.

"She's a twat," Lucy said with such force it was almost comical. "We don't like her. Chapel Crest slut. One of many. All the girls here get on their knees for the watchers. Except me, of course. But Melanie really is their girl. She gets passed around between them like a saltshaker. She's under their protection and all that. Tasha is a close second. If you mess with Melanie, you mess with the watchers."

"Speak for yourself," Devon said. "If Melanie wanted to get on her knees for me, twat or not, I'd let her slob my knob. Might even slob her back."

"And Devon here has no tact," Bryce said with a shake of his head.

"She likes sitting with us. Or she will," Devon said, giving me a wink. "I'm a fun guy."

If I thought the lighthearted conversation would continue, I was wrong.

"She can sit with me," a deep voice said from beside me.

I'd been so intent on willing myself to just disappear I hadn't realized someone else had joined us. The information about Melanie being the watchers' girl did something to my heart. I had no idea what it was either. I didn't want to explore it. My head was already a jumbled mess as it was.

"Oh. H-hey, Seth." Lucy let out a flirty giggle that made me grimace.

Instinctively, I slid closer to Bryce. Seth gave Lucy a quick nod.

"Sirena, hey. It's been a while, huh?" Seth was too close for comfort.

Hell, anywhere within a hundred-mile radius was too close for comfort.

"You know her?" Vic asked, putting down his food to survey the two of us.

"Uh, yeah. We go way back. We used to be neighbors."

"Did she talk then? Care to dish her secrets?" Devon shot me a wink.

"Want to come sit with me? We can catch up," Seth continued in a silky-smooth voice, ignoring everyone else.

I slid a bit closer to Bryce, our legs touching. I didn't know what good it would do. I'd already made a vow to myself to not to get him into trouble again. I reached out and gripped his pant leg.

"She's actually fine here," Bryce said, draping his arm over my shoulder.

I didn't need to see the look on Seth's face because it was in the air. Tension. Anger. Irritation.

"You two together or something?" Seth asked in a clipped tone.

"Uh, yeah. We met before school started, not that it's any of your business." He gave my shoulder a squeeze. "So no, my girlfriend won't be joining you."

Seth let out a soft laugh. "It doesn't matter. *It's doesn't fucking matter.*" He pounded his fist on the table.

Immediately, I was against Bryce, my pulse thundering in my ears, as everyone turned to see what the commotion was. Even Bryce's friends froze, varying looks of confusion and worry on their faces.

Seth backed away from the table. "It doesn't matter," he repeated. "We'll talk later, Sirena. Promise." And with those words, he left.

"What the hell was that?" Devon asked.

Lucy shook her head and blew out a breath. "I have no idea, but he's not called *Asylum* for nothing. He's so hot it doesn't even matter that he's crazy." She let out a sigh.

"I'm so confused," Vic muttered. "You guys are dating?" He didn't seem fazed by Seth.

Bryce cleared his throat. "Uh, yeah. It's cool. I just didn't want to introduce her like that without discussing it with her first. Trying to keep a low profile and all."

"My man." Devon high-fived him as Lucy smiled at me.

They all went back to talking and eating.

Bryce leaned in and spoke softly, "Sorry about that. You seemed uncomfortable. I hope I didn't upset you. Seth gets around a lot, and he was being weirder than usual. They call him Asylum here because he's been here longer than most. Plus there are rumors about the crazy stuff he did that got him sent here after his stay at a state hospital. At least me saying you're my girl takes you off the table, right? I-I didn't know what else to do. I'm sorry. I panicked when you grabbed my leg."

I dragged my stare from the guy in the weird rabbit and chain outfit to see a girl dressed like a cow, complete with an udder, sitting at a table with other students dressed in equally ridiculous outfits.

A petite girl jumped onto a table and started crowing like a rooster and yelling obscenities. Two security guards bustled in and snagged her off like she weighed nothing and hauled her away amidst a few cheers. Most everyone else just carried on with their lunch like it hadn't even happened.

I focused back on the rabbit and cow.

Bryce followed my gaze. "They're being initiated by the watchers. Humiliation trials. It's actually a half-assed job on their part. They're usually much more creative with these. And no, the staff never steps in. The watchers run this place. And those the watchers deem worthless are tossed aside and become the tormented."

When I swiveled my attention from a mousy girl in a frog outfit, I caught Stitches watching us. Bryce's arm drifted lower until it encircled my waist.

"I can't guarantee it'll protect you if we tell people we're together, but it can't hurt, right?" Bryce whispered. "It's not real. I don't want you to think I'm just trying to swoop in on you. I think you and I understand each other and are friends, so consider this one friend helping another. You can break up with me whenever you want. I only ask you try to hold off at for least a week so I don't look like a complete loser." He chuckled softly, but I heard the hurt in his voice.

Bryce had it hard like I did. But I didn't know why. He was handsome and sweet. If there was one thing I knew about people though, it was they didn't need a reason to be cruel.

I winced as I shifted in my seat, my bottom still aching from the beating I'd gotten earlier.

I caught Stitches's attention from across the cafeteria. He popped a grape into his mouth, his dark eyes shifting to Bryce's arm then back to my face again. He lifted a brow and smirked. I swallowed as I stared back at him. But it was Church leveling his gaze on me and licking his lips that really made me squirm. Melanie perched on his lap, her lips at his neck as she kissed his skin. He didn't seem interested in her though. His focus was firmly on me.

I'd left one circle of hell only to fall into another, that much was certain.

CHURCH

The freshman's arms flailed as he struggled beneath me, his face pushed firmly into the toilet, the water sloshing and bubbling as he screamed into it.

"I can't fucking believe Andrews, *of all* fucking people, got her first. Has that guy even fucked before? Does he know how to use his dick?" I shook my head at the guys and jerked the freshman out of the toilet, who sputtered as he choked in mouthfuls of air.

I'd heard the gossip—the hot new girl and Andrews were dating. There was even a rumor Ashes and Andrews tag teamed her and that was why Ashes was seen taking her back to her room. That one pissed me the fuck off. In fact, when I'd heard it, I'd taken to the forest and hunted with my knife until I was covered in blood and out of breath.

Ashes leaned against the doorway of the bathroom stall, his arms folded over his broad chest, his top button undone revealing his ink. "I think you might be jealous she fucked me and him."

"Eat shit, Valentine," I snapped as Sin chuckled softly. "Did you hear the one where Andrews sucked your cock?"

Ashes bristled. "Now you're just being a dick, *Dante.*"

I glanced down at the freshman who'd pissed his pants, the yellow puddling at his feet.

"Listen, you little piss ant." I growled at him. "If I catch you talking about Sirena Lawrence again, this moment will be a fucking cakewalk. Get me?"

The little shit shook and nodded.

"Tell all the cunts you hang with I'll come for them next if they so much whisper her name, got it? I'm itching to kill a mother fucker. Trust me when I say you don't want it to be you."

"Y-yessir," the kid sputtered.

I shoved him out of the stall, and he tumbled forward before getting his bearings and rushing from the bathroom. I shook my head after him. Pathetic little shit. Sin caught him and his buddies trying to rig up the camera on a cell phone so they could look under her skirt and take photos. *Dumb fucks.* Had they succeeded, I would've beaten them all within an inch of their lives. The fact anyone thought they could get near her had me seeing red.

I dragged my fingers through my hair before slipping a joint from my jacket pocket. I lit it and took a hit, leaning back against the stall. I held it deep in my lungs, relishing in the warmth and high, before blowing it out in a cloud of smoke.

What the fuck was happening to me? I was going insane over a girl. One who wouldn't—*couldn't*—talk to me. She'd defied me in the office. It sent me spiraling over the edge, but I'd caught myself before I'd hurt her. Fuck, was it a hard grapple though. I closed my eyes and took another hit as she appeared in my mind's eye. Those long fucking legs. Plump lips. Hair black as night that I could tangle my fingers in. Tits sculpted by the gods. And fuck, those eyes. Blue like a perfect summer day. Green like the brightest moss. Gold like . . . fucking absolute perfection. She was a goddess.

"What's our next move?" Stitches called out, taking the joint from me. "We could dress like clowns and fuck her in the dark."

Sin shuddered and said, "You know I hate fucking clowns."

The door banged open, and the dweeb Sirena and Andrews had been sitting with at lunch entered. He froze like a deer caught in headlights as he stepped in.

Sin reached for him and caught him by the arm, tugging him inside before he could escape.

"You hang out with Andrews, right?" Stitches handed off the joint to Ashes who put it out and stuffed it in his jacket.

"I-I... yeah. We're friends." The guy swallowed, his Adam's apple bobbing as he stared back at us, fear evident in his eyes.

I couldn't remember what he was in for. Something told me he was a klepto though. He took group therapy with Ashes and the impulse control gang. And I only knew that because I'd seen him coming out of a session once.

"Tell us, is Andrews fucking the mute?" Sin asked, giving him a shake.

"I-I guess. I mean, he said they were seeing each other."

"What's your name? Jason?" I asked, stepping forward, the news of Andrews with my specter eating through my soul.

"Victor. V-Vic Meyers."

"Vic Meyers," I murmured, cocking my head at him. "Tell me, *Vic Meyers.* How much does your freedom here mean to you?"

"I... what?"

"Your freedom," I repeated softly. "I could use a little bitch. Do you want to be my little bitch? You know, do my every bidding?"

"I just need to use the bathroom," he said in a shaky voice. "I didn't know you guys were in here."

"Seth Cain was at your lunch table. What did he want?" Ashes asked, ignoring him.

"S-Seth?" Vic's upper lip dotted with sweat.

"Yes, you fucking deadshit," I snapped at him, the very little patience I had remaining quickly leaving me. I was still waiting for him to answer me about being my bitch.

"He asked Sirena to sit with him. Bryce told him they were dating and said she wouldn't be sitting with him. Seth was upset about it and stormed off but said he'd see her soon." Vic licked his lips. "That's all I know. C-can I leave?"

I glanced at my guys.

"I want you to report back to me if anything happens between

Bryce and Sirena. I want to know it all. If Bryce tells you she has a kink, I want to know about it too. If he touches her, kisses her, *fucks her,* I want to know. Got it?" I stared him down.

The little shit looked like he was going to piss his pants like the freshman did. The idea of Andrews even looking at her had my anger at an all-time high. All he had to do was touch her. I'd end him.

"Bryce is my friend—"

"You see, Vic, we're your friends too." Sin gave him a dangerous smile. "Or we could be if you do what you're told. If you don't, I think that would make us your enemies, right?" He glanced at Stitches for confirmation.

"He's right. Fuck up and find out, Meyers. Pretty simple really. So you're going to be a *good friend,* right, and do what you're told. And you won't let anyone know you're taking notes. I'd hate to see you get hurt." Stitches gave Vic a serene look.

"O-OK." Vic nodded. "I-I will."

"Good boy," I said, waving my hand. "Now be gone. You're killing my buzz."

Vic scurried away like he'd been set on fire. The way Ashes was flicking his lighter made me think he was about a cunt hair away from it.

"Think he'll listen?" Ashes asked, staring at the door Vic had scampered through.

"He will if he knows what's good for him" I said with a grunt.

But even if he didn't, I might enjoy teaching him a lesson. I was a nice guy like that.

†

"Mr. Church, I need to see you," Sister May called out as students shuffled out of her classroom.

I got up and approached her desk as the last person left the room.

"God doesn't usually take personal chats, May," I said easily.

Sister May was young, late twenties at the oldest. I wasn't sure why she'd decided to devote her life to a life of no fucking and the insane, but I bet she had it going on beneath her habit. She was a blonde, small tendrils of her hair peeking out.

"Dante, I just wanted to tell you I was rather impressed with your creative writing project. It was deep and meaningful. I really enjoyed reading it."

I smirked at her. "I knew you'd like it. You seem to be the sort of woman who wants to let go and get lost in something new and. . . forbidden." I reached out and brushed my knuckles along her jaw.

She tensed, her brown eyes wide before she pulled away. "I-I just wanted to tell you it was good, and I was impressed. That's it." She shuffled through the papers on her desk.

"I bet I can impress you in other ways. . .Sister."

She paused and licked her lips. I nodded and shifted closer.

"Classes are done for the day. It's been a rough start for me. I bet it hasn't been easy for you. We could help each other out."

She finally turned and looked up at me. "And how do you propose to do that, Mr. Church?"

I leaned in and whispered in her ear, "I could fuck you until you beg me to stop, then I'll just fuck you harder."

She didn't move as I placed my hand on her waist. "I won't tell if you won't. We all need a little release sometimes. God didn't give you that pussy just to wear around. It has a purpose. Don't you want to use it to make me come?" I was way the fuck out of line, but I had plenty of pent-up frustration plus a bet going with Sin that I'd nail this bitch before we graduated or died. Since Sirena wasn't being so friendly, this was as good an option as any and it would win me a bet with Sin. He'd be the one doing a naked lap around campus. Besides, I needed to blow off some steam.

"I-I—"

"*Want to,*" I murmured in her ear. "I bet your pussy is wet just thinking about the possibilities."

She seemed to get her bearings about her because she stepped away from me. "You're dismissed."

I cackled and backed away. "Fine. Next time?"

Her cheeks flushed, and a tiny smile teased the corner of her lips.

Just like I thought. Easy.

The door to the classroom banged open, and Sin stomped in. "Let's go, asshole."

I grinned and winked at Sister May. "We'll do extra credit some other time." And with those sweet words of departure, I followed Sin out of the room, leaving the blushing nun behind.

"Nice." Sin clapped me on the shoulder.

"It's always good to have a nun in my pocket," I said, smirking.

Sin chuckled.

We stepped outside and made our way through the courtyard. I frowned when I saw Sirena and Bryce standing together at a vending machine. He was talking a mile a minute as he pulled items from the machine.

As if sensing us, she peeked over and locked eyes with me. Our encounter in the headmaster's office certainly hadn't left my mind. She tried to be strong. Defiant. She just didn't realize I loved a struggle. She was only pouring gasoline on a forest fire.

She quickly tore her gaze from me and followed Bryce across the courtyard to the dorms. She limped a little every now and then, each of her steps looking painful.

"Rumor has it Sully likes to crack the whip on students. Literally. Bet Sirena learned about his brand of punishment," Sin said, his eyes frozen on her retreating back.

I glanced at him before looking back to Sirena. "You think he really hit her?"

Sin nodded, not looking at me. "Rumor has it and all."

I ground my teeth tightly. *No one* touched what belonged to me. If the rumors were true, there'd be hell to pay.

But the only one who knew for sure was Sirena, and she wasn't talking.

SIRENA

On Friday, I waited outside the cafeteria for Bryce. I stared down at my phone. He sent a text.

Bryce: Running late. Got hung up working on a paper with Lucy.

Lucy and Bryce seemed to hang out a lot from what I'd noticed, which baffled me since she didn't seem his type. But if they had something going on, I was happy for him. He deserved it. Bryce kept his hands to himself and was a perfect gentleman to me, even though the whole student body knew we were *together*.

That just made him even sweeter in my eyes.

I'd been fortunate enough to not have seen Seth around campus the past couple of days. Like a ghost, he'd vanished again on me, and I didn't mind in the slightest. The only real hiccups I faced were the watchers and Headmaster Sully, who I'd learned was a doctor of psychology or something. He came to Chapel Crest ten years ago when he decided to get more *hands on* with his techniques. I was scheduled to see him after class.

My anxiety had spiked sometime around midnight and hadn't released me yet. I didn't want the morning and evening med pass to become my thing, so I'd tried my hardest to calm myself, but it really wasn't looking good.

The watchers had been leaving me alone for the most part. Aside from Stitches's looks during first period and catching glimpses of the others throughout the day, everything appeared fine. I assumed they were too busy with initiating other students. My group therapy sessions had been going OK. I sat and listened while other students spoke about their illnesses and things that had upset them during the week. Overall, it was a free hour for me since I couldn't share my day with anyone.

But just because I didn't hear from the watchers, didn't mean they weren't around. I'd walked past three guys tied to the flagpole in their boxers this morning with the words *pray for us* written on each of their chests. I didn't even want to fathom what they'd done to piss off the watchers. I was just grateful it wasn't me tied to the flagpole in my underwear.

"You look lonely."

I peered up from my phone to find Ashes in front of me, smiling. My gaze flicked down to the lighter in his hand that he flipped open and closed. Open and closed. Open and closed. Five times.

I swallowed thickly.

"Where's your boyfriend?"

I tore my focus from the lighter and stared anywhere but at him, wondering what my best plan of action should be. If I darted left, it was a dead end. Right would send me down the hall for quite a long way. Ashes would catch me in seconds.

My eyes flickered back on his face.

"I'd catch you if you ran," he said, still smirking down at me.

I hated he knew I was thinking that.

"I think we got off on the wrong foot." He held his hand out to me. "I'm Asher Valentine. I like to read and listen to music. I'm not a fan of spiders, but if you need one caught, I'd catch it for you. I have pyromania and set an entire grocery store on fire once. Last year, I set Sully's office on fire. I have impulse control issues, among other things. But I'm not as bad as I used to be. I enjoy coffee, and I wear glasses when I read."

I stared down at his hand.

He set a grocery store on fire? And Sully's office?

To be fair, I wished he'd set Sully on fire, so really, what did that say about me? I continued to peer at his outstretched hand.

Shake it. Be done with it and leave.

Come on, Bryce. Where are you?

Breathe, Sirena.

When I didn't shake his hand, he let out a sigh and ran his fingers through his hair. "Right. So... You and Andrews. How's that going?"

I swallowed and let out a shaky breath.

"How do you guys communicate? Do you write him notes and text?" He nodded to the phone I was still clutching in my hand. When I didn't answer, he pulled his phone out and thumbed through it quickly.

"We can exchange numbers if you want. I won't tell anyone if you want to talk." He stared me down for a moment before tentatively reaching for my phone.

I quickly snatched it back, not sure what the hell he was planning. It was my only connection to home. Cady had loaded a bunch of photos of us growing up on it. I couldn't lose it.

"I just want to put my number in if that's OK. You don't have to use it unless you want to. This is my peace offering to you." He reached out again and lifted his brows at me.

Maybe he'd let me go if I gave him my number. I could always block him if he bothered me.

He eased my phone gently from my hand and quickly thumbed through it before snapping a selfie and inputting something. His phone buzzed a moment later as he handed my phone back to me.

"I sent myself a text from your phone so if you do text me, I'll know it's you, OK?" He pointed his phone at me and snapped a quick picture, a small smile on his lips as he saved my contact info.

In that moment, he looked like any other handsome guy. I'd even go as far as to say he seemed sweet, but I knew the poison that ran through all the watchers. A few nice words and gestures didn't mean shit. Those boys knew how to play dangerous games and win.

"I, uh, should probably warn you that your next payment is going to have to be made soon."

I bristled at his words, fear clawing its way up my throat.

Please, don't lock me in a crypt again. And don't force me...

"That's not the main reason I came over here," he continued, stepping closer. "But it is a reason. Maybe it would be better to submit, Sirena. The fight, the chase is what ignites the fire in Dante. Malachi loves a challenge, and Sin...well, let's just say he's an asshole and gets off on all kinds of shit. They all do."

I frowned at him.

"I'm not much better than them," he admitted softly as he took in my frown. "But I also give a shit in my own way. I've never seen them care about anything like this before or obsess so much. I worry about where they're headed with it. Wherever it is, you're along for the ride. Just make it easier on yourself and do whatever it is without a fight. I honestly don't want to see you hurt. And Seth?"

I shuddered at the mention of his name, fear crawling down my spine like spiders.

"Be careful. I know we don't know one another, and I know I've done less than impress you, but I want you to know that you have my word. If you *need* me, just text." He nodded to my phone. "I'll do whatever I can. Even start a fire if you need me to, but I must warn you, I can get carried away. Sound good?"

The asshole could try to call off his dogs. Or maybe he was a dog too. Probably a mixture of both.

He stepped closer, and I shrank back against the row of lockers as he brushed his fingers along my cheek.

"Why Andrews?" he murmured. "What's he got that we don't? *That I don't*?" He stared down at me for a long moment.

Kindness. And he's not a dick.

My pulse thundered in my ears as we took one another in. We were too close for a friendly conversation. His closeness was intimate as he crinkled his brows and parted his lips, letting his fingers trail along my bottom lip. His aftershave tickled my senses, making my guts tighten as I realized I wanted to breathe him in deeply and hold him there.

I exhaled. *Why the hell am I not pushing him away? Why am I contemplating what his arms would feel like wrapped around me? Or what his lips on mine would taste like?*

Melanie was the girl they were close to claiming. *What would I be? Just some chick they played with in their downtime?* It didn't make sense to me, and I couldn't ask.

"Hey," Bryce called out.

Ashes briefly closed his eyes before snapping them open, a hard look crossing his face as he stepped back, his hand falling away.

"Andrews," Ashes muttered.

Bryce completely ignored Ashes and focused on me. Playing the part with Bryce was easy. He didn't mind holding me or acting like our situation was more than friends. He was natural. I felt like I mattered when he was near me.

So when he reached for me, I took his hand, allowing him to wind his arm around my waist. He'd made strides where so many had failed. I trusted him, and I definitely didn't trust easy. There was just something about him that relaxed me and made me feel human despite the monster clawing to get out of me. I didn't know what my monster was capable of though. I'd been hurt so much. The thought of letting it out scared me. So I beat it down, praying it would stay dormant beneath the surface.

A flash of annoyance clouded Ashes's face briefly as he stared us down.

"I meant what I said." Ashes nodded at me. "If you need anything." His gaze cut from Bryce back to me. He lingered for a moment before turning and walking away.

I let out a deep sigh and glanced to Bryce who'd dropped his arm from around me.

"Was he a dick?"

Like always, I remained silent, but knew the answer in my head.

No. Ashes was. . . nice.

"He's actually the nicer one. The other three are total assholes. Ashes might have a few redeeming qualities about him though. You know, when he isn't setting things on fire."

I thought so too, and maybe that was why I was so damn curious about him.

†

"MISS LAWRENCE. RIGHT ON TIME," Sully said as I stepped into his office after classes ended.

My head screamed at me to run, but my feet refused to move in the opposite direction.

I followed him to his desk, not sure what it was I was supposed to do, but hoping like hell it didn't consist of what happened last time.

"Sit." He nodded to a chair in front of his desk.

I took a seat and swallowed, waiting for the hammer to fall.

"How are you feeling? I see you made it to the rest of your classes this week. And no more fighting, which is. . . good." He winked at me as he leaned forward in his seat and stared me down like a hungry dog. His eyes drank me in as I squirmed uncomfortably in my seat.

"I spoke to Jerry, and I let him know I had to punish you. He was happy with my decision as I figured he would be. Today, I thought we might do some scripture reading. I hope you brought your Bible. In my studies, I've found those closer to God and His word are better prepared mentally for the world. Our core curriculum and *medicine* here is the word of God. God first. Always. With Him leading us, we'll never go astray. That's why it's so important that you take your studies seriously. The curriculum I've designed cures students. I'm going to cure you, Sirena. I'm going to rid you of your demons so your mind works again."

My mind works just fine. Just because I don't talk doesn't make me an idiot. You're the crazy one.

I wanted to shout at him, but that ship sailed long ago, so I leaned down and quickly pulled my Bible from my bag. I settled for sitting back and clutching my Bible.

If he got mean with me again, I'd slam him in the face with the holy book.

A quick image of blood spurting from his nose flashed in my mind.

"Excellent." He got comfortable in his leather chair. "Let's start with Matthew, shall we?"

I flipped to the place he instructed and listened as he read to me, my brain blanking out as he droned forever through the verses, his voice booming around us.

"So the devils besought him, saying, 'If thou cast us out, suffer us to go away into the herd of swine.'" He paused and looked at me.

I quickly snapped my attention back to him, feeling my face heat. I'd been thinking about a hot bath and curling up to watch a good movie.

"Ah, those demons have your attention, don't they?" He rose to his feet.

My heart pounded hard as I stared at him. I tightened my hold on my Bible.

He moved beside me and held out his hand. "Come. Perhaps your demons need an extra lesson today."

I had no place to run as terror coursed through my body. Nervously, I placed my palm against his while I internally screamed.

"I want you to lean over, chest down on the desk." He pointed to his desk.

If you strike him, it might be worse. Take the punishment. Just like you do with Jerry. It won't hurt forever. It won't hurt forever. I can't *hurt forever.* The words repeated in my head as I bent over the desk, wondering if he was going to spank me like last time. The jingling of his belt made my heart raced faster.

He leaned down, his breath hot in my ear. "If you move, if you make a noise, I will punish you more. Do you understand?"

I squeezed my eyelids closed as he shifted away from me, my body trembling.

I didn't know what the plan was, but I soon found out as his leather belt crashed down over my lower back in a hot strike that made me grip the edge of his desk.

He didn't stop at one or two. No, he had to beat my demons within an inch of their lives, so his leather belt connected with my back over and over again as I ground my teeth tightly, praying for relief or even death. Not only was I humiliated, but I was in agony as the belt cracked across my skin, sending electricity through every facet of my body.

My legs wobbled and trembled as I breathed heavily, each strike worse than the last.

Please, God, help me. Please. Where are you? Why me? Why me? WHY ME!

The final hit rang out. *Ten.* I'd counted ten lashes. My eyes burned from the effort of holding back my tears. My nails had cracked and broken as I'd clung to the edge of the desk. I'd made it through without letting a single tear fall.

Because good girls didn't cry. They suffered in silence.

"Get up." He panted.

With trembling legs, I rose, agony searing through my body as I attempted to stand up straight. I rocked to the side, my hip crashing against the desk, sending more misery surging.

"I want you to go straight to your dorm. When you get there, I want you to think about how much your existence displeases our lord. I want you to write out the entire book of Matthew. Turn it in on Monday. Now go. If you fail to turn in a copy, we'll repeat this. If you fail to pay attention when you're in my presence, you *will* be punished. I'll teach you to follow commands, Miss Lawrence. I will teach you to be stronger than your demons. Do you understand?"

I closed my eyes and let out a shaky breath. That seemed to be a good enough response for him before he turned his back on me. With the worst pain imaginable coursing through me, I booked it out of his office and snapped the door closed behind me. I kept my head down as a tear finally escaped and rushed down my cheek.

I fucking hated Chapel Crest.

ASHES

"Line up!" Church shouted at the initiates.

They trembled but moved their asses. I sat on the top step of the deck while Stitches leaned against the railing. Sin sat off to the side in a patio chair, appearing bored as he stared down at his phone and puffed on a joint.

The initiates lined up in their stupid animal attires. They looked fucking ridiculous and like they'd just come from a furry porno convention for the mentally unstable. My mind was elsewhere as I thought about Sirena. How soft her lips had been when I brushed my thumb against them. The way she'd smelled of lavender and coconut. How her body had trembled from my nearness. How much I'd just wanted to reach out and wrap her in my arms and tell her she'd be OK.

I'd controlled it. It was always hard for me to manage my impulses, but I'd gotten a hell of a lot better over the years. It wasn't this place, that was for sure. If anything, being here tested my will. Every damn day was a struggle. I woke up each day wanting to burn this place to the fucking ground. And if a few stragglers happened to be trapped inside, oh well. Collateral damage.

"I'm guessing you all saw what happened to Howard Dean, Sam

Johnson, and Brandon Holmes." Church peered out at the line of students and took in their reactions to the names being called.

Those initiates had decided to not fall in line with their outfits and so had been tied to the flagpole in their underwear. Church had wanted to crucify them out front, but I'd talked him out of it. Tying students up crucifixion style sounded like a lot more work than it was worth. I figured that meant I was making progress.

"Your next task is for you to simply *be.* I want you in your uniforms but with a twist. Accessories are important, so I thought what better accessory than the truth? God fucking loves honesty, right?"

I shook my head. Church's ideas were always out in left field, but this place sucked, and we were all a little bored.

"We're going to give you a marker. I want you to turn to the person on your right and write one word you think describes them. An honest word. Put it on their foreheads." He smiled at the group, who looked like they might puke on one another.

Stitches chuckled softly and shot me a wink as I rolled my eyes. Sin climbed to his feet and moved to stand beside Church, his arms crossed over his chest.

"If you don't put an honest remark on your neighbor, I'll put one on you. Trust me when I say you won't like it. Just write an initial thought. A toxic trait you think the person has. Easy, right? We'll call it therapy. When the marker wears off your forehead, you're free from initiation unless you fuck up and piss us off." He handed the marker to Sin who moved forward and handed it to a small waif of a girl with an eating disorder.

"The asshole on the end will write on you," Sin told her with a grunt, not bothering to cast another look at her as she took the marker. He walked away to join Church.

The girl went up on her tiptoes, her dumb ass bunny tail bouncing as she quickly scrawled *creep* over the guy's forehead beside her.

Stitches let out a soft laugh. That guy, Ronald, had been eyeing her ass since he'd arrived. Clearly, it hadn't gone unnoticed by her. The marker moved down the line. They wrote cruel truths on one another's foreheads until the circle was complete, the small girl getting the word *tease* written on her flesh. *Guess that hadn't gone unnoticed either.*

"OK. Get the fuck out of here. If you try to get rid of the words, I'll gut you myself and throw your body into the lake for the fish to eat." Church turned but didn't get very far.

"Um, C-Church?" a timid, freckle faced guy with messy, brown hair called out.

Church paused before slowly spinning back to him. Everyone stopped to hear what was about to go down. Even Stitches and I moved down the steps to join Church and Sin.

"What?" Church asked in a clipped tone.

"It's just, uh, tha-that one girl i-isn't here. The o-one who d-doesn't t-t-talk."

"And?" Church glared at him.

"I-isn't s-she an initiate too? S-shouldn't she be here? S-she's new."

"Are you questioning how the fuck I run things?"

"N-no, sir. I mean, n-not at all. I-I was just wondering s-since it doesn't seem f-fair—"

"Sin, Stitches, remove this little fucking cock knob from my sight," Church snarled, glaring at the trembling guy in front of us.

He let out a yip as Stitches and Sin seized him by his scrawny arms.

"Dungeon?" Sin looked to Stitches.

Stitches grinned. "Dungeon."

They hauled the trembling kid off, leaving everyone to stare fearfully after them as they disappeared into the dusk.

The mausoleum. The same place we'd put Sirena for the night. I doubted the kid would do as well as Sirena had. I pitied him for that. Anxiety was a real bitch when you couldn't control it.

"Anyone else have any dumb questions?" Church stared out at everyone. When no one said anything, he dismissed them and turned to me.

"The little asshole is right. Sirena is getting off too easy. We should probably fix that."

"We should leave her alone. I think she's pretty stressed out," I said.

The look on her face when I'd approached her was enough to make me realize the poor girl was barely hanging on. I had issues in my own right, but she made me feel all the way to the depths of my charred soul. That had to mean something.

"Not likely. The second we step back, Seth steps up. We're already dealing with fuck face Andrews," Church answered sourly.

"She and Andrews *are* getting pretty close," I muttered, hating seeing him wrap his arm around her like he could actually be a good match for her.

The fact she'd chosen him still baffled me.

Church scoffed and marched into the house. I followed as he went to the bar in the corner and poured himself a glass of scotch, downing it quickly before pouring another.

"It won't last."

"Why not?" I filled a crystal tumbler with alcohol and drank at a slower pace before taking a hit from the vape I had on me.

"Because we won't fucking let it." He stared at his glass before tossing back the contents. "She needs someone stronger than Andrews. Someone willing to go to war for her. Now that we've found someone we're willing to wage war for."

"Andrews seemed pretty willing when he punched Stitches earlier this week," I mused, swirling my liquor before taking another sip.

"Heat of the moment." He waved me off. "You of all people know about impulses. When push comes to shove, he'd crumble before the blood let. We'll get the girl."

"Probably scaring the shit out of her isn't the best way to endear her to us." I raised a brow at him and took another hit off my vape.

He shrugged. "I don't do it to hurt her. Not really, anyway. I do it to see the fire in her soul. It's like she's trapped in there, and only an inferno is going to set her free. Sometimes the flames just need to be stoked a little."

If anyone understood fire, it was me. The splash of the scotch hitting his glass again was the only noise in the space.

"Think about it," he said softly after a moment of silence. "Have we ever had a girl worthy of us all? Imagine having someone who needs and deserves us? She's fucking gorgeous. But it's more than that. She's not a pushover. She's got some sass trapped inside her silent mold. She's smart and sweet and innocent. I want to crack her open and see what makes her tick. And I can't fucking wait to hear her voice. She's just so fucking perfect. Even if I have to bring Andrews in on it, I *want* her."

I nodded, my heart jumping. "I don't think Andrews will come with her. If she chooses us, we'll get her without him."

"Well, I suppose we could make that a reality."

"You're forgetting we were considering claiming Melanie," Sin said as he and Stitches strode back inside. Sin grabbed the booze from me. "What are we going to do about that? I'm not dealing with that shit if she finds out it's a no. I'm not attached to her, so there's no danger with her. Past her pussy, I don't give a shit about her."

Church shrugged. "We let her go. It's not official. She's only been a warm hole to fuck on the regular."

Stitches let out a snort as he flopped onto the couch. "Melanie won't let that happen. You know it. Sin's right. She's nuts. Crazier than we are. She's got that female crazy gene. You know, the one that makes her key your car and piss on your dog. We'll have a fight on our hands if we tell her we were done with her pussy. Plus, she lets Tasha join, who has a fantastic ass. I love how slutty she is. One of these days, we might get some group action going. Isn't that the goal?"

"I'd tell them to both fuck off for Sirena," Church's voice was strong as he gazed intently at us. "I want Sirena Lawrence." He was quiet for a moment before he whispered, "I *need* her."

I glanced at Sin and Stitches. Stitches nodded thoughtfully while Sin scowled. It was strange to hear so much emotion in Church's voice. I'd gone through most of our lives thinking he didn't have any feelings besides anger and cruelty. Sirena brought out an entirely different side of him.

"We still have Cain to deal with," I said, knowing that was the elephant in the room. "We have to get Sirena to talk or scream. If he gets her to first, well, we won't be claiming shit because I'm pretty sure he won't let her go once he gets his hooks in her. We agreed to back off if he wins."

"Fuck him," Church said, leaning against the bar. "There's something there. Something neither are telling. Why is she so scared of him? It doesn't make sense. She knows something. She has dirt on him. I want that dirt so we can bury that fucking asshole. We just need to get her to talk."

"Or scream," I murmured. "It gets us answers and a win."

Church gave me a dark smile. The monster I knew was back from his emotional reprieve.

"Or scream. That's really what I'm going for."

At the end of the day, it was all I wanted too because it meant we'd have her.

I'd have her.

CHURCH

I was at my wit's end.

When I couldn't stand lying here anymore because the dark-haired specter kept haunting my mind, I shoved my covers back, tugged on a pair of dark jeans and a black shirt, stuffed my feet into my shoes, and left the house.

Without bothering to contemplate what the hell I was doing, I made my way to Sirena's dorm. Normally when I was frustrated, I'd race through the woods and cemetery, letting my feet pound out what I couldn't let my fists do, but just thinking about the cemetery made my cock hard because that was where *she* got on her knees for me.

The campus was silent and black as pitch, which was great because it meant no one was out to see me. I went to her room and stopped outside it, breathing hard.

Do I go in? Do I wake her?

I didn't need a lot of time to come to a decision.

Fuck it. It was two in the morning. She had to be asleep. I reached out and tried the handle, letting out a soft snarl of irritation when I found it locked. I hated these fucking auto-lock doors. I supposed they were a good thing with demons like me roaming the halls.

I pulled my wallet out of my back pocket and snagged the master keycard I'd stolen from the office earlier in the week. Her door clicked open within moments, and I slipped inside beneath the cover of darkness only to stop in my tracks as I reached the edge of her bed and saw she wasn't alone.

She was curled up beside Andrews.

That son of a bitch...

It took everything in me not to completely lose my shit as I stared down at them. She lay in pink, cotton pajama shorts, the blanket tangled around her legs, and a white, long-sleeved shirt. Her dark hair was a wild mess against her white pillow. Her lashes fanned across her cheeks as she slumbered.

But it was his fucking arm around her waist that ruined it. It took me a moment to clear the red in my vision as I drew in shallow breaths over and over, my body shaking with barely controlled rage.

Once I had my shit under control, I eased closer and kneeled beside her, studying everything I could in the moonlight streaming through her window.

Absolute fucking perfection. Right down to her soft breathing and plump, parted lips. Lips my cock had the pleasure of touching.

Reaching out, I touched her soft as silk hair, marveling in it as it sifted between my fingers like water. She rolled completely over so we were face to face, and I blew out a breath. She was silent as she continued to slumber, her beauty sending electric currents straight to my dick.

She was sleeping beauty, but I was no prince. I was a devil intent on claiming her soul. My body trembled as I bent closer. I had to taste her lips. I needed it like a starving man needed food. She was sustenance, and I felt like I'd die without her on my lips.

I kept my eyes open as I leaned, my desperation to have her taste on my lips consuming me, my cock hard as fucking steel in my pants. I inhaled, breathing in that flowery scent of hers.

Lavender. Coconuts. Forbidden fruit I had no business wanting, but she was Eve in this garden of darkness, and I was the snake who'd devour her.

I darted my tongue out and ran it along her parted lips. *Fucking sugary sweet. And so deliciously soft.* Just like I knew they'd be. She didn't shift or wake as I did it again, barely tasting her when what I really wanted to do was eat her fucking whole.

Exhaling, I brushed my knuckles tenderly along her jaw. I allowed them to traverse to her neck before I moved to her breasts and swept my fingers gently along the curve of them.

Fuck, she had beautiful tits.

As much as I wanted to sink my teeth into the fleshy goodness, I resisted and pulled back before I went too far. I wasn't so sure I'd be able to stop once I made my move. It wouldn't matter if Andrews was in the room or not. I'd let him watch me fuck her raw if it came down to it.

I swallowed hard and licked my lips, savoring what I could of her before I stood. It was a bold move on my part to get so close. Something had unhinged in my head the moment I'd seen her, and I didn't see it getting fixed anytime soon. I had no right to be in her room, watching her sleep, contemplating kissing her, tasting her, touching her, *fucking her,* but my crazy wanted what it wanted, and unfortunately for sleeping beauty that was her.

I *never* kissed. I fucked. Kissing was reserved for something else entirely, and no one had ever gotten under my skin enough for me to want to.

Except her. *Fuck, I needed her.*

I tensed as Andrews shifted and drew her closer to his body.

I ground my teeth so hard the muscles in my jaw ached. If I didn't get the hell out of there, shit would go south quick. With every ounce of willpower I had, I left the room, making sure to close the door softly behind me.

It was against Chapel Crest policy for co-ed sleepovers. All I needed to do was put a bug in Sully's ear, and it would be game over for sleeping beauty and her prince charming.

Of course, with the rumors of how Sully punished students, I was a bit leery about making that move. Her defiant spirit was part of her allure. The thought of her being turned into a mindless zombie like some of the other students here made fury surge in my veins. My beautiful specter deserved better. So, I'd keep her secret for now, tuck it into my arsenal until I had a better idea of what Sully had planned for my girl. More information would help me decide. I could always just gut Andrews, then there'd be no more sleepovers with him unless she wanted to snuggle a corpse.

I ducked into the darkness once I was outside her dorm and made my way back home. Sirena still needed to be punished for three more occurrences. Seeing her squirm was a big deal to me. It did something to me nothing else ever had. And for that reason alone, I'd come for her and make her do all the fucked-up shit in my head.

And when she screamed, I'd be there to swallow the sound because that was what fucked-up people did. And me. . . I was as fucked-up as they came.

†

"DANTE, why don't you tell us how you're feeling today?" Dr. Oberman encouraged, offering me a smile as she crossed her tanned legs in her black pencil skirt.

"I'm feeling. . . nothing," I said, raising a brow at her. "But judging by how you've been eye-fucking me this whole session, I'd say you should tell me how *you're* feeling."

Crimson crept onto her face as she sat up straighter in her chair. The little shits in my group therapy whispered to one another as I stared down the hot-as-fuck cougar in front of me. I knew her tits had to be fake. I also knew her husband had left her for a younger woman. Not that Doc Oberman was old, late forties at the most. Still hot as fuck and old enough to be my mother. I had mommy issues though according to these quacks, so maybe fucking her would make me feel better. Some Oedipus complex bullshit by Freud. I didn't buy into it too much. My mother was a tall blonde who'd modeled before she died. If anything, I tried to stay away from women who reminded me of her.

"Dante, we've discussed your language before. This is a session where you tell us how you're feeling. We need to stay focused."

I smirked at her, deciding I was enjoying the game. "Well, Doc, I gotta tell you. I feel like I need my cock sucked. Think you can help me out?"

Her cheeks darkened further as a sophomore giggled and eyed me. I winked at her, completely uninterested enough to give her more than that and turned my attention back to the cougar in question.

"Dante, you've said in the past that you hunt in the woods when you feel stressed. Are you still doing that?"

I had to give her credit, she did try to keep my attention diverted. I'd play along.

"Yes. In fact, I killed a rabbit, a raccoon, and a possum last night. I dismembered and disemboweled all of them before making some much needed changes. Racossumbit has been created. I almost feel like Dr. Frankenstein. I just need to figure out how to bring the little guy back to life. Any tips. . . Doc?" I slid my gaze up her body and cocked my head at her. "There was an awful lot of blood."

Her face paled, and she visibly swallowed.

"You didn't really—"

"But I *did*. It helps keep me from doing it to humans. Have you read my chart? I know you're new here, but everyone knows I'm the real deal. Sociopath. Psychopath. Resident mother fucker. Read up on me. Maybe we could do a private session. If you're brave enough, that is."

She cleared her throat and gazed past me after making a note in her chart. I assumed it was something along the lines of *take Dante Church's knife from him*. "Mr. Cain. Care to share how you're feeling today?"

"Same as Church, except I'm not picky—animals, people, doesn't matter to me. Plenty of humans need to die. Also, you should sue your plastic surgeon or whoever fitted you for your bra. Your tits are crooked. I'd still fuck you though."

I nodded. *Good fucking answer*. Still a dirtbag in my opinion though.

Doctor Oberman let out an indignant sound in her throat.

Seth looked at me and smirked.

It was almost like looking into a mirror. Except I didn't hear fucking voices or see shit like he did. But we were definitely on the same page. Plenty of humans needed to die. I wondered just how far he'd go to make that happen.

If nothing else, Mr. Asylum intrigued me.

The bell rang, signaling the end of our session. Everyone got to their feet and shuffled out.

"You really do that to those animals?" Seth asked as he ambled beside me.

I dug into my pocket and withdrew a rabbit paw I'd put on a keychain and handed it to him. I hadn't bothered to wash the blood from its brown fur. "Keep it. It wasn't lucky for the rabbit, but it might be lucky for you. If you're trying to win Sirena, you'll need it."

He chuckled and stuffed the paw into his pocket without bothering with commentary before turning the corner and striding in the opposite direction.

Yep. Just like looking into a fucking mirror.

SIRENA

I let out a pained breath as I shook out my aching hand from writing so much. Over the weekend, I'd copied the book of Matthew from the Bible and had turned it in on Monday. Sully had said that it wasn't good enough, so I was writing it over. Every day. Until he deemed it perfect in the eyes of the Lord because he was a delusional fuck who thought he was overseeing God's work by saving the mentally ill.

I had to see him after classes today for our regular appointment. It had been another week at Chapel Crest, and nothing was getting easier. Group therapy was probably the easiest thing I did there, and that was only because I didn't talk. If I did, I knew I'd be like the others in my group, doing a deep dive inside myself to see what I could change to be a better human. I already knew I was a good person. I just needed. . . well, I wasn't sure what I needed, but it wasn't Sully or Jerry or their fucked-up ways of healing people.

The pain from my aching hand was a welcome relief compared to the pain deep in my soul, though. I was drowning in it. Suffocating. Desperate.

Please, God. Help me. Make the demons go away.

Not the demons within me. The ones lurking in the distance who kept trying to hurt me. They'd eventually kill me, but maybe that was what should happen. Maybe it was God's way of taking me out.

Really morbid to think about.

I wrote another line of scripture and let out a raspy breath at the aching pain. Far too tired to continue, I dropped my pencil onto the notebook. A blister on my hand had popped and was rubbed raw and bleeding.

The truth of the matter was, I'd been bleeding to death slowly ever since Seth had brought that shovel down over my head all those years ago. My wounds had finally come to a head, the infection blistering and boiling over.

I bit my bottom lip, wondering if I'd done enough to appease Headmaster Sully. I couldn't keep writing.

Not knowing what he had planned as punishment made it that much worse because he said if I didn't have it perfect this time, I'd pay dearly. If this was his way of conditioning me to fall in line, it seriously sucked.

After cleaning the blood from my hand, I bandaged the area before taking some pain killers and lying in bed. I stared up at the ceiling, breathing softly, my fingers twisted in my blankets as worry set in over what fresh hell tomorrow would bring.

Would Seth finally make good on his promise to see me? It had been over a week since his promise in the lunchroom. I'd only seen him but once, and it was because I'd caught a glimpse of him walking across the courtyard. He hadn't seen me, which was just as well. Our time would come. I knew it would.

My mind drifted to my other problems. *Would Bryce and I be ousted as fake? Would Headmaster Sully break me? And what about the watchers? Would they come to check one of my punishments off their list?*

I closed my eyes. I willed them to remain that way, but I knew when morning rolled around, they'd pop open like always.

I WAS grateful Bryce stayed by my side as much as possible. It made the interactions with others… less, which was useful because I wanted to interact with the least amount of people as possible, especially Seth Cain, since he was one of my primary concerns.

Even the watchers weren't paying me much attention today. Not that they approached me a lot, but I'd see them watching me when they didn't think I was paying attention. They'd strung some kid nearly naked to a wooden cross in front of the school earlier this morning. Sister Irene and Sister Ellen completely ignore the guy pleading for help through the gag in his mouth. Even security sauntered past. That scared me the most. It was their job to keep students safe. Instead, they'd moved on by like the sobbing student wasn't even there.

If no one was doing shit about the watchers, there was little hope for me if they ever got their hands on me, which gave me mega anxiety. Ashes had warned they were preparing for my *payments*. They just hadn't struck yet, and each day I sat and waited made it worse. Rumor had it, they'd locked an initiate in the mausoleum I'd been in overnight. When they'd pulled him out, he'd soiled himself. Stitches and Sin had photographed him in his own filth and distributed flyers of him throughout the school. The kid was still in the medical ward being treated for his anxiety. If their treatments were anything like what Sully gave me, I worried for him.

That could be me if the watchers wanted. The thought terrified me.

"Hey! Mute!" a guy shouted as I walked with my head down through the outdoor commons area.

I picked up my pace, noting how many students were out this morning.

"I said hey." A strong arm wrapped around my arm and gave a fierce tug.

I stared up at dark-haired guy with a scar running down his cheek. I'd seen him before. His name was Danny, and he was in my afternoon English class. He was always being kicked out of the room. Security retrieved him a few times a week. I didn't know what his issue was, and I honestly didn't care.

Or at least I didn't until I was being pushed against the brick wall of the main building.

"I was talking to you," he said, his dark-eyed gaze trailing over my face as I silently counted in my head, my chest heaving.

I tried to maintain my anxiety as his grip tightened on my arm, the bricks uncomfortable and cold against my back.

"Everyone says you're fucking Bryce and Ashes, and that you don't talk. Is it true?"

If everyone was saying I don't talk, what response are you hoping for from me? Dumb ass.

I swallowed thickly and peeked over his shoulder to find a handful of students pausing to watch. Others continued about their business like nothing was going on.

The one time I needed Bryce, he was MIA.

Danny gave me a fierce shake, causing pain to radiate up my arm from his strong hold.

Where was security?

Conveniently looking the other way like always.

Danny gave me a wicked grin, his eyes darkening further. I breathed faster, my head spinning.

"I'm going to assume it's true. You're a hot piece of ass." He leaned in, his body pinning me to the wall.

I flinched away from him, pressing as deeply into the bricks as I could get and turned my head away.

One. Two. T-three. Fucking GO AWAY! F-five. . .

I squeezed my eyelids closed as his hand moved up and grasped my breast, giving it a hard squeeze.

"I like that you don't talk." His hot breath in my ear made nausea roll deep in my guts as my legs shook. "It means we can have some fun. I've been keeping an eye on you. The watchers haven't claimed you even though they watch you too. And Bryce isn't a big deal. So you know what that means?" He let out a soft chuckle, sending shivers down my spine. He brushed a dark strand of hair off my cheek as I clenched my teeth tightly. "It means your pussy and hot little ass are up for grabs."

He shifted his hand lower until he was pushing my skirt up. His rough hand squeezed my ass cheek before he let out a soft groan into my ear.

I held my breath, willing my body to just fucking die so I could get out of there. I was frozen, terrified. My heart beat painfully against muscle and bone as a silent tear slid down my cheek.

Danny grunted, and his weight fell from me. I cracked my eyelids open to see Stitches pummeling him with his fists as students rushed forward, chanting and cheering like wild animals.

It wasn't much of a fight. Stitches already had Danny on the ground and was kicking him repeatedly as Danny curled into a tight ball. He randomly kicked out a leg to attack Stitches back, but it was useless.

Warm arms wrapped around me.

"Sirena. Hey," Bryce urged softly. "Hey, look at me. Are you OK?" He turned me into his embrace and peered down at me, so much worry on his face it made my heart clench. I didn't want Bryce to be worried.

"Shit, you're shaking. Come on." Bryce steered me away from the fight.

Sin had arrived and managed to pull Stitches away while Danny groaned on the ground, covered in blood from what I suspected was a broken nose.

Stitches gazed at me, his black, shaggy hair hanging in his face as his chest heaved, his lips parted and blood on his knuckles and uniform. My heart jumped in my chest at the hungry look on his face.

Sin clapped him on the shoulder and said something that made Stitches nod before Sin shot me a glare, making me draw closer to Bryce. It wasn't a look of worry or concern. It was one of pure anger and hatred.

But it wasn't either of the watchers who had me picking up my pace.

It was Seth. He stood in front of the gathered students, his focus on Danny bleeding and groaning on the ground. Seth's hands clenched into fists.

And then he looked at me.

In his eyes, I saw the Seth I used to know. My friend. Then he blinked and became the Seth who was always on the edge of madness. The Seth who'd tried to kill me.

SIRENA

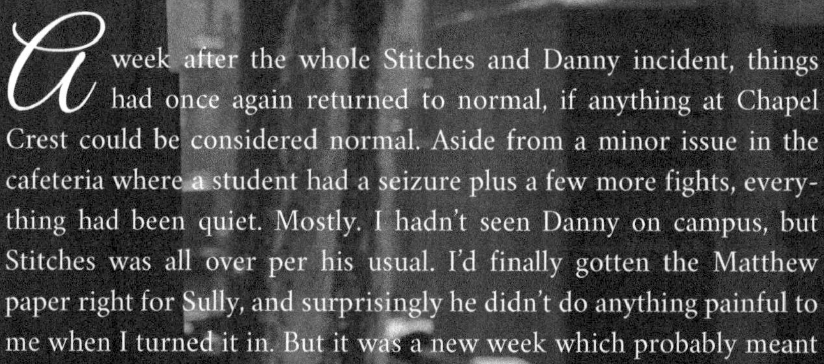

A week after the whole Stitches and Danny incident, things had once again returned to normal, if anything at Chapel Crest could be considered normal. Aside from a minor issue in the cafeteria where a student had a seizure plus a few more fights, everything had been quiet. Mostly. I hadn't seen Danny on campus, but Stitches was all over per his usual. I'd finally gotten the Matthew paper right for Sully, and surprisingly he didn't do anything painful to me when I turned it in. But it was a new week which probably meant new horrors from the headmaster.

"Bryce, want to hang out tonight, man?" Devon asked, jogging up as Lucy and Bryce argued over the layout for the yearbook. Apparently, they were both on the committee. Bryce was involved in pretty much all those sorts of activities—yearbook, student council, newspaper, chess club.

This place operated like a school in most senses, but the dark underbelly wasn't something we could ignore. It was anything but normal. The fact the school tried to hide under a shroud of normalcy sickened me. It was a place for struggling youth with mental illness and behavior issues. It was a place where cruelty oozed—not just from students, but from the staff too. It was hell, plain and simple.

Vic offered me a quick, tight smile as his gaze darted between me and Bryce. He'd been acting a little off lately, or at least I thought he had. I didn't know him well though.

"Uh..." Bryce looked over at me.

I stared back at him, having a silent conversation with him. I wanted him to hang out with his friends. Granted, I was a friend, but he seemed to always worry about me. I felt like he was ruining the fun he could have because of it.

"Yeah, man. Sounds good." He turned back to me after glancing at the guys. "I'll come see you after?"

I gazed back at him wordlessly, but he took it for a yes, which was good because it was the vibe I was hoping for. He grinned and high-fived the guys. They started discussing whatever it was they were going to end up doing. It sounded like they might raid the kitchens.

Lucy glanced at me and gave me an awkward smile. "Boys, right?"

I said nothing and peered at a point over her head at Seth strolling toward us. His gaze locked on mine before it darted to Bryce who was still messing around with the guys. Seth moved past us without a word. I let out a nervous breath and allowed my body to relax.

"Come on, Sirena. Last class of the day," Bryce said, holding his hand out for me.

I stepped forward and slipped my hand into his, giving the show everyone expected, minus the kissing. Of course, that all ended when Vic spoke up.

"Man, why don't you two ever kiss?"

Bryce shot me a quick look before laughing off Vic's question. "We do. Just not in front of people."

"Since when?" Devon snorted. "When you dated Kat Wallace for like three weeks last year, you two were always kissing in front of us."

"Yeah, well, that was then. This is now."

"Come on, man," Vic continued. "Maybe you guys aren't really dating. You're just pretending."

"Shut up. You're being ridiculous," Bryce said, his hold on my hand tightening.

"Then do it. I think you're just trying to keep her safe from all the other dicks around here." Vic leveled his gaze on me. "Right, Sirena?"

"Man, what's your problem?" Bryce demanded.

"Nothing. But people are talking. If you're for real, you'd better prove it. Look what happened with Danny being a dick to her. Stake your claim publicly, man."

"He's right," Devon added. "I heard the watchers, and even *Asylum,* are talking shit. You better cement that shit, or you're going to end up with trouble on your hands."

I felt the tension in Bryce's grip as he turned to me. He'd been so upset after the Danny incident. He'd paced my room for an hour that day without saying a word. It took the entire length of the third *Lord of the Rings* movie for him to calm down. He'd apologized profusely for not being there when I was in trouble. I'd simply squeezed his hand, hoping he knew I didn't blame him at all.

The expression on Bryce's face brought me back to the moment. His eyes said everything his mouth couldn't. Either we kissed and made a show of it, or we let it go to hell. Either way, it was going to be an ugly mess.

Bryce gathered me to him, his hands dropping to my waist as he stared down at me. He leaned in, his voice soft so only I could hear him. "I'm sorry. I don't know what to do." He leaned back enough to stare down at me, his eyes pleading for me to give him an answer.

They were right. This had to be done. My first kiss given as a way to save my ass. In the grand scheme of things, I'd never thought anyone would want to kiss me anyway, so I supposed this was beyond my wildest expectations. On the other hand was the fact deep down inside me I wanted to be kissed by someone who loved me.

And Bryce didn't love me. We were just friends.

Tentatively, I rested my palms on his chest and tilted my head up. This was going to be a damn nightmare.

What if I screwed it up? What if it didn't look real? God, what if I sucked?

"OK," Bryce murmured, leaning down.

I inhaled deeply to calm my nerves, acutely aware of his friends watching us and probably a dozen other students. Bryce licked his lips.

I squeezed my eyelids closed, waiting for the warmth of his lips, but it never came. Instead, I was rocked sideways as Bryce was shoved hard. My eyes flew open as Lucy squealed and Devon cursed.

Dante Church had arrived, and he looked pissed. He wrapped his hands around Bryce's throat, his silver rings glinting beneath the overhead lights.

I darted forward the moment I had my wits about me and tried to wedge myself between Church and Bryce.

"Don't fucking touch her. Do you understand me?" Church roared in a voice that made goosebumps race along my skin. "No one fucking touches her."

"G-girlfriend," Bryce rasped, his fingers on Church's wrists as he tried to free himself.

"I don't fucking care what you're labeling it," Church continued, his lip peeled up in a snarl. "It's not fucking happening. I know all about you spending the night in her room. You're lucky I've let you live this fucking long."

Bryce's face was red as he struggled to breathe. I looked around and saw the other watchers approaching slowly. Bryce would pass out before they even made it to Church to pull him off him. Of course, there was no security to be seen.

I had to do something.

With every ounce of bravery in me, I reached forward and took Church's face in my hands.

His eyes widened, and his lips parted as I turned his face toward mine.

Please. Relax. Don't hurt him. He's my only friend in the world.

"Specter," Church murmured, releasing Bryce, who fell back.

Devon and Vic caught him as Church twisted to me completely. Bryce choked in gulps of air behind me, his breath coming and going in soft wheezes.

I should've dropped my hands. Church's skin was warm, and the rough scruff on his cheeks poked at my palms as I cradled his face. I felt the tension coil in his body as he trembled in anger. He closed the distance between us, his brows crinkled as he practically devoured me with his stare.

His hands went to my waist where he held me in place.

"You just keep surprising me," he said softly before leaning down and running his soft lips along my jaw.

He inhaled deeply. When he exhaled, his warm breath feathered through my hair. Shivers raced down my spine as my breath stilted in my chest.

"My brave girl," he murmured in my ear, his hands tightening on my waist. "It's a good thing because you've also been a bad girl."

I swallowed hard, waiting for the hammer to fall.

"*Four,* Specter."

My heart fell as he pulled away, my hands falling back to my sides. I was back up to four occurrences with the watchers who'd now joined Church.

A wicked smirk turned Church's lips up as he backed away. "If I find out your lips went anywhere near his, there will be hell to pay. You're in the devil's playground, specter. I'd hate to clip your angel wings so soon."

I swallowed and peeked at the rest of the watchers. Sin glowered at me while Stitches's dark eyes took in the scene. I was grateful he didn't launch himself at Bryce the way he had at Danny.

Then there was Ashes. He looked sad.

But shit, he had every right to be. He'd probably be the poor bastard helping to drag me out of whatever hole they dropped me in.

Of course, I doubted any of them lost sleep over any shit they did.

I would though. I knew they were going to bring the pain.

I've endured worse. At least that was what I told myself as they left.

Deep in my heart I knew the worst was yet to come though.

SIN

"I'm going to take care of her," Church said as we sat in our living room later that night. He'd been pent up since he'd lost his shit and attacked Andrews for trying to kiss Sirena. I knew he had a hard-on for the mute, but I had no idea how far he'd fallen in just the few weeks since her arrival. Stitches wanted to steal her for a night and make her sleep with him in his room to fulfill one of her occurrence punishments, but even mentioning the idea made Church fly into a fit of rage and start throwing shit in the house.

"Yeah? When?" Stitches grunted, sinking down into the leather sofa and staring at Church in his chair. "Because last I knew, no one, not even us, had a say in shit regarding her. If I'm not mistaken, this was meant to be for all of us, not just you."

Ashes glanced uneasily between the two as I turned a kitchen chair around and straddled it, watching the scene unfold in front of me. Church was a jealous, possessive asshole. But to be fair, we all were. He'd just never gotten this insane over a chick before. Or ever. It was easy to pass girls around. That was all we ever did with the crazy bitches here. None of them were meant to stick with us. Church seemed to want to keep her all to himself this time. Not that I gave a flying fuck. I didn't want her. I'd fucked some lowly junior in the ass just hours before to prove to myself how much I *didn't* want the mute.

But fuck if she didn't pop into my mind while I was jackknifing into that moaning bitch.

Church's gaze flickered around the room at each of us as he sat forward in his seat. He steepled his fingers and grew silent.

"Just say what you're thinking," Ashes called.

"He doesn't need to," I said, smiling at Ashes and Stitches. "We already know what he wants." Church's gaze landed on me, and he let out a sigh and closed his eyes.

"Well, I don't know what the asshole wants." Stitches shot a glare at Church.

"Do I need to spell it out for you, Malachi?" I laughed, watching Stitches narrow his eyes. His leg bounced and he tugged at his hair in frustration. Ashes looked down at his hands, his elbows resting on his knees. When Stitches didn't answer, I put him out of his misery. "Dante wants her all to himself. He doesn't want to share. She won't be ours to pass around. She'll be his. Only his."

"What?" Stitches snarled, getting to his feet, his hands balled into fists.

I lifted my brows, watching as Church opened his eyes and stared at Stitches.

"Are you fucking kidding me? You want her to yourself? Is that what has you so pissed off and ready to fight everyone?" Stitches bounced on the balls of his feet, looking like he was ready to jump out of his body and fight the devil himself. We'd had a hard enough time keeping him relaxed since the shit with Danny went down. I almost thought he was going to spiral again because he'd nearly stayed up all night long in his bedroom pacing the floor and grumbling to himself. It took us a lot to get him settled. Ashes had to spike his drink with a sedative to get him to sleep.

"What can I say?" Church held his hands up in surrender. "I can't stop what I want." He didn't look the least bit sorry. I had to give him props on that. I wouldn't have either if I were proclaiming my desire for some bitch. I'd been there and done that though. It ended in a whole lot of fucking problems I'd rather not repeat. Spiraling wasn't for me. I swore I'd never do it again.

"We agreed—" Stitches started.

"I called dibs," Church said. "I didn't realize how much I'd want her, but you're right. We did, so I'm going to honor it because I'm not a complete dickhead. Just know that if at any point she tells me she wants just me, that's it for you assholes."

Stitches scoffed. "Eat shit, Church. For one thing, she doesn't speak. *At all.* So there's no way she'll ever say it. Second, she can't stand you. At this rate, we're going to have to send Asher in with all his sweet talk and flowers to win her over *for us*. Because this is for all of us, not just you. We don't need another Isabella thing happening. I refuse. We made an agreement after that. We stick to it."

"I still don't want her," I called out, irritated at the mention of my ex. "So chill on that shit."

Ashes snorted.

"What's wrong, Mr. Candy Hearts?" I challenged, narrowing my eyes at him.

Ashes rolled his eyes at me at the nickname. "I just think you're full of shit. I think once you get close to her, you're going to be worse than Dante. In fact, you've already been pushing people around to keep her away from them."

"Don't read into it too much. I do that shit because I don't feel like cleaning up Stitches and Church's shit when they beat the piss out of someone for touching her. Plus, you do remember what Malachi was like when he spiraled last year, right? Fucking straitjacket and so fucking doped up he didn't even know his own name. The shit with Danny was a real close call."

Stitches shot me the finger, a sour look on his face.

Ashes smirked at me but didn't push the subject which was a good idea because I was sick to fuck of them trying to push her on me. The last thing I needed in my life was some chick who didn't want to talk. I figured that translated into not wanting to fuck. That definitely counted me out. Having to dick around with some shy girl who didn't have the lady balls to tell me what she wanted had no place at my side.

I needed a sexy woman who wanted to do dirty things with me and for me. Sirena Lawrence wasn't that girl. She was real fucking nice to look at, but that was where it ended.

"We need to do her next punishment." Church looked around at us. "I want to fucking crack her open and fuck her with her own tears on my cock as lube. We need to win this shit and be done with it. I can make her scream. I know I can."

"Could just let Sully break her," Stitches said with a laugh. "I mean, if the rumors on Sully and his ruler versus hand beatings he gives students are true, then she won't be able to handle that shit for long. Just gotta get her into his office more. I don't like the idea, but I really fucking want her." His mouth twisted into a deep frown as he tugged his hair again.

"Then we'd just end up killing him," Church said absently. "We don't need to add more bodies to the roster. Yet, anyway."

"I'm not opposed to more bodies." I sat forward, studying him, the ugly memories I had flipping like an Olympic gymnast through my head. There were no regrets, just my anger at everything still.

"I watch everything she does. How she tenses when someone is near her. The way she clenches her hands into fists and how her breathing changes. How her lips part like she wants to scream out the world's truth. She's scared to fucking exist though. It's killing her." Church looked to Stitches who grinned.

"Stalker," I muttered, shaking my head at his words.

"I prefer predator, but whatever." Church shot me a wicked smile. *Fucking crazy bastard.*

"I can start a fight with her and lover boy again," Stitches continued.

"I don't think it'll work. We need something bigger. We can bring her here and fuck with her a bit," I said. "Scare her. Hold her down. Put the pressure on her. That might make her crack."

Ashes shook his head. "I don't want to scare her. Seth will be able to swoop in and be the hero then. She won't trust us if we hold her down and fuck with her."

"She'll never go for him. She's scared of him, so why not punish her by pushing her into his path." I said, an idea forming. Church's eyes glinted with his barely contained madness as he studied me before I continued. "Not a lot. Just keep putting her into situations with him. Her fear will drive her back to us. She'll want to be protected and who better to protect her than us? We get her to beg for our protection, then you fucks claim her."

"That's fucked up," Ashes said. "You already know Seth wants a chance. Hell, we're competing with him over it. I think it's a bad idea. She might scream for him instead and we lose. Veto."

"Fuck off, Ashes." I rolled my eyes, really fucking hoping Seth claimed her before my brothers could. I didn't want my friends near her. I knew the shit that could happen if they fell as hard as I thought they would. "It's not like he's going to kill her. Asylum is crazy, but he's not kill the hot chick crazy. She won't scream for him. She'll scream at our doorstep to save her from him." I didn't believe a word of it. I knew Seth was fucked in his head and would probably do something to live up to his name. I had a feeling she would scream for him and then she'd be out of our hair. My plan could really work to free my friends from the madness she was causing them. My heart ached uncomfortably at the thought, but I shoved the feelings away. Fuck feelings.

"Man, she was faced down with being nearly killed before, and she's scared of him for whatever reason. Maybe he wasn't her friend like he said he was. Maybe he fucked with her, and she hates him for that." Ashes looked to Church. "Don't tell me you're onboard with Sin."

"I'm only onboard to get what we want. What better way to punish someone than by stuffing them into a situation with someone they hate? We want her to scream so we can win. We'll be right there to make sure she's fine. I'm never far behind her. I'm in." Church answered as he ran his hands down his thighs and licked his lips.

"I'm in too," Stitches said. Ashes scowled at him.

"Hear me out, though, man." Stitches held up a hand to silence Ashes before he could argue. "You hauled her out of the mausoleum, so you know what it's like to rescue her. She doesn't run away when she sees you. You've already weaseled in by rescuing her."

"Exactly," Church said. "One of us can save her ass if we arranged for their nearness. It'll be a way to work ourselves into her life. We don't tell her she's being punished. It'll just be a coincidence that they get stuck together. We'll be heroes. Her fear will make her beg us for the protection."

"We should break her and Andrews up," Ashes muttered. "That would be better."

"We will." Church's voice had grown soft. I noted his hands shaking. What did the sick bastard know that the rest of us didn't? I knew he'd left in the middle of the night. I assumed he went to fuck one of the chicks he kept on standby when he was bored with Melanie, but now that I watched him, I knew it was more than that. Something was up. Something was bothering him. If I knew Dante Church like I thought I did, the truth wasn't going to come out until it was necessary.

And it would either be a total shit show or a complete blood bath because that was the only two outcomes to anything Church did. If I had to take a stab in the dark, it all came back to Sirena Lawrence, the girl with no voice.

Fuck me for hoping it was, but fuck me too for the anger it brought me and the terrible thoughts.

SIRENA

"Hey."

I breathed faster as I picked up my pace. I left early like I always did just to avoid this sort of thing, but there I was, my nightmares coming true.

"Rina, hey." Seth grabbed my arm and pulled me to a stop. "Can we talk?"

I shook as I looked around, trying to find a way out. My backpack was heavy. I could probably drop it on his foot and get a head start, but it was open space until the bend where the path curved through the center of a small thicket. Once I made it past there, I'd be in screaming distance of the school. Security had a small hut near there.

If I could still scream. Something told me that wasn't likely.

"Don't run, Rina. You know I'd catch you," he murmured like the fucking mind reader he was. "I just want to talk."

The last time I'd stayed to talk I'd ended up smashed in the head with a shovel and stuffed in a metal box for nearly a week all in the name of saving me from hell. I wanted to shout at him that he didn't save me from hell. He just delivered me to an updated version of it.

I blew out a shaky breath and forced myself to look into his eyes.

He stared back at me through thick, dark lashes, just as beautiful as he'd always been. Probably more so since he'd aged and taken on muscles and height. In a different world, he'd still be my best friend. We'd have shared so much together. But this wasn't that world. In this world, he was the guy who'd tried to murder me. He was the guy who left me, thinking I was dead. He never came back. He'd never had a change of heart. He'd never had any regrets because if he had, the world would have known what he'd done to me because he'd have confessed. He'd simply moved on. When his mom sat with him speaking to the police, he'd told them he hadn't seen me. The liar. *The fucking liar!*

"You're really beautiful," he said softly, not closing the distance between us but not releasing my arm either. "I always thought you would be. Your eyes... I've always loved your eyes."

He studied me for a moment as I stared up silently at him, willing myself to be brave. To face my fears. To stand my ground. I was failing. My breath came in short, fast bursts. My lips tingled. I was lightheaded. My forehead dotted with sweat as I forced myself to stay.

"Everyone says you don't talk. When we were kids, you never shut up." He gave me that playful smile I remembered from so long ago. The one that would make me smile back and feel blessed to have such a great best friend.

Now it felt like a damn curse.

"I suppose life has a way of changing us," he continued, his voice low. "Or maybe we have a way of changing life."

I swallowed and shuffled from foot to foot, my gaze darting around. *I could make it to the bend. I know I could. Shit. I couldn't.*

"We—I'm not going to hurt you, Rinny. You don't need to be afraid. You can talk to me. Just like we used to."

My ass I didn't need to be afraid.

He used an old nickname on me, making my heart hurt. I needed away from here. I remembered I had the cell phone in the side pocket of my bag. I just needed to get to it and text someone. Anyone.

He looked away from me toward the bend in the path, telling me something about how he figured I walked to classes early. I took the opportunity to snake my free arm to the side pocket and pull the phone out. I didn't know who I was texting, but I quickly thumbed over the screen, sneaking a peak at the contact button and hit randomly. At least someone would get my distress signal. I aimlessly swiped my thumb over buttons, not able to look at it and hoped it sent by my various screen probings.

"So. Bryce Andrews, huh?" He turned back to me.

When I didn't say anything, he continued. "He's had a handful of girlfriends, but none of them stick. Few weeks at the most. Probably a problem with him or something. Heard he's gay and hiding it. Standard depression case this place seems to attract. Guy seems weird, though. Figured you should know."

Asshole.

"I'm not seeing anyone," he said after a pause, offering me a smile that said he was a good guy, but I knew better. "I think you need someone at your side who could protect you. It's not Bryce Andrews either. The way fucking Danny Linley touched you made me so fucking angry. . ." His voice trailed off before he licked his full lips. "If I were at your side like old times, no one would come near you."

I winced at the mention of old times. *No thanks.* I'd take my chances with creeps like Danny Linley.

"I know what you're thinking, Rinny. Not like that. I'd never. . ." He blew out a breath, still holding my arm, and raked his fingers through his hair. "I just want to talk to you. That's it. I have a lot I want to say. All this shit in my head. So fucking loud. Damnit. I want to make it up to you. Everything. I owe you. Fuck, just please—"

"Hey, Sirena," the familiar deep rumble of Ashes's voice met my ears. I never thought I'd be so happy to hear from a watcher.

Seth released my arm instantly and glared as Ashes stopped at my side. Immediately, I moved against Ashes. As nasty as the watchers were, they hadn't tried to kill me. Yet. I'd take my chances with them all day, any day.

I shivered when Ashes snaked his arm around my waist and brought me closer, tucking me easily beneath his arm like I was a puzzle piece.

A muscle thrummed along Seth's jaw as he took in Ashes's arm.

"What the hell is this?" Seth demanded, gesturing between us.

"Easy, Asylum. I promised I'd walk her to class today," Ashes said without missing a beat. "I was late, and she left without me."

"Right." Seth's Adam's apple bobbed in his throat.

"So I guess that means your conversation is over. I can handle her from here."

"Sirena, seriously. I want to talk. I'm not going to stop until you listen," Seth said, backing away from us. "I'll prove to you that I'm serious about everything. You'll see."

I stared down at my feet, holding my breath with my eyelids squeezed closed as I counted.

One... two... three...

"Sirena," Ashes said gently, turning me to face him. He reached out and tilted my chin up. "Hey, it's OK. He's gone. Breathe. Christ, your face is red. Come on, Sirena." He gave me a quick shake, snapping me out of it. I let out a whoosh of air, my head spinning. I sagged forward, and he caught me to his chest, his fingers raking through my hair as I gulped in mouthfuls of air.

"It's OK. I got you," he murmured as I clung to him. "I got your text and came as fast as I could. I didn't even know where to look for you. You sent me a frown and *gelp*. I assumed that meant *help*. I didn't even bother going to your dorm. I just never see you in the mornings, so I thought you probably just leave earlier and I'd find you on the path. Lucky guess, huh?"

I sniffled, a tear trickling out of my eye.

"I wish you'd talk," he said with a sigh. "You could tell me what happened to you, and I'd kill the fucker who did it."

The way he said that made my chest ache. As much as I wanted a savior, I knew Asher Valentine wasn't going to be one. He was a watcher. An enemy.

But he came. He's here. That has to mean something... right?

"I'm not as bad as you think I am," Ashes said, cutting into my thoughts. "If I can help, I will. Just know that sometimes I need what I need because I forget I'm human. The things I do—that *we* do—reminds me I am. So forgive me my sins, my sweet little *heaven*."

Heaven.

He called me heaven.

He offered me a small smile that made his eyes sparkle. Where I usually saw malice in the eyes of men, I only saw his sincerity.

It would do. For now.

†

"Movie night tonight?" Bryce asked as we walked through the halls after classes got out. I'd been called on by Sister Francis and when I didn't answer, she'd made me write scripture all class period. My hand was tired, I had a headache, and I still hadn't seen Headmaster Sully for my punishment with him.

I blinked my eyes at the bright fluorescent light overhead as it flickered.

"Me and the guys are going to get into the kitchens tonight and grab some snacks. I know you need a refill on yours. Anything you want? I noticed you really like your granola bars. I can try to grab a couple of those for you and a few sodas and bottles of water."

We stopped outside the library, and he cast me a quick look before looking to the library.

"Studying? On a Friday?"

I blinked at him, and he smiled. I had to see Sully and the last thing I wanted was for him to know what was happening. It would only make things worse because I knew Bryce would tell. Who he'd tell I didn't know, but I couldn't risk it. If word got out, I'd get sent back to Jerry, and Jerry's wrath would be ten times worse.

"OK. I'm going to go meet up with the guys. I can come back and walk with you later if you want."

I swallowed and looked past him.

"Sirena, throw me a bone here." He scratched his head. "I want to keep you safe, but I don't want to intrude if you just want to relax in the stacks. Honestly, I don't like the idea of you walking alone what with the whole watchers being a bag of dicks over you. And then Danny. . . I'll just come back—"

I pressed against him, my head on his chest. He snaked his arms around me and gave me a gentle squeeze before he released me and stepped back and offered me a reassuring smile.

With my hand on his chest, I blinked at him again and looked over his shoulder to let him know to go. I'd be fine.

"I guess if this is the worst you have today, consider yourself lucky. You could be Jake Neiman. I heard the watchers got him and made him fill his underwear with chocolate pudding and walk around in it all day." He shuddered.

Well, glory be I wasn't Jake Neiman. Of course, knowing what I knew about Headmaster Sully and what awaited me behind his closed doors, pudding in my pants would be a welcomed treat.

"Well, I'll see you soon, OK? I guess I won't walk you back?"

I gave a slight nod of my head that made his smile widen.

"We're getting there, huh?" He reached out and gave my hand a squeeze before turning to leave. I watched him go before turning to walk back to Headmaster Sully's office, my own personal ninth level of hell.

Sully was behind his desk when I stepped inside.

"Good afternoon, Sirena. I trust your week has been good." He signed the paper he was reading and looked at me, that wicked smile I hated so much on his face.

I closed the door behind me, knowing the drill, and sat in the seat across from him.

"I spoke to Jerry today. He's wanting a bit more force put into the eradication of the demons in your soul. Tell me, how did you do on your end?" He raised his brows at me. "Aside from the writing assignments?"

My bottom lip wobbled as I stared at him without an answer. He got to his feet and walked to the door. The sound of the lock clicking on it made the nausea roil in my guts.

I struggled harder to come up with something, wanting to show him anything he would deem acceptable before he did something horrible.

He stopped in front of me and gave me a fatherly smile.

"You still don't listen, do you, Miss Lawrence? You don't even try. I don't want to keep punishing you, but if you don't fight the demons too, I'll just have to keep teaching you a lesson. I've been watching you. The reports I've gotten about your group therapy sessions are saying you don't participate. You will fall in line and learn to live in His grace. I think another whipping is in order. So you remember."

I froze, staring up at him.

No. No. No!

Not happening. He could beat me until I died. He could shred my clothes off me and force me to walk in front of the student body and prove he was a monster. There were other ways to scream without making a sound and God help me, I'd do it.

"Don't fight God's will, Sirena. God punishes the wicked. I'm here to make you better." He reached for me, but I jerked away from him. His face went from the fake kind, caring mask to one of outrage.

He reached for me again, this time grasping my shirt. I fought against him until I fell out of my chair. He didn't let go. Instead, he let out a snarl and hauled me kicking and bucking across the floor until we were away from the chairs.

He must have gotten his belt off with his other hand in the tussle, because when he let me go, he followed up by hitting me across the chest with his brown leather belt, making me arch my back off the floor in pain.

And he didn't stop hitting me. The belt came down on my chest, torso, legs. I wept silently, gasping for air, as I managed to get to my hands and knees. It didn't matter where I crawled, he was there, his belt thrashing against my back, ass, and thighs.

His hair was a wild mess as he continued his assault, screaming scripture at me in a garbled rage.

"Withhold not correction from the child: for if thou beatest him with the rod, he shall not die. Thou shalt beat him with the rod, and shalt deliver his soul from hell! You will be saved, Sirena. You will be healed. Your demons will be eradicated. Accept it."

I couldn't even comprehend it after the belt licked my skin several more times. It was all nonsense to me as I fell face first, hitting my head on the edge of a bookcase.

My vision swirled and darkened around the edges as he struck me again, making me finally collapse.

So he was going to kill me.

It wouldn't be the first time someone tried.

STITCHES

"Can I suck your dick?" Melanie giggled as she pressed her lips to my neck.

I took a drink of my whiskey and ignored her as she rubbed against me like a cat in heat. I felt like I was going to jump out of my body as I gave my hair a tug. The backyard was packed with partygoers, all grinding and dancing on one another as music boomed out. I imagined their meds and alcohol didn't mix, but who the fuck was I to tell anyone no. Even I was on my meds and drinking. Pretty sure at this point, the meds were just there to take up space in my veins. I'd keep taking them though, just in case. I was weird like that.

I sat on the patio. Melanie had been on my dick all night. It wasn't unusual, and any other time, I'd have taken her up on her offer, but I wasn't feeling it. In fact, I hadn't been feeling it with anyone since Sirena Lawrence came into my life.

I looked out in the sea of people to see a couple girls giggling around Church and Sin, desperately trying to get them to take the bait. I figured Sin would since he never turned down pussy, but I was curious about what Church would do. Of course, there was also the question of Melanie. If she wasn't getting all the attention from us and being passed around like a joint, she tended to get bitchy.

Church pissed me off with his talk about wanting Sirena without us. I wanted her alone too, but there was something hot about sharing your girl with your friends and watching them fuck her. Or at least I thought there would be. We needed this after Sin's ordeal with his last obsession. Or only obsession. We agreed on it. That was why we fucked Melanie. We kept shit open so we wouldn't have any more mishaps like we had with Isabella, which definitely hadn't been open. She was Sin's girl.

Fuck. I hated even thinking her name. I shoved the ugly memory away as Melanie rubbed my cock through my jeans.

I'd never had a steady girlfriend. We had Melanie, but that wasn't real. She was just a guaranteed fuck for us. Ashes attempted a girlfriend a time or two, but always ended up dropping the girl when she got too clingy. Even Mr. Candy Hearts had his limits. My mind went back to Sin and Isabella. I shoved that nasty memory out of my head again. I couldn't do that shit again. Wouldn't. Refused. Not fucking happening. Ever.

I was pretty sure Sirena could whine day in and day out and all of us would drop what we were doing to make sure she got what she wanted. Even Church and Sin, the two hard asses. Of course, they might make her pay for her whining, but if she were ours, she'd be down for their brand of punishment. *Delicious punishment.* Fuck. *Why couldn't we just take her now?* I wanted her. I needed her. She haunted my dreams. Then she'd run through them away from me, making them a nightmare. What a fucking way to mess up my head further.

"Wanna go to your room?" Melanie breathed out in my ear, her tits pressed against me. "We haven't been together in a long time."

"No," I said, not bothering to look at her. I tugged at my hair again.

"Why? I want you, Stitches."

"And I want a refill." I shook my cup at her, and she pulled away, her bottom lip jutted out. "Fill it, and we'll see about the rest."

That seemed like a fair enough deal for her because she took my cup and scampered off. Melanie liked to feel needed. I blamed it on her narcissism.

It was then that I noticed Bryce pushing his way toward me. I sat forward and let my legs bounce as Ashes came out and stopped at my side.

"Wonder what he's doing?" I murmured, watching as he finally made it to the steps.

"Something's wrong," Ashes said.

"Did you do it?" Bryce snarled, rushing up to us. He shoved Ashes hard in the chest. "Did you fucking do it?"

"Do what?" Ashes pushed him back, making Bryce stumble. He came charging again, his face red.

I intervened and grabbed him by the nape of the neck and shoved him to his knees. I caught Church and Sin making their way toward us, the party still happening around with no one really paying attention to what was going on in our neck of the woods. I caught sight of a security guard having a glass of beer off to the side. Not surprising. Fucking *security*.

"What the fuck is your problem, Andrews?" I snarled, shoving him forward.

He went to all fours, his chest heaving.

"What's going on?" Church demanded, glaring down at Andrews. Sin gave him a light kick to the ribs, knocking him down.

"You were asked a question," Sin snapped.

Bryce pushed himself up and glared at us, his face red. "*Sirena*. You fucking assholes punished her."

"I assure you we haven't touched a hair on her pretty, little head," Church growled as Ashes shot me a worried look.

My chest tightened, all the pent-up energy within me bouncing around violently, desperate to escape. "What happened to her?"

"I don't know. I went to see her tonight, and she wouldn't stop crying. I was going to surprise her and walk her back from the library, but she was gone. I found her in her room in tears. She has a bruise on the side of her face. I couldn't even touch her. She wouldn't let me. Sh-she always lets me."

"And you think we beat your girlfriend?" Sin shook his head. "*Please*. We're a bit more creative than beating on women."

"We didn't touch Sirena," Ashes added.

Bryce climbed to his feet. "Where's Seth?"

"Over there." I pointed to Seth standing around with a couple girls and his friends Coby and Riley.

"Find out where he was," Church grunted. He'd been quiet. Too quiet.

I hopped off the step and went to Seth, the energy buzzing through me. I'd already practically killed Danny Linley for touching her. I knew I would have finished him if I hadn't been stopped. No one should ever touch our angel but us.

Seth looked at me curiously as I approached.

"Where have you been since classes let out?"

"What?" He crinkled his brows at me.

"I said, *where the fuck* have you been since classes let out today?"

"None of your goddamn business—"

"It's Sirena. Where were you?" I was done fucking around. I was so angry someone touched her, I was ready to beat some ass.

Hold your shit together. Don't fucking slip. Don't do that shit again.

"I went for a run with Coby. Then we ate, and I showered. We met up with Riley and came here. Why, man? What's wrong with her?" His eyes were wild as he looked around the party.

"Was he with you?" I glared at his friends.

"Yeah, man. The whole time. We didn't see Sirena." Riley was quick to confirm.

I turned to go, but Seth grabbed my arm. I ground my teeth and turned to look at him. He didn't seem like he cared he was touching me.

"What happened? Was it Danny again?"

Normally, I'd have punched him in the face and walked away, but there was something in his eyes that made me stop. He genuinely looked concerned.

"I don't know. That's what I'm trying to figure out."

"Can...will you let me know if she's OK? She won't let me near her."

I gave him a stiff nod and returned to my group. "Wasn't Asylum. He was with Riley and Coby all night. Unless they're all lying."

"I hope they are. I've wanted to punch him in the face since I met him." Sin looked over his shoulder at the trio as they talked, Seth shooting us worried looks, a frown on his face.

"Look at you, Mr. Protector." Ashes shook his head at Sin who sneered. *Yeah, keep telling yourself you're not interested, big guy.*

"Maybe she's just having a bad day," Ashes offered, wincing.

Bryce shook his head. "Sirena has bad days, but something isn't right. I've never seen her so upset. I want to know what happened to her and who's to blame. She has fucking bruises!"

"We'll handle it," Church said. "Go check on her." I watched as he leaned in and whispered something in Bryce's ear. Bryce stiffened and pulled away, glaring at him. Church merely cocked his head in return.

What was he doing? The problem with Church was he tended to let his crazy out when he shouldn't. Sirena had brought his crazy out even more since her arrival.

"Follow the rules, Andrews. I'll fucking break you if you don't comply. I'll start with her." Church's voice took on a soft, dangerous current that made even my body erupt in goosebumps.

Bryce shook for a moment, his hands balled into fists before he nodded once and left. It didn't take a genius to see how tense he was as he stormed off the patio.

"What did you tell him?" I tugged my gaze from the back of Bryce to Church.

"What I needed to," was all he said. He snapped his fingers a moment later and one of the freshman initiates came running over. A female. The one labeled *Tease*. The big black letters were barely faded on her forehead.

"I need you to get into the infirmary and grab a first aid kit. Take it over to 555 and leave it outside the door," he said, grabbing a bottle of whiskey off the table on the patio and handing it to her. "Leave this too. Come back and let me know once you're done."

"Yes, sir." Tease snagged the bottle from Church and rushed off to do his bidding.

"Does she need a first aid kit? What did Andrews tell you while I was gone?" I waited for Church to answer, but he simply turned on his heel and walked into the house, closing the door softly behind him.

"What the fuck?" I looked back to Sin and Ashes.

"Leave him," Sin said. "He's too angry to talk. Let him plan."

Worry crossed Ashes's face as his gaze shifted between me and Sin.

"Fuck it." I snagged a fresh bottle of beer and popped the top off. I sank down in my seat only for Melanie to come scampering back over, tits half out. I didn't pay her any attention as she slid between my legs and rubbed my cock. All I could think about was what happened to Sirena.

And what would happen to the son of a bitch who touched her once we got our hands on him.

Danny fucking Linley better pray it wasn't him because I'd be back to finish what I started.

SIRENA

My body hurt.

I hugged the toilet as I vomited into it for the third time that night. The pain was too much. Bryce came to my room only to leave, shaking in anger when I wouldn't tell him what happened. I wasn't sure what he expected of me. He'd returned later to lie with me until I fell into a fitful sleep but said he couldn't stay. He seemed angry about that too, which only made me feel more like shit than I already did.

A soft knock sounded out at my door. I shuffled to my feet and lurched toward it slowly only to pull it open to find a first aid kit and a bottle of whiskey propped against the doorjamb.

I took the items and looked down the hall to not see anyone. I snagged everything up and returned to my room, sitting on the bed, wincing.

I ran my hands along the cool white metal of the first aid kit before opening it to find bandages, creams, and pain meds inside. Grateful, I fumbled the pain meds open and swallowed four of them, washing them down with a gulp of the whiskey. It burned all the way down, making me sputter and cough, but if it would take me out for a bit, I would eagerly drink it. Once I'd managed to get a good amount of it down, I propped my pillows around me so my tender back wouldn't have so much pressure on it as I laid back.

My head spun as my phone vibrated. Cady called earlier and left me a voice message saying she missed me and that Mom and Jerry were shopping for new furniture. Weakly, I grabbed my phone and stared at the screen with blurry eyes.

Ashes: Are you OK? I'm worried about you. Bryce came here to tell us you weren't well. Do you need me to come to you? You know I will, heaven.

Heaven. The sweet nickname he'd given me for god knew what reason. *Did he care? Did he know what Headmaster Sully did to me? To other students? Was he helping him somehow?*

I blinked my eyes, my head swimming, trying to force the beautiful man with the sweet smile out of my head. If I'd give into the watchers, they might protect me. *But at what cost?* They already planned on punishing me for just being me.

But I needed someone. Anyone.

I needed them to claim me. I'd end up in a war with Melanie most likely, but if what everyone said was true, the watchers would keep me safe.

I closed my eyes and breathed out. I was sick of being strong. Cady told me to find the biggest, most bad ass guy on campus and befriend him. I needed to give in. I had to.

The warm, fuzziness in my body spread, blanketing me, the pain subsiding enough to make me not want to fling myself out of my bedroom window.

†

I AWOKE SOMETIME AFTER three AM with the strangest feeling of being watched. I cracked my eyelids open and saw a figure sitting in the chair facing my bed. My heart hammered so hard in my chest I was sure the intruder could hear it. My lamp didn't cast enough light around the room to see him completely, leaving him in shadow.

Seth. It's Seth. He's come to finish me off.

The figure didn't move. He simply sat there, shrouded in darkness as I shrank away, deeper into my pillows.

My breath clung in my throat as he slowly got to his feet a moment later, his face coming into view.

Dante Church. Here. In my room.

"You're hurt," his voice was soft, sending goosebumps skittering across my skin.

I swallowed and stared up at him as he towered over me.

"Who touched you?" he continued. "Tell me, specter, and I'll make them pay."

Confusion clouded my thoughts as he cocked his head, his blond hair falling across his face.

"You're just the perfect target, aren't you?" He licked his lips. "You can't tell the awful secrets the monsters try to hide. It's almost. . . sad."

I twisted my fingers into my blanket, shaking beneath his dark stare.

"I brought you something." He turned and walked back to the chair and picked up something before coming back to me. The bed dipped as he sat beside me, a white garment in his hands.

"You see, I think of you as a ghost. A beautiful, broken spirit looking to find her home. I thought this would look nice on you as you slept." He handed the white garment to me. I stared back at him, unmoving.

"It's a gift. I want you to have it and wear it every night. You can start now. I'll turn so you can change." He got up and walked to my window and looked out, his back to me. He wasn't asking me. He was telling me.

Was he serious? He'd broken into my bedroom and was watching me sleep and had even brought me a gift?

Terrified didn't even begin to cover how I felt.

Find the biggest bad ass on campus and befriend him.

Cady's words raced through my mind. He was one of my tormentors though. To be fair, his brand of punishment didn't hurt as much as Headmaster Sully's. And he did say he'd hurt whoever it was.

I swallowed and looked down to the garment in my hands before throwing caution to the wind. If I could get into the watchers' good graces, it might save me a hell of a lot of pain.

Without further hesitation, I took off my long-sleeved sweater and sleep shorts, grinding my teeth at the soreness in my body, and pulled the white nightdress over my head. It reminded me of something out of Victorian times. White. Gauzy. Soft. Long sleeves. It went to my ankles. There was even a small white silk bow on the front of it.

I gasped as I tried to settle back in bed, my body screaming at me. Church turned around, his eyes zeroing in on me. He stalked toward me, his mouth set in a tight line. Terror raced through me but quickly melted away as he adjusted my pillows and helped me settle back. He brought my blanket up around me, tucking me in tightly, his expression never changing.

His fingers brushed my jaw gently.

"If you tell me who hurt you, I'll go and end their life right now. All you need to do is whisper it to me, specter."

I parted my lips, and for a moment, his eyes lit up in the moonlight streaming in through my bedroom window. The words were on the tip of my tongue. They just wouldn't come out. I opened and closed my mouth several times, but my brain, mouth, and vocal cords were out of synch and the only sound I had was silence.

I crinkled my brows, my eyes burning, as I stared up at him. Anger coursed through me. The one time I wanted to scream a name and it wouldn't come out.

"It's OK," Church murmured, leaning down. "I'll find out who did it. You know why?" He skimmed his warm lips along my cheek. "Because I claimed you the moment I saw you. You will never escape me. I own you, Sirena Lawrence. You just haven't realized it yet." He inhaled deeply before pressing a kiss to my forehead. My heart jumped in my chest as his lips lingered.

"Sleep," he said, pulling away from me. "I'll keep watch."

I stared after him as he got up and moved back to the chair and settled in. I couldn't fully see his face in the darkness, but I knew his eyes were focused on me.

Find the biggest bad ass on campus...

Looked like he found me. Just add terrifying to his description.

CHURCH

She lay in bed watching me, her dark brows pinched. I knew it was from the pain she was in, but I didn't press the subject with her. I knew my limits, and something snapped within me the moment I laid eyes on her that first day. All I needed was a fucking name. Even just the initials. I'd hunt down everyone with those initials and gut them all to prove my fucking point.

Don't. Touch. What. Belongs. To. Me.

Some people needed to be reminded.

I watched as her chest rose and fell beneath the white nightdress I'd gotten her. I'd ordered it in only days before, eager to see my little specter in white. Her black as night hair and pale skin made her look like a living doll.

My pretty little plaything.

"You should be sleeping," I said.

She licked her lips before parting them.

My cock came to life in my pants, all sorts of dirty thoughts in my head. I could sink deep inside her and latch on like the fucking demon I was. I could own every part of her body. *Her moans, her trembles, her screams. Mine. Mine. MINE. All of it.*

I breathed out, relishing in the dirty, forbidden thoughts in my head before I shook them away to focus on the breathtaking reality before me.

The moonlight shining in on her after I turned off her light made her look so beautiful it was hard for me not to climb into bed with her and make her scream for me. In that moment, I knew of at least a dozen ways to make her shout God's name and curse mine.

But she remained silent, her mouth turning down into a deeper frown, her brows crinkling further. Frustration and red-hot desire coursed through my body as I gripped the arms of the chair tighter. She was afraid of the dark, but she had the moonlight to guide her. And me.

I wanted to soothe all her wounds. I wanted to tear into her and create new ones and stitch them together with my name while she clung to me, begging me to stop.

But most of all, I just wanted *her*. All of her. I knew as I stared back at her nothing in the world would ever change that. In fact, anything else that happened in her name would provoke the monster I was barely keeping caged.

Sirena Lawrence was mine, and I'd ripped the tongues out of anyone's mouth who said otherwise.

That was how fucking sick I was when it came to my specter. That was how fucking twisted I was. She drove me to the brink of my sanity and then shoved me over the edge with those fucking mesmerizing eyes and pouty lips.

But it was her silence that beckoned my dark thoughts. I wanted to tear into her and strip her of her secrets. There were many. I knew there were.

"If you don't tell me a name, I'll punish every mother fucker who breathes too close to you," I said, my voice a soft snarl as I leaned forward in my seat so she could see me in the moonlight. "If you don't tell me a name, someone could die."

She said nothing, opting to stare at me from beneath long, dark lashes, her blanket clutched in her hands.

"Do you want people to die, specter?" I cocked my head at her, desperate to know what was going through that pretty little head of hers.

Her eyes glistened as she continued to look at me.

If I was looking for confirmation, I got it.

I'd kill for Sirena Lawrence.

†

I STARED out at the sea of faces as I sat in my spot in the lunchroom.

"You going to eat that?" Stitches nodded at the cheeseburger on my plate. He shifted in his seat, his legs bouncing. He was always fucking moving. I wanted to shake him sometimes just to get it the fuck out of him.

I shook my head, my jaw clenched, as I looked out to the mass of students in the hopes of seeing Sirena. I'd stayed in her room all night watching her sleep. Watching as she fought an invisible tormentor. Planning how I was going to take out any fucker who thought about her.

I'd slipped out sometime right before sunrise and had gone back to the sanctuary. I hadn't slept in a long damn time, but I was on high alert, wanting to see her.

"We doing the next occurrence?" Sin shoved Stitches's hand away from his tray as Stitches made to snag his water.

"Yes," I said absently, waiting for any sign of her.

"What are we going to do?" Stitches managed to grab a couple fries from Ashes's tray as Ashes swore at him.

"There are four occurrences left. I think we should each do one," I said. "I want the first one. You fucks can fight out who gets the remaining ones in what order. You plan them, we'll follow."

"Nice." Stitches swallowed and grinned. "I want her in my bed. Her punishment will be a night with me."

"That *is* punishment." Sin wiped his mouth.

"Fuck off," Stitches said, not looking the least bit upset as he tugged at his shaggy black strands of hair. "What about you, Sinclair? What are you going to have her do?"

"Maybe strip her and make her run naked while I chase her through the cemetery," Sin answered in a monotone, not looking like he gave a shit as he slouched back in his chair.

Ashes rolled his eyes. "That's ridiculous."

Sin shrugged. "I honestly don't give a shit what happens. I'm not interested in her. But if I'm thinking it through, it'll be something with Cain like I already said. Maybe everything I said before but with him chasing her. Pretty sure it wouldn't take much to convince him."

"Whatever, man. I don't know what I'll do yet, but I'll give it more thought than getting her naked or making her sleep in my bed." Ashes looked to me as Stitches grumbled how his idea was good before stuffing more food into his mouth. "What about you? What are you going to do?"

"I'm just going to watch her. I'll decide when the time is right," I said softly as the doors to the cafeteria opened and she came in hunched over, looking like she was in pain just walking. Bryce was at her side, not talking. A first, considering whenever I saw him with her his mouth was moving a mile a minute.

"I wish she'd sit with us again at mass." Stitches sighed, watching Sirena as she trailed behind Andrews.

"She learned her lesson," Ashes said.

"Now she just sits with Andrews and his band of losers." Stitches shook his head, his eyes narrowed as he watched her. "She could be a queen, and she chooses to dwell with the pond scum. I'll never understand it. It's crazy. Fucking ridiculous. I hate it."

"That's because she's basically scum," Sin said, not bothering to look in her direction. "Or at least that's the perception I get from her. She just doesn't care."

"You're wrong." Ashes glared at him. "She does care, but can you imagine the shit in her head she's going through? Cut her some slack. Everyone here is battling their own demons. Even you."

Sin rolled his eyes and went back to his lunch. I got up from my seat without a backward glance or explanation to my crew and approached her.

I stepped in front of her path, making her stop, her eyes widening as she looked up at me.

"We're not looking for trouble," Andrews said, reaching for Sirena's hand. She clamped her hand in his.

"Then leave." I didn't pull my gaze from Sirena's.

"Church—"

"If I have to tell you again, there will be trouble." I finally looked over at him. He licked his lips, his gaze darting from me to Sirena, who had taken to staring at her feet, then back to me.

I quirked an eyebrow at him, waiting for him to make my fucking day. Lucky for him, he understood he was fighting a losing battle and released her hand.

"I'll wait for you, OK?"

She didn't answer. She simply continued to look at her feet.

"Don't," I said. "She'll be late."

"Church, man, don't hurt her—"

"You're pissing me off," I said easily. I snapped my fingers and almost immediately my guys were at my back.

"Off you go, Andrews," Stitches said with a smile, moving his fingers in a scamper off gesture.

"Or *off you go,* because we'll fucking bury you for interfering in watcher business. Move it," Sin commanded.

Ashes was too busy watching Sirena to say anything. She was breathing hard, her hands twisted into tight fists. He glanced to me before moving toward her.

"It'll be OK, heaven," he murmured to her. "Breathe. Church only wants to talk to you. That's all. OK?"

He gave her shoulder a gentle squeeze as Stitches and Sin escorted Andrews away. Once Andrews was gone, Ashes backed away and gave me a look. One that meant don't do anything we'd have to clean up later.

But I liked making messes, so I winked at him and held my hand out to Sirena.

"Come, specter. Let's walk."

When she didn't put her hand in mine, I ground my teeth and leaned in to speak softly in her ear. "Allow me to lead you into temptation, specter. I promise it's worth the trip."

And surprisingly, a moment later, her hand slipped into mine, her eyes innocent but full of fear.

Perfect.

SIRENA

Fear pounded in my chest. My body was on high alert as I slid my hand into Church's. His large hand immediately clamped around mine before he led me out of the cafeteria amid stares. Melanie rose to her feet, a nasty look on her face as we passed by.

I sucked in sharp breath after sharp breath, trying not to have a total meltdown, but it was useless. It wasn't working.

Church stopped abruptly and turned to me.

"Hey. Look at me," he commanded softly.

I looked up at him, my body quivering. All I could see in my head was him leading me back to that damn mausoleum and leaving me there. I'd made it through once. I wasn't so sure hanging out with the body of William G. Morse would prove victorious a second time.

"If I wanted to hurt you, specter, I'd have done it last night." He ran his knuckles along my jaw. "And while I do enjoy torturing the beauty in the world, I must admit, I don't feel like that's where we are in this moment. So breathe for me and don't stop. Today we're simply going for a walk. I will return you safely. Cross my wicked heart."

It seemed good in theory, but his words weren't helping me. He noticed because he took my hand and pressed it to his chest. His heart thudded slow and even as he cocked his head at me, drinking me in with those vivid green eyes of his, his nose ring glinting in the sunshine.

"Breathe with me, specter. We'll race to the end of our lives together, using our breath as the markers. And guess what? Death won't find either of us today, so match pace with me. Breathe. In. Out. Feel that?"

I licked my lips, trying to match my breathing with his as I felt the gentle thrum of his heart beneath my fingers.

"There you go, my little ghost. You're doing it," he murmured as he took a step closer. I let out a soft gasp as he pressed his hand to my chest and closed his eyes, his full lips moving silently as he counted my heartbeats.

He was mesmerizing. Beautiful. Saintly. But such a devil. That was how devils were though. They drew you in with all the beauty and promises only to aim for your heart and leave you in tatters.

"I like the way that feels," he finally said as he opened his eyes. "Your heart beneath my hand. It's soothing to me."

I swallowed, my breathing having calmed, and shifted my hand on his chest, feeling that even *lub-dub* of his beneath all those corded muscles that strained against the cotton fabric of his white uniform shirt. His heartbeat never changed. It was always even and calm.

"Nothing in this world or the next can bother you if you don't let fear into your heart." He reached out and cradled my face, his gaze flitting down to my lips and making my stomach twist into a frantic knot.

"Come." He backed away abruptly and took my hand again and led me to the cemetery. Panic filled me once again.

I tried to pull out of his hold, but he turned and hauled me against his body so fast the breath escaped me.

"I gave you my word. Don't make me go back on it," he said in a gravelly voice. "This is not an occurrence fulfillment. We're just walking."

He pulled back and walked, my hand in his, through the tombstones. I looked to the sky, noting what a beautiful, perfect day it was.

It had been that same way when Seth had tried to kill me and shoved me into that damn box.

He walked slow enough that I kept up with him. When we reached an old willow tree whose branches spread out across the graveyard, he stopped at a wooden bench beneath it. The branches and leaves were so thick, you'd never see someone sitting beneath it.

He sank down onto the bench and patted the spot beside him. I shuffled foot to foot before sitting.

"I come here to be alone. To think." He leaned forward, his elbows on his knees and hands folded beneath his chin as he stared through the foliage. "It's the place I go when I need to get away. When that doesn't work, I go into the woods and hunt with my knife."

He didn't look at me. He simply stared ahead as birds chirped overhead and a gentle breeze rustled the leaves.

"I haven't slept," he finally said. "I watched you all night. You have nightmares."

It wasn't a question.

"I don't like it." His hands fell away from his chin, and he looked down. "I've hated a lot of things in my life, specter, but I *hated* seeing you fight your demons without help. Had I been able, I'd have dove in and gutted the fuckers who dared touch you. I saw your pain. I felt it." He pounded his chest gently with his fist. "I didn't like that either. I don't like knowing you're being harmed, and you won't tell. It makes me angry. These feelings are new to me. They're... dangerous."

I swallowed hard at his words.

He finally locked eyes with me. "I meant what I said. Give me a name. *Any name*. I'll fucking kill them so it's one less asshole you wage war with. Whisper it to me. Write it down. Anything. I want to do this for you. *A gift.* Allow me the honor of ending a life for you, so that I may give you a life in return."

I studied him, confused about the sudden turn of character. Was he always this... passionate? I could see the vein of cruelty pulsating beneath his surface, but there was more to it than that. There was more to Dante Church than the wicked bully and leader of the watchers.

He was one of the biggest, most bad ass guys on campus. He could very well be the answer to all my prayers.

He could also be the reason for all my screams.

I wasn't in a position to be choosy though. I needed help. Maybe I'd been praying to the wrong god this whole time. Maybe I just needed to pray to a devil.

"Play by our rules, and you'll be protected beyond your wildest dreams. Always." He reached out and thumbed my bottom lip, his eyes taking in the motion of his gesture on my lips. "Deny me—*deny us*—what we want, and may God have mercy on your soul."

I swallowed, my heart banging hard, as he leaned in, his lips a fraction away from my own.

"Let the little children come to me, and do not hinder them, for the kingdom of heaven belongs to such as these.'"

Matthew 19:14. I'd written it over and over for a week.

Either Church knew more than he let on, or this was the sign I needed.

This was hell, and to survive, we all had to burn a little, so I leaned in and rested my forehead against his. He let out a soft sigh, his warm breath feathering across my lips.

"Such a good girl," he murmured after a moment. "Come."

He got to his feet and held his hand out to me. I took it and allowed him to pull me to my feet before escorting me out of the cemetery and back to the school. Bryce was pacing in front of the cafeteria when we came back into the building. His head snapped up, and he rushed toward us, relief on his face.

"I'll be along to collect payment tonight. Be prepared to pay." Church released my hand and backed away from me, a dark, hungry look in his green eyes, before he turned to leave me with Bryce.

"Are you OK?" Bryce looked me over, a frown on his face.

Was I OK? I'd just made a deal with the devil, and he was coming to collect tonight.

The only thing I happened to be was terrified of what I'd just done.

†

I COULDN'T SEE past the mass of students as I walked beside Bryce later that day after classes got out.

"What's going on?" Bryce said, craning his neck to see if he could find out what was happening. When he couldn't make out what was happening, he grabbed my hand and tugged me through the crowd until we broke through the front to see the medical staff buzzing around, trying to bring someone out of the building.

"Who is it?" Bryce asked a girl standing beside us. Amber Reed. I recognized her from my group therapy sessions. She was abused as a kid and had a lot of traumas plaguing her. She was sent to Chapel Crest when she'd stabbed the boy she was dating in the leg with a pair of her mother's scissors because he hit her when she refused to have sex. I'd heard her recount the story in therapy. How she'd blanked and lost it because his actions reminded her of her childhood. It was heartbreaking to see her cry because she seemed like a nice person.

"Danny Linley," she answered, blinking as they brought out a person on a cot.

His face was a mess of cuts and blood. His arms on the outside of his white blanket were covered in an attempted bandage to stop the bleeding, but it was seeping through like he'd tried to off himself.

So much blood. And definitely Danny.

"Damn," Bryce murmured, watching as the staff rushed him to the small emergency vehicle they kept on campus.

"Heard he tried to kill himself," someone named Alan Jacobs said. I recognized him from my scripture reading class. "He didn't show up to classes today and they did a wellness check on him. He didn't succeed though. They found him all messed up on his floor."

People whispered around us as Danny was loaded into the vehicle. Sully came out of the building with two security guards and stopped in front of the crowd.

"Everyone needs to get back to their dorms. We had an incident here, but it's been taken care of. I can assure you that Mr. Linley will receive the best care at the medical facility. There's no need to concern yourselves with it. I suggest hitting the books or taking a walk. Now go."

I tugged Bryce's hand and glanced around to see the watchers in the crowd. They looked like they were having a deep conversation because they weren't paying attention to anyone around them.

And then there was Seth standing on the edge of the crowd, a small smile on his face. He dragged his attention away from Sully and cocked his head at me, like he knew exactly where I was without looking for me. Chills raced across my skin as he stared back at me.

I knew that look.

I'd seen it on his face eight years ago when he'd tried to kill me.

Pure evil.

CHURCH

"So what went down with you and the mute?" Sin grunted as we leaned against the railing of our house later that evening. We'd seen the staff haul a fucked up Danny out of the dorms earlier that night. I'd like to say I gave a shit, but honestly, the guy deserved to be shredded to ribbons after what he'd tried to do to specter. Even though Stitches had thoroughly kicked his ass, I'd been plotting my attack on the asshole. Unfortunately, it looked like it might have to be delayed so he could heal up just so I could tear his flesh open for him again.

I let out a breath, letting those thoughts go. I could mull them over another time once I knew his status.

The water lapped at the shore, sending a soothing sound at us. I continued my deep breathing, my mind envisioning Danny bleeding out. I felt relaxed for the first time in weeks. Having Sirena give into me had sent much of the tension out of my body. Adding Danny's issues was the cherry on top. Having Sirena wasn't just about winning. It was about owning her. Making her mine. Or ours, I suppose. We still needed to break the news to Melanie though. That would be a screaming, claws out protest. I dreaded dealing with her shit. It wasn't like any of us loved her. We were superficial assholes and wanted a hot pussy to sink into with a decent set of tits. Melanie fit the description, and she didn't mind sharing. Mostly. She wasn't into group activities. She'd let us watch her get fucked by another watcher but joining in was off the table unless we wanted to slap her ass or grab a tit while she was being fucked. We never got to the fun stuff. And she let us watch Tasha eat her out. It had worked for us. It just didn't now.

"We're far closer to owning her than I thought we were. She gave in, for the most part, when I told her we could offer her a certain amount of protection. That only convinces me further we have a fucking snake slithering through campus, causing her harm. I just don't have a fucking name. It could have been Danny. It would make sense, all things considering." I took a hit from my joint and held it, loving that burn and euphoria I felt whenever I'd get high and handed it off to Sin. Getting high was probably one of the only things that kept me sane. Or sane enough to function. None of the fucking meds they pushed helped me. I'd gone off them long ago. Weed always calmed the voracious beast within me. I needed that tonight because I was going to be paying my little specter a visit soon.

I raked my fingers through my hair and blew out the lungful of smoke and let out a cough.

"Do we need a name?" Sin asked after blowing out his hit and handing the joint back to me.

"Not really." I gave the joint a pinch and twirl between my thumb and forefinger before taking another hit and blowing out. "But it'll fucking help. It'll put my mind to ease to know Danny got what was coming to him even if he did it to himself."

"What if it's not Danny? Think it's Cain? He's sketch."

"He is," I murmured, staring out at Lake Superior and watching the moonlight dance along the gentle waves. "I'll figure it out though. If it wasn't Danny, it was someone. The truth never stays buried for long around here. Not when I'm digging for it."

"I'll help."

I looked over at him. "I thought you hated her."

He let out a soft laugh and looked over at me. "I do. I can see the potential and appeal there though. She's beautiful. She's intriguing."

"Then what's the problem?"

He shrugged, looking uncomfortable, a rare look for him. "I could see myself getting lost. I don't like that. I like to be in control, and I think she'd take me to places I wouldn't know how to navigate. I don't want to fall, man. I can't. It'll fucking break me this time."

I nodded, understanding. "You wouldn't be alone."

He stared out at the water. "No, I suppose not, but can you imagine if this doesn't work out? If all four of us fall for a girl who can't function? You know we'd fucking fall. I can see it all over you and Ashes already. Even Stitches looks like his heart is fucking breaking whenever she walks past." He sighed. "She's a fucking mess, Dante. She really is. I don't want to get attached to something only for it to disappear."

"Like Isabella," I said, studying his face.

His lips quirked up into a small smile. "I haven't heard you say her name in forever."

"I still hate the bitch." I shrugged and looked away from him. "And I blame her in part for the fucking turmoil you're in regarding Sirena."

"You always say you hate her, but yet—"

"I said I was fucking sorry, man. OK? I am. It never should have happened." I scrubbed my hand over my jaw, anger coursing through me. "Sirena won't be another Isabella. I promise you that."

Sin didn't say anything else as we leaned forward on the railing for several long minutes. Unable to bear the discomfort any longer, I shoved away and stepped off the patio.

"Have fun," he called out softly as I disappeared into the shadows.

"Always do," I muttered.

✝

I STEPPED into the darkness her lamp didn't reach, taking in her delicate form on the bed in the white nightgown I'd gotten her to wear. Stalking forward quietly, I reached the side of her bed and stared down at her as she slept.

A real sleeping beauty.

I leaned over and turned her light off, plunging us into darkness. It was my favorite place to be. It was where I could be myself. It was where I could let go.

I allowed my fingers to gently trace along the fading bruise on her jaw in the moonlight of her darkened room, letting my anger flow just enough to keep me in that room and determined. Any other girl I'd have fucked and walked out on. No woman was worth such the hassle, but Sirena was no ordinary woman.

She shifted beneath my touch. I sat on the edge of her bed, exploring her face with my fingers as I took in the fullness of her lips. Her long, dark lashes. Her high cheekbones. I trailed my fingers lower until I got to the necklace on her chest. I picked up the delicate silver cross.

Her breathing changed.

"Hello, specter," I said, flickering my gaze up to her face.

She didn't shrink away from me as I expected.

"I've come to collect." I dropped the cross back onto her chest and studied her in the moonlight. Her breathing picked up and her bottom lip trembled.

My cock ached as I reached out and ran my thumb along her lips. "Don't be afraid," I cooed softly. "I'm only going to bring you to the other side of fear so you'll be invincible. How does that sound?" I moved my fingers away from her face and held my hand out to her. "Come."

I thought she might fight me on it, and that would have been great too, but she placed her hand in mine and allowed me to pull her up. Her long black hair cascaded around her in wavy sheets, tickling my fingers as it brushed the top of her blanket on her lap.

I brought her to her feet, and she slid her feet into slip-ons before I led her to the door. She pulled against me, but I turned and cradled her face with both hands. I knew she was afraid of the dark, but I also knew she was afraid of me. There was a war going inside her head as she stared at me fearfully. *Stay in the darkness or go with the darkness.*

"I need this, specter. Allow me this small joy, and I promise you won't regret it. I love the hunt. You're my prey. It's been so long since I've had blood on my hands. I fear I'll wither away if I don't get it soon. I won't hurt you. Let me quell the fear within you. I can change your life if you let me."

Her tongue darted out to taste her lips, and I let out a soft groan at the movement.

"Please feed my demons, specter. And in return, I'll slay yours."

She hesitated for all of a moment before the tension left her. Triumph coursed through me as I led her out of her room and into the night.

"We're going to the cemetery," I said as we walked through the darkness, her hand in mine. Something about the way she clung to me made me feel all sorts of things I couldn't place since they were foreign, but I didn't mind them. Much. "We're going to play a game. I like to run through the cemetery when I'm stressed. I take the trail through the forest usually, but I don't want you to get lost since you don't know the woods like I do." I paused for a moment, licking my lips as Ashes's words tumbled through my head.

She's a secret keeper. You can tell her your secrets and she won't say anything.

I had many secrets. Some I'd never told a soul. But I wanted to tell her. I wanted her to know me. At least this part of me. The rest would come later.

"When I was younger, I hunted when stress overwhelmed me or when I was bored and just needing to get blood on my hands. Small animals mostly. Rabbits. Birds. Other woodland creatures. It's the ecstasy of the chase that got my dick hard. The conquering of life. The submission. Tonight, I want to pursue you. I want your blood, specter."

We stopped outside the cemetery gates, and I looked down at her to see the fear in her eyes beneath the moonlight.

"I won't hurt you. I just want to chase you through the darkness until I catch you. And then. . ." I reached out and cradled her delicate face. "We'll have fun. Can you do that for me?"

She said nothing as her gaze darted from the dark cemetery to me before she frowned and looked down to her feet.

"It'll be OK. You'll love the adrenaline. The fear. *The anticipation*. I'll make it worth your time. In this darkness there's only you and me. Nothing else. Breathe, specter. Face your fear and be rewarded."

Her gaze slid to me, and I nodded, gently bringing her beyond the gate and into the cemetery. I released her hand and stepped away, taking in her chest heaving and her lip trembling. How her hands balled into tight fists. The way the gentle breeze ruffled her mass of black waves. How the moonlight danced along her skin, making her look like my perfect little ghostly princess.

I stopped behind her and pushed her hair back and rested my hands on her slender, quivering shoulders.

My lips skimmed along her soft skin as she breathed heavily. My cock was rock hard as I inhaled that sweet, sugary scent of hers. When I got to her ear, I whispered to her like a devil on her shoulder.

"Run or scream for me. Those are your two options."

I knew which one she'd choose, at least for right now. That only made this more exciting.

SIRENA

I ran as fast and as hard as I could, weaving and dodging behind the granite tombstones, waiting for Church's hands to wrap around my body and bring me to the ground. My lungs burned as I ducked behind a large headstone with a weeping angel and tried to catch my breath.

Dante Church was insane. I had no idea what he had planned once he caught me. But he'd kept his promise to me earlier about not harming me and had promised the same again. Trusting anyone wasn't easy, but there was something about the way he looked at me that made me think that just maybe one more promise could be worked out of him.

"I know you're over here," Dante's deep voice called out into the night.

I peeked out from behind the tombstone to see him in his all-black clothing peering in my direction.

Quickly, I ducked back and swallowed. We'd been at this for a good fifteen minutes already. He was faster than I thought possible, always just a step behind me.

I spotted a small rock on my right and snagged it up before

heaving it toward the dark woods. I watched as his head snapped in the direction of the sound, and he moved toward it. I took the opportunity to dart out and race in the opposite direction. Looking back wasn't an option, so I hauled ass, my feet pounding through the thick grass. Jumping and weaving, I leapt over smaller tombstones and ran full tilt into the night.

I heard his wicked, excited laughter boom into the night, and it sent shivers racing across my skin.

When I arrived at the mausoleum they'd locked me in, I leaned against the cold stone walls and sucked in sharp breaths before peeking around the corner to see the dark cemetery without movement. Thinking maybe I'd lost him, I made to step out, but before I'd made it around the corner, a warm hand snaked its way around my throat, hauling me back against a hard body.

"Gotcha," Church growled in my ear as he gently squeezed my throat, his lips brushing against my ear. "Fuck, that was fun, specter."

He released me, and I stumbled away from him, scared of what this part meant. He cocked his head at me and met me step for step as I backed away. When the backs of my legs met the cold roughness of a gravestone, I stopped.

He loomed in front of me for all of a moment, his green eyes filled with darkness and the moonlight cutting a sinister light over his handsome face.

His hands found me quickly, one on my throat and one on my waist, as he toppled us over the tombstone, putting me to the ground fast. I landed not nearly as hard as I could have had he not steered my fall.

I swallowed as I stared up at him looming over me, his hand gently squeezing my throat as he rested on his other elbow, his body partially over mine.

"I could kill you," he said softly. "Rid you of your misery, but it would make me miserable. What would I do without you? You have awakened something inside me I don't fully understand, specter, but I don't wish for it to go away. I've done bad things. Things that would make you cry your pretty little eyes out if you knew. Things only my friends know. Things I keep hidden from everyone. But you? I want to tell you all of my dark deeds. I want to confess to my specter. What's happening to me?" His brows knit as he continued to study me. Finally, after a few moments of silence, he released his hold on my neck as my mind raced to all the terrible things I knew he was capable of.

"But not to you. *Never* to you," he whispered, leaning in and running his nose along my cheek, his hand still around my neck but without the pressure. *"My specter."*

His hand trailed away from my neck and down to the silk ribbon on the front of my nightdress. My breath hitched as he ran his hand to my breast and gave it a squeeze.

"You can't tell me no. I could take whatever I wanted." He shifted suddenly, moving so he was planted between my legs, his hardness pressed to my heat through our clothes. He pinned my arms over my head as he buried his face in my neck and inhaled me. He shifted, hitting a spot between my legs with this hard length that made desire course through me.

I'd never felt such a rush before. Such heat.

He lifted his head and smiled down as he moved to straddle me. Within seconds, he was hauling me to sit up while pinning my legs with his weight.

I widened my eyes as he withdrew a knife from his pants. With a push of a button, the blade shot out of the handle, glinting in the moonlight.

"This may hurt for a moment," he murmured, taking my hand in his.

I stared in horror as he aimed the knife for my hand, clearly intent on cutting me. I tried to pull away, but he was strong and determined. I fought, smacking at him with my free hand until he let out a snarl and dropped his knife, pinning both my hands down.

"If you fight me, things could progress to a place we won't be able to come back from. I'm sure you can guess how hard my cock is right now. Imagine me pushing myself into that tight pussy and fucking you until you can't breathe." He leaned, his lips at my ear. *"Don't fucking tempt me."*

I ground my teeth as he hauled my hand up again and grabbed his knife from beside his leg. His eyes locked on mine as he pushed the blade into my palm. Electric pain shot through me as he broke the skin open, my blood trickling out.

He dropped the knife to the ground and reached into his pocket and hauled out the tiniest vial I'd ever seen. He held it to the blood oozing from my wound and captured it within the glass confines before sealing it off with a tiny cork and stuffing it into his pocket.

With his eyes locked on mine, he lifted my palm to his mouth where he licked the wound, my blood painting his lips red. A soft groan left him, his breathing heavy.

Butterfly wings unfurled deep within my guts, a wild heat pooling between my legs as he continued to suck from me, his eyes dark and hooded. When he was done, he dropped my hand, my blood still on his lips and leaned into me.

My breath caught as he paused just a fraction of the way to my lips and locked eyes with me. Then, gentle as possible, he cradled my face with both hands and closed the distance between us, his soft, warm lips brushing against mine.

I sat stunned beneath his bloody kiss. My first kiss.

"I want it," he rasped against my lips. "Your firsts. I want them all. And I want your lasts. Give everything to me, Sirena. Be mine. Kiss me back. Seal the deal with the devil. My protection for always. Let me own you, Sirena Lawrence, the girl with no voice."

Something snapped within me. Maybe it was the heat of the moment or the way the fire was building between my legs, or maybe it was the knowledge that Dante Church really was the biggest bad ass on campus and I needed his help, but I leaned into his kiss and parted my lips, kissing him back.

His fingers twisted in my hair as he deepened the kiss, his tongue slipping along my lips and into my mouth to taste me.

"More," he commanded in a low rumble before pressing his mouth harder against mine.

I parted my lips more, allowing him full access. He took it all, his tongue in my mouth, exploring as I tentatively explored his. We shared our breaths as we kissed beneath the moonlight. Nervously, I reached out and ran my fingers through his soft blond hair. He responded by roughly hauling me closer, his lips not breaking away from mine. With nimble fingers, he pushed my nightdress off my shoulders, exposing my breasts to him.

I made to break away, to cover myself, but he let out a snarl and shoved me onto the cold ground, his hand squeezing my breast before he tweaked a nipple, rolling it and pinching it before going back to knead my breast again. He finally broke his lips off mine as I tried to catch my breath. He didn't give me enough time because his lips moved down my neck and to my breasts, licking along the pale skin before sucking my hardened peak into his mouth and biting. I arched against him, breathing hard, as he did the same to the other breast.

His lips skimmed across the soft mounds, licking and sucking until the suck became painful. He moved up my neck again, leaving painful marks on my skin.

When he finally stopped, we were both breathing hard.

"I have to stop," he murmured. "I'll end up fucking your pretty pink pussy until you bleed for me if I don't. *Fuck.* I want it." He rubbed his thickness against my aching center as I clung to him.

"I could bury myself deep inside you, fuck you until you cried, and you wouldn't ever tell anyone, would you?" He licked his lips as he studied me before his warm hand moved up my thigh and inched beneath my nightgown.

"I want a reaction. I want you to tell me no. I *need* you to." His fingers brushed against my panty line at my hip. "I want you to scream when I plow into your drenched pussy. I want you to fight me, specter. Even if you want it, *fucking fight me.* Can you promise to do that for me when the time comes for me to take it from you?" He brushed my hair off my forehead. "Give me an answer."

I didn't know what the hell was happening to me. I'd gone momentarily stupid. He'd tapped into my own insanity it seemed. But he'd delivered on his promise. He hadn't hurt me. He'd succeeded in making me feel something new. He'd turned my fear into pleasure, if only for a moment.

So, I ran my fingers through his hair and pressed a soft kiss to his lips.

"Good girl," he breathed out. "Such a good fucking girl."

SIRENA

I woke up alone in my dorm the following morning, my body still sore from the night before when I'd ran through the cemetery, but I felt good.

Church had brought me back to my dorm after our kiss, cleaned my palm wound, and tucked me into bed before going to sit in the chair, his keen eyes on me as I drifted off to sleep with my bedside lamp back on. I didn't know what any of what happened meant, other than Dante Church was certifiably nuts, but maybe that would be a good thing for me now that I'd enlisted his help. I didn't know if that meant I was in and Melanie was out, or if it meant I was some side piece. I cringed at the thought.

Not sure what was even in store for me from last night forward, I got up, worry twisting in my guts. I quickly got ready for classes and headed out, my mind racing a mile a minute.

"Good morning." Ashes fell in step with me, causing me to jump since I didn't even know where he came from. The fact he could hide his large body without me seeing made me worry more.

"How was your night?"

When I didn't answer, he continued. "I figured I'd walk with you to classes this morning. Not all morning of course. Stitches was going to do it, but he's ridiculously slow in the mornings getting ready. He was still grumbling from the edge of his bed when I left."

I cast him a quick glance and adjusted my book bag on my shoulder.

"Here." He pulled me to a stop and took my bag off my shoulder and slung it over his. "No sense in both of us lugging these damn things."

I studied him for a moment, wondering why the hell the watchers were being so nice to me all of a sudden. They'd gone from terrifying to still terrifying, but with friendlier interaction. Was this what it felt like to be under their protection?

"I know what you're thinking," he said, giving me a quick smile as he flipped the top of his lighter open and closed five times. A pause before he started it over. It almost seemed like a nervous tic for him. I'd never noticed the shaking of his hands before when he did it, but I definitely did now. It was like he was struggling for control. "But accept that you're on our radar and consider the possibilities. They don't all have to be negative."

Of course, they didn't. That didn't mean they wouldn't be. I desperately wanted to believe that everything happening to me was leading me to a place where fear wouldn't rule my life. Where I could smile again. Where maybe I could fit in and not feel so alone.

"We should do something together. Me and you. I'd like to make you dinner. What do you think?" We started walking again.

Was he asking me out on a date?

"I can bring it to your room if that's more comfortable for you. I know you and Andrews are dating, so this wouldn't be me trying to steal his girl. Unless, of course, you want me to steal you." His eyes lit up as we glanced at one another. "I wouldn't be opposed to that."

He was flirting with me. It wasn't making me uncomfortable either. It was endearing and sweet. If I were any other girl, it might work, but I was who I was. I didn't even know how I could respond to him. Did he know I'd kissed Church? He had to. Church probably told them the moment he got back to his place what happened between us. I couldn't even label what the hell happened with Church in the cemetery. He said to give in. I'd sealed it with a kiss. But what the hell did it even mean? Was this it? Was I theirs?

"So, dinner? Saturday night?" He lifted his brows as he looked over at me.

When I didn't answer, he cleared his throat. "Tell you what. Saturday night I'll come over with dinner. We'll watch a movie in your room. I'll be a perfect gentleman. If you don't want me there, then don't open your door when I knock. Deal?"

I blew out a breath that seemed good enough for him because he didn't push the topic as we reached the courtyard. Once there, he pulled me to a stop.

"I want you to know you're safe with me. I wouldn't ever lie to you and make a promise I couldn't keep. In fact, you're safe with all us watchers even though you're afraid." He took a step closer to me, closing the space between us. I stared up into his eyes, my heart hammering a fast rhythm in my chest.

"You matter," he murmured. "Until you do something that we can't stand beside, you'll matter to us. And even then, I'm sure there's room for negotiation. We want you, Sirena. We want to claim every part of you." He brushed a loose strand of hair away from my face. "So. Saturday night? No Andrews. I'm sure you understand." He handed my bag back to me and offered me a lopsided smile. "Can't wait. Maybe we can. . . talk." And with those words, he left me standing there, wondering exactly what the hell was happening with the watchers and where it left me.

†

"Sirena Lawrence. Care to tell the class what year Columbus set sail to the New World?" Sister Esther stood over me as I dropped my pencil onto my notebook where I'd been taking class notes. It had been two days since my experience with Church in the cemetery and with Ashes telling me they wanted to claim me. Two long days of confusion. Of me going back and forth in my head on what it all meant.

"Miss Lawrence," Sister Esther called out again.

August 3, 1492. Say it, Sirena. God, please. Just whisper it. She'll go away if you whisper it.

I licked my lips as my hands shook.

"We don't have all day, Miss Lawrence. Just because you *fake* a disability doesn't mean the rest of us have to play along. Out with the answer." She slapped her ruler on my desk, making me jump as sweat beaded along my forehead. "God is the way to heal the soul. You want those demons in your head gone? Then *speak*."

She glared down at me, her wrinkled skin rosy, like confronting me was getting her worked up. "Many have mental illnesses here. It's what we were created to overcome. If you spoke before your incident, you can certainly speak after. Answer the question or be sent to the headmaster."

"She's a freak." Melanie snickered. A few people in the class laughed along with her. Even Sister Esther smiled at the rude words.

We're all freaks or we wouldn't be here. I wanted to shout it until I was red in the face.

"I bet she'd know the answer if you threatened her with detention," Melanie continued.

"Is that what you need? Detention? Perhaps a writing assignment would work wonders for you along with the visit to Headmaster Sully."

Something in the way she said that confirmed to me she knew what he did to students who visited him for private sessions.

"For fuck's sake, the answer is 1492. Why the hell are you asking her? *You* know the answer. *We* know the answer. Teach the goddamn class because this shit is putting me to sleep." Sin's deep voice boomed out from the back of the room.

I ducked my head, embarrassed and surprised. The last thing I expected was for Sinclair Priest to stick up for me.

"Mr. Priest—"

"Don't *Mr. Priest* me, *Esther*," Sin snarled, getting to his feet. Sister

Esther cowered away from him as he stalked forward, all corded muscles and a big, bad ass attitude. "You know she doesn't speak, so *what the fuck* are you tormenting her about it for?" He glared down at her as she backed up to the chalkboard. Her dark eyes darted to me, her anger and embarrassment clear as day. I tried to fold into myself to make myself smaller from all the attention swiveling back and forth between me and Sin with her.

"I will call security in here, Mr. Priest—"

"Call an entire fucking army, you old bitch. I *dare* you." He glared down at her, dwarfing her in size. When she didn't say another word, he spoke again. "That's what I thought. Watch how the fuck you're talking to her. Got it?" He backed away amid soft gasps from the class and Melanie getting to her feet.

"Excuse me," Melanie called out, her face red with anger. "What the hell are you doing sticking up for her? I'm the one the watchers *claimed—*"

"And you're running dangerously close to being told to go fuck yourself," Sin snarled. Melanie trembled like she was going to cry before shooting me a death glare that meant Sin screwed up on my behalf before she sat down. "You were never officially claimed anyway, so don't start your shit."

Sin looked to me and gave me one nod of his head that meant to get my ass out of my seat and follow him. Hastily, I gathered my things and stumbled forward. He grabbed my arm by the bicep and hauled me out of the room without a word as students whispered in our wake.

I wanted to thank him, but I didn't even know if I had anything to thank him for. He probably just cost me a detention regardless of anything that transpired back there. And the last thing I wanted was more time with Sully.

He didn't say anything as he led me down the hall, his grip painfully tight. When we got to the exit of the school, he shoved the doors open and continued walking while he held my arm. Any normal girl would have asked where we were going by now, but I was silent as a tomb as I sent up internal prayers that he didn't gut me and leave me for dead somewhere.

I didn't fight him. Some part of me, no matter how small, wanted to be able to trust the watchers. Sin didn't strike me as someone who gave a damn about me, but he'd helped me, so I figured I owed him the benefit of the doubt.

He didn't talk the entire walk, nor did he release me. When we finally reached a large home tucked away along the lake and hidden behind the trees, he pulled me up the front steps and opened the door, shoving me through. My backpack slid off my arm and fell to the floor with a loud thud.

The place was nicer than my house back home. A large, open living room and kitchen. Stairs that led up in the back of the living room to a balcony above with a hallway. A few doorways were located off to the side of the living room. Glossy, hardwood floors and leather furniture. A massive widescreen TV with the latest gaming consoles and a stereo system. Granite countertops.

While all of it was immaculate, it was nothing compared to the man who rose from his seat in the living room, his eyes set on me.

Dante Church.

SIN

I didn't know why the fuck I hauled her out of class, or why I even stood up for her, but I did and now we were back at the watchers' house. Our little sanctuary away from the dumb cunts who ran this hellhole.

Knowing Church was back at the house made my decision an easy one once I had her out of the classroom. He'd taken to staying out all night the past few nights and hadn't been sleeping. It was easy to tell with him because he tended to become more pissed off and crazier than usual when he lacked sleep. So wherever he was going, he was doing something. Or someone. And as far as I knew, the only someone who could hold his attention was shaking in our living room.

"Specter," he said in his silky voice as he rose to his feet. It wasn't his movements to get to her that spoke volumes. It was the fucked up look in his eyes. Like he was going to devour her the moment he reached her. I watched as he stalked toward her. Her body tensed at his fast approach, but the moment he was within arm's reach, he slowed his movements and reached out to cradle her cheek. She didn't pull away from him. Instead, she stared up into his eyes like she was trying to whisper all sorts of secrets to him.

He smiled down at her. "To what do I owe the honor?"

"Sister Esther was being a cunt to her in class. Trying to get her to talk. I pulled her out and brought her here," I said, narrowing my eyes at the two of them with their eyes still locked on one another. *I should have fucking let them tear her apart in there.*

"Is that a fact?" he murmured, tilting her head back. "We'll have to do something about that, won't we?"

He released her cheek and took her by the hand and led her to the couch where he pushed her down onto the cushion. A gasp left her pink lips as she stared up at him. "I think you should stay here and relax for a bit. Sometimes a new environment can really help clear the mind." He leaned down and whispered something into her ear I couldn't hear, but when he drew away, he ran his lips along her cheek before pulling away completely and coming toward me after turning the TV on. A house makeover show blared in the background as he approached me.

"I want Sister Esther dealt with."

"And how do you want to do that?" I asked, glancing at Sirena as she stared at the TV, her body stiff. I knew she couldn't hear us since we'd now moved to the kitchen, but I also knew she had to be uncomfortable sitting there watching TV in our place.

"In such a way she doesn't forget her fucking place."

I nodded. I was agreeable to that. I hated that old bitch anyway and had wanted to kick her tits in since I arrived years prior.

"Now, we need to feed specter."

"You know I can't cook." I snorted. Ashes typically did all our cooking if we needed it, but he wouldn't be back until later since he was going to a group therapy session after classes. "Stitches can do it when he gets here."

"I said she needed to eat, not die," Church grumbled, pushing past me to the cupboards and pulling them open.

"Since when do you care if she eats?"

"Since I felt her bones beneath her skin."

"And when was that?"

"Last night, mainly." He pulled out a pot and ran water into it.

"Were you with her last night? All night?" Our voices were too low for her to hear, which was good because I had a feeling I was about to get confirmation on where Church had been spending his nights. While I knew he went to her that one night for whatever messed up reason, I wasn't positive it was where he was spending every night. Knowing him, he could have been off in the woods, terrorizing the local wildlife.

"Yes." He flipped the burner on and leaned against the cupboard and gave me an even look.

"And?"

"And what?"

"What aren't you telling me?"

Don't fucking fall for her, Dante. I can't fall for her. I refuse, but fuck she's beautiful. I stomped the intrusive thoughts to death and watched Church.

"Nothing. I'm only getting to know her. Seeing what makes her tick."

"I'm sure you found it beneath her skirt," I muttered, something hot unfurling in my guts.

This only turned his lips up into a smile. "Perhaps."

I hated the way I had to stop myself from curling my hands into fists at the mention of him beneath her skirt. I didn't want her. *Fuck chicks*. Blow my load in their pussies, asses, or on their faces. That was as attached as I was ever going to get to another one. I chanced a look back to Sirena as she sat on the couch.

Fuck.

"Was it good?" I mumbled, unable to stop the words from falling off my lips.

The tiniest smile quirked Church's lips up as he raised his brows at me. For a moment, I didn't think he'd answer me until he dug around beneath his shirt and hauled out a vial filled with something red. It hung around his neck on a silver chain.

"Is that blood?" I lifted the vial from his fingers and looked from it to his face.

He nodded his head over at Sirena still on the couch. I dropped his new necklace onto his chest and took a step back., that ugly feeling in my guts back.

"How?"

"I went hunting," he said with a shrug as he turned back to the cupboard and pulled down a box of macaroni and cheese. I watched as he opened it and poured the contents into the boiling water.

Fucked up asshole. I wanted to know how exactly he did it, but Stitches stomped into the house and chucked his bag on the floor.

"Fuck these bitches, man. Melanie is all pissed off because I wouldn't fuck her behind the gym after classes. She said you hurt her feelings, Sinclair—"

"We have company." Church held up his hand to silence Stitches and pointed to Sirena on the couch. Stitches's eyes widened, and a grin swept over his face before he strode toward her and flopped down beside her. She flinched and inched away from him, but he only scooted closer.

"Isn't it a joy to watch her?" Church asked softly, his green eyes glittering as he stared at her. "I like the way she's so timid, yet fiery. I never know if she's going to cower or lash out. It's fucking fantastic."

I didn't say anything, opting to watch her and Stitches.

"I want to test her," Church said. "She has limits. I know she does. I need to know what they are."

"I'd tell you to just ask her but considering she doesn't fucking talk." I sighed. This shit was annoying. I wish I'd have just left her ass in the hallway. My mood was shifting from mediocre to pissed off, and I didn't understand why I was letting her make me feel this way.

He wasn't listening. He stirred the pot of macaroni for a moment before turning back to me. "I want to win and have her. We need to get over this shit with Cain. I've been holding back because I'm trying to play fair. I don't want to play fair anymore though. Make some calls. I want willing girls here."

"What?"

"Melanie. She's always down to suck some cock or get fucked. Not Cami though. None of us needs to lose our dicks."

I didn't know where he was going with this, but I didn't much give a shit. Getting off might improve my mood, so I sent out a couple texts to those I knew who'd be interested, Melanie being one of them even if I knew she was probably pissed at me.

Watching Church play Martha Stewart wasn't doing much for my mood, so I went back to the living room and sank down on the other end of the massive leather wraparound sofa and leveled my stare on Sirena.

"Why are you nervous?"

Her eyes widened at me before she averted her stare and looked to her hands.

"She's not nervous, right?" Stitches winked at me. He rested his hand over hers as she twisted them nervously in her lap.

When she didn't answer, he gave her hands a squeeze. Her nervous twisting stopped.

"There you go. See? She's fine. Perfect angel. Just. . . lovely." His leg bounced, jostling against her gently. *Nervous fuck.*

I snorted and shook my head as Church came into the room with a bowl of macaroni and cheese. He kneeled in front of her as Stitches held her hands onto her lap. Church reached out to tilt her chin up.

"I made you something to eat." He scooped noodles and cheese onto the spoon and held it out for her. I thought Stitches might release her hands so she could eat, but he held fast as Church cocked his head at her.

"Open," he commanded softly.

She hesitated for a moment before her lips parted and he fed her. I didn't know why my cock was reacting to seeing her eat and my friends help her, but it was. I adjusted my bulge, not able to tear my eyes from them.

Her eating was slow but steady as Church continued his work and Stitches held her hands. Finally, when Church offered her a spoonful, she jerked her head away.

Stitches released her hands and grabbed the remainder of the food from Church and shoveled it into his mouth. My boner immediately dissipated. Leave it to Stitches to ruin a hard-on.

Church offered her water. She took a few swallows before he

pulled the glass away from her lips and reached for her hands and brought her to her feet, his gaze on her making my chest clench. I'd never seen him react to anyone like that before in my life. Church wasn't a nice guy. Hell, none of us were, but in that moment, I could see him doing far more fucked up things than I already knew he'd done just to keep her.

Pity he'd probably end up killing her because Sirena Lawrence was far too pretty to die. But all pretty flowers die eventually.

STITCHES

I wasn't a jealous guy. I was easygoing. Cool. Collected. Fucking ready for whatever. Usually. We'd exchanged plenty of women between us through the years, but something ugly unfurled within my chest as I watched Church sit with Sirena on the floor between his legs while he reached out and occasionally twirled a strand of her black hair around his fingers.

Look at me, angel. Come on. Please. Fuck.

Her back was to him, her long legs crossed at the ankles as she looked at a point on the wall behind me. He'd had her on the floor, sitting in front of him for a good two hours while we'd played video games.

Ashes had come home, surprised as I was at finding her there, and had greeted her with a warm smile. She hadn't responded other than leveling her gaze on him. He'd walked her to class this morning because I'd been too tired to get my ass moving. By the time I'd shuffled to the door, Sin informed me Ashes had already left. I'd been stewing over it all damn day.

He and Church were on my shit list. They'd gotten closer to her than I had. Sin still claimed he didn't give a shit, but whatever. I'd seen him adjust his cock earlier when Church fed her.

Now, Melanie and Tasha were giggling and drinking with us. Church always had a plan, so I assumed this was another one of his schemes.

Make angel jealous. If I were guessing, that would be my million-dollar answer.

Since my mood was shit, I was OK with giving in and fucking one of the girls. Sin looked the same way, although Sin didn't discriminate when it came to pussy. If the pussy wasn't good, he'd just fuck a girl's ass or mouth instead.

Church lifted a brow at me and inclined his head to Melanie. She was sitting beside Tasha, giggling over some mean, nasty shit they'd done earlier to an underclassman. She hadn't acknowledged me tonight since I'd turned her down earlier. That was before my jealousy had reared its ugly head. Before I felt like I was suffocating. Drowning. Choking on my want of the girl Church had between his legs. *Fucking bastard. Damnit.*

I forced my legs to stop bouncing, all the energy pent up within me desperate to get out.

Fuck it. Maybe Church's plan could work.

I reached over and wrapped my arm around Melanie's waist and hauled her across the couch toward me. She slapped at me until I pressed my mouth to her neck. Immediately, she melted against me, giving in like I knew the bitch would. *Ah, narcissism was such perfect illness.* Melanie loved the power and attention. And I loved to fuck. While it wasn't her I wanted, I could make do and pretend she was my angel. Maybe.

She and Tasha were both drunk as shit, but it didn't matter. They'd do the same shit sober as drunk.

Tasha got up and went straight for Church. Tasha had sucked Church off a few times, but he'd never fucked her. We all knew both Melanie and Tasha wanted Church. More of his cock. More of his attention. More of just him. But Church wasn't like the rest of us. He took what he wanted with an air of unfeeling and walked away after he got what he wanted. He never looked back. He was a drug to these chicks. They wanted to tame his beast. Little did they know he had no beast. He *was* the fucking beast. Sin was almost as bad, but at least the girls knew it. Church liked to draw them in and fuck with them. Sick bastard. He was my hero.

I watched as Sirena stiffened on the floor, Church's fingers tangled in a dark strand, as Tasha leaned down and made to kiss Church. The fact Tasha seemed to have gone momentarily stupid made everyone in the room pause. Church *never* kissed. It just didn't happen. He'd fuck a girl and put his dick in her mouth, but his lips never touched any part of their bodies. I held my breath, knowing this was going to be a shit show. Finally. A little excitement.

He let out a snarl and shoved her away, making her totter back in her high heels. In a flash, he was on his feet, pausing Melanie's hand on the button of my pants.

"Who *the fuck* do you think you are?" Church demanded, his face red as he grabbed her roughly by the arm. "You never come to me unless I say you come to me, and you never fucking try to kiss me. Ever." He shoved her onto Sin's lap as she stared at him with tears in her eyes.

"If you want to suck cock and get fucked, Sin or Ashes, maybe both, will help you out. Not me."

"But that bitch has a boyfriend. That Andrews kid—"

Sin grabbed her and covered her mouth as his hand worked beneath her skirt, so she'd shut the fuck up before she got into more trouble. Her protests turned into soft moans as he rubbed her pussy beneath her skirt.

I chanced a look to see Sirena was staring at her hands again. Something about that lit a fire deep in my guts. I wanted her to watch me. I wanted her to feel the jealousy I felt. Not knowing if she even felt an inkling how I did in the first place with feelings and shit, I decided fuck it. I'd try it out. If nothing else, it would be hot to have an audience. At best, I'd come, and she'd be jealous. At worst? I pushed that thought out of my head.

Seemed like a solid plan.

Church moved back to her and took his spot again, a muscle tense along his jaw. Ashes sat between me and Sin as we went back to making out with the girls we had. He knew he could join either of us if he wanted. Melanie would probably bitch, but Tasha most likely wouldn't. But I also knew he was trying his hardest to impress Sirena.

And me? I was working a whole different angle. If I couldn't have her, then I might be able to piss off Ashes too since my mood was quickly crumbling. My brain couldn't make it believe Melanie was angel. I couldn't take my eyes off her between Church's legs long enough to make it happen. Although maybe I could just fuck Melanie and watch Sirena at the same time. That might work. See if I could get Ashes in on this.

Misery loves company and all that shit.

I pushed Melanie between us and reached over to undo Ashes's belt. He cast me a worried look before he glanced over at Church and Sirena. I dared to look too as Melanie kissed on my neck. Church had his hands on Sirena's shoulders and was whispering in her ear like the fucking devil.

That jealousy grew within me as I jostled with Ashes's belt. He snapped out of his stupor and shoved my hand away and got to his feet.

"Where are you going?" Church demanded. All activity in the room stopped.

"I'm not doing this." Ashes snarled, his gaze darting to a trembling Sirena.

"Really?" Church gave a dark smile. "I was just about to mark my occurrence for specter off the list. Sure you don't want to stick around?"

Ashes's hands balled into fists before he raked a hand through his hair and tugged at it. "With them here?" He jerked his head to Melanie and Tasha.

"You're right. Whores, get out."

"What?" Melanie sputtered.

"You're joking, right?" Tasha let out a snort.

"Do I ever fucking joke?" Church leveled his gaze on the two half-naked girls in the room. "Get the fuck out before I remove you. You've served your purpose. You've upset my specter."

"You're unbelievable," Melanie snarled, getting to her feet and buttoning her blouse. "You're throwing us out for that little, mute bitch?"

Church was on his feet in a moment, me following. Church fisted her hair, and she let out a cry.

"I'm throwing you out because your pussy has run its course. Sirena is in. You're out."

She let out a cry as Church tugged her hair, leading her to the front door. I grabbed Tasha's arm and hauled her crying behind them. Leave it to Tasha to make sure she wasn't left out of the tears.

Church opened the front door and shoved Melanie out. I pushed Tasha out behind her.

"It was fun, but loose. Hope you understand," I said, taking in the furious look on Melanie's face before I shut the door. Church had already moved back to Sirena who had gotten to her feet, her hands twisting nervously in front of her.

"Sit," Church growled, taking her hand and pulling her onto his lap. "It's time to pay the devil."

I couldn't keep the grin off my face.

It was about damn time.

I was a glutton for fucking things up in my life. Self-sabotage and all that shit. Maybe what we were about to do was one of those things. I wanted Sirena so badly it made my chest ache. If I didn't get my way, I fucked shit up until I could feel satisfied. This proved no exception.

Either way, it seemed getting fucked was what I lived for.

SIRENA

Nausea churned my guts as Church pulled me down onto his lap, his arm cinching tightly around my waist.

An occurrence. Fuck my life and Sister Esther for choosing today to torment me in class.

I wanted to ask Church why I had an occurrence to pay for when he promised to protect me. Or at least I assumed that was the deal we'd arrived to. Guess I was wrong. I knew if I were to ask him, he'd tell me he would protect me from outsiders and that it didn't nullify anything I'd done to piss them off.

I swallowed thickly as I tried to keep my breathing even.

"What's the plan?" Sin called out, adjusting himself in his pants. I averted my gaze quickly, my nerves getting the best of me. Having been forced to watch them with the Chapel Crest mean girls made my heart hurt. My feelings involving these watchers were confusing. When Melanie was all over Stitches, all I wanted to do was run at her and yank every strand of hair out of her head. It was the same with Tasha on Sin. I was pretty sure he knew that too because he kept his eyes on me the entire time, making whatever weird feelings I had worse because I *knew* he knew.

Church pulled me flush against his sitting body and ran his tattooed knuckles along my chin.

"I've come into a certain arrangement with our little specter," Church said softly as his hand moved down to brush against my chest. He tapped lightly over my heart in rhythm with the fast thumping.

"What's the arrangement?" Ashes asked, taking a seat on the couch beside Stitches who was watching me and Church with his dark gaze. Something about the way he was staring made my heart beat faster.

"She needs protection from all the bad here on campus. Aside from us, of course." He let out a soft laugh as he reached up and took my chin in his hand and pulled my face to his. "Right, specter?" His lips brushed against mine, igniting a warmth low in my belly.

He pulled away before I could kiss him back and looked to his guys. They all looked like ravenous dogs as they stared back at us. Even Sin sat forward, his eyes locked on me.

"But that doesn't excuse our little ghost from paying for her bad behavior. So tonight, I want to mark off an occurrence." His hand trailed up my bare thigh. Goosebumps followed in the wake of his warm touch. He chuckled softly in my ear, making my stomach tighten with anticipation.

"Trust me?" he murmured in my ear. "Like the cemetery. Let go and explore the possibilities with me. *With us. Be tested, pretty girl."*

I didn't get a chance to react because he adjusted me on his lap and spread my legs, his knees locking so I couldn't get out if I wanted to.

Panic blazed hot in my chest as I sucked in breath after breath, my chest heaving. Church rested his hand back over my heart and tapped the rhythm out.

Ashes sat forward beside Stitches. "What are you going to do?"

"See where she draws the line for us," Church said easily. My guts rolled, sending both excitement and nausea through my body. "See if she'll scream so we can end this."

He said to trust him. He hadn't hurt me last time I trusted him.

He moved his hand to my blouse and undid a button. Then another. And another until it was completely open. My breathing came fast and heavy as he trailed his fingers down my bare skin.

"Do you want them to see you?" he asked softly in my ear. "Do you want them to know what secrets you keep hidden beneath your clothes?"

My bottom lip shook as he opened my shirt. My head spun as I tried to keep my breathing even. I was quickly losing the battle.

"Her skin is like silk," Church called out in a gruff voice. I chanced a look to the guys staring at me and I swore my heart stopped for a moment. This was more than an occurrence. This would be something I knew I couldn't come back from. Something I couldn't fight off. It was happening no matter what I wanted.

This test would lead to their claiming if I passed.

"I'm going to let you go. If you run, I'll force my cock so far into your tight little ass your mother will hear you scream in Detroit. Do you understand me?" Church breathed out into my ear.

I shook. That seemed like a good enough answer for him because he moved his arm from my waist and pulled my shirt off and tossed it to the floor, leaving me in my bra and uniform skirt.

If I thought that was the worst of it, I was wrong.

"Take your bra off," Church instructed, his fingers skimming along the bare skin of my arm. "Show them what I got to see in the cemetery that night."

I dug my nails into my palms as I sucked in heavy breaths. *Please. Please don't make me.*

"You do it or I do it. If I do it, you'll be doing this for nothing because I'll be adding another occurrence to your tab," his voice was soft in my ear. I doubted the rest of the watchers could even hear it.

I squeezed my eyelids closed and reached back and undid my bra, letting the straps fall down my arms. A tear leaked out of my eye as the bra fell to the floor at our feet, taking care to keep my breasts covered with my hands.

"Show them, specter," Church said softly into my ear. "Let them see how beautiful you are."

Slowly, I let my hands fall away from my breasts, feeling the heat creep over my skin from my embarrassment.

"Mm, my very good girl," Church cooed, moving his hands up to cradle my breasts. "What do you guys think?"

"Fucking beautiful," Stitches appraised as his gaze focused on what Church was doing to my breasts.

Ashes nodded and Sin simply watched. Church pulled me back against his chest and kissed my temple, my legs still spread. My uniform skirt offered little coverage, but it was enough to keep my panties hidden.

"They like looking at you, specter." He gave my breasts a squeeze before rolling my nipples with his fingers. A zing of electricity shot to the apex of my thighs, making me squirm. His erection poked me hard in the back. "I think they'd like to touch you."

Oh god. Oh god. Oh god. Please. I can't. I can. . .? Wait, no. Stop. Stop. Stop.

"Malachi," Church called out. Stitches immediately got to his feet. "Come."

Stitches moved to us and went to his knees between mine and Church's legs, his dark eyes fixed on me.

"Touch her," Church commanded in a silky growl. My breath stuttered in my chest as Church's hands moved to my abdomen where he held me in place.

Stitches reached forward and cradled my breasts, his eyes hooded and lips parted. I breathed harder. Faster. My head spun. He pinched a nipple, and I bit down harder on my lip, tasting the blood in my mouth.

"Kiss him," Church instructed in my ear, pushing me forward to Stitches. I turned my head away, terrified of what it meant, but Stitches reached out and turned my face back to him.

"Don't be afraid," he said, leaning in. His lips met mine a moment later, sending sparks of heat between my legs. His tongue tasted and pushed against my lips until I had no choice but to part them for him. He delved inside, a man on a mission. *He has a tongue ring.* His kiss wasn't as rough as Church's had been in the cemetery. It was still strong and commanding though. He was in charge, and he wanted me to know it as he deepened the kiss, his tongue in my mouth, his breath mingling with mine.

Stitches's fingers tangled in my hair as he pushed me back against Church who didn't seem to mind being a slice of bread to this weird, confusing sandwich. With one hand on my breast and the other in my hair, my brain blurred. *This wasn't what I wanted. Was it?* I wasn't this girl.

Could I stop this? Make them understand I wasn't ready for any of this? Would it end in even more torment?

Was this torment? Stitches's lips on mine did feel good. So did the flurry of heat he was setting loose between my legs.

I jerked my head away from him, breathing hard. This wasn't me. I wasn't this girl.

He let out a growl as Church chuckled.

"Maybe she wants to try something different," Church said as Stitches's chest heaved. "Sin?"

If I thought I was nervous before, it was nothing compared to the feeling washing over me as Sin got to his feet and moved forward. Stitches shuffled off to the side, his eyes still locked on me as Sin stopped in front of us.

Tall. Muscular. Fierce. Fear swept through me as I stared up at him. Sin terrified me the most. While Church scared me, he also excited me. Sin just made me shake whenever I was near him.

"Do you want some?" Church asked him.

A muscle popped along Sin's jaw. "No."

"Fucking asshole," Stitches called out. "Yes, you do. It's her punishment. Fucking do it or I'll give you a damn occurrence. She needs to be tested."

Sin scoffed. I thought he'd turn and walk away, but he finally went to his knees before us. He reached out, his eyes flashing with something that both terrified and excited me, and fisted my hair roughly and hauled me forward. His lips crushed against mine, making me wince.

Sin was not gentle.

And his tongue was pierced too, like his septum. I found that out when he pushed it into my mouth and tangled it along mine. He tasted like whiskey and smoke and everything I shouldn't like but did. I tried to kiss him back, knowing the consequences of saying no, but he was in charge and didn't seem to give a shit if I were giving it back to him or not.

He pulled away as suddenly as he'd leaned in, his eyes dark.

"Did you like it?" Church asked.

"Fuck you," Sin snarled, reaching forward and running his fingers beneath my skirt. Church let out a soft laugh as Stitches shot me a wink that did funny things to my insides.

Sin's hands moved up further beneath my skirt, a muscle thrumming along his jaw as he reached my panties. He brushed his touch against the edge of my panty line at my thigh before he swallowed, his Adam's apple bobbing.

I flinched away from him and deeper into Church's hold as Sin's touch moved between my legs.

"Easy, specter," Church cooed. "Let Sin corrupt that pretty pink pussy if he wants to."

I shook as Sin shoved my skirt up and let out a deep sound from the back of his throat. Stitches moved forward, his hand on my thigh.

"Ashes. Get the fuck over here," Church called out thickly. Sin ran his fingers up my heat over my panties as Ashes stopped and stared down at me. I locked eyes with him, noting the worry that clouded his features. He was without his lighter in hand.

"She earned this," Church said, catching the look on Ashes's face. "You fucking know she did."

Ashes nodded tightly and sank down beside Sin who hooked his fingers beneath the lace and gave a fierce tugged. Scared, I reached out and grabbed Stitches's hand. He twined his fingers around mine and held tight as Sin finished removing my panties and dropped them to a tattered pile on the floor, displaying my core to him.

"Fuck," Ashes muttered, swallowing as his gaze swept up my nearly naked body.

"That's glorious," Stitches said softly.

Sin grunted and ran a finger up my bare slit, collecting the moisture their pawing at me had accrued.

"She's mine first," Church said, shifting me on his lap. "Touch her. Kiss her. Do what the fuck ever, but all her firsts belong to me."

"Selfish prick," Stitches muttered as he leaned in and kissed my breasts. I let out a breath and squirmed as Sin ran his finger along my heat again. I tried to fight, but Church got hold of my arms and pinned them at my sides.

"I'll take her," Ashes said softly. "So you can finish this."

Church released me, and my legs so I could close them. Sin and Stitches moved back as Church lifted me to my feet and handed me off to Ashes who pulled me right back onto his lap and spread my legs with his knees, locking me back in place like Church had.

Shit. No. No. No!

"Relax, heaven," Ashes murmured in my ear. "Let this happen. Don't fight it if you don't expect to scream. That's what Church wants. He wants you to scream for him."

I swallowed down the silent scream clawing its way up my throat as Church moved between my legs and ran his fingers through my folds.

I tensed, a tear working its way out of my eye as he pushed a finger deep into my heat and rubbed me.

"Don't move," Ashes instructed in my ear again as I tried to shift away, my throat tight and my chest burning from panic. "Try to relax for him."

Relax? Church was fingering me as I tried to squirm away. No one had ever done this to me before, and he wanted me to relax?

Church murmured something to Sin who nodded. A moment later, Church moved down so his face was between my legs.

"You've never had anyone down here before. You're so tight and wet. Specter, you just made my day. Scream for me if you can," he said before plunging his tongue into my heat and making me claw at Ashes as I tried to escape.

But there was no escape. I already knew that.

CHURCH

She was hard to subdue, but once we managed to hold her down, I dove between her legs and ate her sweet little pussy like it was my last meal. She was silent as she breathed hard, her body tense as Stitches and Sin both held her arms and Ashes kept her secure around her waist.

I lapped at her sweet nectar, my finger buried deep in her tight heat. She was beyond wet for me and that kept me going as I licked her clit. There was no way in hell she'd ever been touched there. I was the first. Fuck yes.

"Close your eyes," Ashes instructed her in a tight voice as she tried to squirm again in his hold. "Close them if you're scared. We can count together."

I chanced a look up from between her legs and saw her squeeze her eyelids closed, her hand in Stitches's as he watched me work my magic.

"There you go. Relax, sweetheart. Let Church make you feel good. It's just us here. No one is ever going to know what we did tonight. You can just let go for a night. Count with me. One. Two. Three. . ."

Ashes's voice almost hypnotized me too. Sirena relaxed a bit against him as I sucked her clit and inserted another finger into her.

She tensed for a moment as she adjusted to the fullness before her body began to shake. Taking that as my invite to make her come, I sucked and licked harder and faster, hooking my fingers deep within her.

Her breathing picked up as she arched her back off Ashes.

"Fuck, she's coming." Sin grunted.

"Not yet," Wolfe said, shifting forward. I worked harder as he brought her hand to his mouth and kissed it.

"Come for Church," Ashes murmured. "Come in his mouth."

Her body shook violently, her clit pulsating in my mouth as her pussy contracted on my fingers. Her wetness gushed out, and I lapped it all up, eager to swallow everything she could give me.

Her pussy tasted like heaven. It was probably the closest I'd ever get to the pearly gates, but it was fucking fantastic enough for me. I'd die happy knowing I'd gotten her off so much that she'd soaked my shirt and face.

"Look at that," Stitches said, mesmerized. "Our pretty girl made a mess."

I pressed a kiss to her pussy as she jerked beneath my lips, her bits still sensitive from my mouth.

Her eyes were still closed when I came up for air and took my shirt off. We hadn't made her scream, but I'd made her come. I'd count it as a victory.

I reached forward to take her, and Ashes sat her up.

"Open your eyes," I commanded, cradling her face as she continued to breathe hard. It took a moment before she cracked them open for me, revealing her colorful eyes. Her cheeks were damp with tears. "There's my good girl."

I ran my thumb along that trembling bottom lip I loved so much, adoring how soft it was from her tears.

"What now?" Stitches asked in a gruff voice.

"She didn't stop us. She didn't scream. That means something," I said, cocking my head as I looked at her. "Right, specter?" I leaned in and brushed my lips against hers before pushing forward and kissing her deeply. Her lips were stiff beneath mine before she melted against me, her bare breasts pressed to my chest which was dampened with her release.

"Fuck, that's hot," Stitches muttered as I drew her closer to me, my hands on her warm, bare skin.

She wanted this. She'd have pulled away and fought me with the kiss. Instead, she'd fallen into it, her tongue sliding along mine in a delicious dance.

I broke the kiss off, my cock painfully hard.

"Kiss Ashes," I said softly against her lips. "He's been neglected."

Her eyes wavered as she stared at me before I placed my hand on her chest and pushed her back against him.

"You don't have to," he said gently, turning her face toward him to cradle it.

"She does," I said, pulling my cock out of my pants and stroking it.

"Think she's on the pill?" Stitches asked.

"Does it fucking matter?" Sin countered.

I shook my head. I didn't give a fuck if she was on it. I only wanted to feel her heat sheathed around my dick. I'd seen her file though, so I wasn't concerned. She was good to go.

Ashes's lips were a fraction from hers when I ran my cock up along her still damp lips. She jerked away from him and struggled to shove me away, her eyes wild.

I grabbed her by the arms and lifted her clear off Ashes. Ashes moved out of the way so I could sit down with her back on my lap, this time with her facing me. I had to bear hug her to get her under control.

"I won't fuck you. I just want to feel you," I hissed in her ear. "Trust me, specter. Have I hurt you so far?"

She shook in my arms before the tension fell away, and she collapsed against me. I loosened my hold on her and reached to my cock between her legs and slid it along her folds.

"Make me come however you can, and I won't fuck you," I said to her. "If you can't get me off on your own, then I'm going to fuck you until you bleed. Let fucking go of everything for a moment and let the good take over and leave the fear behind. Don't hold back. You're in control."

I released her completely as she sat straddling me, my bare cock still against her heat. I lifted a brow at her, taking in her tear-stained face.

"Don't cry," Ashes said gently. "You're almost done."

"Finish it," Sin grunted. He moved back to the couch where he pulled his dick out and stroked it. Stitches stood up and got behind her and pressed a kiss to her temple.

"Do you need help?" he asked.

Her jaw quivered.

"OK, angel. Slide your pussy along Church's cock. He's ready to go. Just keep doing it until it starts to feel good."

She moved ever so slightly along my cock. My eyes rolled back in my head as I suppressed a groan.

"Slide, angel. Kiss him. Touch him. Let yourself go," Stitches instructed as I gripped her hips.

She slid against me again, my cock positioned nicely between her wet pussy lips. She let out a gasp as she did it again. Dry humping wasn't my thing, but for her, I'd do it. And I knew I'd get off by the way my balls were drawing up.

"Good. Keep going if you like it. If you don't, then stop," Stitches said. "Kiss him. Test the waters."

She leaned down and pressed her lips against mine as she moved against me. I groaned into her mouth as I gripped her hips tighter, unable to prevent myself from moving her along my cock.

Her breath came out stuttered as I couldn't stop myself from thrusting against her grinding.

"Fuck. Fuck," I snarled, holding her hips so hard I knew I'd leave my mark on her creamy skin. I bit her bottom lip and tasted her blood in my mouth. Her tits pressed against me as I got lost in the way she felt on me.

And she didn't stop, and she knew she could. Stitches had given her permission. She kept going though.

The tingling in my balls grew and drew up against me, my release teasing my cock.

"Faster, baby," I commanded her breathlessly. "Make me come."

She did as instructed, her body tensing as her own release took over. Her lips parted as her wetness glazed my cock and groin. She shifted back and her hair fell around us in wild tangles, brushing my thighs as her chest heaved. Seeing her that way made my release come to head. I exploded in a delirious whirlwind of bliss, soaking both of us.

We were both breathless as she fell back onto my chest and laid on top of me, her body damp with sweat.

Sin was cleaning himself up and Stitches seemed to have had the same idea as Sin because his softening dick glistened with the mess he'd made on his abdomen.

"Take her," I instructed Ashes who stood nearby, his eyes fixed on us. He'd only watched, apparently. He reached out and pulled her limp body off mine and ran his fingers through her hair as he murmured something to her I couldn't hear.

I stood, dizzy, and drew in a few calming breaths before I pulled my pants back on and scooped her into my arms. She didn't fight me. In fact, she buried her face into my chest and clung to me.

"Can we agree she did well?" I asked.

"Fan-fucking-tastic." Stitches grunted, stuffing his dick back into his pants. Sin nodded silently, frowning, and Ashes remained with his gaze fixed on her in my arms. He hadn't gotten anything. Not even a kiss. Poor bastard.

"Check off an occurrence. We're going upstairs. We'll talk about everything else later."

I didn't wait for them to say anything as I made my way to my room. Once there, I deposited her on my bed and stared down at how beautifully cracked she was. Her eyes locked on mine as I lay beside her.

"You were afraid," I said softly, moving my hand between her legs where I knew the mess I'd made still was. I swept my fingers up her center, relishing in her quivering, before I found my release on her soft flesh. I rubbed it into her skin, marking her in our sins. With my fingers damp, I ran it along her folds. Her breath came out in soft, short gasps.

"I'm going to keep you," I murmured against her lips as I rubbed her gently with my come. "You're mine, Sirena Lawrence."

I placed a kiss on her lips before withdrawing my hand from her and getting to my feet. I went to my attached bathroom and started a bath. When I returned to the bedroom, she was laying in the same place I left her.

Leaning down, I took her back into my arms and brought her to the bath and gently placed her into the warm bubbles. Her eyes were heavy with sleep as she gazed up at me. I removed my pants and got in behind her and held her against my body, something I'd never done with a girl before.

She was different though.

Sirena Lawrence was a miracle sent from the stars to torment my madness. She was a test. She would be my ending if I let her.

"Good girls don't come in bad boys' mouths and keep their boyfriend," I said into her ear. "I want you to break up with Andrews. That's over. Once you do, you'll belong to the watchers. We will claim you. I'm giving you the chance to do it on your own first. Do you understand me?"

She said nothing, per her usual, but I felt the tension in her body.

If she didn't let him go, I'd do it for her.

And I'd not be gentle.

SIRENA

I woke up in Church's bed alone. His side was cold, so he'd been gone for a long time. I let out a breath and stared up at the ceiling. It felt like last night had been a fever dream. I touched my lips, remembering the way the watchers tasted on them. Minus Ashes.

I sat up, knowing I needed to get back to my dorm so I could change my clothes and maybe grab a shower even though Church had taken the time to bathe me the night before. Wincing, I sat up and noted the purple marks on my breasts from Church or maybe Stitches's mouth. Hell, maybe both. Heated flooded my face as I recalled their lips on my skin.

Stitches said I could stop it. I knew I could have. Maybe I'd have gotten another occurrence, but the option was there. I'd let it happen. Not out of fear, but because I wanted it, despite how nervous I was.

I inspected my body further and found fingerprint bruises doted my hips. *Church.* Sighing, I got up and wrapped the bedsheet around me.

"You look like a lost angel," Ashes's voice called out as he came into the room. I stiffened, old habits dying hard, as he approached me slowly. When he stopped in front of me, he gave me a smile.

"Church is working out downstairs in our gym. He does every morning. He's been at it for an hour now."

I swallowed and breathed out. Ashes held his hand out to me.

"I have some clothes in my room if you'd like something to wear. You can dress, and I'll walk you back to your dorm."

That seemed like a sound plan, so I took his hand and followed him to his room down the hall. We entered an immaculately clean room filled with books. Like his own personal library.

"Here," he said, handing me a pair of sweatpants and t-shirt. My bra was on top of the pile, but not my panties. If anything, they were in the trash since Sin had shredded them to bits. I took the clothes and stared at him, not sure how I was supposed to thank him.

"I know last night was a lot for you to take in. I don't want you upset or scared. I was thinking maybe I could still come over to your place Saturday. We could have dinner. I'll bring something. We can watch a movie together and talk. Or I'll talk and sound like an ass and you can listen." He gave me a quick smile.

I studied his face. Ashes was so beautiful. The teddy bear of the four.

"Tell you what. I'll show up Saturday night to your place. If I knock and you don't answer, I'll know you're not interested. If you answer, we'll have a good time. Sound good?"

I blinked at him. It sounded like he was giving me a choice. *Did that mean if I wasn't feeling up to it that I could decline without getting another occurrence from them?*

"Get dressed," he said, stepping around me. "I'll wait outside for you."

He walked away, closing the door with a soft click behind him. Quickly, I dropped the sheet and hauled on the oversized clothes and went to the door.

Ashes was leaning against the wall outside it, and when I stepped out, he offered me that gentle smile of his and took the sheet from my hands and tossed it back into his room.

"Come on. Let's get out of here before those other assholes notice you're gone." He tugged me down the hall and downstairs, only stopping long enough to wait for me to slip my shoes on and then he grabbed my backpack and slung it over his shoulder.

Once we were outside, my nerves began to settle. We walked for a long time before he finally spoke.

"For what it's worth, I'm sorry about last night."

I glanced at him quickly and averted my eyes to my feet when he looked back at me.

"I know you were nervous," he continued. "I was a bit too if I'm being honest."

That didn't come as a complete shocker. I'd seen the worry on his face when Church started pushing me for more.

"Just so you know, you were fucking beautiful even if you were scared. I don't want you to think we used you because it's not like that."

Ashes pushed open the door to my building and led me inside and up to my room, remaining quiet in the elevator. When we reached my room, I unlocked the door and stepped inside, him following me. He placed my bag on the floor and closed the door.

"I hope you want more of what happened," he said softly, taking my hand and bringing me close to his body. "But that would mean you'd have to let Andrews go. Can you let him go for us?"

Did *us* mean I'd be with all four of them? Would I just be a plaything to them? I didn't want to be the girl they brought back to their place to screw and push out the door before the next one entered. Hell, I wasn't even sure I wanted to be their girl. I was so confused about how I felt. Terror flooded every fiber of my being before pleasure did, but terror always returned. I was scared of them. Scared they were going to hurt me if I didn't comply and since I couldn't get the words out, it made everything even worse.

Church knew I couldn't scream. That was why he kept pushing for more. And god, we'd been so close. Embarrassment flooded my body as I remembered how exposed I was to them again. They'd seen all of me. They watched me do things I'd never done before.

But how did I feel?

In this moment, ashamed. Scared of it happening again.

Desperate for more.

That last feeling terrified me more than anything else.

Ashes brushed his fingers through my hair tenderly as he gazed down at me.

"You don't know what you do to people, do you?" he mused softly. "You have no idea of your beauty or your magnetism. You don't even realize how many people watch you and wish they could have you. You, Sirena Lawrence, are a unicorn. Rare. Beautiful. Magical." He leaned in and pressed a kiss to my temple. "An angel sent from heaven to make the wicked weep."

I swallowed as he pulled away.

"Figure out what you're going to do about Andrews. As much as I did enjoy seeing you last night, I don't want you to get another occurrence with us. I know it's going to be hard for you to cut ties with Andrews since he's really a decent guy, so I'll try to keep Church off your back for a bit. I can't guarantee it'll work. You'll need to figure it out quick though. Accept the offer or become the prey. I'm pretty sure you know how it works with us."

He made to step away, but I grabbed his hand and pulled him to a stop. He turned back to me, his brows crinkled. I opened my mouth to, well, I wasn't sure what, but it didn't matter anyway because no words came out.

"What's wrong?" He moved back to me, the concern from last night back on his face.

I blinked at him, unsure about how to communicate what I needed to say to him.

"Tell me," he said softly. Urgently, as he squeezed my hands. "Whisper it to me. Text it?"

I closed my mouth and opened it again, imagining I looked like a damn fish out of water. He licked his lips before he turned my hand over and traced words onto my palm with his finger.

It's OK.

One letter after another.

I breathed out as he released my hand and turned his hand over, palm up.

I hesitated for a moment before I forced myself forward and took his hand. With a trembling finger, I began brushing my finger along his palm, writing letters he'd hopefully be able to piece together to know what I was saying.

He licked his lips as I finished. I dropped his hand and looked at him through my lashes.

Thank you.

It took him a moment to speak, but when he did, he wore the sweetest smile.

"You're welcome, heaven," he murmured, placing a soft kiss on my cheek. He backed away a moment later, his eyes on me. When he got to the door, he opened it and left the room without another word.

But he didn't need to say anything. I knew by the look on his face he was happy.

And that made me happy and washed away my worries, inflating my heart with feelings for the watchers that had no business being there.

It was something else too though.

I'd spoken. Maybe not with my voice, but I'd communicated to Ashes with words. I hadn't used words with anyone in so long.

They were changing me. I couldn't—wouldn't—deny it.

ASHES

I couldn't get the grin off my face. She communicated. *To me.* No one else. Church may have been able to control her, but it was me she chose to speak to. I mean, if what she did counted as speaking.

"Why the fuck you so happy?" Sin grunted as I came into the house. Stitches glanced at me from his spot at the table where he was stuffing cereal into his mouth, his leg bouncing.

I shrugged.

"Did you take Sirena home?" Church demanded, coming into the room looking like he'd just had a shower.

"Yep," I said, popping the p.

Sin folded his arms over his chest as he leaned against the kitchen island, his eyes narrowed. "He's gleeful. He knows something we don't."

I shrugged again, the grin spreading on my face.

"She kiss you?" Stitches demanded, pushing his empty bowl away.

"Better."

"Did you fuck her?" Church advanced on me, a sinister look in his eyes that really pissed me off. I knew he said he got first on everything, but what the fuck. This time, I got a first. Fuck yeah, I was going to gloat.

"No," I scoffed, not entirely turned off by the idea. But with Sirena, I didn't want to just jump between her legs. I legitimately wanted to get to know her first. That was why I didn't dive in for the kiss I knew I could've had. I let it go because I really wanted to do it just her and I when the moment felt right. I was a prick, but I wasn't an asshole. Not really, anyway.

"Then why the fuck are you smiling like the cat who got the cream?" Stitches asked.

I glanced to Church, noting his hands were balled into fists.

"First, I want to say that I know last night was great and all, but I don't think you should push her on ditching Andrews."

Church opened his mouth to say something as Stitches let out a groan and Sin shook his head.

"Hear me out," I said, holding up my hand. "This is a huge step for her. She doesn't know our intentions. She doesn't know us. She knows him and knows he's a good guy. She needs that. Let me talk to her on our date on Saturday, and I'll get it all out for her so she can decide."

"Date?" Church snapped. "What date?"

"The one I asked her on," I said.

Sin rolled his eyes as Church's Adam's apple bobbed in his throat.

"What a load of shit." Sin shook his head.

"Don't act like you didn't enjoy last night, Sinclair. I saw you with your dick in your hand and your mouth on hers. That come on your stomach wasn't because you didn't enjoy watching," Stitches called out.

"Man, fuck you," Sin shot back. "My dick was already hard because I was going to fuck anyway."

Church held his hand up to silence the room. "Asher, I know you well enough to know you aren't telling us everything. What's going on?"

I sat down at the table and looked at the three of my friends, smiling.

"I walked her home. I talked to her. More of a lot of reassurance and all that. Then I asked her what was wrong. I told her she could tell me." I paused, watching the guys. Church took a step closer, and Sin watched, the tension rolling off him in waves. Stitches stared back at me, waiting for me to drop the bomb as his legs bounced and he twisted his fingers together.

"Get to the fucking point," Sin snapped.

I rolled my eyes at him. "I took her hand and wrote a word on her palm with my finger. I said *it's OK*."

"Lame," Sin muttered.

"Continue," Church said, shooting Sin a look that said to shut the fuck up.

"Well." I grinned. "She answered me."

"What?" Stitches demanded the same time Sin's arms fell to his sides and he took a step forward. Church simply stood staring at me in stunned shock.

"What did she say?" Sin asked.

"She took my hand and wrote *thank you* on my palm."

The room was silent as I looked back at my friends. It seemed to last forever before Church cleared his throat.

"She spoke to you."

I nodded.

"She communicated."

I nodded again.

Church looked to Sin and Stitches. "She hasn't screamed."

"So that shit doesn't count then," Sin grunted.

"It counts, and Asher is a lucky mother fucker. We're lucky because he's lucky." Stitches sat back and ran his fingers through his black hair. "We win, right? We said get her to talk or scream. This counts, right?"

I looked to Church who wore a frown.

"It doesn't count," Sin said again. "It has to come out of her mouth. She did communicate, but it wasn't actual words you could hear. Asylum will argue it, so let's just call it as it is. Not enough." He looked relieved, which confused me.

Church let out a breath. "Sin's right. She didn't speak it. That doesn't mean she isn't going to because if she did that, it means there's hope for more. Plenty more. So let's take that shit and run with it. We pushed her and that wasn't her limit. I say we push more." He looked at each of us in turn.

"Fuck yeah," Stitches said. "I'm all for it."

Sin shrugged. "Whatever."

Church looked to me. "Asher?"

"Yes," I said in a soft voice.

And maybe I'd just signed her death warrant, but I was desperate for more of her.

That said a hell of a lot.

SIRENA

"Today we're going to read Genesis," Sully said as he settled behind his desk. "I thought the story of origin would be of use to you. I sat around contemplating what I could use to get through to you. I figured reminding you of your roots would be a great way to start our evening."

I swallowed and stared straight ahead.

He seemed content in my nonverbal answer because his voice began droning as he started his reading.

I hadn't had any interaction with the watchers since Ashes left me at my dorm. It had been days now. I hadn't broken anything off with Bryce because what would I do? Tell him we couldn't be friends anymore? And how would I tell him that when I didn't even speak? Unless I could write it on his palm like I had Ashes, but that didn't seem right.

I breathed out and focused on Sully's droning voice. The last thing I wanted was to be beaten again. My body was still sore from the last time. Luckily, his brand of medicine didn't leave me with a whole lot of marks. Just ugly memories.

Regardless, I couldn't stop my mind from wandering back to the night with the watchers. The way Church's mouth felt on my heat.

How Stitches kissed me. The way Sin touched me, hatred warring in his eyes with another emotion I couldn't place.

I swallowed and ran my hands down my skirt.

"Your assignment this week will be to write me a paper on your beginnings," Sully said. "Tell me about your early life. Where you were born, siblings, favorite thing to do as a child. Think you can handle that?"

I stared back at him. Our hour was up. It had flown by, and I hadn't been hurt.

"I'll take your silence as a yes." He got to his feet. If I had to guess, I'd say he looked distracted and wanted me gone, which was completely fine by me.

I stood and followed him to the door.

"You will have your paper on my desk by Monday morning. No exceptions."

I stepped out of the room, and the door closed on me. A breath of relief rushed from my lungs, and I darted away in case he had second thoughts. I was nearly to my locker to pick up a few things when I was shoved hard from the back.

My face smacked hard against my locker door, making my ears ring from the impact. The taste of blood met my tongue.

I turned to see who had attacked me only to find myself face to face with Melanie and Tasha.

I stared up at them as I shrank as far back as I could into my locker.

"Listen you fugly, little bitch," Melanie started, her eyes flashing with malice as she jammed her manicured finger hard into my chest. "Stay *the fuck* away from the watchers. They were claiming me. *I'm* theirs, not your fucking weird, disabled ass. If I catch you near my guys again, I swear I'll make you pay. Smacking your head on your locker will be the least of your worries. Tasha and I are going all in with them. We don't need you to ruin it."

She fisted my hair and slammed me back into the locker so hard my vision blurred from smacking my head.

"I'm *not* playing." She snarled in my face before she backed away from me as I wiped at my nose and saw the blood on my shaking fingers

Ah, so that's where the blood taste was coming from.

"You're a disgusting freak with your weirdo eyes and the fact you don't talk," Tasha added, giving me a hard glare as she took her turn to shove me. "Stay with your own kind or get buried, you creepy bitch."

They turned and walked away from me, hips swinging. I stood trembling, staring after them. They rounded the corner and were gone, but I hadn't moved, my body still quaking from the encounter.

"Hey, you OK?" Seth's deep voice called out. "Rinny?"

Shit.

I turned abruptly, putting my back to him as he stopped and stood behind me. I still suspected he had something to do with Danny getting hurt.

"Sirena."

Breathe. Just breathe. You're safe here. He can't touch you here. You're going to be OK. You won't die today by his hand. Not in the hallway. Breathe. One... two... three...

He grabbed my arm and spun me roughly so I was facing him. I didn't even realize I was crying until he reached out and thumbed the tears from my cheeks. His lips parted and his brows crinkled. A tic went off near his eye as he tilted his head and brushed his fingers through the blood on my face.

I swallowed hard, my lip trembling, my chest aching as he stared at the blood on his hands.

Please, Seth. Don't hurt me again. I wanted to scream it at him. I wanted to run. I wanted to hide. I wanted to be free from this nightmare.

"Who did this to you?" he asked softly as he rubbed my blood between his fingers, a mad glint in his blue eyes. "Who made you bleed?"

I continued to stare at him, my head spinning as I attempted to slow my breathing.

Help. Help. HELP! I opened my mouth to scream it, but the words weren't there.

"Fuck," he snarled. He reached forward and cradled my face between his hands. "Talk to me, Rinny. It's me. It's Seth. Your Seth. *Your best friend.* Please fucking remember what we had." He stepped closer so his warm breath feathered across my face. "I've never forgotten."

I closed my eyes, tears streaming down my cheeks, as he continued to cradle my face.

"I've missed you. I have so much time to make up to you. So much to share with you. Fuck, you're so beautiful even when you're bleeding. Maybe even more so," he whispered in a hoarse voice. "Come with me. I'll take care of you. No one will ever hurt you again. I promise."

I wept harder, silently, at his words. I remembered his promises. I fucking remembered all of them.

"Angel," Stitches called out.

I kept my eyelids squeezed tightly as heavy footsteps approached. Seth's hands fell away from me only to be replaced by warm arms that I knew had to be Stitches's. I collapsed against his chest, clinging to him.

His deep voice rumbled against my ear as he spoke. "Get the fuck away from her," he said in a dangerous voice.

"You don't tell me what the fuck to do," Seth shot back. "She belongs to me."

"The fuck she does. She clearly doesn't want anything to do with you. Get the fuck out of my sight before bad shit happens," Stitches returned, clutching me tightly to his body.

"We had a deal, Malachi."

"We do," Stitches snarled, his typical upbeat personality not shining through. Only darkness emanated from him. "And you're losing. So fuck off."

Seth let out a soft laugh. "I almost just won."

I had no idea what the hell they were talking about, but I honestly didn't give a shit. I just wanted Seth to go away.

"He's gone, angel," Stitches murmured moments later, backing away so he could take my face in his hands and angle my head up. "Open your eyes."

I snapped my eyes open and stared up at him. His dark hair had fallen forward, and a look of concern swept over his features.

"Why the fuck are you bleeding? Did he do this? Did Cain fucking do this to you?" He pulled away from me, but I reached for him and twisted my fingers in his now blood smeared white uniform button down.

He gripped my face tightly. "Did he do this, Sirena?"

I sucked in gasping breaths before giving the slightest shake of my head.

He studied me for a moment before he sighed. "I don't suppose you'll tell me who it was either, huh?"

I bowed my head as he released me. I felt empty in his absence, something that confused me. He reached for my hand and tugged me from my locker without a word. I followed along, keeping my head down, aware of the drying blood on my face and lips.

Even if I could talk, I didn't need to ask where we were going. He was taking me back to the watchers' house. He didn't say a word to me the entire walk there. When we reached the house, he flung the front door open and hauled me through and pushed me down onto the couch.

Judging by the silence, no one was home. Stitches stomped away from me, and I heard him rustling around in the kitchen for a moment before the sound of running water met my ears. A moment later, he was kneeling in front of me and pressing a warm rag to my face as he cleaned me.

Stunned, I sat still, letting him take care of me. If I wasn't experiencing it, I might have thought I was dreaming. I didn't think Malachi Wolfe had a compassionate enough bone in his body to wipe the blood from my face.

"If Church gets home and sees you a mess like this, he will kill someone. Doesn't even have to be the person who did this. He'll kill someone just to prove a point," Stitches murmured as he finished wiping my face.

"Lucky for you, pretty girl, he's doing a group therapy session tonight before him and Sin head off campus with Ashes." He grabbed an ice pack and wrapped it in a tea towel before he pressed it to my nose. "I was supposed to go too, but I'll stay behind with you. Keep you safe," his voice became gruff as his Adam's apple bobbed in his throat.

Keep me safe. But who would keep me safe from him?

†

STITCHES WAS RIGHT when he said he'd stay behind. I guessed that meant I'd be staying with him while the guys left. He'd sent off a text telling them apparently because no one came back for him.

"Do you want something to eat?" He moved off the couch where we'd been sitting for hours watching TV.

My stomach growled in response, making him chuckle. He rattled around in the kitchen for a few minutes before the smell of pizza filled the air. When he came back into the room, he was holding a bottle of water. He twisted the cap off and handed it to me.

I sipped it nervously, noting his eyes were locked on my every movement.

"We can watch something different if you're not into action movies," he said, taking the water from me when I'd finished. He capped it and put it on the glass coffee table in front of us and grabbed the remote. "You want to watch a chick flick? Ashes probably has something on the DVR," he muttered, thumbing through shows.

He settled on Legally Blonde, a movie Cady adored, before he got up and rustled around in the kitchen some more. The smell of butter and popcorn filled the air before the popping of kernels met my ears. I sat watching the opening credits before he returned with a bowl of popcorn and sat down beside me again and draped his arm over the back of the couch. He stuffed a fistful of popcorn into his mouth.

"Have some," he said, glancing over at me.

I was simply too nervous to reach over and get some, so sensing that, he took a piece in his hand and turned to me.

"Open, angel," he said.

I hesitated for a moment before parting my lips for him. He placed the popcorn inside my mouth and smiled.

"I'll keep feeding you if you want," he said. "I like watching you eat. Probably speaks volumes about my mental state, huh?" He let out a chuckle and grabbed another piece of popcorn. I opened my mouth, and he placed it inside, his eyes locked on my mouth as I chewed.

I followed his hand with my eyes and watched him grab a third piece. I thought he was going to give it to me, but he placed it on his lips and raised his brows at me.

He wanted me to take it from him.

My pulse roared in my ears. This was a test. Would he give me an occurrence if I didn't do it?

He let the popcorn fall into his mouth and chewed.

"We're going to do that again, angel. This time, you're going to take the popcorn off my lips with your lips," he said, confirming what I thought. "If you're brave enough to."

I swallowed hard as he put the popcorn on his lips. I twisted my fingers nervously in my lap.

Just do it. You've already kissed him before. Besides, Stitches is a good kisser. His lips are soft. Maybe he'll kiss you again.

But what if. . .

No what ifs. Just be brave for once in your life and take a chance!

I leaned forward and brushed my lips against his as I took the popcorn from him. He immediately threaded his fingers through my hair and pressed his lips against mine as I furiously tried to swallow the popcorn, a feat I was proud of doing. He chuckled softly against my lips as he deepened the kiss, his other hand moving to my waist as he hauled me closer to him.

What was happening? Was I doing this? Was I really going to make out with Malachi Wolfe?

This wasn't like me. I was terrified of men. But these men. . .these insane men who brought me to the edge of fear and hauled me back made me want more. I couldn't explain it. It still terrified me, but I was quickly becoming a crazed addict around them.

Stitches's tongue slid along mine as he prodded my lips open, his kiss growing fiercer.

"I could kiss you all night." He breathed out against my lips before pecking my mouth again. "Angel, you're an enchantress." His lips met mine again, our tongues dancing along one another's.

I jerked away from him as the timer on the pizza went off.

"Hold that thought," he murmured, getting to his feet and going into the kitchen. He banged around in there for a moment before he returned to me and held his hand out.

"Come here."

I stared at his hand for a moment before sliding mine into it, not knowing where this was leading and a little scared of the fact.

He brought me to the second room down the first floor hallway and led me inside.

His bedroom.

Panic clawed at my chest, but he towered over me and walked me backwards to his bed until the backs of my legs hit the edge of his mattress and I fell back onto my ass.

"I'm going to be right back. We'll watch the movie in here. Don't move." He cradled my face for a moment before he left.

I swallowed and looked around. Stitches's room was a typical bedroom. Bed. Desk. Chair. Dresser. Dark blue walls. Large TV. An adjoining bathroom. Closet. Car and motorcycle magazines. His walls were bare though with the exception of a shovel he had hanging on the wall.

My breathing picked up as I stared at it. I twisted my fingers in his blue duvet, my lips going numb as I raked in my breath too fast for my body to handle.

A murder weapon. A fucking shovel to my head. The dark. The fucking dark.

Stitches came into the room with the pizza and drinks and placed them on his desk.

"I made just cheese because I figured that was safe. It's a frozen one, so I hope you're OK with that," he said, turning to me. He took me in for all of a moment before he crossed the room in quick strides, his hands landing on either side of my face as he blocked my view of the shovel.

"What's going on?" he demanded softly, his brows crinkled. I shook, my breathing still ragged. "What the hell?"

He looked over his shoulder at the shovel and blinked several times before his hands fell away from my face. He stalked to the shovel and snagged it off the wall. I flinched back and went to my side on his bed and curled into a tight ball, my eyelids squeezed closed as I waited for the impending THWAK of the shovel on my head.

I heard a door open and close before Stitches's warm hands were on me.

"Hey. Sirena. Listen. Hey." He pried my hands away from my head and forced my face upward. "Open your eyes. It's gone. I got rid of it. At least I think I did. I assumed it was the shovel."

I breathed out and peered through my lids to see he was telling the truth. The shovel was gone.

He frowned as he stared down at me. "You're a mess," he whispered. "Why the fuck do I love that about you?"

I breathed out, feeling slightly calmer. His words sent a flurry of emotion through my body. These feelings were so foreign. I never imagined I'd have an inkling of feeling for a man after what happened to me, or what was continuing to happen to me, but there I was actually feeling something that confused me.

"Was it a shovel that hurt you?" he asked gently.

I didn't answer him as he swept his fingers through my hair.

"I spiraled last year," he continued softly. "Went off my meds. I was stressed out. My mom. . .she tried to contact me. I haven't seen her in years. I grew up bouncing around in foster homes until Dante's dad took me in. You'd think that would be the fairytale ending for a poor, abused kid from the streets, but it wasn't. It only fed the monster inside me because Dante was a lot like me. I was Dante's gift because his father knew how twisted he was. He wanted to keep him in check. He thought having a brother might help him. I think he knew it made both of us worse, but in a good way."

I stared up at him, taking in his glittering eyes and the serene look on his face.

"I never knew my dad. He could have been anyone. Mom was an addict who let men into the house. Those men would beat me and do whatever they wanted to me as payment so she could get high. I was currency. When I was younger, one of the guys tried to gut me with a kitchen knife. Took forty stitches to piece me back together. Ashes gave me the nickname Stitches after he saw me in the hospital. It stuck and worked out because I get in fights and people usually end up with stitches too."

My heart clenched at his words.

"I was supposed to be the companionship Dante needed since he has his own issues. And I was. We're best friends. Brothers. Sin and Ashes came into the picture when we were just toddlers. You see, I lived near the guys. We grew up together. Same school, despite the wealth Dante had. I guess growing up near him helped with my way into Dante's family. I wasn't a stranger. Before Dante's mother died, she'd take us for ice cream. I think we both got worse after her death. All of us have issues, so we just fit." He gave me a shaky smile for a moment before it faded away. "I inherited money last year from my grandfather. He hated my mother. Must have hated me too, or so I thought, since he left me with that bitch. But he passed away and left me cash and his house in Traverse City. She heard about it. She contacted me. Told me all sorts of shit I should have known better than to listen to. I craved my mother, Sirena." His eyes locked on mine as I watched him. He continued to rake his fingers through my hair as his leg bounced.

"She has dark hair like you," he murmured. He gripped my hair tightly at the roots and gave it a tug. I winced at the pain that brought, but he was quick to loosen his hold. "You remind me of her. She was beautiful too. She used to be a good mother. You see, I was born addicted to heroin. I was taken away. She went into rehab. She came out and raised me like a mother should until she slipped and fell right back into the pit she'd been struggling to get out of. I was six."

I swallowed as a muscle thrummed along his jaw.

"I gave her the money she asked for. Few thousand. He left me plenty, so it wasn't like I was hard up from giving her the cash, plus Dante's family is loaded. I haven't gone without in a long time. At least in the money department." He shook his head, his fingers still in my hair. "But she fucking left me again. Promised she was going to set something up for us so I could have her back. . .she fucking lied to me. She lied to me, Sirena. I lost it. I was already under a lot of pressure with other shit going on in my life. She was the last straw. I dug for three days straight in my mania with that shovel. The guys kept it because I dug enough for the pool Dante had put in. Gifted it to me when I got out of *the hole*." He let out another soft laugh. "It's my participation trophy."

He finally stopped touching me and got to his feet. I watched as he went to his desk and pulled open a drawer and dug out a bottle of pills. He opened the container and poured a pill onto his hand and tossed it into his mouth before uncapping a bottle of water and swallowing it down. I watched, fascinated, as he medicated himself.

"Lithium. It seems to be the only thing that keeps my shit together these days." He placed two pieces of pizza on paper plates and brought them back to the bed and settled in beside me. I sat up and looked over at him. He offered me a smile and the plate of pizza. I took it with shaky hands.

"You make me feel better," he said softly. "Probably shouldn't give away my secrets, but there they are. I know we haven't spent a lot of time together or anything, but this is the first time in my life I've actually felt anything for a girl. I typically just fuck them and never have feelings. Never connected before. Wanted to, but shit. It wasn't in my heart. My head. I don't know." He paused for a moment and tucked a strand of hair behind my ear. "But you? You brought something to life inside me, and I don't want to let it go. So I guess that's me telling you I really fucking like you, Sirena." He bit into his pizza and chewed quickly as I stared at him, my heart thudding hard at his words.

"Eat," he said softly. "Dante will kill me if he finds out I had you here and didn't feed you."

I looked back to my plate and lifted the pizza and took a bite of it and chewed. I wanted to ask him what that meant. Maybe he was a mind reader because he answered me without the question.

"Dante doesn't know you're here. No one does. If he finds out, he might kill me. He was already suspicious because I didn't want to go off campus with them tonight. But you're mine too, so I'm rolling with it. He already kissed you and tasted you. As long as I don't go further than that, it'll be OK." He had a faraway look on his face, like he was trying to convince himself of what he was doing was acceptable. "Good thing you can't tell, right?" He looked back to me and grinned before stuffing the pizza into his mouth and hitting play on Legally Blonde.

I blew out a breath and relaxed against his pillow, having seen a different side to him tonight.

One I didn't entirely hate. One that I was drawn to and could cause me a hell of a lot of trouble if I didn't watch myself.

Because I realized deep down, I really fucking liked Malachi Wolfe too.

SIN

I leaned against the front of the car beside Church as we watched Ashes set the contents of the metal barrels on fire. Ashes was a different person when he got to light the fires. Every week we'd leave campus to come to this abandoned warehouse on the edge of town so he could set shit on fire in the safety of the metal containers. I knew it was just a taste of what he really wanted—like burning the entire fucking place down—but it was enough to hold him over until next week.

"Why do you think Stitches didn't want to come tonight?" I asked as I watched Ashes drop more shit into the barrel and grin at the flames, his lighter clenched tightly in his fist.

"Specter." He grunted.

I figured as much. The bitch really was working her way beneath my friend's skins. I was the only one fighting it. I already knew what would happen if I let her in. She'd set my world ablaze like Ashes did with his barrels. Kissing her was all I needed to do to confirm everything was fucked. I had to distance myself. In fact, I knew my friends well enough to know this could break them if shit went south. And it always did with chicks. ALWAYS. I needed to do something to get a handle on the situation. We didn't need her. It didn't matter how much we wanted her, it had to stop.

"Are you sure he stayed for her?"

Church didn't look at me. With his arms folded over his chest, he continued to watch Ashes throw shit into the fire. "No. I just have my suspicions."

"And if he's with her?"

"Then I'll kick his fucking ass." Church finally looked over at me, his moss green eyes glittering. "I get all her firsts. So if he fucks her, I'll kill him. If he gets her on her knees to suck his cock, I'll kill him. I might even kill her too. Or just kill her and make him watch."

I scoffed, hating the venom in Church's voice. Hating the pain I heard in it. Sirena brought out the emotions in us that didn't need to be brought to the surface. We were dangerous as it was. Add in emotions and the world was fucked. I definitely needed to put a stop to this. Church and Malachi were brothers. Adopted, but just the same. Hell, we were all brothers. I wouldn't have another bitch come into our lives and tear us apart. Been there. Done that with Isabella. I'd already been stupid to kiss Sirena. To touch her. *To fucking feel.*

Enough was enough.

"We need to end this, Church."

"No," he said softly. "I'm not ending it. I want her. I'll have her."

"She's going to tear us the fuck apart—"

"She won't."

"She already is," I shot back. "You just said you'd kill Stitches if he's with her. If he touches her. You know damn well he will. We made a vow we'd only be with girls together after Isabella. We didn't vow to fall in love with them—"

"That hasn't changed," he snapped, glaring at me. "The only thing I want is to be her first. I want to say when and where. I'm in control. That's it."

"You realize how fucked up you sound? You can't control everything."

"I can and will," he said, looking back at Ashes who was now dousing the flames with gasoline. The flames arched into the sky as he whooped and danced around the barrels. I let out a sigh.

"You like her too," Church finally said.

"No, I really fucking don't. She's beautiful. I get the appeal. I just don't want to feel the shit I feel. I don't want to get attached. I don't want to fall down after I worked so hard to climb out of that deep, dark fucking chasm, Dante. I'm asking that we just walk away. Finish off her occurrences and let her be a fucking zero to us."

"I'm not letting her go," he said, not bothering to look at me. "I'll never let her go."

The soft orange glow from Ashes's flames danced over Church's face as he stared straight ahead, his body tensed, and a muscle popping along his jaw.

Fuck it. I wouldn't be able to get him away from her. And if I couldn't get him away from her, that meant getting Ashes and Stitches away would be just as hard.

I guessed I had to take matters into my own hands.

SIRENA

I awoke tangled around Stitches's body to the sound of yelling and crashing. I snapped my eyes open to see a really angry looking Church barreling toward us from the doorway.

Stitches immediately shoved me behind him and got to his feet. He'd removed his shirt sometime in the night, so his tattooed torso and jagged scar were on display. A large wolf's head in black and white was tatted on his back, covering the entirety. It was a beautiful piece, but now wasn't the time to be admiring artwork.

Church's fist connected with Stitches's face, sending him stumbling back. Stitches shook off the hit and charged forward, his fist smashing into Church's jaw. I scrambled away and fell off the bed and hid on the other side, searching for a way out as they cursed and beat on one another.

"Stop! Knock it off!" Ashes's voice called out, followed by more footsteps as I caught sight of Sin's black boots enter the room.

"What the fuck," Sin shouted, getting into the fray.

"You know the fucking rules," Church yelled, the sound of another hit connecting sounding out. "She's mine! She's fucking mine first!"

"I didn't fucking touch her," Stitches snarled back. "I kissed her. That was it! But fuck you. You aren't the boss of me or any of us—"

"You know damn well I'm who leads," Church said. "If you don't fucking like it, you're free to leave, *brother.*"

"This ends now," Sin said. "Where the fuck is she? Sirena? You mute bitch, where are you?"

I scrambled beneath the bed, my heart in my throat as Sin stomped forward to try to find me.

"Don't call her names, prick," Ashes called out. "I swear to fuck, Sinclair—"

Sin's hand wrapped around my ankle, and he yanked me hard. I clawed at the hardwood floor, but I was easily removed and brought out.

Immediately, Sin reached down and snagged me off the floor by my hair and hauled me to my feet. I gasped at the pain his tight hold brought. Without an ounce of care, he threw me roughly to the floor in the center of the group. I hit the floor hard, my knees connecting with the hardwood with a loud thud. Tears stung my eyes at the pain that shot through my body.

I shook on my hands and knees before the four of them.

Church squatted in front of me and tilted my chin up. "Did you let Malachi fuck you?"

I sobbed silently, wanting to get the hell out of there.

"I didn't fuck her," Stitches snarled. "Fucking *asshole.*"

"I'm not asking you. I'm asking her. Did he fuck you, specter?"

When I continued to cry, he let out a snarl of frustration and took my face in his hands and shook me so hard I thought my brain would disconnect. He released me, and I fell forward. In an instant, he was behind me and pulling me upward to my knees so his hand was wrapped around my throat and my back was to his front.

I fought against him as he moved his hand beneath my skirt and ran it up my thighs to my heat. He tightened his hold so much that my breathing came in sharp, wheezing gasps. I stilled against him, knowing if I fought, he probably would choke me out.

His hand moved beneath my panties, and he plunged his finger into my heat. I opened my mouth at the painful intrusion.

He grunted, his hold so tight now I absolutely couldn't breathe. He withdrew his fingers and sucked them into his mouth as my vision dotted with sparkles.

"I told you I didn't fuck her," Stitches said softly.

Church released me, and Ashes caught me as I fell forward. I shoved him away as I tried to suck in my breath, my pulse thundering in my ears.

He was crazy. He was really going to kill me for no damn reason. I'd been insane to think I was safe with him. Or any of them because they let him do it.

"Heaven, don't," Ashes called out, the smell of smoke reaching my nostrils. He smelled like he'd been in a fire.

I shoved at him again, making him hiss. Church's hands wound around my waist, and he pulled me to my feet. I turned in his arms and smacked him as hard as I could across his face, my chest heaving as I struggled to catch my breath.

"Are you mad?" he asked, slowing turning his head back to face me.

I glared at him, shaking.

"I'm fucking mad too," he snapped. His hand caught my throat again and this time he lifted me off my feet and shoved me against the wall. I clawed at his wrists, kicking my swinging feet as he held me in place.

"You don't stay with anyone unless I say you do. You don't fucking kiss anyone unless I say you can. You don't come into my fucking house without me being here and crawl into bed with my. Fucking. *Brother*." His face was so close to mine I could feel the warmth of his breath. "You fucking do it again, I'll tear your heart out and fuck it while you die watching. You think you can't breathe now? Just wait."

He released me, and I slid down the wall to my knees and sucked in more breath.

"You're a fucking asshole," Ashes said, shoving Church aside as he backed away. "The fuck is the matter with you? You hurt her!"

He didn't answer. He stormed out of the room, leaving me behind with the guys.

"Get her the fuck out of here," Sin said. His gaze fixed on me. "Go back to Bryce. None of us are good for you, Siren. You'll only meet your end with us."

He walked out of the room, leaving me with Ashes and Stitches. I pushed Ashes's hand away as I got to my feet.

"Heaven, please—" Ashes reached for me, but I backed away to the door. A look of pain swept over his face.

"Don't. OK? Let me walk you back."

I reached the door and turned and rushed through it. Luckily, no one was in the living room. Not that it would have mattered. There was no way in hell I'd stop.

"Sirena, wait!" Stitches shouted, following me into the living room.

I didn't stop. I slammed the front door behind me and ran as fast as my feet would carry me away from them.

SIRENA

A week passed without contact from the watchers. When Ashes turned up at my door on that Saturday night, I didn't answer it. I didn't want to see him. I didn't want to see any of them.

My neck was bruised from Church's hands. My eyes were bloodshot. My knees hurt. Lesson learned. I was fortunate enough that Sully was gone, so I didn't need to do my special therapy session with him.

Instead, I sat in my room alone after having brushed off Bryce for the third time that week. I didn't even bother eating lunch with him. I was avoiding him as much as I was avoiding the watchers. When he came to my door, I wouldn't answer it.

I sat alone and painted most of the time I was alone. Or I cried.

The following Friday, I sat in Sully's office and stared straight ahead as he commended me on writing such a good paper on my beginnings.

"Very detailed. I am curious. Where is your father?"

I said nothing.

"Jerry tells me he doesn't even call. Do you think maybe he knew you were unwell and didn't want to deal with you? They say some have a sixth sense. Perhaps he knew what a burden you'd be on him and cut his losses. Although, I do hear your sister is just as beautiful as you are."

I snapped my attention to him, his mention of Cady sending anger reeling through me.

"Ah, your sister is the way in, is it?" He chuckled softly from behind his desk. "Jerry says she's troublesome. He's considering sending her here. A year younger than you, right?"

I could tear the skin from his face. I envisioned myself smashing his head in with the lamp on his desk, his brains and blood spewing out of him like a goddamn volcano.

"The demons have you again, child?" he asked in a silky voice. "You're thinking impure thoughts, aren't you?"

He rose from his seat and approached me. He moved behind me and placed his hands on my shoulders. I stiffened beneath his cold, rough touch. When he leaned down to speak into my ear, my breath caught in my chest.

"You're not a child anymore though, are you? Eighteen now. Stayed in your room and didn't celebrate it. Alone." His hot breath blew across my jaw as I sat frozen beneath his hold.

"I've heard the watchers have taken an interest in you," he continued. "I don't get wrapped up with them because of a deal I have with Dante Church's father. They get free reign here. That doesn't extend to you, Miss Lawrence. You do not belong to them. You belong to me. To this school. I will let them play their games because I know they'll break you for me. That's when I'll sweep in and save your soul. Just like God intended." He released me, and I breathed out.

"We're done for the day. Today's assignment is self-reflection. I want you to think about exactly who you are, Sirena, and what you want to be. Then I want you to write it all down for me and turn it in next week." He walked back to his desk. "Go. You're dismissed."

I scurried out of the main office like my heels were set on fire and ran straight into Ashes. He caught me at the waist and looked beyond me for a moment before locking eyes with me.

"Hey, Heaven," he murmured. "What are you doing in the office?"

I shoved him away, but he held tight.

"Don't do this. Please," he said, his voice shaking. "I want to talk to you. I won't hurt you. I swear I won't. I will leave when I'm done if you want."

I swallowed as I stared up at him. He smelled of smoke and a rich cologne. For some reason, his scent calmed me.

He backed away and took my hand in his and gave it a gentle tug. Reluctantly, I followed along. We passed Seth along the way. I quickly ducked my head before I could see his expression.

"Sirena?" Bryce called out.

Shit. I really couldn't do this today. All I wanted was to be left alone. By everyone.

"Hey, come on," Bryce shouted. I thought he'd stop, but he didn't. He got in front of us and halted the journey.

"Sirena, what are you doing? Why haven't I seen you? You're avoiding me," he said. I swallowed hard and took in the hurt expression on his face as his gaze traveled to Ashes's hand clutched around mine.

"Oh," he said softly, backing away.

No. No! I wanted to scream it from the rooftops. This wasn't our "break up". This was just a damn mess I needed to get out of.

"Sorry," Ashes offered. He at least sounded it.

"Yeah. No. I get it. Nothing great lasts forever. Friendship. Love. Yeah. I got it." Bryce cleared his throat and backed away. I tried to tear my hand away from Ashes's to go to Bryce, but he held fast.

Bryce. Don't. Don't go! Just. . . shit! Wait. I have to explain. I can't explain. God, help me!

He turned and walked away, his head down. My heart cracked as I watched him leave.

"It's better this way. Trust me," Ashes said softly. "Rather it be me and you who broke the news to him than Church. You already know how destructive he can get. I wasn't going to be able to hold him off on you about Andrews forever."

I knew he was right. Bryce would be safer without me. It still fucking hurt though.

But there was no me and the watchers. They'd just left me completely alone. I figured that meant something.

Ashes led me to my dorm, thankfully, because there was no way in hell I'd go back to his place. He'd have to carry me if that were the case, and I wasn't so sure I wouldn't bite, kick, and punch the entire way.

We stepped inside my room, and he closed the door behind us.

"Wow," he murmured looking at all my paintings. I'd long run out of canvas and was using sheets of notebook paper and anything I could get. My paints were nearly gone, so I'd taken to sketching.

My face heated. I'd have thrown everything out if I thought I was going to have company. I watched as Ashes stepped forward and stared at a portrait of him I'd painted. His hair was a mess. There was a smear of soot on his cheek. I captured the light perfectly in his eyes with twin flames.

I watched as his Adam's apple bobbed in his throat as he reached out and ran his fingers along the soot I'd painted. The small burn scar at his hairline.

"Sirena, you're an amazing artist," he said, his gaze roaming along my walls to my other paintings. There was one of Bryce. Each of the watchers. Abstract work. He stopped at the painting on canvas of a little girl holding a white mouse and staring up at a boy.

"Asylum," he murmured, drinking in the picture. "*Seth.* You knew each other for a long time, huh?"

I turned away from him and sat on my bed. He joined me a moment later. We were both quiet as we sat there.

"Church fucked up. He knows he did. He's sorry in his own messed up way."

I sat stiffly.

"Heaven, we're all fucked up, OK? He overreacted. I'm not going to cover for him. He's violent and possessive. Incredibly jealous. I can't just say it's his mental shit and gloss over it. What he did to you was wrong. He's aware of it. Him and Stitches aren't talking right now. Hell, none of us really are. We know nothing happened between you and Stitches. He said he kissed you. Nothing else."

I didn't move an inch.

"I'm here on behalf of everyone to offer apologies to you. We didn't let you go. We let you have a break. You still have three occurrences to fill." He cleared his throat as I flinched. "I'd like to fulfill mine tonight."

I jerked away from him and got to my feet. He followed me, watching, assessing, as I paced.

I need to get the hell out of here. I need to run away. I could always just off myself—

Ashes's hands covered mine as he stopped my pacing.

"You're hurting yourself," he whispered, gently unclenching my fists. "You made yourself bleed." He released my hand and ran his thumb along my bottom lip. It was only then that I realized I'd bitten my lip so hard I'd bled.

He cradled my face and tilted my head up so I was staring at him. "My occurrence won't be like theirs. Not tonight. Tonight it's just me and you. Unless you tell me no, then it's you and the watchers. So I'm really hoping I don't have to do that."

Bastard.

He led me back to the bed and pulled me down beside him. "I want my date with you. That's what the occurrence is. I want a night with you."

I blinked at him in surprise.

"I'm really not as bad as you think I am," he said with a laugh. "I mean, I keep some shady friends around, but I love them. They're my family. So what do you say? Me and you. A date. I'll show you how I live."

I hesitated for a moment. As if sensing what I was thinking, he held his palm out to me. I noted the burn scar on his wrist and licked my lips.

"Don't be afraid," he whispered.

I blew out a soft breath and reached for his hand and wrote words onto his palm.

Church will be mad.

He smiled as he took in each letter. "He will be mad. I'm really hoping he is. He won't hurt you this time, though."

You. I wrote on his palm.

"Not me either, heaven. He needs this just as much as the rest of us do. Trust me?" He gave me a sweet, serene look that broke down my carefully erected walls. Ashes was the sweet one. The nice one. Well, maybe not completely nice, but I felt at ease with him.

Maybe this would be a faster way to my ending.

So I wrote a word onto his palm that made him grin.

Yes.

ASHES

I knew what she was thinking without her saying a word as she stared at my motorcycle. Her pretty eyes were rounded as she grimaced down at the sleek black bike. I'd given her time to change and had gone back to the empty house and threw on a pair of jeans, black t-shirt, and my leather jacket before returning to her room to get her.

"I promise you'll be safe," I said, handing her a helmet. With trembling hands, she took the helmet and put it on her head. I chuckled, taking her in. She was so tiny and delicate. Having Church lose his shit on her had really taken its toll on all of us. No one was talking much, especially to Church. He'd taken to holing up in his room and hardly coming out. When he was out, he was angry and throwing shit.

I knew he wanted to apologize even if he didn't know he wanted to apologize. It was eating him alive. Stitches wasn't his typical lighthearted self either. He grunted a lot and stared at his phone more than anything. And Sin. He almost seemed happy. That worried me the most because Sin was hardly ever happy. His moods stayed pretty even with his melancholy. With Sirena out of the picture for the last week and a half, he wasn't stomping around pissed off. He even tried to make dinner and get everyone together. It only worked for a few minutes before Church and Stitches got into it again, and Church threw his dish of spaghetti against the dining room wall and stormed out.

I reached out and fixed her helmet and tightened it on her.

"You look really pretty," I said, enjoying the way her cheeks reddened. I couldn't help but take in how she was dressed either. She looked completely different without her school uniform. Her ripped skinny jeans hugged her body in a way that made me want to pant. The pink V-neck gave me just enough of a glimpse of her cleavage to make me want to bite my damn knuckles to keep from touching her.

I swung my leg over the bike and turned back to her. She hesitated for a moment before she followed.

"Students aren't allowed off campus. Except us," I said. "And since you're with me, that means you. Our protection extends to you, heaven."

She shifted behind me.

"Hold on." I took her hands and wrapped them around my midsection. "Ready?"

She trembled against my back. I started the engine, throttling it to make it purr beneath us. She flinched against me. I reached down and patted her hands, which were twisted tightly in my black t-shirt before giving them a gentle squeeze.

We raced out of the parking lot, her hold on me tight. She pressed her body against mine, her warmth radiating through me.

Yes. Definitely heaven.

I took it easy, enjoying just cruising with her on the back. We took some winding roads along the lake before jetting off outside of town to my favorite place in the world.

Pictured Rocks.

It was cut along Lake Superior. Gorgeous miles of scenery and a blue lake. Thick trees. She'd love the ride. I knew she would. Her hold on me lessened as she grew curious. I smirked, knowing I was making her feel that way.

I pulled off down a trail I knew all too well and rode slowly through until I got to the spot where I could go no further. I parked the bike and cut the engine before hopping off and grabbing a pack from my saddle bag and offered her my hand.

She took it tentatively. I helped her take her helmet off and placed it on the bike before reaching back out to her and fixing her hair.

"Perfect," I said, offering her what I hoped was a reassuring smile. Taking her hand, I led her through the forest. We stopped when we reached a cliff overlooking the water. Her lips parted as she took it in.

"It's my favorite spot," I said, opening the pack and pulling out a blanket. I laid it over the ground, and she sat on it, her eyes never deviating from the water. I grabbed out two bottles of water and some granola bars and sat beside her and offered her one of each. She took them. As beautiful as the scenery was, it was nothing compared to her.

Finally, she tore her gaze away from everything and looked back at me.

"Do you like it?" I asked, holding my hand out to her.

Yes.

Her delicate fingers traced the words onto my palm.

"I thought you might. Sorry about the dinner. I'd have made us a candlelight picnic, but I tend to get carried away with fire," I said, giving her a smile.

She cocked her head at me, taking me in for a moment before she traced letters onto my palm.

Thank you.

"You're welcome," I said, brushing her hair away from her face.

She turned back to the water, and I followed, breathing in the fresh air. We sat like that until the sky turned a deep shade of orange, the setting sun casting its colors across the blue sky.

For the first time ever, a tiny smile graced her lips. My heart raced as I took her in. I took my phone out and snapped the photo of her without her even acknowledging me. She was far too lost in the beauty in front of her.

"You're cold," I murmured, noting the goosebumps on her arms.

She finally turned to me and crinkled her brows before looking down to her arms. Immediately, I took off the leather jacket I had on and wrapped it around her. She snuggled into it before laying on her back and staring up at the sky.

I couldn't help myself. I took more pictures of her.

I paused when she finally focused on me. I snapped the picture and laid beside her, staring up at the darkening sky.

"I've always loved fire," I said softly as we laid beside one another. "I love watching the sky change here because it reminds me of fire. So many oranges and reds." I brushed my fingers against hers on the blanket. "I had a sister. A twin. Her name was Abigail. We grew up in Detroit, but my parents had a summer home on Lake Michigan near Petoskey. We were ten when she died." I breathed out, never having told anyone but the watchers my story. But I wanted to share it with her. I wanted her to know me. She needed to know the monster I was. She didn't move. She simply continued to stare at the sky.

"One summer, we went to our summer home. Abby was so excited. Hell, I was too. I'd been getting into a fair amount of trouble at school. I'd set a trash bin on fire for the third time and had been expelled. My parents were at the end of their ropes. I was doing all sorts of bad shit. I didn't know why I was doing it, just that I couldn't stop myself. I always scared Abby, but no matter what, she stood by my side." I swallowed before continuing. "It was late. We were supposed to be in bed, but I'd spent all day collecting leaves, twigs, and branches. I'd left them near the house. When it got dark out, I went outside after my parents went to bed and took out a lighter I'd stolen from my cousin and lit everything right next to the house on fire. It was fucking beautiful," I said, remembering how quickly it burned. "I watched it until Abby found me. She scolded me as we stomped on the flames, and she dragged me back into the house. Mom and Dad were going to send me away. We both knew it. I needed help."

I closed my eyes briefly before continuing. "We went to bed. A few hours in, I smelled smoke. I got up and couldn't see a damn thing. I could barely breathe. I rushed to Abby's room down the hall. There were flames everywhere. I managed to get inside. I could hear my dad calling for me through the smoke and flames. He tried to get to me first since my room was closer, but I wasn't in there. I was with Abby.

Her room was blocked off by the fire. She was scared and had gotten in her closet. I found her curled up at the bottom. I sat with her, hoping Dad would come. When he didn't, I knew it was up to me. I pulled her out and tried to carry her. She wasn't breathing like she should. I tried *so fucking hard*. She caught fire though."

I stopped my story and looked over to Sirena who had turned her head to stare at me. I couldn't tell what she was thinking as she continued to watch me. The lack of pity on her face strengthened me to finish the tale.

"I managed to get Abby in my arms. I carried her through her room to the window. I busted the window out to get her out. It cut me pretty badly. I hadn't even realized her nightgown had caught my pajamas on fire and that I was burning with her." I turned onto my side to face Sirena. She mirrored my movement and rolled onto her side, her vibrant eyes drinking me in.

"I dropped Abby through the window and jumped out behind her. The fire department was already there, spraying the house. My parents were screaming, and Mom was on her knees as the house engulfed in flames. I came through the night carrying Abby. I collapsed before I made it to my mom and dad. But I saw the look of horror on their faces. They knew it was me. They knew Abby was gone and that it was my fault." My bottom lip trembled, and a tear snaked down my cheek. "I saw the look in their eyes when they realized I was the monster who survived. That Abby, my sweet sister, had been the one to die. She loved to sing and dance. She wanted to be a ballerina. She worked so hard. Always at rehearsals. But when she wasn't, she was with me. She tried to keep me on the straight and narrow. Always saying to me, "Asher, I'm not going to tell on you, but I won't leave you." I didn't leave her either. Not in that fire." I paused and braced myself for the next part. "At Abby's funeral, I tried to crawl into the casket with her. I knocked it over in my struggle to be with her. Her body rolled out. My mother wailed. My father struck me so hard I lost consciousness. She looked so pretty, Sirena. She was in her ballerina outfit. Her favorite pink tutu and leotard. But she was so cold. So fucking cold. It didn't matter how much makeup they used on her, they couldn't cover the burns. Burns that I'd put there."

I closed my eyes for a moment before I forged on. "After Abby's funeral, I was sent away. My mom couldn't look at me. She blamed me. Dad swore they'd come back for me. I bounced through the foster system for a long time before I found a stable enough home. Monica Havers. Her brother was a pyro. He died in one of his fires when they were kids. In a way, we were similar. She got me into Chapel Crest at a young age. I did rounds of therapy and shit for a few years before I got here. I set fire to my school, and it was pretty much the last straw, but here I am." I finished my story. "She didn't abandon me. She tried to help me. I haven't seen or heard from my real parents since they left me with the social worker."

Sirena reached out and thumbed another tear off my cheek that had sneaked out. I closed my eyes, relishing in her warm, tender touch.

Her fingers drifted to my arms where she ran her delicate touch over the burn scars I had from that night. Over the scars from the broken window. The burns were on my chest too, but she didn't need to know that right then. Her fingers drifted to the scar along my hairline.

Then there it was. The pity in her eyes. I reached for her face and cradled it.

"Don't you dare feel bad for me, heaven. I made my own hell. I have the watchers to keep me in line now. I haven't slipped in a long time. They take care of me. They take me off campus to a safe place where I can let loose. Things are better now. *I'm* better. Mostly."

I didn't want to tell her about the night terrors of watching my twin's face melt away or the way she wept my name in that smokey closet until the smoke and flames overtook her and she died in my arms. I didn't want to tell her about the crippling depression or the number of times I tried to kill myself because of the agony I felt inside at what I'd done to Abby.

But her fingers trailed up the jagged scar on my wrist, evidence of the knife I took to it two years ago. Her lips parted as she realized what it meant.

"I haven't tried since," I whispered. "I think about it all the time, but I haven't done it. No one knows about how often I wish I were dead. How I wish I was brave enough to finish the fucking job God forgot to."

She took my hand in hers and traced letters onto it.

Me too.

My heart clenched at those words. I watched as she brought my palm to her mouth and pressed her warm lips against it.

I couldn't help it. I pulled her closer and brushed my lips against hers in a soft, gentle kiss. She melted into it immediately, her tongue tentative as I tasted her. I gathered her closer to my body as I kissed her, getting lost in what was quickly becoming a drug to me. Soft. Warm. Perfect. She tasted so sweet. I knew I'd never get enough of her. When we broke apart, I rested my forehead against hers.

"I hope God forgot about you too, because I need you here with me." I pressed my lips to hers again, meaning everything.

I was selfish like that.

CHURCH

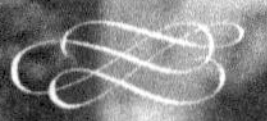

"Where's Ashes?" I demanded, coming into the living room.

"Don't know," Sin said. "I haven't seen him since lunch."

I looked to Stitches who sat staring down at his phone. He was still pissed off at me over attacking him and Sirena in his bedroom. There wasn't shit I could do about it. I wasn't a time traveler.

"Malachi—"

"Fuck off," he muttered, not looking up from his phone.

"Do you know where Ashes is?" I finished.

"I hope he's fucking angel, honestly. I hope he's balls deep, blowing his come all up in her tight pussy. Maybe he'll get her pregnant. Out of all of us, pretty sure Ashes would be the best dad. Not you. You're a prick."

My hands shook as I breathed in and out, the image of Ashes taking my specter's virgin pussy as his own. Even though I knew Ashes probably wouldn't do that even if given the chance, it still didn't help calm me. I was obsessed with having it first. I fell asleep to the image of her pretty pink mound covered in my release. I rubbed it into her skin, watching as she squirmed beneath me, her breasts—

I stopped the thought as my cock began to harden.

I looked out the window. Night had fallen long ago. It wasn't like Ashes to stay out. Last time he did, he'd set fucking Sully's office on fire. We'd caught him and had it put out, but just the same. Sully wasn't too happy.

"I texted him," Sin said. "He's not answering. Maybe he just needs some alone time. I don't hear sirens, so everything must be OK."

I gritted my teeth for a moment before turning and going upstairs to my room. I showered and flopped onto my bed, my mind on specter.

I'd watched her every day since I'd snapped on her. I've never in my life felt regret, but I was pretty sure that was the feeling in my chest. The way her colorful eyes wavered as she stared up at me. The tears. Her trembling lip. Her hands on my wrists as she tried to pry my fingers off her neck. How her body was so shaky as I choked her. The way her breath stuttered out of her as she struggled to breathe.

I loved all of it. And I fucking hated myself for it too.

I'd never hurt my specter enough to kill her. But I was no fool. I knew what I was capable of. But not to her. I'd never hurt her.

Would I?

I certainly didn't want to.

I hated the fucking muddled thoughts in my head. My heart ached because all I wanted was her. And I wanted her to want me too. It was a feeling I'd never had before. I didn't know how to navigate it. I was going crazy as I tried to unpack it all.

The red lights on my clock illuminated the darkness. Minute by minute. I finally glanced to see it was just after one in the morning. I didn't hear Ashes come home, but that didn't mean he didn't sneak in.

I flung my blanket back, already dressed in all black, and made my way to his room. I knocked softly on it, my heart thudding unevenly in my chest. When he didn't answer, I cracked the door open to find his room empty and his bed made.

I swallowed thickly and went downstairs to the front door and slid my shoes on.

"Where are you going?" Sin called through the dark living room. I hadn't even seen the fucking lurker sitting on the couch in the dark.

"To find Ashes. You want to come?"

"No." He took a swallow of whatever he was drinking. I assumed it was alcohol since he'd been drinking every night since Sirena ran out of here.

"We need to make sure he's not doing anything stupid," I said. I cared very much for my brothers. They were the only ones in my life I cared about. Until Sirena arrived. But I cared about her so differently it was frightening.

"He won't kill himself. And even if he decided to, it's been hours. He'd already be dead."

I ground my teeth at the idea of Ashes slipping and bleeding out. I'd already been to that fucking circus.

"Try Sirena's," Sin continued softly before taking another drink.

"Sirena is pissed at all of us—"

"She's pissed at you for choking her. She's pissed at me for the words I said. I very much doubt she's pissed at either Ashes or Stitches enough to ignore them. The difference between the two is that Ashes doesn't mope around. He continues to go for what he wants." Sin fixed me with a look through the darkness. "Try her room. And if he's there, don't do something stupid."

I didn't hesitate. I tugged the door open and disappeared into the night.

So many things went through my head as I ran to Sirena's through the cover of darkness. What if I got there and it was Bryce? What would I do? I told her to get rid of him. I hadn't seen him around her, but I knew if she wouldn't have gotten rid of him then I'd have to do it. What if it was Ashes? What if he fucked her?

Stay calm, Dante. He's your best friend. Even if he did—

No. Fuck that. I'd kick his ass. Might put him out of his misery with her fucking pillow.

My hands were shaking by the time I got to her place. I pulled the master key card out of my wallet and crept into her room.

I stopped at the foot of her bed and stared down at her wrapped in Ashes's arms, both sleeping soundly. Her bedside lamp was on, casting a dull yellow glow on her and him. I swallowed hard and breathed out.

Ashes was still in his street clothes. She was in a tank top. I couldn't see what she had on beneath the blankets though. All I knew was it wasn't the fucking white nightgown I told her to wear. That really pissed me the fuck off.

I watched for several long minutes as they slept peacefully before I moved to her side of the bed. She'd done some decorating since I'd been gone. I couldn't see it all in the darkness on the edge of the room, but she'd been painting by the looks of it. Looked like a crazy person had drawn on any scrap of paper they could get their hands on and had taped their artwork around the room on the walls.

I admired that. It was fucking beautiful.

Now wasn't the time though. I'd come back and look at her pictures another time.

I clicked off her lamp and sank onto the overstuffed chair in the darkness and watched her sleep. Ashes's arm was tight around her tiny waist, his fingers touching her bare skin. I glared at the offending hand, willing myself not to tear it off him and beat him with it.

She finally shifted and broke away from him. Her black hair was out of its braid and looked beautiful as it blanketed her. Her bare leg slid out from under the blanket. Tiny pink sleep shorts. The ones she wore the first night I watched her sleep.

I allowed my eyes to skim up her exposed body. Her top had ridden high up her torso. Another fraction of an inch and I'd see her breasts.

My çock was rock hard in my pants. I rubbed my hand over the fabric as I watched her sleep. She twitched. Then her head snapped side to side. Her lips parted. She shifted her legs as her breathing picked up.

She was having a nightmare.

I slid my hands into my pants and brought my cock out and stroked it as she breathed harder, fighting an invisible force.

Fuck, that was beautiful. I wanted desperately to make her fight me as I sank inside her. As I fucked her virgin pussy until she bled for me, my name a silent scream on those delicious lips of hers. She promised she'd fight me. The night in the cemetery. She sealed it with our first kiss.

There was no going back. I wanted it.

I stroked my dick faster as I watched her struggle. Her chest heaved, pushing her breasts against the thin fabric of her top. Her body trembled. Her lips parted. Her brow crinkled. The scream was right fucking there. I pictured myself making her do all those things as she struggled beneath me. My release came hard and fast, spilling over my hand as I choked down my groan. She stopped moving. Her body relaxed.

It was over.

I breathed out and got to my feet and went into her bathroom and cleaned my hand off before I returned to her room. She was still on her back and Ashes's arm was now around her waist.

Standing over her, I stroked my dick, a bead of my leftover release coming to head. I ran my cock along her soft lips, smearing my come onto them.

I hoped she fucking dreamed of me.

I tucked my dick away and turned and walked to the door, but before I got there, I heard Ashes call out softly to me.

"You're fucked up, Dante."

I let out a soft chuckle and looked at him over my shoulder. "Did you fuck her?"

"You know the answer to that."

I nodded tightly and opened the door.

I did. She was still mine.

SIRENA

Ashes was gone when I woke.

I reached over from where I lay and brushed my fingers along the cool sheets where he'd been. He must have left a long time ago.

I rolled over and sighed. I'd had an incredible night with him. Learning what happened to him and his sister broke my damn heart. I'd spent so much time wrapped up in my own problems, I failed to realize how bad others had it. Now I knew both him and Stitches's stories. And Even Bryce's. Chapel Crest really opened my eyes to people around me.

The text notification on my phone flashed, and I grabbed it and looked down at it to see a message from him.

With shaky fingers, I opened it.

Ashes: I had an incredible night with you. I'll make sure the occurrence is knocked off. I want you to know it was more than that to me. I want to spend a hell of a lot more nights with you like that.

I closed the message and stared at my ceiling. Ashes was a mess. I was a mess. He said the watchers were sorry. Maybe they were. It wasn't like Stitches had done anything wrong. Sin had been cruel with his words. And Church. . . he hurt me. He scared me. But damn if I didn't miss him.

Sighing, I got up and showered and pulled on a lavender sundress and black ballet flats Cady had sent with me. I felt good, except for the empty feeling in my chest when I thought of the watchers. I attempted makeup, trying to mimic everything Cady showed me. I managed to get mascara, winged the black liner after three attempts, and lip gloss on without incident and figured I'd call it good.

When I was done, I sat at my desk and began sketching. I was out of paint, so all I had left was my pencil and paper. I drew the cemetery. I drew Ashes and flames. I drew Stitches smirking and Sin scowling. I drew Church reaching for me on my knees.

I didn't stop. I sketched for hours, not moving from my seat. Growing tired, I laid my head on a fresh sheet of paper and closed my eyes, allowing myself to drift off to sleep.

When I woke, the sun was setting. I'd wanted to see Bryce. I needed to see him. It wasn't sitting well with me that I hurt him. I hadn't meant to hurt him.

I left my room and went to his dorm and knocked on the door. He answered a few moments later and blinked at me.

"Sirena?" Another blink. "Uh, sorry. Come in. I-I wasn't expecting you." He stepped aside for me, and I entered his room and looked around. Tidy as could be. Two beds. He had a roommate. I'd forgotten that.

"Vic isn't here. He ran out to get some dinner for us from the kitchens."

I followed him to his bed and sat beside him.

"You look really pretty," he said softly. "I've only ever seen you in street clothes when you arrived here. You usually wear your uniform or pajamas. A-are you meeting Ashes?"

I reached for his hand and twined my fingers with his.

"I know I reacted poorly last night," he said softly, squeezing my hand. "I'm sorry. You've just been avoiding me. I'm worried about you. I care about you, Sirena. You're my best friend. I have Vic and the guys and Lucy, but you're the only person I've ever felt like I could be myself with. You don't care about all the bullshit. You just care about me, the person. It's hard to find people like that in the world. Especially this world at Chapel Crest. We're always labeled by our reasons for being here."

I stared at him. He offered me a smile.

"Are we good?" he asked.

I gave his hand a squeeze. His lips quirked up again.

"Good. Best break up I've ever had." He laughed, his face lighting up. "Most of the time they hate me for one reason or another. Not that I have a lot of exes. Not sure if that's a good or bad thing."

Definitely good, Bryce.

He leaned in and hauled me against his body, his arms wrapped tightly around me.

"You don't know it, but you were a godsend to me," he murmured as he hugged me. I hadn't hugged anyone in years, but I found myself winding my arms around him in return and holding him back.

He breathed out. "You've come a long way. Your sister would be proud."

He pulled away and placed a gentle kiss on my forehead just as the door burst open.

"Man, they were out of burgers. All that was left were boiled eggs," Vic grumbled.

I jerked away from Bryce quickly and jumped to my feet like I'd been set on fire.

Vic's gaze swept between us quickly, a frown on his face.

"Were you two just making out—"

I was already at the door. I wasn't sure why the anxiety had swept over me so suddenly, but the room felt smaller, and I needed to breathe.

"You don't have to go," Bryce said, getting to his feet. "I know it's early, but you look so pretty. I can, I don't know, see if I can get something else from the kitchen and we can watch movies—"

"I heard she's dating Ashes. Lucy said she saw them holding hands yesterday. And Church. . ." Vic's voice trailed off. "Man, let her go. You don't want to be wrapped up in that shit. That's too dangerous."

Bryce ignored Vic and came at me.

"Are you OK?" he murmured.

Was I OK? I wasn't feeling OK. I felt like I needed to get out of the confined space. Maybe it was because Vic was there in the small room with us. I hadn't been in small space with him like this before. I felt too trapped. These shared dorms were way too small. I was suddenly grateful that Jerry was such a prick for wanting me rooming alone.

I sucked in sharp breaths as I stared up at him. I grabbed the doorknob.

"OK," Bryce said. "I'll walk you back."

I pressed my hand to his chest.

He frowned and stepped back.

What was wrong with me? Why was I having this breakdown? The day started out so good too.

I pulled open the door and rushed off without looking back. The moment I was outside, I leaned against the brick wall and hauled in calming breaths and closed my eyes. When I was younger, I'd get panic attacks out of nowhere. I wasn't always able to explain them. It had been a long time since I'd had one that wasn't triggered by anything. The only thing I could think was the small space with someone I didn't know well.

Once I had myself back together, I made my way to my dorm, wondering if maybe Cady or my mom would call. Usually, they'd video chat me, or at least Cady would, and Mom would pop in and tell me how much she missed me. I'd watch Cady show me a new dress or gush about some boy at school or the latest gossip. I'd always just stare back at the screen, wishing I were normal.

I spotted Church in the distance in black pants and a black, long-sleeved top. I watched as he ran in the direction of the cemetery. He told me he liked to go there to think beneath the willow. He also told me he hunted in the woods. This didn't look like a hunt. Maybe he was going to think.

It would be dark soon. The last thing I wanted was to be out in the middle of the night, but I couldn't stop myself as I took step after step in the direction he'd gone in.

By the time I made it to the cemetery, dusk had fallen, casting dark shadows around everything. Swallowing hard and gathering my courage, I stepped through the creaky cemetery gates and walked to the willow in the back.

I wasn't sure what I'd do if I saw Church. Or what he'd do. Ashes said he was sorry. I wasn't sure if I believed him since Church hadn't come to me and said it. I pushed the low hanging branches aside, expecting to see Church sitting on the bench, but no one was there.

I wandered forward and sank onto the seat and looked around.

Church was right. This was a nice place to think.

I closed my eyes as the gentle breeze made it through the thick branches and rustled my hair. I'd left it down today. The dark tendrils tickled my skin as I sat there, letting the calmness wash over me.

"You're beautiful," Church's soft, deep voice called out.

I snapped my eyes open to find him standing in front of me, his green eyes locked on me. I inhaled sharply at the look in his eyes as he stepped forward.

He stopped and kneeled in front of me and brushed the hair away from my face. "You're a brave girl for following me."

I flinched away from him as he reached for me again.

"You were with Andrews today."

How did he know?

"You were with Ashes last night."

I licked my lips.

"You're scared of me because I hurt you."

I breathed out, my hands trembling in my lap. This was probably not a good idea.

"I like that you're afraid of me," he continued softly. "But I also hate it. I hate myself for it. I don't want you to fear me and flinch away from my touch." He rose to his feet and leaned over me, caging me in my spot as he rested his hands on either side of me on the stone bench. If I wanted to get away, I'd have to go backward.

"I'm sorry, Sirena. For hurting you. For scaring you. Forgive me?"

I chanced a look up at him to see his eyes shining with sincerity.

I faltered in my fear. Church just had a way of calming it when he wanted to. Maybe that just meant I was crazy too.

Nervously, I reached out and cradled his cheek. He closed his eyes for a moment at my touch before they snapped open. His hands caught my waist, and he hauled me to my feet without any effort and smashed his lips against mine.

"I saw you sleeping with Ashes. I was so angry," he said between kisses. "I wanted to hurt him. Hurt you. I didn't. I knew you'd come to me. I've been waiting."

I parted my lips for him, allowing him to delve deeper. His tongue slid into my mouth and tangled with mine.

He'd been in my room again. He watched me sleep again. I should have been upset, but I wasn't. God help me, I wasn't.

"The wait was killing me." His breath feathered across my lips. "*You* were killing me, specter." Another kiss. His hands moved from my waist to my face to my hair. He tugged the strands roughly, tilting my head back as his lips moved from mine to my jaw. To my neck.

My heart thudded hard as he sucked against the skin on my throat, leaving his mark behind.

"You look so fucking beautiful in this dress," he growled, nipping at my earlobe. "I saw you coming back from Andrews's. I watched you go there. I'm always fucking watching when I can, Sirena. Do you think I'd have let you see me if I didn't want you to? Everything is a test."

His words sent a chill through my body. Instead of pushing him away, I drew closer, earning a growl of approval from him that only made my heart race faster.

In one quick, easy movement, he lifted me off my feet and put me onto my back. The grass poked my bare shoulders as he leveled himself over me. I cast a quick look around to see night was falling.

"That's not the darkness to be afraid of." He breathed out, running his nose along my jaw as he spoke. "*It's me. I'm* the one you should be afraid of tonight."

I trembled beneath him at his words, my brain cloudy and my stomach twisted into tight knots.

He pushed the straps of my dress down my arms, exposing my breasts to him.

"Fuck, I've missed these," he murmured before he began kissing the soft mounds. I breathed heavily as he licked around my hardened nipple before sucking it into his mouth.

I twisted my fingers in his hair, only causing him to suck so hard it began to hurt.

He popped his lips off one only to move to the other and do it again.

My breath hitched as he looked down at me, his hand trailing up my thigh until he was at my panties.

He pulled them slowly down my legs before stuffing them into his pocket.

"I'm not supposed to claim you just yet. I'm finding it really fucking hard, specter. Your soul beckoned to me the moment I saw you. Your heart. Those gorgeous eyes and kissable lips. I need you to scream for me. Fuck, you need to do it so I can have you. You're tormenting me," he said thickly as he ran his finger up my damp slit.

I jerked beneath his touch, the heat uncoiling deep in my belly as he continued to gently touch me.

"Once I have you, I'll let the watchers have you. All four of us will take care of you. You'll be our girl. We'll never let you go. Do you want to be my girl, specter? Forever?"

I trembled as he slid his fingers forward to my entrance and breached it with the tip of a digit.

He leaned in and brushed his lips against mine before whispering in my ear, "You just need to scream for me. Say my name. Summon me, your demon, and I'll be yours forever, baby. I will save you."

He shifted down and his mouth met my heat, sending my back arching off the ground as his expert tongue lapped at my clit, his hands tight on my hips as he ate.

My breath came in sharp gasps. I twisted my fingers in his hair and bucked my hips forward to meet his mouth. He licked and sucked, making my eyes roll back with each sweep of his tongue.

When the heat grew to a boiling level, I came undone silently, my release rushing out of me and onto his waiting tongue where he swallowed everything. His lips and chin glistened when he emerged.

"You're fucking delicious," he said softly. "You come so hard. I've never seen a girl come like that before. I fucking love it. I love tasting it and swallowing it down. I love making you a part of me."

I swallowed as he pulled his cock from his pants and stroked it, his eyes locked on mine.

"You're going to return the favor for me tonight," he continued. "I'll teach you how I like to come."

He got to his feet and reached down for me and tangled his fingers in my hair and brought me to my knees. I made to pull my skirt down and my top up, but he knocked my hands away.

"No," he said sternly. "I want to see you."

He took his cock in hand again and stared down at me. "Open."

I'd never sucked dick before. It couldn't be too hard to learn, though.

And I really wanted to please him. Call me crazy, but it was eating me alive. I wanted Church's approval. I doubted many ever had it.

I parted my lips, and he smiled before pressing his cock against them.

"Wider, specter."

I opened wider, and he slid his thick dick between my lips, filling my mouth. I gagged as he pushed in further, hitting the back of my throat. There was still more dick to fit. I was pretty certain I'd not thought this through enough. There was just no way.

He slid his cock out and pushed back in. I gagged again. A soft chuckle left his lips.

"Too much cock for my girl?"

He slid in again, this time slower. I didn't gag this time. He cocked his head at me and pushed in deeper. My eyes watered. Deeper. The gag was right there. I couldn't. Further. Further. He was buried completely in my mouth and cutting off my oxygen.

He stayed that way for a moment before pulling out.

"Good girl," he praised softly before pushing back in. "Good fucking girl. Do it again. Faster."

I tried again and looked up at him. His gaze met mine, making a thrill rush through me.

"That's it. Look at me. Don't look away," he murmured, thrusting in and out gently. "Just like that, baby."

I coughed and gagged again, making him laugh softly once more.

"I don't typically enjoy it when someone can't suck cock," he mused as he rubbed the head of his dick against my lips. "But you might make me come if you keep gagging on me."

Humiliation raced through me. I wanted to do this with him. I felt the heat in my cheeks as I stared up at him.

"Don't be embarrassed," he cooed. "I like teaching you."

He pushed his dick into my mouth again, not as deep. I could handle this. I sucked against his velvety length as he breathed out and twisted both hands tighter into my hair.

"Make my cock hurt," he said in a shaky voice. "I want to feel your teeth, specter. You don't need to be gentle. Make me hurt."

I allowed my teeth to scrape against his cock, earning a moan from him that did something to my insides.

"That's it, baby. That was perfect. Now suck me hard. Harder. Yes. Fuck, that's good," he said breathlessly as I hollowed out my cheeks again. He pushed in deeper and didn't stop when I started to gag.

"Take it," he choked out. "Fucking make me come."

Tears from holding back my cough streamed down my face as he ruthlessly fucked my mouth. His cock twitched against my lips for a moment before his release jetted out of him and down my throat. I tried to pull away as the salty thickness made my gag reflex worse, but he forced my mouth to remain on him as emptied himself into it.

I couldn't possibly swallow all of this. He pulled his dick from my mouth and tilted my chin up.

"Swallow," he said in a soft, dangerous voice. "I ate yours. You eat mine. That's the deal."

I shook as I tried to swallow. I got some of it down before I coughed and gagged again, sending the rest over my lips and down my chin. It dribbled down and landed on my breasts.

He went to his knees in front of me and smiled.

"Poor baby," he murmured. "Let me help you."

He pressed his lips to mine and kissed me deeply before he kissed my chin, licking up his release at the same time before kissing me with it in his mouth. He pushed it forward with his tongue, forcing it onto mine. I couldn't break away from him since he had a firm hold on me. I had no choice but to swallow.

He nipped my bottom lip as he pulled away from me. His eyes raked over my nearly naked body before he reached forward and rubbed the bit of his release on my chest into my skin. He moved his damp fingers to my nipples and rubbed it around each of them before offering me his fingers to suck.

I opened my mouth for him and sucked like he wanted, the remnants of his taste on my tongue. When I was done, he pulled my top up, not bothering to fix the straps, and my skirt down, but he didn't give my panties back. Instead, he brought me to my feet before lifting me off of them and sweeping me into his arms. I rested my head against his chest. His heart rate was slow and even as we walked through the night.

"You know what I think, specter?" he said softly as we moved through the darkness. It really wasn't so scary in his arms. "I think God knew he lost me to the devil and decided to send me an angel. I think you're supposed to make me better, but I think his plan backfired because you make me feel things I've never felt before. You make me crazier. In my head. My heart. My soul. I hope you pray, sweetheart, because you're going to need a miracle to get rid of me."

I clung to him tighter, making his hold stronger on me as he brought me out of the cemetery.

I knew he wouldn't let go.

I was OK with that.

STITCHES

"Her and Andrews broke up," Ashes said as Bryce walked into the cathedral for mass with Vic and Devon. Church narrowed his eyes at Andrews as he passed by. Church had been in an exceptionally good mood over the weekend, even going as far as apologizing to all of us for his outburst in my bedroom. I'd forgiven him. Mostly. It was hard to stay mad at him. I did try though. He was my brother. One of my best friends. I couldn't leave him hanging.

"Where is she?" Church murmured, not bothering to tear his gaze away from the door where students were pouring inside.

"That shit's not over?" Sin said, frowning. "We need to move on from her. You know she isn't the one. We can get Melanie back—"

"I'm not fucking Melanie again," Ashes interrupted, shaking his head. "I've tasted heaven and *it is sweet.*"

I high-fived him as Sin shot us a scowl.

"Come on, Sinclair," I said, tugging my hair. "You kissed her too. We've been over this. You're just scared." I grabbed a Bible and tossed it into the air and caught it.

"Fuck you," he snapped. "I'm not scared. But I'm also not a fucking idiot. Doing this shit created a fight. You and Church threw punches. I'm not going to deal with another fucking Isabella situation."

"To be fair, I don't think we're going to knock up Sirena. We learned our lesson after you two fucks screwed up," I pointed out, tossing the Bible up again and catching it. I bounced my leg, the energy buzzing through me. *Fuck, these pills didn't work as good as I wanted them to.*

Sin glowered at me. I knew my friend was barely keeping it together. Even after all this time, Isabella was still a sore subject for him.

"Besides, three on one. We voted. You lost." I grinned and grabbed Church's Bible and attempted to juggle them. They crashed down and one hit Sin in the thigh before dropping to the floor. A muscle popped along his jaw as he glared at me.

"Damn, and they say I'm the fucker with the mood swings," I muttered, reaching down to grab the Bible on the floor. I just sat up when Sirena walked in looking cute as a button in her uniform.

Her gaze darted around uncertainly.

"Gotta be hard," I commented. "Breaking up with the shit head who let you sit with him. No worries. I got this. Stitches to the rescue."

I jumped out of my seat at the pew and pushed Church back down as he made to get up and rushed to her. She took a step away from me, her eyes wide.

"Hey, there, angel," I said, trying to slow my movements so she wasn't scared. "You look lost."

Her gaze roamed back over the crowded room before coming back to me.

I offered her a smile. "I heard Ashes marked off an occurrence for you. He likes to go easy, huh?"

She simply stared back at me.

"We had a good time, though, right? In my room. I mean, I thought we did." I raked my fingers through my hair and gave it a tug. "You know. Until Church ruined it."

She reached forward and rested her hand on my chest. It surprised me so much that I stared back at her, blinking rapidly.

"Do you want to sit with us?" I asked, getting my shit together and wrapping my hand around hers.

"She can sit with *us*," Seth said, coming up behind her alone. She immediately moved to me, her face paling. She tucked herself firmly beneath my arm.

What a change.

"Oh, tough luck there, Asylum. Looks like Sirena is going to sit with us today."

"Do you remember Oscar?" Seth asked suddenly, completely ignoring me. "I found him after you left. I still have him."

Her body shook so hard I had to hold her up. Her lips parted as horror spread over her face.

What the fuck was happening?

"Do you want to see him?" He reached into his pocket and pulled out a dead white mouse. It was clearly a poorly done taxidermy job, but it was definitely a dead mouse.

I couldn't catch her as she went to her ass and rocked, her lips moving but no sound coming out. Her face was drenched in tears as they cascaded from her eyes.

"Get the fuck out of here," I snarled, shoving him hard in the chest as Ashes and Church rushed over. Ashes scooped her into his arms as two security guards took awkward steps forward. I knew they were scared to tangle with us. In my last tussle with them during my fit of mania, I'd broken a guard's arm and had practically gutted an orderly when he came at me with his needle.

"What the fuck are you doing?" Church spat, shoving Seth again.

"She won't talk to me," he snapped, glaring at Ashes as he lifted her and walked to the door with her in his arms. "We're still playing, aren't we? Get her to scream and all that shit. Figured I'd jog her memory." His hands shook as he stood before us, a sad look crossing his face. It wasn't so much sad as it was heartbreaking. Like the love of his life was just declared dead and all he had left was the blood on his hands.

"What the fuck is that?" Church demanded, pointing to the mouse Seth held.

"Oscar," he whispered. "He was ours when we were kids. I just wanted her to remember."

"Real shit job on preserving him. Fucking novice," Church said, snorting at the poor, lopsided thing.

"Fuck you, Church. I'm winning this. I don't care what I have to do. She was mine in the beginning before any of you fucks. I didn't get here because I play nice. I'm never nice when it comes to her." He took a step back. "Sirena is mine."

We watched him turn and walk up the aisle to his usual spot and sit down. The two security guards moved back to their places as Church shook his head.

"Fucking douche. We should just kill him and have you dig his grave."

"I go manic and dig a fucking pool and suddenly I'm the gravedigger?" I scoffed. "Do you know how many blisters I got from that shit? My hands were raw for weeks."

"Thought that was from you pulling your dick too much," Church muttered.

"Just my right hand, dick head," I shot back. I turned to leave and saw Sin still standing where we'd left him. He wasn't looking at us. He was looking at Seth, and if I had to guess, nothing good was going through his head.

"Let's go. Fuck this place," Church said, nodding for me to follow. I gestured for Sin to join us. He fell in step behind us, and we followed Church out the door and into the sunshine.

"Ashes took her to the sanctuary," Church said, putting his phone back into his pocket.

"You think that fucking mouse had something to do with her trauma shit?" I asked as we walked. "Like maybe she's scared of mice or something. Seth would know that if they were friends when they were kids."

"I don't know. Must be. Might have to beat the answers out of him." Church said, his pace fast. He didn't look opposed to the idea. "I saw she drew a girl and boy with a mouse in her room. She has the picture hanging on her wall. So clearly, Asylum isn't lying."

Weird. Maybe it really did mean something.

Sin hadn't said a word the entire time. He seemed to be deep in thought. I hoped seeing her freak out like that would bring out the nice guy in him and make him see that she was the one for us.

When we reached the house, Church flung the door open and went straight to Sirena who was still shaking in Ashes's arms on the couch.

"I can't get her to calm down," he murmured, raking his fingers through her hair. "She just keeps crying."

Church reached down and lifted her into his arms and sat with her on the couch.

"Get her water," he murmured, brushing her hair out of her eyes with his fingers. I went to my knees between Church's legs, frowning.

This was more than a simple mouse phobia. I tore my attention from her and looked to Sin who was still frowning. He must have been putting the pieces together.

He didn't say a word. He simply glanced at me and shook his head before going to his room and closing the door softly behind him.

I sighed and took the water Ashes returned with and pressed it to Sirena's lips.

"Drink," Church commanded softly. "Please."

She sipped the water, her breathing slowing.

"There you go. There you are," Church said as he held her tightly. "No worries. I have you."

"*We* have you," I corrected him.

A muscle thrummed along his jaw. "We have you."

Ashes sat beside Church and rubbed her feet, humming softly.

"Are you fucking humming *Row, Row, Row Your Boat*?" I hissed at him.

"I don't know what the fuck music she likes," he hissed back. "It's not like I have a fucking roadmap here, dick."

I shook my head and looked to the angel in Church's lap. Her gaze shifted to me, her tears now gone. Her hand brushed against mine. I took it and brought it to my lips and pressed a kiss to it.

"You're safe with us," I murmured. "Promise, angel."

That seemed to do the trick because her body finally relaxed, and she squeezed my hand.

The final nail in my coffin. That was it. I was done for. Her reaching to take my hand as she lay on one of my best friend's laps sealed the deal for me.

I would never break a promise to this girl. So help me God.

SIN

I watched for three days as my friends doted over Sirena. They'd walk her to class. Back to her dorm. Bring her snacks. Walk beside her in the hallway as students whispered. I knew Melanie was pissed and plotting. I'd overheard her tell Tasha she wanted to take the mute bitch down. Her words, not mine, at least this time.

I said nothing to the guys about Sirena. I'd disappear to my room, knowing I had to end this. I couldn't lose my friends over a girl. I'd almost lost them once before. They were all I had in this fucked up world, and I wouldn't let some piece of ass ruin it. We fucked girls and left. We never got attached. Not anymore.

"Sinclair," Doctor Oberman said, giving me a smile. "You look like you have a lot on your mind."

I scoffed. I hated this bitch.

"We're here to listen. We're all friends here."

"We're really not, *Janet*," I said, glaring at her. "My female friends spread their legs and let me fuck them. So unless you're going to hike up that twenty-dollar skirt and let me into that pussy and take a ride with me to pound town, I'd say we're more like acquaintances."

She dropped her pen and reached to pick it up, looking completely flustered as her glasses slipped down her nose.

"Nice," Riley Danvers snickered. I didn't bother looking at him. He hung out with Asylum. Pretty sure he might be a fucking schizo too, albeit a sane one, if there were such things. Or maybe he was the ADHD one. I got these fucks confused a lot.

"Mr. Priest, please be respectful when you're in session—"

"So do you want us to express ourselves or not?" I demanded. "You asked. I answered. If we're supposed to lie to you then what the fuck is the point in any of this?"

She opened and closed her mouth several times.

"Fuck this. My number is in my chart. If you feel like changing our friendship status, shoot me a text. Not after ten though. Meds make me tired." I got up and stomped out of the room to the sound of laughter and whoops and Oberman trying to calm everyone.

I went to the bathroom and leaned against the wall and pulled a joint out of my jacket and sparked it up. I inhaled deeply, needing to take the fucking edge off.

"Feel like sharing?" Seth called out as he came into the bathroom.

I stared down at my joint for a moment before handing it off to him.

He took a hit and leaned on the adjacent wall and stared at me before he took his second hit and handed it back to me.

"Nice trick fucking with the mute with that dead mouse bullshit." I grunted and inhaled deeply as I sucked on my weed.

"Yeah. It fucked her up pretty good?"

I nodded and blew out the smoke. "Sure did. She sobbed like a baby on Church as the other two dumb asses took care of her. She's a hell of an actress."

"She's not acting," he said sharply, his tone changing.

I eyed him curiously. "Yeah? How would you know? You guys were like eight the last time you saw one another."

"Ten," he murmured.

"Ten. Whatever."

"Ten is the magic number," he said.

Seemed to be. Most of the big shit in my life and the guys' happened at ten.

"She was always so happy," he continued in a low voice, pulling me from my morose thoughts. "She had loads of friends, but she always chose me over any of them. She'd have given up anything for me. I guess in a way she did."

"Did you love her?" I asked, studying him. "You sound like you fucking loved her."

"Always have. Always will," he answered, locking eyes with me. "I wanted to save her."

"From what? You guys were kids."

"From the world. From me," he said softly. "You know I'm crazy. I-I fucking hear voices in my head. I see shit sometimes. I'm not *me* all the time. Sometimes I slip and let them in. *The others.* I'm a lot better than I used to be. The meds help." He chuckled bitterly. "She knew I was fucking haunted. She never gave up on me. Even at the end—"

"The end?"

"Right before she went crazy too. We did that, you know. Made her the way she is. I left her. I should have fucking stayed."

I nodded. "Yeah, regret is a bitch."

"I spent every night thinking she was dead. The police came to ask us questions after we moved. They asked me when was the last time I'd seen her. I didn't tell them the truth. I lied like a fucking piece of shit. I fucking hate myself for it."

I narrowed my eyes at him as he continued to speak.

"She loved that mouse. Oscar. I even let her name him. We'd build mazes and shit for him. We'd make bets. I always let her win. Her eyes would light up. Fuck, she'd light up my whole world when she smiled. I don't think she smiles anymore."

"Then what darkened it?" I asked, my curiosity over him growing. I'd never had a full-blown conversation like this with him before. He was always an enigma, the stories of how he ended up at Chapel Crest just rumors.

He shrugged. "Life."

"Heard you popped one of your stepdad's eyeballs out with a fork and that's what got you sent here."

He let out a soft laugh. "Nah. Those are just rumors." He smiled at me. "I dug them both out with forks after I spiked his drink with my mother's sleeping pills. He screamed. Guess those pills weren't strong enough to keep him asleep when the pain started and all that. It was a fuck of a mess. I wasn't strong enough to carry his ass to the dinner table, so I got a tv tray and placed it in front of him. He wasn't going anywhere. I had him tied to the headboard. I screamed at him to finish his meal or get the rod. Just like he used to do to me. I cooked those eyes to fucking perfection before I made him eat them. He passed out before he could get the second one down. The neighbors heard his screams and called the cops. They took me away."

"What the fuck, man?" I said, my stomach clenching at his story. I wasn't the squeamish sort, but seriously, *what the fuck*. I'd done my fair share of fucked up shit, but I'd never made a mother fucker eat his own eyes.

"He lived. Divorced my mom." He laughed. "I was doing her a favor. Hell, I was doing myself a favor. He couldn't hurt me anymore."

"He fucked you up, huh?" I grunted.

He nodded and looked at his feet.

"My old man fucked me up too. Beat the shit out of me. Shot me in the chest before he blew his own brains out. Ain't life fucking grand?"

Seth chuckled and took the joint back from me when I offered it. "It's really fucking beautiful."

I watched as he smoked again, looking serene.

"So you and Sirena."

"Me and Sirena," he said softly, handing the joint back and blowing out the smoke. "Love of my fucking life."

"Really?" I took the last hit and relished the burn and high.

"It doesn't matter how many chicks I fuck. She's always the girl I think about. Of course, she's not a little girl in my head. I envisioned her just as she is now. Fucking beautiful. Perfect. Her eyes. God, I've always loved her eyes. I have a thing for eyes." He smirked at me before continuing, "Her hair. The way her cheeks flush when she's nervous. How she parts her lips when she's thinking. I told her when we were six that I was going to marry her. She would be a mommy and I'd be a daddy. She said she wanted a girl and a boy. Two dogs. A fucking parrot she could teach all her favorite songs so it would sing with her." He laughed again. "She had a beautiful voice, man. *Gorgeous.* Like an angel. She used to sing all the time. Her dad got her lessons. Her mom continued them after he left their family. I could sit and listen to her sing for hours. Now she doesn't even whisper." His voice grew hard. "She won't talk to me. I've tried everything I can think of, but I fucking broke my Rinny. I loved her so fucking much."

I swallowed. "What if I can get you alone with her?"

He snapped his head up, a crazed look in his eye that made chills rush down my spine.

"How?"

"I don't want to claim her. She's going to ruin everything with us. Isabella," I said thickly. "My ex. She ruined everything. I almost lost Church and the guys because of her shit. I can't go through that again. Sirena's already coming between us. I don't think she means to, but she's got this *thing* I can't pinpoint that makes you want to fall to your knees and worship her."

"And you don't want to fall," he finished softly.

"You need to win. You need to make her scream. Church will honor the bet. I know he will. It's part of who he is."

"What do you suggest? I thought bringing Oscar to see her would help."

"She was locked in a box for a few days. She's scared of small spaces and the dark. She's scared of you." I swept my gaze over him, shoving the niggling thought out of my head about why. "I have an occurrence left for her. We all have one. Church and Ashes both used theirs. Stitches won't do this, but I will. I suggested a while back to get you involved. They were against it, but fuck it. How about you meet me at the mausoleum Friday night. Midnight. I'll have something for you."

"Rinny?" He pushed off the wall, his blue eyes filled with darkness. "You'll give her to me? In the dark?"

I licked my lips, my stomach sick. *Why did I feel like I was giving away the world?*

"Yes. If you promise you'll make her scream."

He nodded eagerly. "I promise."

"Deal." I held my hand out to him.

He took it immediately and shook it before pulling me close so he could whisper in my ear.

"Don't fuck with me, Priest. If you don't bring her to me, I'll let your boys know you were playing both sides. Then you really will lose them. And her. She drew you in. I can tell, you know. You want her, but you're afraid. I'm *not* afraid. I'll love her enough for *all of us.*" He bit my earlobe.

I released his hand and shoved him away. *Fucking weird prick.*

"Midnight. Don't be late or deal's off."

He said nothing as I backed away from him and left the bathroom.

There was one thing I knew. I just made a deal with the fucking devil.

God rest Sirena Lawrence's soul.

Something about knowing I was going to lose her before I even had her raced through me and crashed into my heart.

It didn't matter if I felt anything for her. What mattered was keeping my family together. I made a vow I'd never let another woman come between us. This was me keeping that vow, regardless of how fucking much it hurt.

CHURCH

"Do you like chocolate?" I asked as I watched Sirena nibble on a carrot from beside me on the couch. Eating a carrot for dinner seemed bland as fuck to me.

"At least put ranch on it," Stitches said, crinkling his nose as she bit again and chewed. He crouched in front of her.

"Ashes, do we have chocolate?" I asked.

"I don't have any," he said, taking a hit from his vape on her other side and flipping his lighter open and closed. His eyes were locked on her.

"Malachi? Chocolate?" I asked.

"It's not my time of the month," he said absently as he handed Sirena another carrot.

I rolled my eyes at him and got up to go into the kitchen. I rummaged around in the drawers until I found a bar of chocolate. I came back into the room and unwrapped it and offered it to her.

Her brilliant-colored eyes flicked to me before she looked back to the chocolate.

"Bite," I instructed.

She took a small bite from the chocolate and chewed.

"Better than fucking carrots," I said, shooting a glare at Ashes.

"You said to hurry and get her food. That's nature's bounty, man. It was as fast as I could go, OK?" he said indignantly. "Besides, I think she likes them."

"It's like having a little alien baby," Stitches murmured, reaching out and wiping a bit of chocolate from her lip. "A little pet we have to figure out."

I offered her more chocolate. She made to just take it from me, but I pulled it back and tutted at her, liking that I could feed her. *She was like a little pet. My little pet.*

She bit into the bar again and chewed.

"Where's Sin?" Ashes asked.

"Said he was going off campus for a bit." Stitches shifted forward and brushed her hair behind her ear. "Said not to wait up for him."

I frowned. Sin was being exceptionally weird the last few days. After we'd gotten Sirena back, he'd gone off the deep end and avoided us like the plague. I knew he was concerned about us, but if he'd just fuck her with us and make her scream, then maybe we could move past it and be one big, happy, fucked up family.

I knew him well enough to know it would take a hell of a lot of work to get him onboard. Isabella fucked him up good. Hell, so did I.

We all did.

Sirena pulled her head back from the chocolate when I offered it again. Ashes offered her another carrot that she took, making Stitches roll his eyes.

"So we have a pet rabbit. Don't let Dante know, angel. He likes to do bad things to cute, defenseless things."

She looked over at me as if asking me to confirm.

"It's true," I said, not bothering to deny it.

Her eyes widened before she turned away from me and stared at the wall and swallowed her carrot.

"Nice. Way to scare her." Ashes sighed.

"We should watch a movie. We have that new action shit with zombies in it." Stitches grabbed the remote and went through the movies we had downloaded. He stopped on the zombie flick and turned it on and settled on his ass next to Sirena's bare legs. I'd brought her here straight after classes, so she was still in her uniform.

"Every time someone dies from a zombie bite, specter should take off a piece of clothing," I said, running my hand up her thigh. She looked over at me with innocent eyes that made my dick stiffen. "And take a shot."

"Hell yeah." Stitches was on his feet in a moment and grabbed a bottle of whiskey and a couple shot glasses. "We'll all play."

I smirked at Sirena as she looked around wildly.

"No escape, my sweet ghost. It'll be fun. We'll make it worth your time," I said into her ear. She shivered against me but didn't try to get up. That meant yes in my world.

Within the first thirty minutes, her shirt and skirt were off in a pile next to our pants and shirts.

"Drink," I instructed, holding out a shot to her.

She grimaced and turned her head away. Stitches went up on his knees and grabbed her face and forced her back to me. I smiled and pushed the shot to her lips. She'd already done three. It didn't take a rocket scientist to figure out she was a lightweight.

She wrapped her fingers around my wrists but parted her lips and swallowed it down.

I nodded my approval and took my shot and pushed my boxers off.

Her eyes shot to my dick as her cheeks flushed.

Stitches was already out of his boxers and sporting an impressive hard-on. I looked to Ashes and raised my brows. He shot a look to Sirena and visibly swallowed.

"Man," he started.

"Specter." I turned her to face to me. "Help Ashes. He's nervous."

"Fuck you. I'm not nervous. But the first time I show my girl my cock, I don't want it to be during a fucking zombie movie."

I grabbed the remote and turned it off, earning a grunt of discontent from Stitches.

"There. No fucking movie. Take your dick out," I commanded.

Ashes looked to her again and chewed his bottom lip.

"Do it." I pushed her toward him, hating the feeling of wanting to rip her back to me and keep her in my arms. I was a selfish prick, wanting her to only myself, but I knew to get through this, I had to let go.

She fell into Ashes who shot a glare at me but held her gently.

"You don't have to, heaven. Church is just being a dick."

"They're the rules," I said, hating them myself. I was a stickler for rules.

"I'll help you," Stitches said, moving to his knees and going to Ashes who swatted at him as he hooked his fingers in Ashes's waistband.

"Don't act like I've never undressed you before," Stitches said, winking at Ashes.

"I was drunk and had vomited on myself, prick."

"Potato, Pa-tah-to." Stitches tugged against Ashes's boxers and got them off. He helicoptered them over his head before letting them go. They landed across the room on a bookcase.

"What do you think?" I asked Sirena as her cheeks flamed red. "Do you like what you see?"

She sat stiffly between me and Ashes.

You shared her before. You can do it again. Just kissing and touching. That's all. She's not going to get fucked.

She looked down at her hands twisted in her lap.

"Relax," I said, wrapping my hand over hers. "Remember coming in my mouth? Maybe this time you can come in Stitches and Ashe's mouths. Or maybe all over their hands."

She shook against me, making my dick harder.

"Here." I handed her another drink. "Open."

She parted her lips and drank the shot without protest.

Ah, so she needed the liquid courage.

"Who do you want to kiss first?" I asked softly, running my knuckles gently along her thigh. "We can start there and move to the next one."

She said nothing as she sat stiffly between me and Ashes. I was just about ready to tear her pink panties off and chuck them across the room and just let them watch me fuck her, because damn, I was really restraining myself, when Ashes held his palm out to her.

"Tell me," he said gently.

I watched, fascinated, as she began tracing letters onto his palm.

"Scared," he murmured. He reached out and took her hand and pulled her to him. His lips met hers in a soft kiss that looked like a fucking Lifetime movie commercial. He was gentle and sweet with her. But I could see it. The restraint as his hands twitched. Mr. Candy Hearts may play all sweet and nice, but he wanted to tear her apart just as much as I did.

I rose from my spot beside her and moved to my leather chair and watched as Stitches took my spot. When Ashes broke off the kiss, Stitches was quick to pull her face to his to pick up where Ashes left off.

I watched as she fell into it easily, my dick in my hand as I stroked myself slowly.

Ashes's hand roamed up her bare thigh before he got to her panties. He crept his fingers forward beneath her waistband as Stitches continued to devour her mouth. I could see her tremble as Ashes dipped into her heat and rubbed against her clit.

She broke away from Stitches's kiss and looked to find me.

"It's OK. I'm OK," I murmured, knowing she was checking for my permission since I'd lost my shit on her and Stitches in his bedroom. "Let them make you feel good tonight."

She licked her lips as Stitches's mouth descended on her neck. The purple marks I'd left when I'd kissed her there were beginning to fade.

I'd have to fix that.

Ashes kissed her shoulder and pulled her bra strap down. Her perfect, full breast came into view before he pressed his lips to the soft mound and sucked her hardened peak into his mouth.

She sucked in a sharp breath at the action, Stitches's lips were still on her neck. I watched as his fingers moved to join Ashes's beneath her panties. She squirmed beneath them as she tried to clench her thighs together.

Stitches grunted and hooked his leg over hers and spread her wide for them. Her chest heaved as she breathed quickly, but she didn't push them away. In fact, when Ashes's lips found hers, she parted them immediately for him, allowing his tongue to slip in.

I watched, completely mesmerized as they touched her. As they made her breathe harder. As they brought her close to release, working in tandem beneath her panties. It drove me nuts to not know whose fingers were doing what, but it also turned me on to the point that my cock was weeping precum down my shaft.

I stroked faster, wanting to come with her.

Her body began to tremble as she closed her eyes. Sensing her impending release, the guys worked her over harder, both sucking on her nipples as they fingered her.

Her back arched off the leather couch as her panties darkened with her release.

Fuck, I loved how she squirted like that.

I groaned as my release came to head, shooting onto my stomach as I watched her tremble before she went limp, her breathing slowing.

Ashes was the first to withdraw his fingers, then Stitches.

"Goddamn, what a beautiful fucking mess," Stitches said in awe. "Fuck, angel."

She cracked her lids open to look over at him. I watched as she cradled his face for a moment before she turned her attention to Ashes. She did the same for him.

She finally looked to me.

"Finish," I said hoarsely, my chest clenching as I realized the permission I was giving.

I guessed in this fucked up world of straitjackets, prescription drugs, self-medication, and restraints, this was called progress.

I was making fucking progress.

STITCHES

I typically hated it when Church lost his mind. In this instance, I was kind of loving it. He was giving his permission. If we didn't jump on this fucking train now, we'd be left with a nasty case of blue balls. I had a lot of pent-up energy pin-balling through my body. I needed the release. Fuck. Fast.

"Come here," I murmured, reaching for Sirena. She came to me without protest, and I guided her down to my dick. She stared up at me all innocent.

"Suck me empty, angel." She hesitated for a moment before she tentatively leaned forward and sucked along my shaft. Goosebumps scattered across my skin as her tongue darted out tentatively against my flesh.

If this wasn't fucking heaven, then I didn't know what was. Fingering her tight pussy made me feel like a god. Then to get her off and have her soak the fucking couch? Oh yeah. Definitely fucking heaven. Add Church not punching me in the face for touching her, and it really was perfect. Probably one of the best dates I'd ever had if this counted as a date.

"Fuck, her mouth is so warm." I let out a soft groan.

"She's new," Church called out, watching her from his darkened corner like some fucking cuckhold lunatic as my cock slid between her lips.

"Feels good to me," I answered, laying my head back against the cushions and letting her suck me.

She coughed and gagged a few times, but I didn't give a shit in the slightest. I just liked the feeling of her warm mouth on my dick. She found her rhythm finally and bobbed up and down, making heat unfurl low in my guts.

Ashes stroked his cock slowly beside me, completely enraptured by her as she took my cock in her mouth like the good girl I knew she was.

"There you go. Just like that. Suck a little harder. Fuck yeah. Keep doing that." I grunted, my abs tightening. "Suck the head a little."

She whirled her tongue around the head of my dick before she sucked me in again.

"Holy fuck." I breathed out as my body tightened. Mother fucking hot damn. Maybe it was the tentative sucks. The soft licks. The way her hand gripped my dick as she tried to please me, but fuck was it good. I loved her inexperience. That just meant we could mold her and not have to break any bad habits. I was so eager to train her that the thought nearly had me blowing my load.

I took her head between my hands and moved her on my cock how I wanted, blissed the hell out that she was so pliable in my hands. No bitching. No annoying banter about her jaw hurting or the eye roll because I wasn't coming already. Just her sweet mouth trying to make me happy.

"Baby, harder. Fuck. *Please.* Suck harder. I'm going to come. You're going to make me come." I twisted my fingers in her hair as the heat flourished low in my guts. I let my head fall back and groaned like a whore in confession as I unloaded in her mouth, every fucking nerve fiber in my body on fire as euphoria swept through me.

"Swallow me," I whispered in a shaking voice as I came down from my high. "Please, swallow for me." Something inside me needed her to taste me like that. It was dirty and primal, and shit if it didn't make me want to come in her mouth again.

She shook as she tried swallowing. That only made me want her more. She'd swallow for me even if she didn't like it.

I cradled her face as she looked at me.

"Swallow," I whispered again, thumbing her bottom lip. "For me. It'll make me so fucking happy, angel."

She swallowed.

"Show me," I murmured, my heart racing.

She opened her mouth to show me it was empty. My heart swelled. I pulled her to me and kissed her hard. She melted against my body as I explored her mouth with my tongue, tasting myself on it. I kissed her until my lips were numb. Until her lips were swollen from my kisses. And no one tried to fucking stop me.

She was breathless when I broke away from her.

"Next time, we sixty-nine," I said, grinning at her.

She bit her bottom lip for me, her warm hands on my chest, all her hair tumbling around her in wild waves. And those eyes. She didn't need words when her eyes were so expressive.

Yeah. I was in fucking love.

ASHES

I was a patient man. Fires never started themselves, but shit if I wasn't ready to pull Sirena off Stitches and tell him to go fuck off somewhere because he was hogging her.

The moment his hands fell away from her, I grabbed her and hauled her to me.

I wasn't a complete asshole, though. I knew she was probably tired and maybe a little tipsy like I was. It hadn't escaped me how difficult this had to be for Church who watched silently from a spot on his leather chair.

Seeing him kiss a girl was one thing, but him letting her go when I knew he was head over heels for her was another.

But I'd take care of her. He'd never have to be concerned when she was with me. I'd never lose control with her like I used to.

At least I hoped I wouldn't.

"Hey, beautiful," I greeted her softly, placing a soft kiss on her lips. She kissed me back, and I pulled her against my chest so I could relish in her warmth as she pressed her breasts against me.

I ran my nails gently down her back, feeling the goosebumps left behind with every gentle swipe. With our lips still fused, I guided her hand to my dick. I wrapped my hand over hers and around my shaft before I pumped it slowly. I wasn't too far off from blowing all over the damn place, having watched her give Stitches his blow job.

"My turn?" I asked softly, knowing I'd be OK if she refused. Just having her like this would be good enough for me. When she slid slowly down my body, my breath caught in my chest.

I closed my eyes and breathed out as her warm mouth sucked the head of my cock.

Tentatively, she ran her tongue along a vein, making me hiss.

She stopped and looked up at me with wide, confused eyes.

"It's good. I-I like it," I stammered as she sucked me into her mouth again. "Can you take me deeper?"

I wasn't a small guy, hell, none of us were—not that I looked, but you didn't get naked and fuck girls in the same room with your guys without noticing—but she slid my cock deeper into her mouth. I felt her throat tighten, and I pulled back, knowing that was her limit. For now. She just needed a little training in that department. I would eagerly sign up to teach her.

I thrust upward gently, knowing not to go too far.

"There you go," I said softly, sweeping her hair around my fist and guiding her with it wrapped around my hand. "Yes, baby. Hell yes."

I knew we had an audience who were stroking themselves again, and fuck if that didn't turn me on more.

I took her hand that wasn't wrapped around my cock and guided it to my balls.

"I like them squeezed," I said hoarsely. "Not too hard but make me feel it."

She obliged, giving them the perfect amount of pressure as she continued to suck me.

"Faster. Hollow your cheeks more. There you go. Fucking perfect. Keep going. Little faster. God. Fuck." I groaned as my dick tingled with my oncoming orgasm.

Just before I was ready to blow, I pulled out of her mouth and jerked my release onto my stomach. Long white ropes of my come streamed onto me as I kept my eyes on her.

She watched, fascinated as I finished on myself. I reached out with the hand that wasn't wet with my release and brushed my knuckles against her jaw. Her jaw had to be hurting.

"I'll be right back," I said, sitting forward and kissing her quickly. I got up and stepped around her to see both Church and Stitches were cleaning up too. Stitches gave me a knowing smirk as I grabbed my clothes and went off to the bathroom. I quickly cleaned myself up before returning fully clothed to her and hauling her onto the couch as Stitches and Church both got up to clean themselves.

I kissed her shoulder as I fixed her bra. Then I dressed her like she was the most delicate thing in the universe, making sure all the buttons on her white blouse were done up before I braided her hair and laid it over her shoulder.

"Perfect," I murmured as Church came back into the room in his clothes. I knew my time with her was over for now because Church would take her away from me.

And just like clockwork, he reached out and pulled her out of my lap and brought her to his chair where he hauled her down onto his thighs. She curled against him, and he wrapped his arm around her and planted a fierce kiss on the top of her head before he pushed play on the zombie movie and the sounds of the squealing, brain starved, walking dead filled the room.

Stitches returned a moment later and settled next to me fully clothed.

"He loves her," he murmured as he watched Church nuzzle against her.

"He's not the only one," I answered softly. I caught Stitches's eye, and he smiled at me.

Yeah, he definitely wasn't the only one.

Now, we just needed to convince Sin.

SIRENA

The guys didn't have me stay with them. I figured it had to do with them wanting to give me space, which I was grateful for.

I curled beneath my covers later that night as Stitches tucked me in. Church told him he could walk me home, but that he needed to return right after.

"Good night, angel," Stitches said, leaving a kiss on my temple. "Dream of me. Make it dirty."

A smile teased my lips beneath the covers as he chuckled and backed away to the door. I heard it click closed behind him.

I breathed out, my body still feeling like Jell-O. But in a good way. How the watchers could go from what I feared to what I wanted didn't make sense to me, but maybe it didn't have to. Maybe this was how it was supposed to be, given each of our situations.

Sin wasn't there. They didn't seem overly concerned at his absence. I didn't know Sin all that well. In fact, I didn't know him at all other than he kissed roughly, saved me from a nun once and scared the shit out of me.

But so did the watchers in the beginning. They still scared me, but they also intrigued me, making me desperate for more. Maybe Sin was like that. He was just harder to reach. Maybe he'd come around. I wasn't sure how I felt about it, so I didn't ponder it. In the grand scheme of things, I genuinely wanted what would make any of them happy. We all deserved a slice of happiness, even grumpy Sinclair Priest.

To make things even better, I'd been fortunate enough that Sully was just reading the Bible to me and making me write ridiculous essays. He hadn't hurt me since the belt beating, but he did give me looks that made my guts twist.

So far, life was going well.

I closed my eyes, feeling at peace for once in my life.

†

I WOKE up in the morning and showered before dressing in a pair of leggings and a black tunic. I slid my feet into ballet flats as a knock sounded out on my door. I opened it to find a massive package wrapped in pink paper and tied with a large, fluffy white bow.

I brought it into my room and placed it on my bed and pulled the card off the top.

Specter

Ashes mentioned you were out of paint and supplies. I didn't like that, so here is my gift to you so that you may paint your dreams. No one should be without their dreams.

Yours

Dante

Mine? I swallowed thickly and unwrapped the package to find a new art set, complete with fresh canvases and paint with new brushes. Eagerly, I took the new items to my painting spot and set to work creating a new masterpiece, one that centered around the three watchers. I painted Sin off to the side.

He's just protecting us from a distance. That's all. That's why he hasn't joined.

At least that was the lie I told myself.

When I finished the painting, I set it aside and yawned. There was a knock on my door again, so I went and peeked out the hole to see Bryce leaning against the doorjamb. Quickly, I pulled the door open.

"Hey," he greeted me, offering a lopsided smile. "Want to get dinner? I have it on good authority it's pizza."

I stepped out of my room, letting the door click closed behind me.

"You look nice," he said, walking beside me. "Like, you even look happy."

I bumped my arm against his playfully, causing him to grin.

"It's a damn good look on you, Sirena."

My face heated at his words. He fell into an easy one-sided conversation, telling me about how Lucy and Devon had been caught making out and decided to just come out with their new relationship.

"I'm happy for them," he said as he grabbed plates and handed me one. "Like, I did like Lucy, but I guess we're probably better as friends now that she's been with Devon. He'd never let me live it down anyway."

I held my plate as Bryce laid a slice of cheese pizza on it and followed him to the usual table. I had been taking lunch in my room after our "break up" just because I didn't want anyone to say anything to make Bryce feel awkward. It was all over Chapel Crest though. Everyone knew it happened.

We sat side by side and ate, Bryce continuing to tell me all the things I'd missed over the last several days.

"And then Jack grabbed all the damn sodas from the fridge. Security came jingling down the hall. Jack made to run but tripped because his laces were untied. Soda everywhere. So now he's in detention with Sister Esther. She's an old bitch."

I could agree with that.

We finished our pizza just as Vic approached. He gave us an uneasy smile before scurrying away.

"He's being exceptionally weird," Bryce muttered, watching as he disappeared through the large double doors. "He stole my damn iPad a few nights ago. I found it under his mattress after he denied it. I know he has a problem, but does he think I'm stupid?"

He grabbed my plate and put it away before holding his hand out for me to take. I clasped it and let him lead me out of the cafeteria and back outside.

"It's the weekend. What do you want to do? I'd say we could go back to my dorm, but chances are, Vic will be there. You just saw how weird he was. We could always just go to yours and watch *The Hobbit*."

That worked for me.

I tugged his hand toward my building, and he fell in step beside me.

"Vic has impulse control issues. Don't know if you knew that. He takes things. Kleptomaniac. He's not as bad as a guy who was here last year though. Brandon O'Hara. That guy was bad. He stole my damn shoes right out of my room. I know it was him because he wore them the next day. He was a big guy, so I didn't bother confronting him, but can you imagine? I don't even know how he got into my room. Probably swiped the master key card from the office. Wouldn't surprise me."

We'd reached my dorm and went upstairs to my room. I opened the door and led him in and went to my bed and sat. He immediately set up the movie for us and settled in beside me.

I dozed off midway through and woke up to his spot on my bed being cold and him gone. He'd left my bedside lamp on for me. I sat up and went to my dresser and pulled out the white night dress Church got me.

I changed into it and brushed my teeth before crawling back into bed. My eyelids grew heavy as I drifted off, the watchers on my mind.

†

I AWOKE to someone touching me. My eyes popped open, the weight from their body heavy on me. Kisses along my jaw. Hands on my bare breasts. A hard length pressed between my legs with my night gown shoved up my waist.

I pushed against him, my heart in my throat.

"Easy," Church growled in my ear as he pinned my arms over my head.

The light was off. We were in the dark.

I squirmed beneath him, desperate to illuminate the room. With just the moonlight, I needed more. "No," he said, giving my breast a squeeze.

I stared up at him, our eyes locking.

"You wore it for me," he said softly. "My gift."

I swallowed thickly as his hand drifted down my cheek to my throat. He flicked his gaze up to me and smiled.

"I'm going to let your arms go, OK? Be good, specter." He released my arms, and his other hand squeezed my breast again before he pinched my nipple between his index finger and thumb. I swallowed, breathing heavy at the slight pain his touch brought. He wasted no time in peppering kisses along the sensitive skin.

"I saw you today. With him. Bryce Andrews." He bit against my breast, making me flinch away from another painful touch.

"I told you that was over," he murmured, giving my nipple a harder pinch. I grasped his biceps as he reached up and gripped my face tightly.

"What do I have to do to prove to you that you belong to me? I actually sat around and thought about it all day after Vic came and told me you were with Andrews. I had to see for myself, so I followed you. I waited until he left your room. Then I came in here and kissed your lips. I breathed you in. I fucking touched you. You know what I realized?"

I stared up at him, my heart in my throat.

"That I'm *obsessed*. That I want to make it official and claim you. I don't give a fuck anymore. I know you're not as sick as me, specter. You probably don't really even belong here, but let's change that, OK? Let me infect you with my sickness. *Be like me.*" He pulled his black shirt off and brushed his lips against mine. The vial of my blood was still around his neck, and it swung above me, his tatted chest the backdrop, as he pushed his pants off.

"I can't get you out of my head. Do you have any idea what that's like for someone like me? I'm slipping. I'm losing control. I need you to fucking understand how much I want you." He shoved my panties down. I squirmed against him, but he pressed me down firmer into the mattress.

"I know your meds." He shifted so his cock was positioned between my legs. My pulse roared in my ears.

"I know you're on the shot." He kissed me again. I didn't kiss him back, conflicted about the current situation.

"Remember what you promised me?" he asked, licking my bottom lip. "When you gave your soul to me? I said to fight me when I took it. Now's the time, specter. Fucking fight. Your life depends on it."

My heart jumped into my throat. I pushed against him, earning a deep growl that made heat sweep between my legs. He caught my arms and pinned them over my head again as I bucked beneath him.

"Scream. Fucking scream my name," he snarled, his dick slipping through my damp folds. "I need to win. I need you. Fuck."

My panic grew as he began to overpower me. Did I want this? No. Yes. No. Yes. Yes, I needed him to do this.

No, Sirena! Just tell him you want it slower. Sweeter. You want to know his secrets first.

You can't tell him. Your voice is broken! He knows it too.

I arched against his hard body as he shoved forward, breaching my entrance. A silent sob left my mouth at the painful intrusion.

He pushed in deeper, spreading me, burning me as he stretched me.

"Oh, fuck," he choked out. I couldn't even struggle beneath him to get him to stop because his body was so heavy, and he had my arms pinned above my head. "Sirena. Baby. You're so fucking tight it hurts me. I love it."

I swallowed down a sob. He shifted and stared down at me, a sad look on his face.

He thumbed the tears away before he kissed each eyelid.

"I-I can't stop. Don't make me," he whispered, pushing in deeper until he bottomed out, our pelvises touching. I'd never felt so full before.

"But I will if you say my name. I'll make everything go away if you just say my fucking name for me. Please, baby. Scream. I need you to. I need you to do this for me. Please, Sirena. Please. I have to have you. I'm breaking all the fucking rules. Just do this for me. For us."

I opened my mouth for him. His Adam's apple bobbed in his throat as he held my wrists tightly over my head.

The word wasn't there. The goddamn sound wouldn't come out. I wanted to do this for him. I wanted to give him whatever he wanted.

His bottom lip wobbled as he stared down at me. He shifted, sliding out slowly as my breath hitched. He slammed back into me hard and fast.

I trembled beneath him as he did it over and over, his eyes locked on mine with each rough thrust, my body jostling beneath his.

"Say it," he commanded, fucking me harder. I was so wet for him that I couldn't stop the shame at listening to the sounds in the room. My cheeks heated with it.

"Don't be embarrassed by it. Your pussy wants my cock. And I want you. All of you," he said, slowing his movements and kissing me. "Show me how much you want me. Fight me. Please, baby. If you can't scream for me, then fight me."

He released my arms. I swallowed hard and did what he wanted. I struck him hard across his face, snapping his head to the side. His blond hair whooshed around his face with the impact. Slowly, he turned back to me, his green eyes glinting in the moonlight.

"There's my girl," he said, slamming into me.

Oh god, why did that hurt so good? Why did I want him like this?

My monster. Dante Church was my monster.

I bit his lip hard when he kissed me. His blood painted my lips red. He pulled his dick from me and slammed in again and let the blood drip from his lip onto my breasts. He pulled out and left a trail of bloody kisses on my chest.

I dug my nails into his back as he bit my breast so hard it made my eyes water. He snarled as I pulled his hair and tried to keep him from traveling further south. But there was no winning with him.

His mouth met my heat, and I twisted my fingers into the sheets as he bit my clit, sending a burning ache through my body. Tears sprang to my eyes as he did it again.

I ground my teeth as he struck my pussy, slapping it so hard I almost came undone from the pressure.

"You're fucking soaked." His deep voice vibrated between my legs. "You deserve to be rewarded for being such a good fucking girl."

He lashed his tongue rapidly over my clit, making me claw uselessly at my sheets, my hips bucking up to meet his mouth.

"Dirty fucking girl." He growled, biting me again before he pushed the pain away with more pleasure. He shoved a finger into my heat and then another before hooking them in place and rubbing me hard.

My eyes rolled back as he sucked my clit into his mouth.

The heat swept over me before it crashed down on me, the euphoria so good I went momentarily stupid as my body gave out and I soaked him in my release. He lapped it up as I quaked beneath his mouth. He continued to coax the feeling from my body until I was a boneless heap on the bed, covered in a sheen of sweat and my bedsheets wet.

Slowly, he crawled up my body and took his cock in hand and slid it up and down my wet folds before he pushed forward and breached me again.

He kissed me, nipping gently at my bottom lip. I kissed him back, completely letting go and giving him anything he wanted, the coppery taste of his blood in my mouth.

His movements weren't as violent as he slowly thrust in and out of me. He twined his fingers with mine and brought them over my head again as he pecked my lips over and over.

"I know you're mine," he whispered. He pulled out and pushed back in, his hips rolling into me like a tidal wave. Dante Church had moves. He wasn't just fucking me. He was making love to me.

He rested his forehead against mine as he continued his onslaught. His cock thickened as I clenched around him, the deliciousness sweeping through me like a hot fire before it incinerated everything inside me.

I clung to him, my nails tearing his back to ribbons, as I came on his dick. He groaned, his cock twitching deep inside my body as he filled me. He gave a few uneven thrusts before he slowed and remained still.

"I'm yours too. You own me, Sirena." He breathed out as his body relaxed. "I'm fucking yours."

I wanted to say it back, but I had no words. Instead, I cradled his face when he released my wrists and pressed my lips to his, hoping he understood. He kissed me back in a slow, deep way that made my heart jump.

"So this is love," he murmured, breaking off the kiss. He didn't give me time to react before his mouth was on mine again, his tongue sweeping inside.

So this was love. Unconventional. Crazy. So fucking stupid. But I wanted it.

Damn me to hell, I wanted it, and I was in it.

CHURCH

I held her naked body against mine. There wasn't an inch of her that my body wasn't touching. Seeing her with Andrews fucking sent me over the edge. I restrained myself from ending his fucking life and let him walk past.

Of course, he didn't see me. I told myself I'd just do it. I'd claim her body without the fanfare. I didn't care if she were awake or not.

But then she opened her eyes as I prepared to push the limits of what good boys do and what bad boys do. I still fucked her. She gave me what I wanted though. Her body. Her fight. I knew deep down she was terrified of what it meant, but I'd take care of my little ghost. I was created to torment her just as much as she was created to haunt every facet of my fucking existence.

I kissed the top of her head and raked my fingers lightly through her black waves as she slumbered on my chest. I'd never slept with a girl before like this. I'd fuck them and kick them to the curb. The last thing I wanted to do was kick my specter away. If anything, I wanted to eat every last delicious piece of her and keep her inside me forever where no one else would ever touch her. Look at her. Want her.

Because she was mine. All fucking mine.

Well, and the watchers.

That was a hard pill to swallow because when I'd agreed to sharing a girl with them after Isabella, I honestly didn't think we'd find one I could stand past midnight, but here specter was, wrapped in my arms.

I'd gone off the deep end though. I wasn't supposed to fuck her until she screamed. Then she could be claimed. I'd completely bent the rules there. But if she wouldn't tell, neither would I. If I were being honest, I thought maybe shoving my cock inside her pussy might have earned me a scream or seven.

Have to try her ass next time.

I smiled at the thought of breaking her in from behind. Gripping her hips so tight I'd leave my bruises on her creamy flesh. I'd make her wince when she walked. She wouldn't fucking sit right for a week. Maybe more if I did it twice.

My phone buzzed from somewhere on the floor.

I ground my teeth. I didn't want her to wake up. I liked her sleeping on me. I liked watching her. Touching her. Knowing she wouldn't say no.

Not that she could anyway.

Really, she was the perfect girl for a guy like me.

My phone stopped buzzing, and I relaxed, my hand trailing over the dangerous curves of her waist to her supple ass. I shifted her leg gently over mine and ran my hand over her soft ass cheek.

I wanted to smack it. Spank her until she couldn't take it anymore then ram my cock into her tight little asshole.

My dick hardened as the thought took hold.

My phone buzzed again as I shifted to put her on her stomach to try my luck. She stirred, and I cursed softly beneath my breath.

Her pretty eyes opened and locked on mine as my phone continued to buzz in the background.

"Good morning, specter," I said softly.

Her cheeks flushed pink as she blinked up at me, so much fucking innocence I almost came right there. Who'd have thought a little virginal pussy could awaken the gentleman in me.

Or demon.

It was debatable.

And I knew she was a virgin because I'd seen the sheets she'd painted with our sins. Blood red. My favorite color.

I kept her dirty last night. The last thing I wanted her to do was wash away our sins, so I made her sleep in them.

I ran my hand over her breasts beneath her nightgown before looming over her and licking her soft lips.

My phone rang again. Whoever the fuck was calling me was going to regret it. I groaned and pulled away from her and scooted my naked ass out of bed, my hard cock bobbing in the effort. I winked at her as she watched me go, her cheeks pink.

"What the fuck do you want?" I snapped into the phone.

"Where are you?" Sin demanded.

I said nothing, watching as my specter slid out of bed and went into the bathroom.

"Hello, mother fucker? Where are you?" Sin called out, an edge to his voice I hadn't heard in a long ass time.

"Getting my dick wet. Why? Ashes set the house on fire?"

"Sirena?" his voice grew soft. "Did you fuck her?"

"I did," I answered.

"Did you make her scream?"

I stared at her closed bathroom door. "No. She took my cock like a champ."

"What the fuck are you going to do if Asylum wins this? Huh? You fucked her before anyone won. You're too fucking attached—"

"He's not going to fucking win. What is your problem? We got the girl. I fucking got us the girl while you were out stomping around crying over shit we stopped caring about after we covered it in fucking dirt." I snarled softly into the phone.

"I told you I didn't want her."

"And I told you that you're a fucking liar."

He let out a soft huff of air. "So that's it? You're really doing this?"

"Already done it."

He was silent for so long I pulled the phone away from my ear to check to see if we were still connected.

"Fine. Then I want to use my occurrence."

"It's yours to use," I shot back, wondering what the fuck he had planned. Sin wasn't exactly a saint when it came to the shit he did to punish offenders. In the grand scheme of things, it didn't matter. She knew she had them coming, and I relished in the thought of soothing her tears away when it was over.

But if one hair was harmed on her head, I'd beat the fuck out of him.

"Just say when," I added.

"Soon. I want to do mine alone like Ashes got to."

I was silent for a moment before I nodded. Maybe some alone time would get him feeling better about her. She had that effect on people. "Fine."

"Great, now get home. Alone. We don't need to deal with her getting bitched at for having you in her room," he whispered before the call dropped.

I pulled the phone away from my ear and frowned down at it before dressing. I didn't give it much more thought as Sirena came back into the room looking like the pretty little sweetheart she was.

Moving to my feet, I stalked toward her and cradled her face. I wasted no time as I pressed my lips to hers, urging her to part her lips for me. She was such a tiny wisp of a thing. I towered over her by a foot and had to really bend to kiss her. But it was perfect. She was fucking perfect.

"I need to go." I breathed out against her lips, really fucking hating Sin's mood swings and his bitching. I needed to take care of this shit once and for all. I pulled my clothes on. "Paint me a picture while I'm gone. I'll be back tonight. Maybe I'll bring a guest," I said, thinking that maybe Sin would give in and finally get his dick sucked.

I released her and went to her door and didn't look back as I stepped out of it.

I knew if I did, I wouldn't leave.

And I really would work on making her scream for me.

SIN

The last thing I wanted to do was hurt my brothers. *My family.* I learned in life that blood didn't always equate to family. A bullet to my chest as a kid taught me that early on. But I knew I was doing them—us—a damn favor.

I'd spend the last few days preparing for Sirena's occurrence.

It was probably my most elaborate yet.

After Church returned home and screamed at me for ruining his morning, I'd stormed out of the kitchen and gone to my room, more than ready to just get this shit over with.

When dusk hit, I checked to make sure the guys were still home. Church and Stitches were in a fierce game of Madden while Ashes flipped his lighter open and closed, his eyes on the screen as he watched them play.

I'd overheard Church say he'd be seeing Sirena tonight.

Not if I could fucking help it.

I walked through the living room in my all-black clothes and didn't say a word.

"Where you going?" Ashes called out.

"For a walk," I muttered.

"Don't get eaten by Sasquatch," Stitches shouted, not bothering to look at me.

"I'll see what I can do." I pulled open the door and stepped into the night and hit SEND on Seth's name as I walked.

"I've been waiting for your call," he said softly, like I'd given any inclination on when I'd be giving Sirena to him.

"I hope you took your fucking meds tonight," I said gruffly, walking toward Sirena's dorm.

"Why do you think I ever take them?"

Christ.

"Meet me in the cemetery—"

"At the mausoleum near the oak. One hour," he finished for me before disconnecting.

I stared down at my phone in confusion. *How the fuck did he know I was going to even say that, right down to the time?*

Whatever. I picked up my pace and went straight to Sirena's dorm and knocked on her door. She opened on the third knock in that fucking white night gown Church always wanted her in.

Her eyes widened at me as I stood in her doorway.

Fuck, she's beautiful.

Not fucking now. Head in the game.

"Hey, Siren," I said softly, drinking her in.

She made to back away from me, but I grabbed her arm and tugged her forward so hard she crashed against me. I caught her around the waist as the door slammed closed behind her.

She pushed against my chest, and I gripped her biceps tightly and gave her a shake.

"Stop. Stop it," I snarled. "I know you know what time it is. Save your strength. You're going to need it." She stopped her fight as she stared at me through her wild black hair. My heart caught for a moment before I did something really fucking shitty.

"Trust me. I won't hurt you, Siren," I said, lessening my hold on her arms and really fucking hating myself in that moment because the reality was, she was definitely going to be hurt tonight. I had a sinking suspicion Seth really knew what happened to her all those years ago and that was why she was afraid of him.

Fuck it. I was doing this for my family.

I kept my hand around her arm and led her to the elevator and down the stairs to the outside where night had finally fallen.

Her body shook as she kept pace with me, stopping every now and then to adjust her feet in her stupid ass bunny slippers. I was sure if Church had seen them, he'd have gotten a kick out of them.

I thought she might fight me when we got to the cemetery, but she didn't. Instead, she looked around wildly, probably hoping to see the guys.

"It's just us for now," I murmured, leading her deeper through the stone garden. When we got to the mausoleum, I bypassed it and went to a granite bench beside a weeping angel headstone and pulled her down next to me.

I wanted to atone for my sins before we started this.

I stared up at the moon and blew out a breath. Ashes said she was a secret keeper. I may as well tell this precious creature how atrocious I really fucking was. If she died tonight, maybe she'd carry my message to God and let him know he could go fuck himself for the life he'd given me.

"My father and mother had a nasty divorce," I started. "My dad drank a lot. Sometimes, he'd hit my mom. He'd tell me she deserved it for some fucked up offense. He never hit me though. In fact, he doted on me. I thought that's how things were supposed to be. He taught me the wife falls in line and when she doesn't, you put her there." I chanced a look in her direction to see her watching me, her vibrant eyes shining beneath the moonlight.

"Mom left dad. She took me with her. I was scared for her. For the first time in my life, I feared my father. I was at Dante's house. We always went there after school before Chapel Crest. My dad called and said he was going to pick me up. He knew if I wasn't home then I was at the Churches's estate. I waited for him. He said we were going on a fishing trip. Mom kept warning me to stay away from him since she had the courts involved."

I raked my hand over my face and went back to staring at the moon because looking at her made me feel things I didn't like.

"He took me to this place we'd never been to before. He didn't have any of his fishing gear. He made me stay in the room with him while he drank. He started talking gibberish in his drunken state. Then he called Mom. I could hear her screaming on the other end. Begging him to bring me home. He punched me. Kicked me. I called out for my ma. That's when he pulled out the gun and handed me the phone. He told me to tell my ma the best goodbye." I paused and rubbed my chest, the memory still strong within my mind. "I told Ma I loved her. She said she loved me. She said to run. That she would find me. I was going to, but Dad pointed the gun at me didn't say a word. He pulled the trigger."

She flinched beside me, and I wanted to hold her to keep her from hearing this shitty life story, but I couldn't. I was trying to escape her. Putting her back in line as my old man would say. I dragged in a breath.

"It fucking hurt. The bullet hit me in the chest." I tugged my black Henley up and showed her the nasty scar on my chest through the tattoos. Her brows crinkled as she stared at it before she looked back into my eyes. I let my shirt drop and looked to the moon.

"I lie dying on the floor, trying to call for my mom. I watched as he picked up the phone and said something into it. *This is what you fucking get.* Then he put the barrel into his mouth and pulled the trigger. I watched as his brains left his body. He dropped beside me, his eyes locked on mine. He was the last thing I saw before everything went black."

It was silent in that cemetery as we both sat beside one another breathing.

"I ended up coming off life support. A real fucking miracle since I should have died. Mom met Rudy and married him. I scared him. I wasn't the same kid anymore. Shit fucked me up." I pulled a joint out of the front pocket of my Henley and lit up, inhaling a deep hit. I blew it out into the night.

"I got into some trouble. Had some fucking psych issues. Docs all said PTSD. Borderline personality bullshit. A result of the trauma." I took another hit. "I got sent to Chapel Crest after Everett Church, Dante's father, suggested it to my mother. His family started this place years ago. It was a regular ass school then. Shit's changed so much since then. Everett sits on the board now. He's got his hands in plenty of pots. Guy's a real tool bag."

I hated Church's father. Hell, Church hated his father. Dude wasn't nice despite the face he put on for those who didn't know him like we did. Church probably inherited his crazy from his old man. Hell, looked like my old man left me the same gift.

"We were here a few years when Isabella arrived. She was beautiful. Not like you though," I said, turning to look at her. The truth rolled off my tongue quickly as she studied me, no emotion on her face. "You outshine her in beauty in every single way, but she sank her claws into me. I fell. *Hard.* I thought I was in love. Hell, maybe I was. I had abandonment and trust issues. Still do, apparently. They say it's just part of my trauma. My personality disorder. It's so bad it affects the relationships I form." I shook my head. I never opened up like this to anyone. Maybe it was because she didn't speak. Maybe it was because I knew she might not come out of where I planned to put her tonight. My ugly sins would die with her.

Fuck, I hated the thought of such a delicate creature leaving the world.

Focus, Sin.

"She had issues. We all fucking do. She liked to play games though. I never knew what her issues were. I assume she was narcissistic and maybe just fucking twisted. She enjoyed carving my fucking heart out and stomping on it." I took another hit of the weed. This was the hard part.

"I fucked her," I said. "Bare. I thought she was on something. And why wouldn't I? She told me she was. She came to me a few weeks later and said she was pregnant. I-I was happy. For the first time in my miserable fucking life, I was happy. Maybe I would be good for something. But I was scared too. I told her I was. Neither of us were prepared to be parents. I was terrified we'd have a fucked up kid, but I really fucking prayed we didn't. I kept that faith. We started to fight a lot. Her meds changed or something. She got really depressed and violent." I held my arm out and pointed to a long, jagged scar on my forearm. "She caught me with a knife in my sleep once."

Sirena raised her brows at me, her gaze raking quickly over my face.

"Shit escalated after that. I still loved her. I loved our baby. I tried to make things work. She kept pulling away from me. Then I came home from classes and her and Church were together. He was fucking my girl. She was doing all the same shit for him she did for me. Or used to. I lost it. Church and I fought. She screamed at me and told me I was ruining her life. That she hated me. That she hated our baby." I wiped at my nose and inhaled some weed again. I could still see her blonde hair tumbling around her shoulders, her dark eyes alit with hatred as she screamed at me and told me I was a worthless piece of shit who should have died.

"She left. I called and called her. She wouldn't answer me. When she finally returned, she met me and handed me a bill for her abortion. She ran off and killed our fucking baby. I'll never forget her words. *Since you didn't die, I killed your fucking kid.*"

I finished my joint and looked to Sirena who had tears in her eyes. I reached forward and swiped a fallen one from her cheek.

"She tried to tear me and my family apart. Church and I didn't talk for a long time. She'd told him I wanted him to fuck her. That I had a fantasy about coming home to find it. Church always did have a fucking wild streak." I chuckled softly. "Ashes and Stitches didn't know which side to join, so they separated from us too. It was a fucking nightmare. But we figured it out in the end."

I pulled a tiny pill from my pocket. "I want to tell you the rest, but I need you to take this. It's part of your occurrence." I held the pill out to her. She immediately flinched away from me, the tears now dried on her cheeks. I gripped her arm with my free hand tightly.

"Don't fucking try to run. Just take the damn thing. It'll make tonight easier. At least in the beginning."

She jerked away from me and got to her feet. The fury radiated off her in waves. I anticipated this though. In seconds, I was on my feet and grabbing the back of her head. She kicked and bucked against me as I struggled with her until I had her backed against the stone walls of the mausoleum. I pressed her body against the cold rock and forced the pill into her mouth and covered her nose and mouth with my hand.

Her eyes grew wild as I held her in place.

"Swallow it, Siren. Trust me when I say you're going to want this."

Tears slipped down her cheeks as she cried silently. Finally, her throat bobbed with her swallowing. I waited a moment longer before I released her. She sagged forward, and I pushed her back against the wall.

"As I was saying. We figured it out in the end. Isabella had to go. She came between me and the guys. We agreed to only fuck girls together after that. We hadn't found one to love until you arrived. I'm too scared to go through that again. I don't want to love you, Siren. Fuck, I don't, but when I look at you, I know I will. I know I'll end up hurting and broken again. I know my friends will. I can't lose them." I pressed my lips to her forehead as she trembled beneath me. "They're all I have left in this world. When Stitches slipped last year, it was hell. I never want to see him like that again. In a fucking straitjacket and fucked to hell on pharmaceuticals. I never want to see Ashes in tears because he burned everything he loved to the fucking ground or Church. . . well, he always overcomes, but it isn't without losing another piece of his fucked up soul."

I rested my forehead against hers as her breathing slowed.

I licked my lips. "She's dead. Isabella. We scattered her ashes in the lake."

She jerked against me, but I shoved her back against the wall and forced her face up to look at me.

"You don't deserve that fate, Siren. I'm giving you an out. I'm giving you away. Maybe it'll save us all."

Her expression changed, her eyelids drooping as the pill took hold. Fear shone in her eyes just before her eyelids fluttered closed, and she went limp. I continued to hold her against the wall, tears sliding down my cheeks.

I placed a tender kiss on her lips before I deepened it, tasting her for the last time before I lifted her into my arms and brought her into the mausoleum. I'd spent all week setting this up.

I'd moved old man Morse's bones out of his cement prison and cleaned it up inside, adding a layer of cushioning and white velvet. Siren deserved to at least be comfortable.

I lifted her limp body into the large tomb and adjusted her so she looked like the prettiest sleeping doll. I fluffed her black waves and folded her hands over her abdomen, watching as she breathed in and out deeply.

She'd hopefully be out for most of it, but if she wasn't, I hoped it wasn't long until she succumbed to the torment.

"She looks beautiful," Seth said softly from behind me.

My heart jumped. I hadn't even heard him come in.

"The box I put her in was smaller," he continued, moving to stand beside me. "She bled so much. She cried. She tried to escape. I only wanted to save her. They said she would be better off that way."

I gripped the edge of the cement tomb as he revealed what he'd done to her.

"I only want her to talk to me again," he murmured. He looked at me. "If she screams, she's mine, right?"

I nodded tightly, really fucking hating myself more.

Why don't you stop this? Why are you doing this?

Because I fucking care. I. Care. I'm protecting my family.

He smiled and turned back to look at her. I watched as he reached out and brushed his fingers along her lips. Her lashes. Her hair. The look on his face screamed crazy, but it was his touch that made me step away.

"I'm coming with you this time," he whispered, smiling down at her, the moonlight from the door cutting a sinister streak of pale light over his face. "Wait for me, OK, Rinny?"

I didn't move as he crawled in next to her and curled up at her side and wrapped his arm around her sleeping form.

"Thank you," he said softly to me before he closed his eyes, his head beside hers on the white velvet pillow, and a small smile on his face.

I didn't say a word. I simply slid the heavy cement lid over them and backed away, closing the door behind me.

EPILOGUE

SIRENA

It was hot. Too hot. The air felt thin. It wasn't easy to breathe. My head hurt so much. Where was I?

I fluttered my eyelids open, only to be greeted by darkness. My heart jumped into my throat as I tried to sit up but found I couldn't.

I clawed at cold stone above me. A silent sob left my lips.

Hot. So hot. Dark! God, it's so dark! Small. Too small. I can't. I can't. Help. Help me! Someone!

What did Sin do?

The mausoleum.

The pill.

The tomb inside the mausoleum.

Realization came crashing down on me. I squirmed again, panicking inside the small, dark space, freezing when I realized I wasn't alone.

"I'm so glad you're awake, Rinny," Seth's soft voice called out beside me. "I was beginning to worry about you." His fingers snaked through my hair. I sobbed silently, trying desperately to get away, but there was nowhere to go in this fucking stone prison.

"You can't run from me now. You can't hide from me. Now, you have to face me," he murmured. He brushed his lips against my cheek.

"I've thought of you every single day since we—I—left. I should have come for you. I should have found you." His hand moved lower until it was around my neck. "I thought you died. I was too afraid to look. I tried to make it up to you. With Danny because he hurt you. He touched you when you didn't want it. He scared you. You saw the blood, right? The cuts? I made sure he knew not to mess with my Rinny. He will never forget it either."

Help. Help. Help! SOMEONE! HELP ME!

Breathe, Sirena. One, two, three. Fuck. Shit. One, two, three, four. I can't breathe. God, please! Not like this. Not like this.

I clawed at him as he tried to shift me closer to him. My nails met his face, and I tore across his skin, making him hiss.

"Scream, Rinny. That's all you need to do. Just scream for me. I promise it'll be OK after that. You can't hurt me any more than I already hurt myself."

I did my best to fight him as we grappled with one another's arms in the tight space.

"You keep it up, we're going to run out of air," he snapped, his voice changing. My heart thrashed violently in my chest.

He was right. I hated it, but he was right. Fucking Sinclair Priest. The memory of him taking me was foggy, probably due to whatever was in that pill he shoved into my mouth. Our time together came in blurry chunks.

I stopped struggling, and simply shook, drawing as much into myself as I could.

"You were always smart," Seth whispered into the darkness, his lips at my ear. "Do you remember the box I put you in? It was so small I wasn't sure your body would fit. I tried not to make it worse."

One. Two. Three. Four. Five. Six. Seven.

Stay calm.

It's just a dream. It's a nightmare. It's not real.

"Maybe we'll go to heaven together this time, Rinny."

Eight. Nine. Ten. Eleven. Twelve.

"Or maybe hell since I've done a lot of really bad things. You were my greatest tragedy though. I missed you when you left."

Thirteen. Fourteen. Fifteen. Sixteen. Seventeen. Please God. Eighteen. Breathe.

"I'll never have to miss you again though, Rinny. We're here. Together. Forever." He began humming our song from when we were kids softly into the darkness. The fucking song he tried to murder me to. The song that would be our death march into the afterlife together.

"Roses and whiskers

Don't stop the purrs, mister.

This world is too big

To go it alone"

I breathed in deeply, my mind slowly breaking apart as I realized I wouldn't be getting out of this box. That my fate was always entwined with Seth Cain's.

I wept silently as Seth continued to hum, his fingers in my hair, his body pressed against mine as the air grew thinner.

"So follow me through the thicket

And just try to fit through the thorns.

I'll be right behind you.

No need to be alarmed."

Seth's song—our song—continued in my ear as the darkness grew heavier.

It's over. It's fucking over.

Church's face flashed in my mind. Ashes. Stitches. Sin. My watchers. The smiles. The touches. The kisses. The lies.

Seth's hand shifted low on my abdomen before traveling south. He continued our song, his voice soft and perfectly pitched in the darkness.

"I'll always *be right behind you.*

No need to be alarmed."

His soft lips brushed against my jaw as he softly sang an additional verse.

"I'll be right behind you.

Always beside you

Scream for me, Rinny

It's time for our monsters to play."

My body shook violently as Seth kissed along my jaw in the darkness.

I-I can't. I'm going to die. One. Two. Three. Four. Church. Church. Church.

The memory of Church's words echoed in my head.

You just need to scream for me. Say my name. Summon me, your demon, and I'll be yours forever, baby. I will save you."

I parted my lips, and I screamed as I succumb to the madness inside the box.

"CHURCH!"

To Be Continued in Ashes: The Boys of Chapel Crest
Get it here:
https://books2read.com/ashervalentine

Want to read Bells: The Boys of Chapel Crest? It's Sin and Isabella's story and explains why Sin is the way he is. Best read after Church and before Ashes.
Get Bells: The Boys of Chapel Crest
Skip ahead for a preview!

Thank you for reading Church: The Boys of Chapel Crest. Please consider leaving your review.
Did you enjoy this dark reverse harem? Thirsty for more?
Check out Black Falls High.
It's complete.
https://books2read.com/inruins

ABOUT THE AUTHOR

Affectionately dubbed Queen of Cliffy, Suspense, Heartbreak, and Torture by her readers, USA Today bestselling author K.G. Reuss is known mostly for making readers ugly cry with her writing. A cemetery creeper and ghost enthusiast, K.G. spends most of her time toeing the line between imagination and forced adulthood.

After a stint in college in Iowa, K.G. moved back to her home in Michigan to work in emergency medicine. She's currently raising three small ghouls and is married to a vampire overlord (not really but maybe he could be someday).

K.G. is the author of The Everlasting Chronicles series, Emissary of the Devil series, The Chronicles of Winterset series, The Middle Road (with co-author CM Lally) Black Falls High series and Seven Minutes in Heaven with a ridiculous amount of other series set to be released.

Follow K.G. at the links below and on TikTok!

https://vm.tiktok.com/ZMexyRPcE

Sign up for her newsletter here:

https://tinyletter.com/authorkgreuss

Join her Facebook reader group for excerpts, teasers, and all sorts of goodies.

https://www.facebook.com/groups/streetteamkgreuss

BELLS

Before I found a love I was willing to die for, I had to survive one I had to kill for.

Chapel Crest wasn't a place of solace. It was made for suffering.

I would know.

I'd been locked inside ever since my mother tossed me away like I didn't matter.

In my suffering though, I found her.

Isabella.

The girl who made me believe I mattered.

The girl I gave everything to.

The girl I loved.

The girl I would do anything for, even kill for.

Or just plain kill.

Because you don't betray a watcher and live to tell about it.

This is the prequel to Chapel Crest and is best read AFTER book one. It tells the tale of Sin and Isabella through multiple POVs before Sirena. This is a dark tale of greed, deception, and all things that hurt. Please read the foreword.

ONE

SIN

"I don't like her," Stitches said, glancing over to the blonde at the table next to us. She was staring down at a book and completely ignoring us.

"Not really your call," I muttered to him as she popped a pretzel into her mouth. "She likes me. I'm trying to get my shit sorted. She listens."

Church scoffed next to me. "She sucks your dick. That's about the only communication you two have with one another."

I gave him the finger, which made Ashes snort from beside Church who simply gave me a look that said he didn't give a fuck one way or the other what I did or why I did it.

We were students here at Chapel Crest. Or patients. I supposed it depended on how you looked at it. Chapel Crest was a fucking asylum academy, and I'd never let anyone tell me differently. We were all a million shades of fucked up here. There was a medical ward on campus where many of us went for therapy or an extended vacation if we lost our shit. It's where meds were handed out like candy and religion over science choked you.

If the pills wouldn't cure you, God would.

At least that's how it seemed to be here. Religion was a fundamental study for us all. It was the core of treatment and the core of recovery.

Good boys and girls who don't lose their shit and kill people got to go to heaven.

The rest of us got to go to Chapel Crest.

Our headmaster was a practicing doctor and a complete fucking cocksucker we hated. I knew the fuck was into experimental treatments and probably other shady business, but I'd never be able to prove it. None of us would unless we slipped and fell hard and ended up admitted into the medical side.

"I'm not saying it's my call, Sinclair. I'm saying I don't trust her. She's fucked up even more than we are," Stitches said, bringing me back to the moment as I stared at her from my seat. "I'm just trying to save your fucking heart, asshole. And your sanity."

"Ah, fuck sanity," Church said, getting to his feet and heaving his orange across the courtyard. It smashed into the side of Danny Linley's face. He immediately reached for his bleeding nose and stumbled away from where he was sitting.

Church looked back over at us and grinned, his blond hair falling into his eyes. "He was playing with his cock under the table over his pants. Fuck that guy. I'm trying to eat my hot dog here. He was ruining the fucking experience for me."

Stitches let out a huff of laughter. "Rumor has it he fucked some passed out chick at a party and got sent here instead of jail time because his old man is loaded."

"Aren't you into fucking the unconscious?" I asked, finally looking to Church who didn't look the least bit ashamed of who he was. Church was dark and twisted, much like the rest of us. He didn't display many emotions, at least not ones that brought warm and fuzzy to mind. If he could hurt it, smash it, break it, or kill it, that was what he'd do.

He leveled his green eyes on me. "The difference between Danny Linley and me is that the chick would fuck me awake and scream no to him."

Stitches jerked his thumb at Church. "He's got a point. If she'd fuck you awake, she'd fuck you sleeping. It's science."

I rolled my eyes at the two nut jobs as they high-fived.

I got to my feet, my sights set on the blonde.

"Be careful," Ashes said, his blue eyes roving over to the girl I was eyeing.

Isabella.

A complete fucking basket case, but she fucked and sucked and that's what I needed. I'd say she checked all my boxes. I liked her a hell of a lot, and I wasn't about to just overlook that since I never felt shit for girls before. Because of the way being with her made me feel, I kept at it, hoping maybe she was the cure for all the bad shit in my life.

"Fuck being careful," I said, turning to grin at my friends. The watchers. My ride or die posse. We ruled this place with an iron fist and giant cocks. No one fucked with us.

"Atta boy!" Stitches shouted. "Go get mentally fucked up. You need more of that."

I shook my head and gave him the finger as I walked away from our table. The moment I was at Isabella's table, a smile spilled onto my face.

"Hey, Bells," I said, grinning down at her.

"Sin," she answered in her silky voice, her dark eyes trailing over me. I liked her blonde hair spilling around her the way it was. Made it fun to twist my fingers in.

I nodded my head slightly. A playful smile spread over her pretty face as she got to her feet and followed me.

Lead me not into temptation but deliver me from evil.

A-fucking-men for crazy pussy.

ALSO BY K.G. REUSS

May We Rise

As We Fight

On The Edge

Into The Fire

When We Fall

Double Dare You

Double Dare Me

Church: The Boys of Chapel Crest

Ashes: The Boys of Chapel Crest

Stitches: The Boys of Chapel Crest

Sinful: The Boys of Chapel Crest

Asylum: The Boys of Chapel Crest

Emissary of the Devil: Testimony of the Damned

Emissary of the Devil: Testimony of the Blessed

The Everlasting Chronicles: Dead Silence

The Everlasting Chronicles: Shadow Song

The Everlasting Chronicles: Grave Secrets

The Everlasting Chronicles: Soul Bound

The Chronicles of Winterset: Oracle

The Chronicles of Winterset: Tempest

Black Falls High: In Ruins

Black Falls High: In Silence

Black Falls High: In Chaos

Black Falls High: In Pieces, A Novella

Hard Pass

Kings of Bolten: Dirty Little Secrets

Kings of Bolten: Pretty Little Sins

Kings of Bolten: Deadly Little Promises

Kings of Bolten: Perfect Little Revenge

Kings of Bolten: Savage Little Queen

Barely Breathing

The Middle Road

Seven Minutes in Heaven

Printed in the USA
CPSIA information can be obtained
at www.ICGtesting.com
LVHW022026090524
779584LV00007B/502